The Cunning Man

BAEN BOOKS by D.J. BUTLER

The Witchy Wars Series
Witchy Eye
Witchy Winter
Witchy Kingdom

To purchase any of these titles in e-book form,
please go to www.baen.com.

The Cunning Man

D.J. Butler
Aaron Michael Ritchey

BAEN

A Baen Books Original

Baen Publishing Enterprises
P.O. Box 1403
Riverdale, NY 10471
www.baen.com

ISBN: 978-1-9821-2416-8

Cover art by Dan Dos Santos

First printing, November 2019

Distributed by Simon & Schuster
1230 Avenue of the Americas
New York, NY 10020

Library of Congress Cataloging-in-Publication Data

Names: Butler, D. J. (David John), 1973– author. | Ritchey, Aaron Michael, author.
Title: The cunning man / D.J. Butler and Aaron Michael Ritchey.
Description: Riverdale : Baen Publishing Enterprises, 2019.
Identifiers: LCCN 2019029051 | ISBN 9781982124168 (trade paperback)
Subjects: LCSH: Paranormal fiction. | GSAFD: Fantasy fiction.
Classification: LCC PS3602.U8667 C86 2019 | DDC 813/.6—dc23
LC record available at https://lccn.loc.gov/2019029051

Pages by Joy Freeman (www.pagesbyjoy.com)
Printed in the United States of America
10   9   8   7   6   5   4   3   2   1

*This book is dedicated
to our wives,
Emily and Laura.*

We would like to thank Tan Smyth for her sensitive early read and comments, and Jason Huntzinger for helping us envision Helper in the 1930s.

Many thanks also to this book's *two* editors, Toni Weisskopf and Tony Daniel. Thanks also to J.R. Dunn, for busting us on a few anachronisms.

And again, we are grateful to and for our wives.

"*Magus* is a Persian word primitively, whereby is exprest such a one as is altogether conversant in things divine; and as *Plato* affirmeth, the art of Magick is the art of worshipping God."
—*Henry Cornelius Agrippa, His*
Fourth Book of Occult Philosophy,
"Preface to the Unprejudiced
Reader," Robert Turner, 1655

"And it came to pass that there were sorceries, and witchcrafts, and magics; and the power of the evil one was wrought upon all the face of the land."
—*The Book of Mormon,* Mormon 2:19

Chapter One

"I'VE HEARD DISTURBING THINGS ABOUT YOU." BISHOP SMITH WAS the youngest of the three men who made up the Presiding Bishopric, and his Van Dyke beard certainly made him the jauntiest. It jutted forward like a knife.

Hiram Woolley felt his heart lurch like a toad in his chest.

Bishop Wells, sitting in a chair beside Bishop Smith, had a face round as a pie and a cream-colored complexion. Behind round spectacle lenses, his eyes smiled, though the line of his mouth was flat. Smith and Wells were the counselors, number two and number three respectively; the Presiding Bishop himself, Bishop Cannon, wasn't with them.

They had heard Hiram was a magician.

Smith and Wells both wore slacks and waistcoats, their jackets slung over the backs of chairs; Hiram was in his overalls, with his faded olive-green wool coat and his hat on his knee. The Bishops wore polished black shoes, and Hiram had dirty Redwing Harvesters.

"Oh?" he said.

"About you and your grandmother."

"Hettie," Hiram said. "God rest her soul."

"She was a witch."

"No," Hiram said immediately.

Bishop Smith leaned forward, nostrils flaring. "And *you* have magical powers."

1

Hiram ran the fingers of one hand through his thinning hair. He wanted to stand, put his fedora back on, and leave, but he owed respect to Bishop Smith. To the office at least, if not to the man. "No, I don't."

"Jedediah Banks said you caught a thief. Found out who it was using balls of clay that dissolved in a dishpan." Bishop Smith smirked.

Hiram said nothing.

"And Beulah Wiseman said you dowsed her a new well when her old one dried up."

"Hiram wouldn't be the only dowser in Utah." John Wells spoke in mild English tones. He and Hiram had met at a barn-raising in Butlerville, several years earlier. Hiram had taught John how to drive a straight nail, in the process of which he'd seen a protective lamen, an amulet written on paper, around Wells's neck. He'd driven Wells home that night, and Wells had told him of his experience as a child in Nottinghamshire, being healed of an abscess in his foot by a cunning woman named Granny Jenkins.

"There's more than one adulterer, too." Smith squinted at Hiram. "Well?"

Hiram could repeat the simple truth that he didn't have magical powers, but that would make the final admission worse. "I helped Beulah. And Jedediah, too. And the thief, for that matter. Got him to return Jedediah's mule and ask forgiveness."

Smith steepled his fingers before him. "And do you believe God gave you magical abilities?"

Hiram carefully controlled his breath to avoid sighing. "Yes," he said. "And no."

"You're being evasive." Smith frowned. "Do you know James Anderson? In American Fork?"

"At the People's State Bank," Hiram murmured. Jim Anderson was his loan officer.

"James Anderson is a faithful brother." Smith's frown twisted slowly into a smile.

"He is." Hiram's heart was thumping.

"I don't think Brother Anderson would want to have anything to do with witches."

Like any farmer, Hiram was sometimes late in his payments, and his personal relationship with his bankers was the only thing that got him the days—and sometimes weeks or months—of grace he needed to stay afloat.

"I'm not trying to be evasive," Hiram said. "Look, you're a healthy man with two legs, you walked into this room. Did God give you the power to walk?"

Smith looked suspicious. "This is irrelevant."

Wells smiled slightly. "Let's hear him out, David."

Hiram continued. "Without God, you wouldn't walk. You wouldn't have legs, the earth you stand on wouldn't exist and wouldn't be spinning around to generate gravity—anyway, that's what Michael says makes gravity. You can walk because of God, but that doesn't mean you have a special power of walking. You're just an ordinary man, doing an ordinary thing—walking—in the world as God made it. In the same way, you could say that God gave you the power to read, or swim, or drive a car."

"I'm not a witch." Smith's voice was cold.

"Neither was Grandma Hettie." Hiram avoided making eye contact with John Wells, feeling he might implicate his friend. "And neither am I. A witch is someone who hurts others, but I help people. That's what Brother Banks and Sister Wiseman both told you about me."

"So you would call yourself what, then?" Was that a hint of triumph in Smith's eyes? "A wizard? A charmer?"

It was a trap. Those words were both associated with condemnation in the Bible.

Hiram shrugged. "If people ask, I tell them I farm sugar beets. Which is the truth."

"I would hate to have to drive home past the bank, Brother Woolley," Smith said. "On the way here I stopped to talk with Brother Anderson, and he told me you're late on your payments as we speak."

The egg-shaped, red-flecked green stone Hiram always carried in his pocket—his bloodstone, or heliotropius—lay inert. So Bishop Smith was telling the truth.

"I'll catch up on payments. Harvest should be good this year."

"I hope you catch up in time."

What could Hiram say that was safe? "Grandma Hettie said that the things she did made her a 'cunning woman.' I suppose that makes me a 'cunning man,' though that's not a term you hear so much anymore."

"A wizard."

Hiram shook his head. "Just someone who knows how things work. And who uses his knowledge for good."

"And this knowledge . . . these things you do . . . you're convinced they work?"

Hiram nodded. "Ask Beulah and Jedediah. In the mouth of two witnesses."

"Do they *always* work?" Smith smirked. "Or do they only *sometimes* work?"

"Well," Hiram said, "sometimes a man who knows perfectly well how to walk trips over his own feet anyway, or steps into a puddle, or isn't looking where he's going, so he walks into a wall, or someone else kicks his feet out from under him. You wouldn't say his walking only works some of the time. And some things depend on faith, or a pure heart—mine, or the person I'm helping—so yes, sometimes my lore fails."

"And does your lore include the use of . . . sacred things?"

The hair on the back of Hiram's neck stood up. This was a dangerous question. Certain sacred names or gestures were very effective against illnesses or wicked spirits, especially if repeated multiple times. He shrugged slowly. "If making the sign of the cross over a sick person, or singing a psalm to an excited mule, helps a person in need, then yes, I do it."

"Is this *nineteen* thirty-five . . . or *eighteen* thirty-five?" Bishop Smith leaned back in his chair and looked at Bishop Wells. "You really want to send this man to the Kimball Mine as our representative?"

"To say 'representative' is a bit much." Wells smiled softly. "We need someone to take food to the miners, and Hiram is ready to go. And he does this sort of thing for me often. I trust him."

"The food's loaded on the back of my Double-A," Hiram said. "Three different Lehi congregations pitched in. But I can unload it. I'm not the only man in town with a truck."

Bishop Smith looked at the two other men through slitted eyes. "Take the food to the men of Kimball Mine, Brother Woolley," he said. "And then come back home. Don't do anything else, and don't imagine we won't hear if you do. Even in godforsaken Helper, there are those who will tell us what happens."

Smith stood with a dancer's grace—back erect, heels snapping sharply together—and left. The door fell shut behind him and Hiram heard the clicking of his heels on the wooden floor of the halls.

Hiram Woolley and John Wells stood more slowly, then shook hands.

"Maybe I should stop trying," Hiram suggested. "Keep to myself. Farm beets."

"*Can* you?" Wells asked, the dark eyes in his cheeselike face glittering.

Hiram grunted.

"Listen," Wells added as they walked together to the exit. "The Kimball family, they followed . . . older ways."

"Heber Kimball saw signs in the heavens, back about eighteen thirty-five." Hiram nodded. "Or . . . do you mean polygamy?"

"Both," Wells said. "Teancum was a polygamist like his father."

"Are you saying . . . there's something more than a closed mine happening here?"

Hiram had been acting as unofficial assistant to John Wells since nearly the day they'd met. Sometimes, John called on Hiram because of Hiram's farming skills, or because he owned a truck. Other times, he needed Hiram because Hiram was a cunning man.

"I don't know for sure," Wells said. "Teancum Kimball was said to have had prophetic gifts, and at least one of his children is mad. Keep your eyes open, and stay out of trouble."

Hiram grunted again and nodded. Could he stay out of trouble? He had to . . . for himself and for Michael.

They left the building, and Wells turned right, walking toward his dusty white Terraplane parked under a black walnut tree. Hiram turned left, and found his adopted son Michael waiting beside their Ford Model AA pickup truck, strumming on his Sears, Roebuck guitar.

Michael's birth parents had been Navajo, so the two looked nothing alike; Michael was stocky, with a solid chest and a dark complexion, where Hiram was thin, rangy, and naturally pale. Hiram tended to introduce him as my son, Michael, not including any surname in order to avoid the thorny question whether Michael's last name was *Woolley* or *Yazzie*.

Michael ended the blues song he'd been yodeling and put the guitar away.

Hiram checked the apple crates and brown sacks of groceries in the back of the truck, piled so high the Double-A looked like one of the gypsy family vehicles he'd seen in France. He found them all secure, tightly roped to iron rings along with Hiram's shovel, water cans, spare gas can, camping gear, and toolbox.

Michael drifted over.

"You could have come inside," Hiram said.

Michael snorted. "I'd feel like a hypocrite, Pap. What did they want to do, tell you who to give the food to?"

"I already know that. There's a mine foreman. Name of Sorenson." Hiram climbed into the shotgun seat and Michael got behind the wheel. Michael drove because Hiram had fainting spells. Only occasionally, but often enough that he preferred Michael to drive.

"Anything else they want to talk about?" Michael asked.

Hiram tried to avoid lying directly to his son. "They had the idea that I've been carrying on Grandma Hettie's craft. Her special skills."

Michael started the truck. "You mean *magic?*"

The sudden note of disdain in Michael's voice stabbed Hiram in the belly.

"Yeah," he said, as the truck rolled from the church parking lot and turned south. "Crazy, I know."

Chapter Two

DRIVING DOWN FROM LEHI FELT GOOD. HIRAM LIKED THE ROAD, the blue skies, and the mountain ledges dotted with sagebrush, gambol oak and pine, and tall yellow grass. Snow sat in nooks of orange stone, hiding from the sun and the nearly-warm breeze. He also liked the engine smell of the Double-A. The dirt road was graded, but scarred by plenty of washboard ruts. The government had been paving all the highways until the stock market had jumped off a cliff, dragging the rest of the economy with it.

They were descending through Price Canyon toward Helper when Michael asked, "So, how long do you plan to keep running these errands for Bishop Wells?"

Ye have the poor always with you, Hiram thought. "You hear back from any of those colleges?"

"No," Michael admitted. "I wrote to a few more. Mahonri helped."

Hiram had known Mahonri Young all of his life. They'd played on Sundays in the marshes around the mouth of the Jordan, slipping out of the white-slat chapel on any pretext whatsoever. They had whiled away many days racing off into the mountains to swim, fish, and memorize the stars. Mahonri was still his best friend and, other than Michael, the smartest man Hiram had ever met. Smart enough he'd gotten schooling. Then he'd gotten a job working at Brigham Young High School, in the library.

Hiram gripped his son's shoulder with pride. He would have

tousled Michael's hair, once, but Michael was too big for that. "You decide what you want to do with a degree? You can't say 'spaceman,' there are no spacemen. No Flash . . . Flash . . ."

"Flash Gordon."

"Right. No Flash Gordons."

"There'll be spacemen soon enough, Pap."

"Hoping to meet a blue-skinned beauty of Venus?"

Michael's grin collapsed. "Well, Jenny Lindow turned me down for the Mutual Improvement Association dance. That makes three girls in a row."

"Jenny's a nice girl," Hiram said.

Michael nodded. "And she turned me down, anyway."

"You know, I was never very handy with the girls."

"Yeah, Pap," Michael said. "But you're white."

"You're my son," Hiram said. Maybe that was why Jenny had said no. Maybe her parents didn't want her going to the dance with the cunning man's son.

Michael nodded. "I grew up with you and Mamma and Grandma Hettie. I went to church, I worked the farm, I learned my ABCs. But I'm not like you, Pap. Not . . . *quite.*"

Hiram's heart ached. He saw his son's world diverging from his as fast as Flash Gordon's rocket. "A spaceman, then?"

Michael grinned again. "Probably a scientist first. Geologist, maybe. Or entomologist. Or . . . there are just too many choices."

Hiram clapped a hand gently on his son's shoulder. "You'll find your place in this world, Michael."

"So will you, Pap."

Hiram chuckled.

Rounding a corner, Michael hit the brakes. A heavily rusted Model T lay stopped across the road, blocking it. Three men in overalls, thick gray sweaters, and boots clustered around the open hood. Black streaks marked their sweaters, and where undershirts peeped out, they were gray, rather than white.

The Double-A threw up dust as it stopped. One of the men removed a hat and fanned away the cloud, revealing a hairline rising steeply from a widow's peak. He settled the hat over his face; he kept his dark heavy-lidded eyes on Hiram and Michael.

The other two men huddled over the engine, faces hidden.

On Hiram's right rose a steep hill, thick with pines. To the left a slope fell into the ice-choked Price River.

"Well, I'm having no luck finding a girlfriend." Michael laughed. "But I'm having a better day than those poor shmoes. Let me guess. We're going to help them?"

Widow's Peak lifted a hand, keeping his hat over this face. He had dark eyes, dark hair, and skin that looked tan despite the winter. A Greek or a Turk, maybe? Hiram had known both in the war.

Hiram touched the pocket of his overalls. His bloodstone clicked softly against his clasp knife.

"Pap?" Michael asked. "Are we going to help them?"

Hiram reached up and tilted the rearview mirror so he could see behind them. Another dark-haired man, this one in work pants and a gray-stained sheepskin coat buttoned all the way up and covering his face below his nose, came ambling out of a stand of pine trees, about a hundred feet away.

Had he been relieving himself? Or was this the lookout, and the extra muscle?

"Maybe," he murmured.

"Jeez, Pap, what's going on?"

Hiram opened the door and stepped out. "Did your car break down?" he called.

He pressed the bloodstone against his thigh.

"Yes, yes, the car, she is broke," the man said.

The bloodstone pinched his leg.

The Greek was lying.

"One second," Hiram said.

The Greek nodded. The fourth man stood stock still, watching.

"Michael," Hiram said in a low voice, "I'm going to move their car. When it's clear, you're going to drive past them. I'll jump in the back. If you see trouble, and I can't get to you, drive on to Helper and get the police."

Michael lowered his voice. "You mean...these guys are bandits?"

"These guys are hungry."

Michael gripped the steering wheel. "What is this, cowboy times?"

"Just watch for an opening. Then give her the gas, son." Hiram slapped the roof and got down. He didn't reach into the glove box to grab the Colt M1917—Hiram's other great reminder of his friend from the war, Yas Yazzie.

Hiram walked up to them, smiling widely. "Bad luck with your car." His breath came quicker, and a thick sweat oozed down his sides, cold against his skin. With the first two fingers of his left hand he tapped his breastbone, drawing comfort from the metallic feel of the round iron chi-rho talisman that bumped against his skin. It was the very same amulet Grandma Hettie had given him the day his mother had disappeared. It was a disk of pure cast iron, forged at the new moon and well-fumigated with the Spirits of Mars before ever being worn. Its front and back faces were identical, bearing the chi-rho symbol, the great icon of Christ's victory, in the center, and around the outer rim at the clock positions of midnight, three, six, and nine, the four Latin words IN HOC SIGNO VINCES. The amulet protected the bearer against his enemies.

He hoped these men weren't his enemies.

Widow's Peak nodded. His eyes were fixed on Hiram. Hiram smelled liquor.

"Can I help you move her so me and my son can get by?" he asked. "We're on our way to the Kimball mine."

Something flashed in the Greek's eyes. He grunted and reached into his pocket. "She no move."

The bloodstone pinched Hiram again.

Hiram saw a smudge of white wood—ax handles hidden in the engine, within reach of the two men standing there.

Hiram's heart filled his ears. He fixed his eye on the Greek. "Your car isn't broken, and you're thinking about robbing us. I won't let that happen, but I guess you might have families. I can give you some bread and canned vegetables."

"Maybe...maybe that's okay." Widow's Peak looked uncertainly at his companions.

The two men spun. Red bandanas covered their face. They pulled out the ax handles and barked words Hiram couldn't understand at their friend.

Widow's Peak dropped his hat, revealing a mustache like a Fuller brush. From out of his pocket he pulled a gray sock sagging with something heavy in its end.

A bag of groceries wasn't going to resolve this conflict.

Hiram charged Widow's Peak, raising a fist. The Greek flinched, and Hiram plucked the sap out of his hand.

Behind him, the Double-A growled. What if the fourth man on the road attacked Michael, rather than Hiram?

Hiram spun the sap over his head like a sling and released

it into the face of one of the ax handle men. It struck him in the forehead and he dropped.

The second man darted forward, raising his ax handle over his head.

Hiram showed him his right fist, and then hammered the man's face with his left. His knuckles crashed right into the red bandana, and sent the attacker staggering away.

Hiram didn't dare look back. He hurled himself on the seat of the Model T, pushed the clutch down with his left, and shifted the car into neutral with his right.

The Model T didn't move. Hiram glanced at the hand brake to the left and under the steering wheel. It was set.

Hands grabbed Hiram's left arm. He threw himself right and kicked backward like a mule. He saw his Harvesters connect with the nose over the Fuller brush, and then blood sprayed onto the Model T's window. Widow's Peak fell.

The fourth man charged the car.

Hiram released the brake and the Model T lurched forward.

A sharp scream cut through the air.

Michael pulled the Double-A past the Model T on the right side, as the rusted car rolled toward the river.

Hiram squeezed out of the car. He stepped over Widow's Peak, who lay hollering in the road and clutching his leg. The men with bandanas were standing up, and the fourth man was yelling urgently at them.

Hiram jumped onto the running boards of the Double-A. He slammed a hand onto the roof. "Go, son!"

The men stopped chasing Hiram, and jumped into the Model T to stop it from rolling downhill into the river.

Michael gave the truck gas and they sped away.

When they were around a corner and out of sight, Hiram plunked himself back down on the seat. He let out a long breath.

Michael drove with his mouth open. Sweat dripped off his nose. "Those guys, they would have robbed us. How did you know? What the hell, Pap?"

Hiram closed his eyes, feeling light-headed. "Nice work, not running them over."

"You surprised me as much as you surprised those guys." Michael laughed. "What were you saying to that guy before you took his sock away?"

Hiram gave his son a weary grin. "I offered them a bag of groceries. Maybe I should have offered two?"

Michael laughed in spite of himself. "I think they wanted the whole truck. Where did you learn to fight like that?"

Hiram sighed. He needed a long cool drink from the water jug in the back. Should he tell the police there were bandits in the canyon? But they might be the very men he had come here to help. At least he should tell someone about the injured fellow.

The man *he* had injured.

Hiram said a silent prayer for the hungry men who had attacked him.

Michael finally had to answer his own question. "Yeah, the Great War. Punching out the Hun."

Chapter Three

THE TRUCK CLIMBED UP SPRING CANYON, THE LONG VALLEY ABOVE Helper that was home to many coal mines. The interior of the Double-A quickly became stifling, and stayed hot even when Hiram cracked a window. Hiram fished a green bandana from the bib pocket of his overalls and mopped at the sweat on his forehead. There wasn't enough room in the cab of the truck to shrug out of his coat.

Hiram was intensely thirsty.

The road turned right in a broad loop around a stand of pine and the canyon opened. Three smaller canyons continued like splayed fingers, the yellow rock like skin and the junipers cloaked with snow like skinned knuckles. On the left side of the road a two-story white clapboard building hove into view. The two-foot tall wooden sign running the length of the building, above a deep porch and three rocking chairs, read DOLLARS.

"Hey, Pap, in these errands we do," Michael said, "maybe we could arrange to go somewhere exciting. Like, I don't know, Denver. Or California."

"I'm not sure I'd call them errands," Hiram objected.

"Would you call them . . . *quests?*" Michael asked. "We deliver groceries, we try to help people find jobs, we settle family disputes. Or anyway, *you* do those things. I'm more of a servant, really."

"We're both servants," Hiram said. "It's a ministry. We're trying to help people in need."

"I, for one," Michael said, "need a drink."

"I could use a Coke, myself." Hiram generally drank water, but at the moment, a cold Coca-Cola sounded inviting. This was a fasting day—Hiram tried to fast one day a week—but he drank when he fasted. A man had to, when his living included physical labor.

Michael stroked his chin. "If you were driving this truck, I guess you could pull over and get a dope, if you wanted."

Hiram kept his gaze mild, but didn't back away from Michael's challenging eyes.

Michael looked away first. "Coke. You know I just mean a Coke."

Hiram nodded. "I was thinking *you* might like a Coke, too."

"It's like you're a magician, reading my mind." Michael grinned and eased over into a gravel drive beside the store.

Hiram cringed at his son's words.

"Keep your boots on." He climbed out of the truck, shutting the door and smiling in through the window.

Was that a train whistle he heard, or the sound of distant music from one of the town's bars or bordellos?

But no, he was too far away to hear either. It had to be the wind.

"It's February, Pap. It's freezing, and I'm driving the Double-A. Am I really going to take off my shoes?"

"It's just an expression," Hiram said.

"No one says it but you." Michael grinned. Even wide open, his eyes seemed to be all dark brown iris. Like his father's.

Wide open, like Yas Yazzie's eyes had been in the moment he died, in Europe's frozen mud, thousands of miles from his red-rock home.

"Old-fashioned, I guess." Hiram loped toward the store with his long, bone-rattling strides.

"Don't I know it!"

Stepping up onto the porch, Hiram sneaked a hand into his right pocket to touch the cool heliotropius.

The other objects in the same pocket were his clasp knife and his Zippo lighter. He didn't smoke, but many others did. A quick offer of a light could soften a heart.

He stopped, hand on the doorknob. Hanging in the window, on the other side of the glass, were bunches of herbs. They hung stem-up and leaf-down, and many men would have simply walked past them, oblivious.

Hiram knew the herbs, and he knew their uses. Peppermint and bay.

You could cook with bay, and peppermint made a lovely tea. But both had a further use: they warded off hexes.

The lead holding the shop's windowpanes in place was twisted into irregular patterns. No, a single irregular pattern, repeating in each window. What was the meaning of the pattern? The planets, as well as angels and demons, each had a unique written sign. The signs were like the drawn equivalent of secret names.

This kind of lore was beyond Hiram, though. It was book-lore, and his lore had mostly come to him by word of mouth.

He turned back to see Michael, head lolling back against the seat, eyes closed.

Hiram shook his head, chasing away baseless fears. He touched the Saturn ring on the ring finger of his left hand. He'd never worn a wedding band while Elmina was alive, but shortly after her death, he'd put the Saturn ring on. He'd never taken it off since.

The night before, Hiram had dreamed of driving slowly on a desert road and calling Michael's name, to no response. But not all dreams were prophetic. Hiram hadn't bothered to consult the little dream dictionary in the bottom of his toolbox.

And in the case of a truly dire emergency, Michael knew Hiram's revolver was in the glove box, loaded with five rounds, one empty chamber for safety. There were six more bullets in a full moon clip beside the Colt.

Hiram opened the shop door.

He heard the chainsaw-like sound of two large dogs growling. Two black beasts leaned in his direction, snarling and yipping. Hiram recognized them as Rottweilers—he'd seen them in Germany.

"Down, boys!" called a voice.

The dogs retreated and Hiram entered.

A second sign hung over the counter inside. It read: *Scrip from all Spring Canyon mines accepted at eighty percent of face value, credit extended only to those who don't need it.* The short counter held a cash register, a book of accounts, and a dog-eared copy of the Sears, Roebuck catalog. Three walls of the room, floor to ceiling, were covered with deep wooden shelves, groaning under the panoply of goods a miner's family could use to make a life, from Clabber Girl baking soda and White King soap to bolts of cloth and carpentry tools. Washboards and metal basins hung between the windows, and shovels leaned into the corners of the room. The shop floor was occupied by mannequins in Sunday frocks, iceboxes, and a washing machine with a very large drum.

The Rottweilers slunk behind the counter, growls subsiding.

A man in a white shirt and red suspenders stood at the register. His hair was white and so bristle-thick that Hiram thought he could count the hairs on the man's head from across the room. It shot straight up like a rooster's comb, without the glisten of pomade.

"Hallo!" the old man bellowed. "Welcome!"

Hiram nodded, squeezing the heliotropius and forcing himself not to touch the chi-rho talisman. "German?"

The old man laughed merrily. "How did you know? I didn't slip and say *velcome*, did I?"

Hiram shrugged. "I knew a few Germans."

"My name is Gus. Gus Dollar. And yes, I'm German. Or at least I was...in another life." The old man pointed at Hiram's coat. "You were a Doughboy?"

Hiram nodded.

With an explosion of laughter, two small children rushed into the storeroom from an open door in back. They were tow-headed balls of mercury, skittering back and forth across the planks, giggling at each change of direction.

Would Hiram and Elmina have had children such as these, had she not carried such a fatal darkness within her?

Stepping out of the way of the tumbling children, Hiram bumped a shelf and knocked a poppet off it. He caught the poppet in his large, callused hands and carefully placed it back into position, sitting on a shelf beside cans of Gibson and Maxwell House ground coffee.

Next to the coffee, and not next to other toys.

He looked at the poppet again, smiling blandly. It was made of orange wax and nearly featureless. It wore tiny overalls cut from calico, and tucked within the overalls and also wedged into the poppet's wax was a buffalo nickel. It was a new coin, with the bison on one side and the Indian head on the other.

It was a hex, an old shopkeeper's charm for drawing customers into any business. Grandma Hettie had pointed out similar poppets in a tack and saddle shop in Santaquin and a greengrocer in Provo.

Hiram bit back a laugh. It hadn't been the heat inside the truck's cab that had made him want to come inside and buy two Cokes, it had been this poppet. The idea was a tad disturbing, despite the fact that the charm was fundamentally harmless.

He turned to look again at Gus Dollar. The old man chased the two children in one final circle around the room. He looked sixty, but he moved with the agility of a much younger man. Something was not quite right with his eyes.

His left eye, Hiram realized. It didn't move, it was fixed forward.

A false eye? An injury?

But for all that he had a bad eye and was old, Gus Dollar's shop and his charm and the two children racing around him struck a deep bass note of envy in the bottom of Hiram Woolley's soul.

Gus chased the children out and met Hiram at the counter again. "Forgive me."

Hiram forced himself to smile. "Children. Nothing to forgive."

"You don't look like a miner," Gus said. "Or a doctor, or a deputy sheriff."

"Is that who usually visits Spring Canyon and the mines?"

Gus nodded. "Undertaker, once in a while. Peddlers. And I heard some of the miners talk about a union man, which I didn't believe until I saw it with my own...*eye.*" He rolled his good eye in a circle, the inert one staying fixed on Hiram.

"Is that glass?"

Gus leaned forward, gripped the eyeball in question with the fingers of one hand, and popped it from its socket. Setting it on the countertop, he rolled it toward Hiram.

Hiram caught the eye. The sphere lay warm in his hand, staring up at him. It might have been a large marble. He handed it back to Gus. "Might want to wash that off."

The shopkeeper laughed, his eye socket now a sunken pit with mostly-closed eyelids hanging loosely over it. He tucked the glass eye into a breast pocket. "Old injury. Now, what can I do for you?"

"Two dopes." Hiram instantly regretted the word. "Cokes, I mean. From the icebox, if you have any."

"Cold day outside, though. You sure you wouldn't rather have a hot coffee?"

Hiram in fact would have preferred a hot coffee. Black, and if sweetened, then with a little beet syrup. The way Grandma Hettie had always taken it, and the way Hiram had grown up taking it, with bacon, eggs, and fried potatoes, before going out to work the farm. Food that filled your stomach, food you could work on.

But he'd promised John Wells he would give up coffee, and Hiram Woolley kept his promises. Wells had made it clear that Bishop Cannon felt strongly about the matter, and that as the bishop's second counsellor, Wells would sustain the man.

"Two Cokes, please." Hiram hesitated. The herbs, the strange windows, the poppet, all made him wonder if he should reveal himself to Gus Dollar.

Or had Gus already guessed?

"I've heard men say," Gus said slowly, his accent becoming more German with each word, "that drinking Coca-Cola, instead of coffee and wine, helps a man keep a chaste and sober mind."

"Hmm," Hiram murmured.

"Or on the other hand," Gus said, "you could just be one of these Mormons."

Hiram smiled. "Maybe both things could be true."

"Maybe." Gus chuckled. "So, what are you doing, driving up to the coal mines, dressed like a farmer in those overalls, and your old soldier's coat over the top?"

"I'm looking for the Kimball Mine. I didn't see a sign."

"Left fork," Gus said. "But that doesn't answer my question."

"I'm buying two Cokes. And I *am* a farmer."

Gus retrieved two bottles from the icebox in the rear corner of the store. "Your business."

The shopkeeper's nonchalance embarrassed Hiram. Was he being rude because he envied the man? "I'm delivering food. To a man named William Sorenson. Food for the miners out of work."

"That's every miner at the Kimball Mine. Caring for the widows and the fatherless, eh? Pure religion and undefiled?" Gus set the Cokes on the counter. "Five cents. *Bill* Sorenson. The mine foreman. His real name is actually *Vilhelm*, but he insists on being called Bill."

"Shouldn't that be ten cents?" Hiram gestured at the price, clearly spelled out on the bright red door of the icebox. "Vilhelm Sorenson...is he a Swede, then?"

"A Dane. If you personally plan to drink both these bottles, the price is ten cents." Gus Dollar smiled. "But if one of them is for the young man sitting in that truck outside, then I'll accept a nickel."

Hiram wanted to refuse the gift, insist on paying the full dime, but he didn't. It would be an act of foolish pride to refuse another man the opportunity to do a kindness.

"And if I get a Snickers, too?"

"Then a dime in total."

Hiram tendered a dull coin and took the Cokes and the candy, putting the cream-paper-wrapped square into his pocket. He wouldn't eat it today, but Michael might need it later on. "Why would you...what would make you say that thing you said, about a chaste and sober mind?"

"You look like a man acquainted with fasting," Gus said with a faint smile.

Hiram smiled back. "President Roosevelt might say we've all become better acquainted with fasting in recent years."

Gus nodded. "White man and an Indian traveling together. Maybe he's your teacher. Your master in the mysterious arts."

"He's my son." Hiram felt his brow furrowing, against his will. "He was a baby when his mother died from the Spanish flu. I knew his father in the Great War, so I adopted him."

"I'm joking." The word sounded very German, like *choking*. "I saw the way you looked at my charm."

Involuntarily, Hiram shot a glance at the poppet and blushed. "My grandmother raised me. She...read the almanac. Understood the true meanings of the Psalms."

"A *hexe*. A cunning woman. Knew the properties of stones?"

Hiram nodded.

"Had a library of strange books?" Gus pressed.

Hiram rushed to change the subject. "The miners need food." He gestured at the sign over the counter. "You could give them credit."

"I do," Gus said. "Despite what I wrote on the sign. But I've given just about all I can give now. A storekeeper who offers everyone credit starves to death. Or his children starve."

"The mine will be open soon." Hiram said it hopefully, willing it to be true.

Gus Dollar nodded. "The mine will be open soon. And if not, soon enough the men will take to the rails. The good thing about being so close to Helper is that there's always a train to catch."

"And if the men go hoboing, what happens to the families?"

Gus shrugged. "The good men send money back. But you can't ride the blinds with a small child, or a pregnant woman."

"Bad time to be looking for work."

"Bad time." Gus nodded. "And what food are you bringing the miners, then?"

"Ham," Hiram said. "Flour. Tinned vegetables."

Gus reached across the counter to clap Hiram's shoulder. "You'll do alright, cunning man. You'll do alright."

Hiram wasn't so sure.

Chapter Four

HIRAM AND MICHAEL CONTINUED UP THE LEFT FORK OF SPRING Canyon, the Double-A rattling on every stone. A sharp turn to the right brought them to a steep hill. Michael tried to take it in third gear and the engine protested.

"You'll want to drop into second gear, son."

"Just have to go faster is all," Michael insisted.

Michael might damage the truck. Or worse, spill the pile of groceries strapped to the Double-A's bed. Hiram kept those worries to himself. "You're driving."

Michael stomped on the accelerator pedal and the engine cycled faster.

Hiram's thoughts lingered on Gus Dollar and his store, the wax poppet, the herbs in the windows, the curious lead shapes. Hiram was uncomfortable that the man was so open about his hexing, and yet he was... content. His business thrived and his family prospered.

The cab of the Double-A again grew chill, and Hiram shrugged down into his green overcoat as far as he could. No Model A or Double-A left Henry Ford's factory with a heater, but there was a jobber you could install after the fact. Hiram kept meaning to get one, but it seemed just as easy to keep an extra coat and gloves in the truck.

Hiram glanced behind him to check that the crates of beets and groceries were okay, given the steepness and roughness of the road. Michael had done a good job roping them down to the wooden slats of the truck; knots were one of the things he'd mastered before dropping out of the Boy Scouts.

The engine sputtered and they lost speed, a little short of the top. Michael set his sweating Coke bottle between his legs to shift back into second. "You were right. Fortunately, you're the kind of father not much given to rubbing my nose in my mistakes."

"And you're the kind of son who always holds his tongue."

Michael laughed out loud. "Bullseye, Pap."

Hiram smiled.

"Once again, you've taken me to the middle of nowhere." Michael shook his head and grimaced. "I'm fairly certain that there are families in San Francisco that could use groceries. Los Angeles is also probably low on sugar beets."

"What about Tooele?" Hiram grinned.

"We've already been there," Michael said. "That was the time you were out all night, messing with the well on that one guy's farm."

"Abramović's ranch." Hiram had lied to Michael about the reason why he hadn't slept that night. The farm had been plagued by the spirit of Mr. Abramović's mother, who had been cruel in life and vengeful in death. Hiram had eased her transition with a charm, but he had a scar on his back from her cold fingernails.

He hated lying to Michael. Guilt filled his pockets like stones.

They turned another corner and Hiram got his first look at the Kimball mining camp.

"Stop for a second, son." To the right was the camp itself, a city of irregular, leaning buildings. Hiram saw single-room houses and larger dormitories, all of their roofs and many of their walls tacked against the weather with tar paper. There were also tents and other larger buildings: a school maybe, or the company store, a church, a union hall. At the very top, pressed into the crack of a narrow stone-walled side canyon, was the mine entrance itself, surrounded by a handful of more solidly-built yellow stone buildings. Two tracks of rails led from the opening to the right and a long wooden structure with a metal chute, crouching above the canyon atop a skeletal tower of thick timbers like a giant mountain lion, ready to pounce; the tipple was where the coal would be sorted and dumped into big trucks to be driven down the canyon to the train.

Electric wire jostled up the canyon on low poles, but it only seemed to connect to the larger buildings. Outhouses sprang up among the houses like weeds in a neglected furrow. Cars—mostly Model Ts, battered, dirty, and rusting—squatted in front of the many of the houses on a track that was more a stream of mud than a road.

If the food on the back of Hiram's truck had to feed all those people, it would be gone in forty-eight hours.

A gaggle of red-faced children ran past, waving carved sticks at each other. They were stick-thin and dirty, their coats too thin for winter. "Bang, bang, bang!" one group shouted.

"Bang, bang! You're dead, Butch!" the others yelled.

"Nobody kills Butch Cassidy! Ain't you heard? He's still alive and living in Urgentina!"

The gang and pursuing posse both skidded through dirty snow and dropped out of sight down the hill.

The north-facing side of the canyon had far more plant life; below the camp were clusters of willows and cottonwoods, leafless and gray along the creek. Across the water and the road, the south-facing canyon cliffs collected big boulders and few plants. The Kimball house perched there, a shadowy red against the washed-out red rock cliffs like a vulture fresh from its feast. The house didn't even flirt with trees, a lawn, or a garden. Someone had hammered the wood together in front of a dusty driveway, painted it red, and called it good. Telephone lines reached from the eaves to the rocks and wooden posts jammed into the rocks above.

That would have been the work of Teancum Kimball, the man who opened the mine some thirty-odd years ago. Teancum was gone now, and his children owned the mine.

"Know why those rocks are red, Pap?" Michael asked.

Hiram didn't respond. The bishops had also said that Teancum had been a polygamist. How did a man with three wives end up building a house without a single tree or a garden?

"It's the iron in rocks," Michael said. "Hematite is a common mineral, an iron oxide, found in Utah. It comes from the Greek word 'haema' which means blood. Blood rocks."

Blood rocks. In his pocket, Hiram carried a bloodstone.

He stepped out of the truck, feeling slightly ill.

"Are you listening to what I'm saying, Pap?"

"Yes." Hiram stepped to the front of the truck and leaned

on the hood. That red house surrounded by the blood rocks had dark windows the color of pitch.

Hiram's ears started ringing. He blinked, trying to resist a sudden dizziness. A sweet smell with a hint of spice, like onions, garlic, and maybe horseradish, filled his nose. He was on the edge of falling into the smell, and the ringing grew harsher in his ears. Or was it the loud, sharp whistle that wasn't the wind, wasn't a train, might not even be anything outside of his own senses. His vision narrowed.

Hiram blinked. The cold bit his cheeks.

"Rupert and Giles," he murmured. "Rupert and Giles..." He couldn't remember the charm to stop fainting spells.

He couldn't catch a breath. The ringing in his ears got louder, only it wasn't a ringing, it was a buzzing. A fly a quarter-inch long, black as ink, hummed slowly through past Hiram's face and then landed on his neck. He whipped his hand back to smack it.

And missed.

Suddenly, the phantom odor dissipated. Hiram's knees buckled, but he caught himself, and his hearing returned to normal.

"Pap, are you okay?" Michael was leaning out of the truck.

Hiram squeezed his eyes shut. "Yes."

He got back into the passenger seat, Michael squeaked the gears into first, and they trundled off.

Michael knocked Hiram's thigh with the Coke bottle. "Were you having a spell, Pap?"

"Not quite. Almost."

Michael sighed. "Jesus Christ, you're lucky I'm here."

Hiram took a deep breath. "I *am* lucky. No need to cuss."

"I tried saying cripes, and you objected to *that*, too."

"Yes, well. I'm not crazy about that word."

"'Cripes'? It doesn't mean anything."

"It means the same thing as the curse word you're pretending not to say."

Michael snorted; that might be as close to an acknowledgement as Hiram would get. "I might sing some blues while you unload."

Michael was trying to get his goat. "That jazz music is dangerous." Hiram grinned to lighten the mood. Jazz music didn't really bother him, though some jazz *musicians* did.

"Pap, I'm seventeen years old. I'm in my prime. I'm *supposed* to be rowdy, and engaged in all manner of unwise behavior."

"Not your prime," Hiram said. "You're just starting out."

"Mahonri says you're giving me good guidance, and that you're just trying to save me heartache later. That does nothing to soothe me, I can tell you."

"Mahonri Young is a smart man," Hiram muttered. "It's why he works in a library. Slow down, son, to save on the dust."

"The dust is behind us. What do you care?"

"Butch Cassidy's behind us, too."

They reached the camp. Men sat on rough wooden stools beside a long leaning building. It must be a boarding house, but it looked more like a poorly-built chicken coop. Coal dust blackened both the men and the buildings.

On the opposite side of the track, a row of houses leaned against each other to remain standing.

An orange streak—a cat—flashed across the road. Michael slammed on the brakes and the Double-A bounced to a halt. The tabby sped under the steps leading up into a little shack, leaning hard to the right.

Michael exhaled and pushed himself back from the wheel. The car seat springs squeaked. "Well, that was a close one."

Five kids ran across the road, following the cat. They all looked to be under ten, wearing patched clothes and shoes that were too big or held together with twine. The oldest was a girl in a formless dress that might once have been white but was now a sooty gray. The dress's lace looked like a spiderweb torn apart by a rainstorm. She carried a long cottonwood stick, the end sharpened to a point.

The other children followed the girl. She yelled something in a foreign tongue; the children fanned out. A pair of young greasy-faced boys crouched on either side of the house's steps. The girl calmly carried her spear forward.

Hiram clambered out of the truck. "Hey, girl, easy there. Let's not hurt the cat."

She glared to him, shouted something he didn't understand, and waved her spear. Then she pointed at the steps.

The cat yowled and hissed.

"You don't want to torture that animal," Hiram said.

One of littlest children in the group wiped at his mouth. He might be five years old, and the whites of his eyes were bright pink. He was stick-thin.

They all were.

The door swung open and a lean woman emerged, muscular arms busting out of a gray dress with dull red flowers printed on it. Her thick black hair was held back in a red bandana. Gray cotton long john pants peeped out below her dress, and her feet were bare. She glanced at Hiram and the truck behind him, and then shouted to her children.

Her shouts didn't make the cat any calmer.

"Mister," the woman said, "what is it you want?" She had furious brown eyes and her mouth slanted downward to the left.

Hiram swept off his hat and smoothed down the sparse hairs on his head. "I'm Hiram Woolley. I just don't want anyone to hurt that cat."

The woman's frowned jammed further down her face, slanting like her home. "What business is it of yours? Are you the sheriff?"

"No," Hiram said. "I have groceries. I'm taking it to Bill Sorenson, but...I'll happily give you some now."

The girl with the spear went on a run of foreign jabber, pointing at Hiram, at the cat, and then at the woman.

The woman must be her mother; they had the same eyes.

She squinted at Hiram for a long time.

"Medea Markopoulos," she finally said. "My warrior daughter is Callista. Most of these others are my children, too. Park. We'll take the food."

The daughter wouldn't stop talking. Medea plucked the spear out of Callista's hand and used it to shoo her sons away from the steps.

The cat skedaddled.

Hiram went back to his truck and walked with Michael as he parked it in a scraggly patch of weeds. Hiram lifted an apple box of food, as did Michael. They followed Medea into her house.

Without her spear, Callista folded her arms across her chest, glaring at Hiram. With dark eyes and dark hair, and the look of defiance in her face, she reminded Hiram of how Michael had looked, six or seven years earlier.

Around the time, say, that Elmina had died.

Callista's brothers stood with her, but their eyes went to the tins of beans, the long green stalks of root vegetables, and the sacks of flour. The little one drooled down his chin.

Inside, the only light came from a single window in the back of the room. A man lay on a stuffed mattress on the corner of the floor; pillows and blankets were stacked under him, propping his head up. His eyes were closed and his leg was wrapped in bandages. Two other mattresses leaned against the walls.

A stove in the opposite corner radiated heat. Shelves made of long slats of wood nailed into one wall held dishes, eating utensils, pots, pans, and other necessaries. A table and a cluster of chairs were pushed against the wall between the door and the stove.

Hiram set the food down and took off his hat again. Michael set down a sack with more food in it; Hiram smiled at his son. The woman backed up against the homemade cabinetry. Leaning against the shelves were an ancient rifle and a curved sword.

The man on the bed coughed.

"Pap," Michael said, "it's the . . . guy . . ."

Hiram recognized the man's widow's peak and Fuller brush moustache. The man's thigh turned at an unnatural angle.

Medea moved to stand beside Widow's Peak. "My Basil. He hurt his leg."

"Yeah." Hiram's heart was heavy. "Basil needs to see a doctor. If his leg heals like that, he'll be lame for life."

Medea's eyes flashed pride and anger. "This is none of your business."

Hiram nodded slowly. "Have a good day, ma'am."

"Nice meeting you," Michael mumbled.

Medea nodded once.

They returned to the truck. The kids poured into the house. Those beans weren't going to last long against those hungry mouths. Callista stood last in the open doorway, watching them.

Michael drove them away. Hiram sat with his hand covering his mouth. A heavy feeling hung in his stomach.

"And they can't pay for a doctor, right?" Michael said. "Because the mine is closed?"

Hiram nodded. "Maybe the mine won't stay closed. And at least they're eating today."

"Gee, that's just great," Michael said. "Until the food runs out. We have to get that mine back open. Or . . . something. This isn't right."

"Even though they tried to rob us?"

"They were hungry, Pap. You said it yourself. And did you see those kids? They weren't just playing with that cat, Pap. They were going to eat it."

Hiram looked out the window and they drove on through the camp.

Men in denim stared at them. Children played.

But no chickens, no goats, no pigs.

Hiram lifted two fingers in a greeting at a knot of men.

They spat on the ground.

"This place is making me feel lucky to be a farmer." Michael licked the mouth of the now-empty Coke bottle.

"You're not a farmer. You're a future geologist."

"Or spaceman."

"Turn left there," Hiram said, and they left the main track. He was looking for the biggest houses in the camp itself, trying to find Vilhelm Sorenson.

They trundled down a slope, across the bridge, and up the other side. Laundry, streaked and mottled gray with soot, flapped on lines around the hastily-made single room clapboard houses. The houses had tar-paper roofs and siding but very few had windows. They did, however, have gardens, limp and yellow with weeds and winter. As the track became narrow and Michael's driving slowed, Hiram could smell the wafting reek of the outhouses.

They made a turn, following the road as it twisted up through houses that seemed abandoned. Michael and Hiram fell silent. Even the Double-A seemed to putter a bit more quietly.

Three men walked up the road, blocking it. Michael was forced to stop. All of the men wore dusty overalls and long-sleeved shirts. The fedoras on their heads were black with coal-soot. Each of the newcomers had a shock of blond hair on his head; one wore a red waistcoat and had a thick goiter on his neck. They were solid working men, driving their heels into the mud of the road at each step. In their hands they held ax handles.

Everyone in this camp seemed prepared to fight.

Hiram stepped out of the truck, kept the door open, and tried to stay calm. "I'm looking for Vilhelm Sorenson."

The three men stopped and glowered. Two of them turned to their comrade Goiter, likely the one who spoke the best English. "*Ja*," he said, "up the hill. *Einundfünfzig*. One and fifty."

Hiram nodded. "Thank you...*danke*."

"You a friend of Sorenson's?" the German asked.

"I try to be everyone's friend. I brought food for the camp." He gave them a final nod and retreated to the truck.

He slid in and Michael got the truck going again. The boy muttered under his breath, chanting through the steps of starting the vehicle. They took another turn, drove past a school and a company store. Worried women in dresses talked, ragged children played, and lean men sat in groups. Hiram saw Serbs, Croats, more Greeks, more Germans, and a few Orientals.

The house numbered 51 had a pig-shaped piece of wood nailed to the door.

Chapter Five

A HUGE MAN BURST FROM THE HOUSE. HE TROMPED HEAVILY, stooped, left shoulder lowered, swatting at unseen enemies with a rolled-up newspaper in one fist. His thin hair showed a forehead like a limestone cliff; the tangle of eyebrows rose as high as a full inch and his smashed nose dangled slightly sideways. "Hey, dere, mister. You want to see me? If you're from de railroad, you turn around, or else I bloody your nose."

"We got everyone's attention," Michael said. "Perhaps you should run for local office, Pap."

Hiram eased out of the truck and raised his hands. "I'm looking for Vilhelm Sorenson."

"And who sent you?" The giant's left hand was missing its last two fingers.

"I have groceries for the camp," Hiram said. "It's got some beets on account I'm a beet farmer, in from Lehi." He must be nervous; he felt his grammar slipping. "But some bishops in Utah Valley let me into their storehouses, so I have other groceries, too. Ham. Flour. Beans. About two days' worth, maybe." The camp was bigger than Hiram had expected.

"Bishops? Catholic bishops?"

"Mormon bishops," Hiram said.

The man-cliff lowered the newspaper. "I'm Sorenson. I'm de foreman here. And you are what, Mr. Mormon? A do-gooder?"

Hiram knew that he stood in the least Mormon part of the

State of Utah, and *do-gooder* sounded a lot like *meddler* and maybe *hypocrite.*

"I'm a man with a truck full of food," Hiram said. "Do you want to help pass it out? Or shall I just leave it at your door?"

The Dane lumped his way forward to the edge of the porch. "A Mormon beet-farmer, on my doorstep. *Gud,* what a world."

Even stooped, the Dane stood eye to eye with Hiram. Hiram smelled pomade in the giant's hair and smoke on his clothes.

Sorenson softened further. "Maybe you should come inside. We can talk a bit. I'll tell de men to come for de food. We'll take it. Gratefully. Your boy can park de truck dere." He waved to men across the track, then pointed to a space in front of the house.

"That's Michael, my son," Hiram said.

Michael flicked some fingers at the Dane, then clutched and shifted. He eased the Double-A into the offered spot.

"I hear the mine is closed." Hiram said, and immediately regretted it. His words would only make him sound like a meddler.

"You a friend of de Kimballs?" Sorenson smacked the newspaper into his left hand.

Hiram repeated what he'd said to the men. "Never met them, but I'd like to think I'm everyone's friend. Do-gooder, remember?"

Sorenson smiled, revealing a big cracked front tooth, blackened where it wasn't yellow. "*Ja,* funny guy. I like guys dat make me laugh. Like Charlie Chaplin, he's always funny."

"Michael's the funny one." Hiram motioned for Michael to join them and he followed Sorenson inside. Despite his limp, the Dane moved with a quick step.

Hiram gave the pig-shaped design nailed to the door a long look.

Sorenson noticed. "De Germans, dey think de pig and de numbers bring luck. Something about de three kings. We need de luck now, dat's for sure, and my wife believes."

Memories of Elmina's smile and the way she looked at him while he washed the dishes flooded over Hiram, wiping the smile from his face. Bitter, gut-punching echoes of her final screams, as she lay dying of some hidden sickness on their marriage bed, followed. Six years. Had six years passed, since her death and the Crash?

He took off his hat and finger-combed his hair.

The house had three rooms: a parlor; a bedroom on the left,

bed just visible through the cracked door; and a kitchen on the right. Needlepoint images of boys and girls playing hung on the parlor walls and a little side table was covered with a lacy doily. Heat radiated into the parlor from a cast-iron wood-burning stove in the kitchen. A hissing kerosene lamp hung from a hook. The camp had electricity, and the Sorensons didn't seem poor. Did Bill Sorenson prefer not to have electricity in his home?

Hiram and Michael followed Sorenson into the kitchen. Below the kitchen counter, which was little more than a shelf fixed to the wall, stood a wooden keg. On the counter lay a bowl of yellowing milk and a crust of white bread. Sorenson drew out two chairs from a small table. Both Michael and Hiram sat.

Hiram motioned to the bowl and the crust of bread. "Is that for Robin Goodfellow?"

Sorenson raised an eyebrow, a feat of strength that would have crushed a lesser man. "What? De wife again. But we are not here to talk about bogeymen and spirits. We have problems. You bring food? Fine. But dat won't fix us for long. De men need jobs, or dey need to leave. Maybe I tell you, and you tell de bishop, and he talks to Ammon Kimball. And we fix dis for good."

Sorenson gripped his newspaper roll with both hands. "You want beer, boy? Or are you Mormon, too?"

"Officially, I suppose I am," Michael said. "Really, I'm unaffiliated. However, I'm not one to touch intoxicating liquors."

"Water would be fine," Hiram said. "And I agree with you. It's not good for men to be idle. Food only solves the problem for a couple of days."

Sorenson rose and went to a bucket next to the stove. "Ammon runs de mine. No, he doesn't run anything, he sits over dere in de big red house, scratching his boils. De mine is closed while de Kimballs claw each udder's eyes out. Teancum disappeared two years now, him and his new wife. My wife says he is dead. I say he had wife number four, who was younger dan his daughters, what man wouldn't want to run away with her? But she dreamed he was dead, but den she dreamed about de ghosts of de eastern seam. Dreams." He snorted.

Hiram listened closely. Without meaning to, he found himself fingering his Saturn ring. "Is that what Robin Goodfellow does? Does he bring your wife dreams?"

"*Gud* help me if I know. I thought he killed mice." Sorenson took the bucket and poured water into three tin cups. "My men always talk of de haunts, too. Some of de men say dey heard whispers in de eastern seam, and of course, dere are shadows and laughing. It sounds like a bad movie, no? Not a funny movie, with Charlie Chaplin. And den dere are stories of strange animal things running around on top of de mesa. If dat weren't bad enough, robbers are on de roads. Nothing is good. Nowhere is safe."

Hiram thought of Basil and Medea Markopoulos and their hungry children.

Sorenson splashed the bucket down on the counter. "Robbers are real enough. Ghosts? I think not. Before de mine closed, I had to pay Chinamen extra to go down dere. We got it done. I always get de work done, when dere is work."

Hiram closed his eyes. A haunted mine was probably just overactive imaginations, gossip, idleness, and liquor.

But if not... Wells had told him to keep his eyes open.

"If the mine is closed, what are the men still doing here?" Michael asked. "I'd have figured they'd take off for greener pastures."

"What green pastures?" Sorenson stood with his arms crossed. "Farmers come up from de fields to mine in de winter. Dey wait. Might as well wait here, radder dan wait at home in dead fields. Dey're okay, dey gotta go plant soon, anyway. But de real miners? Dey're in deep to de company store. We pay rent here, and dat works as long as we're getting paid. But when we don't get paid, we still owe rent. We owe, and we can't leave, not until we're paid off. No paychecks, dough. And every week, more rent."

Hiram sighed.

Michael jumped from his seat. "Come on! How is that fair?"

Sorenson laughed. "Boy, maybe somebody promised you life will be fair. Instead... rich men drink cream and eat beef, arguing with each other, while we get poorer."

"It's *Michael*, not *boy*." If Michael's mind was sharp, his tongue was sharper. "But... at some point, you have to cut loose and take off, and try to find work somewhere else. It's not like the Kimballs could come after you."

The big Dane turned to Hiram and rumbled out more laughter. "Oh, your boy is quite a talker."

"Always has been," Hiram admitted. Maybe he should have taught Michael to curb his tongue more, but he'd never had the heart for that fight. Especially after Hettie and Elmina had died.

Sorenson nodded. "My boy, Anders, he says we should go to de lawyers. He works in de big city now, over in Price. All my udder children moved off. Michael, my friend, we live in bad times, and dere is little work. Udder mines are busy, and dey have problems of deir own. You get a reputation as a trouble-starter, or a debt-dodger, you won't find anyone to hire you." He turned to Hiram. "You don't talk much. Not de funny guy I thought. But now you see, a few groceries won't do a thing. Can you fix dis, do-gooder?"

Could Hiram fix it? Was the mine closed because some people thought it was haunted? Maybe he could consecrate the mine, or perform an exorcism. Or if it was a matter of setting the men's minds at ease, maybe he could invite a Catholic priest in to do it. How did the Chinese do exorcisms? "My son's the funny one."

"True," Michael said.

"Funny don't open de mine."

Hiram let out a long breath. "You said the Kimballs are fighting. What are they fighting about?"

Sorenson rose and tried to pace the kitchen, but it was too small a space. He wound up leaning against the back wall. "Dat's not so simple. Ammon is an okay joe. He's a mean boss, but dat's okay, I understand dat a mean boss gets de work done."

"Hold on there, old-timer," Michael said. "All the names are running together for me. So Ammon is Teancum's son. Is he the oldest?"

"No, Eliza, de sister, she's de oldest. She was born when Teancum ran cattle here, before de mine. The Kimballs are Mormon, and dey used to have all de wives around here. First wife, first child, Eliza. But old Teancum liked 'em young." He raised his eyebrows at Hiram.

"I only had the one wife," Hiram said. "Don't know what I'd do with two."

He tried not to think about the dark day when he'd learned two things at the same time. One, that the reason he saw his father so rarely was that Abner Woolley was a polygamist, and spent most of his time with other wives and children. And two, via a letter postmarked from Phoenix, that Abner was leaving for Mexico and wouldn't come back.

That day, Hiram had staggered to the edge of Grandma Hettie's farm and stared southward across the lake until well after midnight.

He shook off the memory.

Sorenson laughed some more. "Agreed. Second wife, and out came Ammon. One child per wife, or one living child, anyway. Lots of babies born dead. Dat's how it goes, sometimes. Third wife died giving birth to Samuel, but by dat time, Teancum's wives weren't so happy. So dey all leave, and Eliza, she leaves too. Ammon and Samuel stay, but only for a time. Samuel was always de strange one, an artist. Soft in de head. He leaves too and it's just Teancum and Ammon."

"How long ago was that?" Michael asked.

"During de Great War," Sorenson said. "Dat's what? Seventeen years now?"

Hiram felt the years. He felt the war, too. That was where he'd met Michael's father, in the trenches of Verdun.

"And Teancum got a fourth wife?" he asked.

"She was pregnant when dey ran off." Sorenson nodded. "Two years ago, it was. And Ammon took over when Teancum went." Sorenson drew a thumb across his throat and made a quacking sound. "We work through de change, no problem. Den Samuel comes back, and he says Ammon is doing everything wrong. Den Eliza comes back, and she fights, too. For what? I don't know. Ammon comes to me and he says de mine must close. He gets de Germans on his side, some of de Croats, de Serbs, and den Samuel gets de Greeks, de Chinamen, de Japs, to go for him, and everything stops."

Hiram furrowed his brow and squinted. "There's still coal in the mine?"

"*Ja.* But Ammon says we got to dig in one place, and Samuel says he wants a new shaft entirely, and each of dem got a gang. So we don't dig nowhere. We stopped and can't start again until de family decides what to do, since dey all own it togedder. Your bishop wants to fix things, maybe he can get de family to stop fighting."

"Or at least get two of them to agree," Hiram said.

"And every damned day, you owe the company more rent." Michael shook his head.

"That's not much better than *cripes*," Hiram murmured.

"Yes, cursing is fitting in dis case," Sorenson shot back. "You know what I think?"

Hiram said nothing.

"Tell us," Michael said.

"I think it is de railroad, again, damn railroad, and I curse when I say it, you hear me?" He smacked the rolled-up newspaper into his palm. "Dere's a man, Naaman Rettig, and he works in de Hotel Utah. Denver and Rio Grande Western, de D and RGW. He comes into town, and maybe he talks to Eliza, since she is in de hotel as well. Pah! She has de big house across de way, and she spends de money de miners should be getting to live in a hotel. Eliza and de Rettig railroad man, maybe dey talk. And maybe I'm out of a job."

"How's that?" Michael asked.

"I don't have such a good history with de railroad," Sorenson replied.

Hiram sighed, trying to find a handhold on the problem. Where to start?

"That doesn't make sense," Michael insisted. "Spring Canyon is useless to the railroad. It doesn't go anywhere, so there's no point running tracks up here."

"Papa Charlie Chaplin, what do you say to dat?" Sorenson asked.

Hiram leaned forward, elbows on his knees. "If the railroad had the mine, they'd get the coal at cost."

"And damn de miners." Sorenson slapped the newspaper against the wall. "You think our debt is unfair now? Wait until de Denver and Rio Grande Western railroad comes. Dey will pay us pennies. Dere's a woman, McGill maybe, and she says de boys gotta form a local of her union. She says we can make it fair, and she tries to help, but what can a woman do?"

"Vote, for one thing," Michael said. "Finally."

The door to the Sorenson house was thrown open and filled by the three large blond men. "Bill, ve make you stay here," Goiter said. "Zere's a meetink, and you aren't invited."

Sorenson sprang to his feet. "You mean, something's happening, and you been sent to keep me out of it. Who did dat? Wagner, wasn't it?"

With the foreman looming over them, the three men with ax handles looked embarrassed and small. They said nothing.

"You idiots!" Sorenson lurched through Michael and Hiram, spilling them off their chairs. The Germans raised their weapons, surprise evident in their faces, and the foreman battered them back with his rolled-newspaper club, then disappeared out the door.

Hiram stumbled for the door, the cowed Germans scattering at his approach. "Stay here, Michael. Don't leave the house."

Michael was speechless, for once, but he wasn't any more obedient than usual, and bounced right into Hiram's wake.

Hiram broke out of the house and went to the truck. The groceries were gone. He snatched the Colt from the glove box, praying he wouldn't have to use it.

With Michael following at his heels, Hiram headed toward the mine.

Chapter Six

MARY MCGILL FOUND HERSELF TROTTING, SWEPT ALONG WITH
the crowd of German miners. The sky overhead was a pale blue,
devoid of clouds. The mob surrounding her stank of the anger
and sweat of working men. It was a familiar smell.

The tipple sat unused, no trucks under the scored chute, and
the conveyor belts inside silent. No cars carrying coal emerged
from the mine entrance.

"You've got to save your outrage for the main event," she said.

Hermann Wagner was a paunchy German with a perfect cube
of a head, its symmetry only barely disturbed by tiny, constantly-
blinking eyes and crumpled ears. The ears weren't even opposite
each other—Wagner looked as if he'd bobbed for apples in a bin
full of cauliflower, and come up with two florets stuck to random
sides of his squared-off noggin.

He had no official title, but by popular deference Wagner was
the Head German of the Kimball Mine.

"I can give it to those Greek bastards all night and still have
enough for Sam Kimball." Wagner chuckled. "What did you call
it, Gil? A body shoot for young Sam."

"Body *shot*," Mary said. "But Sam isn't the main event. It's
all the Kimballs. You need the mine open, you need better prices
for the coal you pull out, you need no interest on advances at
the company store and for your rent, you need the child labor
law actually *enforced*—"

"Hold on," Wagner said. "My Klaus is a good boy. He don't mind the work."

Mary sighed, lengthening her stride to keep up. McClatchy hadn't wanted her to come out to the mining camps around Helper, but when he'd enumerated the list of reasons why, it had consisted mostly of physical dangers to which his fading sense of chivalry didn't want Mary McGill exposed: bandits, the remoteness of doctors, bad roads, restless Indians, rockslides, and rattlesnakes. He'd never suggested she might encounter miners too eager to side with the mine owners for their own good.

"If you made enough for your own work," she said, "Klaus wouldn't have to sort rocks out of the mine carts and carry messages up and down the mine. He could go to school. Maybe become a doctor. Doesn't that sound good?"

"*Ja*," Wagner agreed. "*Ja*, Gil, okay. But first we got to get the mine open, and that means digging out the east seam like Mr. Ammon says. None of this stupid new shaft nonsense like Sam wants. That guy gets a body shoot, him and all his Greek friends."

Mary bit her tongue.

They passed through two tarpaper shanties and into the open space below the mouth of Kimball Mine. The mine buildings, mortared sheds of the yellow and orange stone poking through the juniper all around Kimball Canyon, lined an avenue that tumbled down from the gaping mine-mouth and then opened into a rough and muddy plaza. Behind a coal shed, and stretching away on two earth shelves that had been created by splitting a long slope in two with a retaining wall of railroad ties, stood the tarpaper shacks and the rickety boarding houses in which the miners lived. The Kimball Mine was the shaft, Kimball was the name of the shantytown in which the miners lived, the Kimball Corporation held the deeds, and Kimball was the name of the family that owned it all. The red Kimball house brooded on the north side of the canyon, across the road and the seasonal Kimball Creek.

Ammon Kimball stood in the lane leading up to the mine. He was a heavy man, all shoulders, whose hanging head and perpetual frown made him look like an angry bull. He wore plain blue jeans and a navy work coat, and he shifted from foot to foot as if he were in discomfort. His eyes were sunk deep in dark pits, like all his family's were.

The two plaster strips on his neck were probably covering shaving cuts, but they nevertheless made Mary feel abruptly self-conscious about the fact that the entire left side of her face was marked with a large red blotch. An angel's kiss, her mother had called it. *Damn, but that must have been one enormous and excitable angel*, her father had said while drunk.

She forced herself not to touch her own face.

Ammon stood glowering at a crowd of Greek miners. Mary recognized Dimitrios Kalakis with his single enormous eyebrow and the waves of eastern cologne he favored; that stuff smelled like cloves and oranges on the verge of going bad. With him stood club-footed Stavros Alafouzos and a third man Mary didn't immediately recognize; he was small, but he had well-muscled arms crossed over his chest, and a red bandana covering his face.

"Go home," Ammon growled. "Unless you're prepared to dig the east seam."

"Or stand aside and let Germans do the work!" Hermann Wagner thumped a fist to his sternum, then stepped to Ammon Kimball's side.

Ammon snorted.

That was when Mary noticed the gun.

There was nothing unusual about firearms in Kimball. Even in good times, many of the men hunted deer, rabbits, and elk to supplement the canned peaches and biscuit flour they bought from the company store. But the Kimball Corporation was strict about firearms anywhere near the mine. In addition to the obvious risk of shooting other employees, any kind of spark might ignite the coal dust and the coal in the mine. The miners were forbidden to smoke within a hundred yards of the mineshaft, for the same reason.

So the fact that Paul Schneider—Mary thought of him as "Stinky," despite the delicate carpentry work he did, because the man apparently never bathed and lived on a diet of the strongest available cheese—carried a rifle over his shoulder was not strange. The fact that he had the rifle within a dozen steps of the mine shaft opening was odd, and would have ordinarily gotten him docked pay, if not fired.

But if Ammon noticed the rifle, he said nothing.

"Strong Germans, my feet!" Dimitrios Kalakis trilled. Despite his heavy features and the single eyebrow like a black caterpillar slung ear to ear across his face, he had the high-pitched, trilling voice of a nervous woman. "If you want to dig, the only thing to do is to get a Greek, always! Have you heard of Herakles? One of his greatest feats was rescuing the three thousand cattle of King Augeas, who were trapped in their byre, how do you say it? Their cattle shed. And how did Herakles do it? He *dug!* He dug a hole so vast that in one day all three thousand cows could walk through it! And Herakles, was he a German?"

"If he had been German," Hermann Wagner bellowed, "he would have done it in six hours!"

Dimitrios waved his fist. "He was a Greek!"

"Stand aside and let us work!" Wagner shouted.

Mary kept her eye on Stinky. The man shifted from foot to foot and licked his lips.

"You do not decide what work gets done in this mine!" Dimitrios shrieked.

"No!" Ammon roared. "But *I* do!"

The door of the shed behind Dimitrios slid open, revealing Samuel Kimball, flanked by two more Greeks. Samuel looked like a lighter version of Ammon; they were the same height and had the same eyes, but the younger brother might have had fifty percent of Ammon's weight removed from each limb. Where Ammon glowered and stared into each step he took, Samuel stood as if perpetually recoiling, his long, pale, stained fingers fluttering over his chest.

Black feathers protruded from the neck and sleeves of his shirt. Had he pasted them there, or had Samuel Kimball been sleeping in a literal crows' nest?

"Samuel!" Ammon snarled. "Get off my land!"

"No, brother!" Samuel's sudden arm movements looked like the flapping of a bird's wings. "I'm a Kimball and I will have my say! And you know as well as I do that the east seam is petering out. Not to mention the things, Ammon, the things we've seen down there in the deep, in the dark, down, down, down below. It's a poisoned place. We need to sink a new shaft. You *know* it to be true! *You know!*"

Mary wanted to slap him.

"I know no such thing," Ammon growled back at his brother.

"You know it." Samuel stroked his own nose. "*You* know it the same way that *I* know it."

"Nonsense," Ammon snarled.

"He must have told you." Samuel stared with large eyes magnified by his glasses.

"Gil," a German miner at her elbow whispered, pointing. "Look!"

The crusty old foreman, Bill Sorenson, charged to the edge of the ring, just a few steps to Mary's right. Behind Sorenson came someone new. He was tall and lanky, and he would have been handsome if he'd had a little more meat on his bones. It was hard to tell with the fedora he wore, but Mary guessed he was in his forties. He wore a faded Army coat over blue overalls, and his hands were in his pockets. Behind him came a tall young man—slightly taller than the fellow with the fedora, and with a solid chest—whose complexion and features suggested he was some kind of Indian. Navajo, maybe? The kid wore a sneer, and looked around at the entire mining camp as if he couldn't believe his surroundings.

"You've been smoking that horseshit again!" Ammon's faced was turning red and the muscles in his neck stood out like the straining lines of a ship running before a strong wind. "No wonder the money ran out!"

"The money ran out because of you, you, all because of you, and your pig head! Your big, pig head!" Samuel crowed. "I know you know! It's time to sink a new shaft!"

"Everybody calm down dere! Right now!" Bill Sorenson bellowed.

Hiram surveyed the two groups of miners. The Germans clustered around the larger of the Kimball brothers, Ammon. With them was a woman who was strikingly free of the black coal dust that stained all the miners' clothing. Hiram didn't know what to call her outfit, but she had a kind of navy-blue woolen suit coat with a matching skirt that dropped to below her calves—he tried not to look too long at her legs—and a wool coat over the top. She looked like she belonged in a city.

Plumes of white breath rose from all present. The place smelled of rough men, lathered up for a fight.

What had gone wrong between the two brothers?

Why did Samuel seem to believe that he and Ammon shared a secret?

A flicker of black caught Hiram's eye, standing out in this grim world in which almost everything was coated with a thin layer of gray. Downhill from the mine entrance, a woman stood beside the passenger's seat of a Model T on the camp's main track. The woman's dress was as black as the paint job of the car; her eyes were sunk in two dark pits below her brow and her face was angry.

Hiram turned back to the fighting men.

"I'm going to mine the east seam," Ammon growled. "Hermann Wagner and his men will mine it for me, ghosts be damned. Dimitrios, if you and your men don't want to get paid anymore, you can clear out." The older Kimball shifted as he talked, an expression of discomfort and irascibility on his face. Caused by the boils Sorenson had mentioned? "Just pay your bills before you leave."

A German with a cube for a head folded his arms across his chest and nodded. Hermann Wagner, presumably.

"Not ghosts be damned!" shouted one of the Greeks in the crowd. "I have seen them!"

There was a round of nodding among the men, and not only on the Greek side of the mob.

"We have families!" This came from one of the Greeks, a lean man whose face was covered by a red bandana. Maybe the bandana filtered out the coal dust from the air to protect his lungs.

"If you go down into that mine," Samuel Kimball said to the Germans, "you'll be trespassing. I'll have you shot as you come up." He waved an arm, and black feathers drifted to the ground.

"I'll do the shooting personally," a Greek with a single thick eyebrow over his entire face and a woman's voice said. Was the smell of wassail coming from him? "Greeks are wonderful shots. Do you know the story of story of the great hunter Orion?"

"You wouldn't dare, Dimitrios!" Wagner told him.

"It would give me joy!" the Greek answered. Beside him, a Greek miner paced back and forth with a traipsing, curious gait; some kind of club foot.

"No one will do dat!" Bill Sorenson bellowed, hurling himself into the ring. "No one will go into de mine without my direction. Anyone who does will answer to me."

"And if I fire you, Sorenson?" Ammon Kimball shouted.

Bill Sorenson laughed. "If you fire me, den you will have to deal with all dese pigheaded sons of bitches on your own."

Ammon and Samuel both glared, Samuel stroking his own temples.

And then Hiram realized who the woman in black must be. He turned just in time to see her getting into the Model T. An unseen chauffeur then drove her away, and as the car turned Hiram saw the word TAXI painted on the side of the Model T in bright yellow.

Eliza Kimball.

"I can replace you, Bill," Ammon growled.

As if that was a signal, Hermann Wagner reached into his pockets and stepped forward. When he pulled his hands from his pants, he held a short length of iron bar in each fist. The bars were too short to swing as clubs, but by holding the iron in his hand, he was weighting his punches.

With a nod to Samuel Kimball, Dimitrios stepped forward, too. He drew a sock from his coat pocket and gave it a swing to test its heft. Hiram heard the jingle of coins in what had become a makeshift sap.

The Greek and the German advanced on each other.

Michael bounced at Hiram's side, antsy.

Sorenson laughed and got between the miners. "You know what de word 'chickenshit' means, boys?" He shoved both sleeves up over his elbows and swatted the air with his newspaper.

Hiram hung back, not sure what to do. Michael stood close to him. Again, a motion drew Hiram's eyes away from the unfolding fight. In the same dirt lane barely vacated by the Model T taxi, a Ford Model B with HELPER CITY POLICE painted on the side threw open its doors and disgorged two men in blue uniforms. One was a tall, scowling colored man, and the other was a pink-faced gasping white man weighed down by a thick ring of belly fat. The white man staggered with the fingers of one hand splayed open, crawling his way through the air as if by main force, and the fingers of the other clenched tight into a fist.

Hermann let out a yell. "Ammon!" His side echoed him.

The others, led by Dimitrios, responded with a battle cry of "Samuel!"

Sorenson shoved Hermann back, raising his newspaper in warning. Dimitrios took that opportunity to whirl the sap around to strike at the Dane. Hiram leaped forward; he spun the Greek about and knocked the weapon out of his hands.

Dimitrios snarled and grabbed at Hiram's throat. Hiram feinted back, drawing the man in, then punched the miner in his breadbasket, knocking the wind out of him.

By that time, Hermann had dodged his foreman to go after an Oriental miner. The German's fists were still loaded with the iron bars. His punches could prove deadly, and the very last thing Kimball Mine needed was a murder.

So when Hermann charged forward, Hiram kicked his legs out from under him.

"No!" the woman in blue shouted. "Don't shoot!"

Hiram whirled. One of the Germans had stepped forward and was now pointing a bolt-action rifle at Samuel Kimball. The woman had grabbed the rifle with both hands and struggled to get control of it.

Time seemed to slow down and accelerate at the same moment.

Hiram threw himself toward the woman.

"The gun, Pap!"

Hiram touched his left hand to his protective amulet and grabbed for the rifle. The chi-rho amulet protected Hiram from enemies. Were these miners his enemies?

They were if they shot at him.

With one hand only, Hiram was at a disadvantage in the three-sided struggle. He succeeded in jerking the barrel away from Samuel Kimball's direction. Hiram ended up in front of the rifle.

Bang!

The shot was loud in Hiram's ears. He smelled the powder and felt the shock of the gun discharging. Something stung his left arm and he lost his grip. Stepping forward, he balled his right hand into a fist and coldcocked the shooter with one punch to the jaw.

As the man collapsed to the ground, Hiram smelled the stink of sour milk.

The woman was left holding the rifle.

The gunshot had stopped the fight. Germans, Greeks, and others drew back as Sorenson stormed about, swinging his newspaper to keep both sides apart.

One of the cops bellowed, "Stop right there! This is the police!"

"Quite the haymaker," the woman said.

Hiram shrugged. "I didn't have much choice."

"My name's Mary." She worked the lever to eject the shell and then pointed the rifle at the mud. "Some people call me Gil."

"Hiram."

"You're under arrest!" the white policeman blustered.

Dimitrios and Hermann glared at each other, surrounded by their countrymen. Sorenson spat on the ground. "You two started dis. I won't forget it."

Hiram expected to see the policemen taking away the Greek and German leaders. He was shocked when, instead, the colored man grabbed him and roughly twisted him to one side, looking at his arm. "This fella's been shot."

The sting. "I must have just been grazed," Hiram said. "I barely noticed it."

"You're under arrest," the white policeman said again. He grabbed Mary, dragging her down toward the Model B.

"She didn't shoot me," Hiram said.

The colored policeman squinted at Hiram.

"No?" the white policeman said. "Then she can explain it to us in the station. She's trouble, this one. Organizing labor to try to force honest businessmen out of business."

"That's nonsense!" Mary cried. The Germans looked embarrassed, but none of them moved to intervene. "I just want them to pay a fair wage and to stop sending children down into the mines!"

"Explain it at the station!" the policeman said again.

Hiram touched his arm where it stung and found blood on his fingertips. "Officer, she's telling the truth."

The pudgy white policeman turned to Hiram. "You wouldn't happen to be Hiram Woolley, would you?"

Hiram nearly snorted in surprise. "I am."

The officer pushed Mary over to the colored policeman and the pair marched toward the Model B. She didn't fight.

The white policeman reached into his pocket and took out a card. "Naaman Rettig, from the D and RGW, is looking to talk to you. He heard you might be arriving today. Lucky I found you, huh?"

Hiram took the card; it was white, with raised gold lettering. "Look, officer, I'll let this man know you gave me his card, but about this woman, she didn't do anything wrong."

The fat cop harrumphed. "She's done plenty wrong." He turned and followed his comrade down the hill.

"I'll come to the station!" Hiram called to Mary as she was pushed into the back seat of the police car. "I promise!"

Chapter Seven

THE MINERS WERE DISPERSING, BILL SORENSON CHASING THEM away. Ammon and Samuel stood staring at each other across foot-churned mud.

Hiram wanted to follow Gil...Mary...the arrested union organizer, but he was afraid that if he left, Ammon Kimball would grab his brother and snap him in two.

"Pap," Michael said. "The gun."

"It's only a flesh wound," Hiram murmured. "There's hydrogen peroxide in the car." He probed the wound with his fingers again, and was pleased; the blood flow had virtually stopped.

That was his heliotropius at work. The dark green stone with blood-red streaks prevented him from being deceived and also stanched the flow of blood. It was also said to drive out poison, prevent deception, and bring rain.

Also fame, which made Hiram reluctant to carry it. He didn't want fame.

He slipped Naaman Rettig's card into his pocket. The railroad man might be able to do something about Mary McGill.

"You've corrupted Dimitrios Kalakis, I see." Ammon Kimball glowered at his brother.

"No more than you've corrupted Hermann Wagner. I bet you promised him Bill Sorenson's job!" Samuel's face flushed bright red, sweat dripped from his round eyeglasses, and spittle speckled his lips.

"You never cared about the mine," Ammon growled. "Father's disappearance wasn't enough to bring you back, so what did it? Is it money? You've run out of money again and you've come home to beg, only you're too proud to ask for anything, so you've talked poor old Dimitrios into helping you try to steal my inheritance?"

Samuel let out a yowl. "The mine belongs to all of us! And so do, so did, so will, Father's other things. His other things!"

Ammon's eyes narrowed. "It was you. You were the thief!"

Hiram stepped forward, putting himself between the two brothers. They ignored him. He closed his fist around the blood-stone and concentrated. Which brother was lying?

"Pap." Michael's voice was soft, but insistent.

Samuel's flushed face darkened further. "I have taken nothing, nothing, nothing that didn't belong to me." His mouth worked soundlessly for a moment. "What I was given, I have returned! You know, Ammon, you know, but you hate me. You hate me and it's blinded you!"

Ammon laughed, a single bark like a dog losing interest. "Go back to your paint squirts, and get the hell off Kimball Corporation land. Before one of the monsters you're so anxious to believe in gets hold of you!"

The bloodstone lay inert throughout the conversation.

The older Kimball stomped away, shouldering past Hiram and heading down the hill and across the canyon toward his house. Samuel stared after Ammon, the round glasses unable to hide the rapid fluttering of his eyelashes. Then the younger brother moved, with less certainty, feet dragging in the mud-crusted snow, and seemed to fade into the landscape in a cloud of his own frozen breath as he moved down the canyon.

"Pap," Michael said, "you should have shot that guy with the rifle. This is the whole reason to have a gun, so you can shoot someone who's threatening you."

"There were too many innocents standing around," Hiram said. "And that's not the reason I carry the pistol."

Michael looked skeptical. "Well, you don't carry it to let me target shoot."

"I carry the revolver so I can shoot someone who's threatening *you*," Hiram said.

"Thanks for that, I guess." Michael frowned, hands on hips.

"You want to go down to the jail to try to rescue that lady unionist, aren't you?"

"Don't you?"

They turned and headed down to the Double-A.

"Yeah. Only the difference is, I want to do it because it's the right thing to do, and you want to do it because you made a promise."

"Keeping promises is not a terrible thing, Michael." One of the large promises Hiram had kept in his life was his vow to Yas Yazzie to take care of Yas's son. Michael. He'd promised it in Yas's dying moments, as he'd accepted Yas's revolver, and, at Yas's insistence, scratched his own initials next to his friend's on the barrel—an *H.W.* next to a *Y.Y.* Yas's wife Betty, Michael's mother, had died of the Spanish flux shortly after Michael's birth.

Michael had never known his birth parents. He'd lost Grandma Hettie while he was quite young, and then his adopted mother. The boy had grown up surrounded by tragedy. Maybe that was why Hiram had never been hard on Michael. Maybe that also explained the young man's tendency to lash out.

"I'll drive," Michael said. "You're so righteous, the truck might wither at your very touch."

As they descended to town, the late afternoon sun gave a blue cast to the snow frosting the hills around Kimball Canyon. Beneath the blue-white caps, the canyon walls tumbled down in yellow and orange scree, split by horizontal shelves of stone.

Michael explained how the forces of erosions cut the canyon through the layers of rock, wind and rain, ice and sunshine. He pointed out that south and west, the layers were cracked into multiple thin slices. On the north and east, the stone remained in larger blocks, rounded divots scooped out of the stone.

For Michael, it was all the action of wind and rain on the stone.

To Hiram, the divots made the stone appear as if dozens of skulls lurked just behind the façade of the rock and were straining to push through. The land felt haunted. He remembered how he'd almost succumbed to one of his spells when he'd gazed into the dark windows of the Kimball family home.

What had gone wrong in the Kimball family?

And should Hiram do anything about it? He had delivered the groceries; his job was done.

Or was his work truly done, if he left the mine unopened? Did that make him like a doctor who only dispensed morphine to relieve the pain, and didn't try to treat the underlying disease? If he only gave the men food, but left them idle and without means to feed themselves in the future, he had only delayed the pain and violence that must result.

And there were Medea and her children. He had personally run over Medea's husband. Could he really leave while that family was in such dire straits?

And if the problem at the root of all this trouble was a haunted mine, could Bill Sorenson or Ammon Kimball or any of the others really do anything? Or would it take someone with the wisdom and lore of a cunning man?

Hiram sighed. In any case, he had to get Mary out of jail. Surely when he made a formal statement that she hadn't shot him, she'd be released.

Though that might mean he'd have to implicate the German fellow as the shooter. He didn't relish that idea. But surely he could say the shooting had been an accident.

There was some truth in that.

Kimball Canyon opened into the larger Spring Canyon at the site of Dollar's.

"I kind of want to stop and get a Coke, Pap."

Hiram, too, felt hot and thirsty. He thought of Gus Dollar's wax poppet, though, and wanted to push on. "Let's wait until we get down into town."

He looked at Dollar's as they drove past. Three cars were parked beside the clapboard building. The other canyons opening at this crossroads into Spring held other mines; this was the coal center of the state, and, together with the railroad, that made the area the industrial heart of Utah. Gus Dollar made his living selling things the company stores didn't provide, and he drew traffic in by a charm. He must talk to many miners, and miners' wives and children.

Could Gus tell Hiram what had happened to the Kimballs?

But the thought of talking too much with Gus made Hiram uneasy. He examined his heart to find the cause. Was it that he disliked another man knowing that Hiram knew hexes and charms, or that his father had had other wives? That surely was a part of it. Hiram was private by nature. Grandma Hettie had taught him to be even more discreet than he was already naturally inclined to be; a person who worked charms was often misunderstood, and easily accused of being a witch.

What else, though?

Hiram laughed out loud. Michael stared at him, swerved slightly, but managed to stay on the road.

"What's so funny?" his son asked.

"Mankind," Hiram answered. "The Fall. Me."

Envy. Wasn't that it? Envy, pure and simple. Gus was wealthy and successful and by every indication better at hexing than Hiram. Their very first encounter has consisted of Gus besting Hiram with a charm, drawing Hiram into his store to sell him Cokes.

And then, as if to rub in his superiority, the man had given him one of the Cokes for free.

But no, that hadn't been Gus's purpose. He'd given Michael a free drink out of generosity.

Though...could a free bottle of chilled Coca-Cola be a vehicle for a hex? Was it possible that Gus Dollar had given Hiram the second Coke for free as a way to bewitch Michael?

Hiram laughed out loud again.

Envy.

"You're weird, Pap," Michael said. "I'm not saying I don't love you. But you're an odd one."

Hiram took the revolver from his coat pocket and put it back in the glove box, along with the loaded full moon.

Spring Canyon was broad and green. Junipers and lodgepole pines climbed up the canyon walls, and the gambol oak and cottonwoods clustering along the banks of the water flowing down the canyon's center—Spring Creek, probably?—would add further green, come spring. The canyon twisted gently this way and that, revealing small herds of cattle sheltering in each new bend and drinking at man-made pools. The canyon opened for the final time sinking down toward the Price River.

Michael continued his geology lesson. "And this decline is known as a high alluvial fan. The creek grew wider and dumped more sediment out as it slowed down."

"And I wanted you to stay in school. It seems you got schooling."

"Libraries are fun, teachers aren't, and I can talk to girls at church, which might be the only good reason to go."

The road wound down the fan, past a row of small bungalows and then a wooden sign that read *Helper*.

"That's us," Michael said. "Professional helpers. Only we don't get paid. So volunteers, I guess."

"The town got its name from the railroads," Hiram told him.

"The Helper Railroad?" Michael frowned. "I thought it was something longer, the DGGWR, or something."

"The D and RGW. Denver and Rio Grande Western. No, a helper locomotive is an extra engine car they attach to a train when it needs additional push to get it uphill. West of here, the railroad goes uphill steeply."

"Back along Highway 89," Michael said. "The way we came."

"Right. So they have to attach a helper locomotive here. Or more than one helper, sometimes. And they called the railroad station where they did that *Helper*, and then that became the name of the town."

"Surely," Michael said, "such prosaically minded town fathers must soon rename the town Brothel. Or Prostituteville, that sounds very scenic. Or maybe they could use the French word for a prostitute. Is that something you learned in the war, by any chance?"

"Michael," Hiram said.

"I'm just going by what you told me. Far more brothels than Lehi, you said."

"Well, that isn't hard." Hiram took the card out of his pocket and examined it. The front of the card had both Price, Utah, and Denver, Colorado addresses. On the back, scrawled in tight, almost illegible penmanship, were the words: Hotel Utah. "Anyway, we can ask this Naaman Rettig what he thinks the name of the town should be. We talk to him first, because maybe he can help us get the union lady out of jail."

"And then drive home?" Michael asked.

Hiram didn't respond.

The road followed Spring Creek until it joined the Price River. Crossing the river on a bridge made of railroad ties, the Double-A was struck by a sudden fierce breeze, blowing from the north.

Michael laughed.

"You think it's funny we might get pushed into the river?" Hiram asked.

"No, I think it's funny because it's like Salt Lake City is huffing and puffing down the canyon, trying to blow Prostituteville right out of the state. Wait, is it *Putain*?"

"Helper." The Double-A left the bridge and bumped down onto dirt again. "Stop the truck for a moment."

Michael dutifully braked.

Ahead of them and stretching away to their right was Helper. It was a town organized in parallel strips. Immediately to their right, along the river, was a tangle of bare trees and brush. Beside that stretched a field of desert grass, beaten brown by the winter. Across a gravel road stood the backs of the brick buildings of Helper's Main Street. From this side, Hiram saw iron fire escapes, back doors, loading docks, and private parking spaces. Beyond Main Street and slightly uphill of it ran the railroad tracks. A train puffed westward now, its second and third "helper" engines pushing right behind the first and a line of coal cars stretching out behind. On the far side of the tracks, on a gentle slope rising up and away from town, stood several streets of brick, adobe, and wooden bungalows. He smelled the coal smoke and cinders along with the dry winter grasses and the river. Above it all and to Hiram's left rose a stark white and yellow cliff, hundreds of feet tall. Without a doubt, Michael would know the geology of the cliff.

When Michael had quit school, Hiram had been uneasy; some of Michael's teachers had looked relieved, liberated from the boy's constant challenging. But Michael had attacked book after book on his own, most of the volumes provided by Mahonri Young. Mahonri had assured Hiram that Michael could get into a good college by taking written entrance exams, and Hiram had relaxed.

Somewhat.

Michael tapped the wheel and flashed Hiram a smile. "You don't want to drive onto Main Street and see the brothels. And you don't want to talk about them, so now you're trying to distract me with trains."

"I wish you didn't know what a brothel was," Hiram said.

"I'm seventeen, Pap, not seven."

"When I was seventeen, I had no idea there were brothels in the world." Hiram sighed and then pointed along the river to a pair of tall cottonwoods surrounded by a clump of scrub oak. "Let's just park it here, so we can be a little more discreet."

Michael parked the car. "Maybe we can sleep in this thicket too, Pap."

"Only if we have to."

The wind buffeted them again as they crossed the weeds. Passing between a stone wall and a gravel parking lot, they entered an alleyway. The sun dropped below the hills behind them, and the way abruptly transitioned from shade to near darkness. Ahead, on Main Street, Hiram saw passing automobiles and the harsh red and yellow glows that suggested neon lights.

Lehi didn't have neon lights. Hiram braced himself for what he knew was coming.

Gravel crunched beneath Hiram's and Michael's Redwing Harvesters—they wore boots that were identical, though Michael's were slightly larger.

"What do you think they charge at these brothels?" Michael asked.

"You and I are not going to find out."

"That's not the right answer."

Hiram shook his head. "Yes, it is."

"No, you should be saying *ooh-la-la*. Did they teach you nothing in Paris?"

They exited the alley onto the main street of Helper. Main Street was full of neon lights: Hiram saw two, no three, movie theaters, and a bowling alley, and restaurants of various kinds. There were bars, and sidewalks full of people laughing and drifting from one entertainment to the next, but it wasn't the full-blown bacchanalia he had feared.

"That one." Hiram pointed at a signboard that read *Hotel Utah*. The words were spelled out in a cross, centering on the shared letter *T*, and that struck him as a good omen. It made the sign of the cross, and also it reminded him of the *Sator Arepo* charm, the Abracadabra pyramid, and other written charms, in which words intersected in meaningful combinations.

"I'm following you, Pap."

Hiram stepped toward the hotel. First Naaman Rettig, then Mary McGill.

Chapter Eight

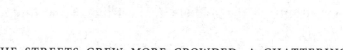

THE STREETS GREW MORE CROWDED. A CHATTERING HERD OF men spilling from one of the town's movie theaters jostled Hiram and Michael at the door of the hotel. The letters on the movie marquee spelled out *The Mystery of Edwin Drood*.

Hiram and Michael struggled past the filmgoers and into a warm, dark foyer.

But...could this be the Hotel Utah? It was a crowded space, the wallpaper fraying, the carpet underfoot unevenly worn into tangled ruts. The front desk was slapped next to the bar and somewhere in the building, frying fat emitted greasy smoke.

A man with a handlebar mustache walked, elbows locked with a cool-eyed, gigantic woman, her arms as big as Hiram's thighs. Her caramel-colored dress tented off her in a wash of thick perfume. The man wore a turquoise and silver bolo tie, a bright orange waistcoat, and tightly-cut trousers the color of a ripe lime over cowboy boots polished to a dull red shine. His snapping, roosterlike strut suggested that he was dressed to impress.

The couple moved toward a back hallway.

A man with two older women on his arms started up the steps to Hiram's right. The women wore black lace gowns with plunging necklines and their lips were bright red.

"Pap," Michael said. "Pap?"

❖   ❖   ❖

Hiram's mind was elsewhere.

He remembered a town called Rouen, a couple hours' drive from the sea and on the Seine. He was thinking of a red lamp he'd seen, casting a rosy glow on dozens of women in silky lingerie.

Brits, Aussies, and Yankees were lined up fifty feet deep to get in, every man filthy from the trenches and most looking forward to a bath and a shave as a prelude to the other services on offer. Hiram and his friend Yas Yazzie stood in the back of the crowd, unable to look each other in the eye.

Yas was a big Navajo, broad-shouldered, with dark eyes and jet-black hair. His skin was a smooth brown and when he smiled, his face glowed. But Yas wasn't smiling then, in Rouen, when some British lieutenant went careening by on a bicycle in a cloud of gin. He wasn't smiling a few minutes later, when one of the women admitting the soldiers at the front of the line let her lacy robe slip open.

Hiram wasn't smiling, either. He felt ill and embarrassed. He wanted a bath, but he figured he'd get the bath and then bow out from any other kind of encounter. He had a wife at home, as did Yas, but then, many of the boys in their unit were married. Charlie Casey insisted that being at war, five thousand miles from home, gave them all a free pass with the ladies. And besides, the women were French. It wasn't like they were sleeping with American girls.

And back home, who would ever know?

Those arguments seemed hollow from the start, but especially when Hiram found himself looking at a half-naked French girl, walking along the line of Doughboys to encourage them. Hiram had made a promise to Elmina Shepherd to be true when they'd wed, a promise for all time and all eternity. Yas had done something similar.

"Yas," Hiram said, "we're not over here for this."

The two men weren't exactly in the business of soldiering either, at least not in the normal sense of the word. Both of their wives had wondered why they'd signed up at all. Neither man had been drafted...again, at least not in the normal sense of the word. They were as much as ten years older than the other fellows in the platoon. Older than most of the guys in the regiment.

Older, and wiser.

Yas nodded. "I'm only sad you said it before I did. Maybe we can find a bath somewhere less crowded."

It took them six hours. They found a bathtub on the second story of a wrecked hotel, half the walls gone and the roof open to the sky. They built a fire of shattered hotel furniture under a soup pot from the hotel's kitchen and shuttled pans from hand to hand until they could fill the tub with water that very nearly passed for hot. They took turns getting clean while looking up at a clear night sky.

Seventeen years later, Hiram stood in the crowded lobby with Yas's son, Michael, now *his* son. Hiram wasn't sure he'd grow to be as tall or wide as Yas, but he had the hands and feet for it. And he was sprouting like a weed, a bit taller than Hiram and not done growing yet.

What could Hiram tell the boy? That it wasn't what Michael imagined? That he regretted bringing his son along to Helper? Not to look?

"Remember that every woman deserves respect," he found himself saying.

He expected a sarcastic response, but Michael only nodded.

Hiram led his son to the front desk. The clerk was a stick-bug of a man, thin and slow-moving, with an Adam's apple that looked as if it had come from a foundry. A mustache overflowed his upper lip.

"Can you ring a suite for me?" Hiram asked. "I'm here to see Naaman Rettig."

The insect man grinned and a gold tooth winked from his smile. "Wrong hotel, Captain. But if you and your Indian pal want some fun, this is the best place in town."

Michael raised his hands. "Aw, Pap, am I your Indian pal? Though I'm thinking this doesn't seem like that much fun, after all." He walked away, through clouds of perfume, and Hiram followed him to the sidewalk.

The Hotel Utah was one door down. The crowd emerging from the theater had made Hiram miss his door. That same crowd was now packed into the hotel's bar to drink, voices raised to the pitch and volume of a stampede.

In front of the hotel stood parked a row of cars. Most of them could have belonged to miners or railroad engineers or local farmers, but one stood out: it was a bright red Chrysler Phaeton, the carriage of a rich man, with its whitewall tires and its leather ragtop. The Phaeton was polished to a shine that hurt to look at, and it was deliberately parked straddling two spaces, as if to keep lesser cars away.

This lobby had brown and gold wallpaper down to a wainscoting of polished wood. Cigar smoke residue oozed from the wood, and a berrylike hint of old wine made Hiram feel that merely to inhale was to risk intoxication. Underfoot was thick red carpet that swarmed with golden bees and hives; out of respect, Hiram avoided stepping on the gold thread. When he asked about Naaman Rettig, the clerk, an older man in a gray suit, rang the railroad man's room.

"Go right on up," the clerk said.

Hiram wondered why Rettig wanted to see him. And where had he got Hiram's name? Had Hiram's heliotropius finally betrayed him to fame?

He and Michael started up the stairs, climbing through the tobacco smoke from the bar and the watery electric lights.

Michael was chuckling. "That was hilarious. My first brothel and I go there with my straight-as-a-shovel Mormon father. Quite the rip-snorting place, but none of those gals were ginchy enough for me."

Hiram didn't want to ask what "ginchy" was.

"It's fine, Pap," Michael said. "I'm not going to become a sex maniac or a boozer."

Hiram sighed.

They walked up four flights of stairs and down a red-carpeted, golden wallpapered hallway to a door. The bees and their hives were banished from this floor, with nothing to replace them and break up the oxblood of the carpet.

A man without a neck stood at the door, arms crossed over his chest. Instead of tall, nature had made him wide, so wide that Hiram doubted he could walk through the door without turning sideways first. The sides of his heads were shaved, while the rest of his thick black hair was greased forward. He wore slacks, wingtip shoes polished to a mirrorlike shine, and a black sweater. And he didn't look happy.

"I'm Hiram Woolley. I'm here to talk with—"

The big man pushed open the double-doors.

The first room of the hotel suite had been transformed into an office. A corkboard covered one wall, next to the door to the bathroom, and push pins, papers, and all manner of receipts were transfixed there. On the other wall, beside the bedroom door, was a map of the region, more pushpins, and some string.

A desk dominated the space in front of the wide windows letting in the multicolored light of Main Street. Stacks of paper clipped or stapled together littered the top of the desk, along with more maps and several coffee mugs, their bottoms stained dark.

A slightly short middle-aged man rose from the desk. His thick shock of hair was so blond it was almost white. Pale hair also burst out of the collar of his shirt above his cravat.

Hiram removed his hat and held it in his hands.

Rettig's desk job had widened him a bit, but his shoulders and arms had the muscles of a fit man. He wore a frock coat and waistcoat. He pulled on soft gray kid leather gloves.

Before those gloves went on, however, Hiram saw the twisted pink skin left by burns, severely disfiguring scars, marking the man's hands and wrists.

Rettig squinted at them with light green eyes far too small for his face. He slapped a hand down on his desk. "Welcome, welcome, Mr. Woolley. I just have to find my cheaters."

Michael moved forward to the desk and lifted handled glasses, a lorgnette, so Rettig could reach them. He put them to his face, which made his eyes look even tinier. "Much better," the railroad man said. "But Lord, where are my manners?"

He walked to the front of the desk, forcing Michael backward. Hiram stepped forward to shake Rettig's hand. "Naaman Julius Rettig, that is my full Christian name, and remember, it's *Naaman*, but I *won't* take 'nay' for an answer. I'm glad Chief Fox found you so quickly."

"I'm Hiram Woolley, but you know that." And *how* did the railroad man know it? "And this is my son, Michael."

Holding his glasses on his nose, Rettig shook Michael's hand. "Yes, yes, the Navajo son." Rettig dropped Michael's hand abruptly. "Now, Mr. Woolley, I appreciate your accepting my invitation. For we have business to discuss, not only the business of my railroad, but the business of humanity. I believe I'm quoting Dickens."

They all sat, Rettig behind the desk, Hiram and Michael in chairs, a bit too close to the ground. The chairs were so short, their legs must have been sawed. Rettig sat tall, and they had to look up at him; his desk sat on a low platform.

"Your office is impressive," Hiram said. Then he guessed: "Is that your Chrysler parked out front?"

"It's even swankier on the inside." Rettig smiled. "Do you like it?"

Hiram shrugged. "My truck suits me."

Naaman dropped his glasses to his desk to squint furiously at them. "I got a telegram from your Bishop Smith, who is very concerned about the Kimball mine situation."

That was how Rettig knew. "He asked you to help me?"

Naaman Rettig laughed. "Oh, in a manner of speaking. He said you were bringing food to Kimball Mine. The Kimballs are known to him. It's a prominent name among your people, and he worried about them. As he should. He said you were bringing food, and asked if my trains would carry more food down to the Kimballs, from Utah Valley."

Hiram wanted to feel relieved, but something warned him he shouldn't. "That's good to hear."

"What is a 'presiding bishop'?" Rettig asked. "Is Bishop Smith the head of your church?"

"There are three men in the presiding bishopric," Hiram said. "They don't run the church. They run the physical side, the secular things. Such as the buildings. And now they're trying to figure out how to deal with the Crash. I help them. Bishop Smith is... he's the second man of the three."

"Very good. As for the use of my trains, of course, I had to tell him no." Naaman Rettig nodded and smiled. "I'm the trustee of the railroad's investment here, and I can't go squandering that investment on some mine. Not unless, of course, the railroad owned the mine. I'm glad you're here, Mr. Woolley."

"You don't have to call him Mr. Woolley, sir," Michael put in. "*Hiram* is fine. And thank you for being such a good steward of your shareholders' money."

"Easy, son," Hiram said.

Rettig licked his lips and blinked, obviously caught off guard. "Yes, I am a good steward. Now, let's talk about the Kimball Mine, the Kimball Corporation, how much do you know about the Kimballs?"

Michael answered as if rattling off a list of facts out of a book. "It was a ranch, back before the railroad. Teancum did well with the mine, until all the wives and most of the kids left, or died, and he was left all alone with Ammon. Teancum disappeared a couple years back, maybe with his new fourth wife. With old Teancum gone, Samuel and Eliza came home. The kids fight over how to run the mine, and it's shut down. And we brought them beets. We're beet farmers when we're not serving the good people of the State of Utah."

Rettig plucked up the lorgnette and looked through it at Hiram. "Beets?"

"We brought more than beets," Hiram said. "These being hard times, it wouldn't be right for us not help out."

"I can respect that." Rettig put his glasses back on the desk. "Here's more of the story for you to consider. Teancum Kimball was a rancher in 1881, when the D and RGW first made Mr. Kimball an offer on his land. Kimball proved there was coal in the hills, and our railroad needs coal. Kimball refused. Actually, the story goes, he had an old blunderbuss that he waved around, saying he'd rather be damned than sell his ranch. I wasn't there myself, you understand, but the incident made such an impression on the director at the time that he recorded it in the company's minute books. And Teancum never did sell. Instead, he started mining the land himself. Eighteen ninety-one, that's when Teancum Kimball opened his mine."

Michael sat straight up and cocked his head to one side. "Sir, thank you so much for the history lesson. I had no idea 1891 was so fascinating. What happened in 1892?"

Rettig let a scowl cross his face, but only for a moment. "Nineteen oh-three was the year of the great mine riots. Men were killed. Again, the D and RGW offered to help Teancum with his troubles. Again, he refused to sell. And that was the same year his wives ran off, all except for one, Samuel's mother. Samuel came the next year, but alas, Teancum's remaining wife died. If anything, that hardened him."

"You know an awful lot about the wives of Teancum Kimball," Hiram observed.

"Kimball is a prominent name here in Helper, too." Rettig paused. "Some say Ammon himself had been in love with the young woman, Samuel's mother, that sweet young sister wife. And when Samuel sprang into the world, Ammon swore to hate him forever. A family drama, Biblical."

"Biblical?" Michael asked. "Do you mean there was a plague of frogs next? Or did the Price River turn to blood?"

Rettig frowned at Michael. "Others believe it was Teancum who turned Ammon's heart against his little brother because he was weak, a fancy boy, who didn't want to dirty his hands with anything but paint. Regardless, no one around here was surprised when Samuel left."

"Let's cut to current events, Mr. Rettig," Michael said. "Two years ago, Teancum and his new wife disappeared—"

"God rest their souls," Rettig cut him off and directed his tiny-eyed gaze at Hiram. "Though a man that age taking a girl scarcely into her twenties to wife is perhaps not looking for rest. Again, the D and RGW made an offer. Ammon refused. No firearms were involved, thankfully, and that brings us here, today. You want to help the men of the Kimball Mine, do you not, Mr. Woolley?"

"*Hiram* is fine. And I do want to help. That's why Michael and I are here."

Rettig squinted through his lorgnette and found a manila envelope. "This is our thirteenth offer to purchase the Kimball Mine. My predecessor's failure to convince Ammon Kimball to sell might be one reason he lost the confidence of the board, and then his job."

Hiram's heart felt heavy. "How can I help, Mr. Rettig?"

"I'm hoping you might take them the offer."

Michael laughed out loud.

"Why me?" Hiram didn't relish the thought of getting between the feuding brothers.

"You and the Kimballs share a faith. I hope that you'll be able to talk with Ammon and Samuel, get them to bury their differences."

Hiram ran his fingers through his hair.

"As the Lord is my witness," Naaman Rettig said, "my motives are pure. I'm only in town three more days, because, believe it or not, I have much larger issues to deal with on the Denver end. A faulty survey means one of our lines is in danger of falling into the river. The chaos in Helper can be easily ended. Instead of a family torn asunder by feud, the mine should be owned by a solid business with a clear-eyed Board of Directors, with the united purpose of giving the men of Kimball steady jobs with good pay."

"I think that calls for a God bless America, sir." Michael sat tall, with his shoulders back.

Rettig scowled. "Don't mistake me; the railroad wants to profit. But the railroad's profit requires it to have coal, and obtaining coal requires the work of miners, so the D and RGW's desire for profit will lead it inexorably and directly to re-opening the mine. And in the meantime, yes, I would bring food down from Utah Valley for the men and their families. So yes, my boy, God bless America. Now, I'm a busy man, Hiram. Will you take my offer to the Kimballs?"

"Mr. Rettig," Hiram said, "I heard from Sorenson, the foreman at the mine, that Eliza Kimball was staying at this hotel. Perhaps she might be a better messenger."

Rettig shook his head. "She refuses to see me."

Hiram surrendered. "I'll try."

"Don't fret, Mr. Rettig," Michael said. "We Mormons have secret handshakes. We'll get them to sign."

Rettig burst into laughter. "Your son has a quick wit, Hiram. I believe he's been funning me, and none too gently. I thank you for agreeing to help."

Hiram wasn't sure if it was the right move, showing up on the Kimballs' doorstep with the railroad's man's offer. But maybe even an offer they rejected could unite the Kimballs. Maybe Ammon and Samuel could come together against a common enemy.

And Eliza?

"I'll do this as a favor to you, Mr. Rettig," Hiram said, "but I'm going to ask for something in return. There's a woman in jail here in town, Mary McGill. I was wondering if you could do something to help her out. She's innocent."

Rettig lifted his lorgnette back up to his eyes. "Hiram, I truly am sorry. But that is between her and the local authorities. I have no power."

Hiram found he had nothing to say, so he took his leave with Michael in tow.

Chapter Nine

HIRAM AND MICHAEL LEFT THE HOTEL. THE CHILL AIR DROVE their hands into their pockets, where Hiram felt Rettig's envelope.

The police station was a solid cube of heavy brick, like a bank with all the grandeur stripped away. Its windows were sealed with black iron bars and its blinds were drawn, but the doors were open. Light spilled out onto the sidewalk, splashing into yellow puddles in the blue of the early evening. Two police cars were parked in front. A train chugged by the distance in a rush of engines. A long whistle blew. The scent of the coal burning and the hot metal of the wheels on the tracks were brought to Hiram by the breeze.

A woman laughed raucously from inside a nearby saloon.

"*Ooh-la-la,*" Michael said.

"You know why I don't ground you when you make comments like that?" Hiram said.

"Because I'm seventeen years old, practically a man, and soon hopefully going off to college to become a physicist?"

"Because you're funny. I like that in a fellow."

"Also, who would drive the truck?"

"I would drive it myself. I know how, believe it or not. And my license is just as valid as yours."

"But you would fall asleep and crash."

"Only once in a while. It might still be worth it."

"I guess I'll keep being funny, then."

"*Ooh-la-la,*" Hiram said.

"Now you're getting the hang of it."

Hiram walked up the steps and through the open door, and Michael followed. Inside, a wide waiting room with hardwood floors was dominated by a single desk. On the desk rested a logbook and a pen. Benches for waiting lined three walls. Closed doors at the back of the reception room, and wooden stairs leading up, hinted at other spaces.

Through a large window of pebbled glass set in a door, Hiram saw and faintly heard two policemen interviewing someone. The third person sounded drunk and belligerent.

The colored policeman sat at the desk, watching Hiram and Michael. His head was shaved bare beneath his uniform cap. His eyes were set wide in his face, and his ears were large, and maybe just a tiny bit pointed. His expression was emotionless; did that reflect cruelty? Fatigue?

"My name is Hiram Woolley," Hiram said.

"I remember you," the policeman said.

"I'm not from here," Hiram began.

"I know who you are. A Mormon farmer come down from Salt Lake with food for the miners. You and your boy here. You drive that Ford Double-A. Only *he* drives it, not you. Maybe your eyesight is bad? But you don't wear glasses."

"I have occasional fainting spells." Hiram shot Michael a glance before his son could say anything. "*Very* occasional." Who had the policeman been talking to? Naaman Rettig? "I'm sorry, you have me at a disadvantage."

"You mean you don't know my name." The policeman blinked slowly, as if it were a conscious act. "I'm Sergeant G. Washington Dixon, but most people call me Shanks."

"Because you're tall?"

"On account of my long legs."

"Sergeant Shanks," Hiram began again, "the woman you have in custody, Mary McGill, didn't shoot me."

"That's what you said up at the mine. What I can't figure out is, this is the least Mormon town in this whole state. Those miners you brung food to ain't Mormons, they're Orthodox and Catholic and Lutheran. At least their wives are, since most of the men are just godless sons of bitches slugging out their lives underground to add a little *oomph* to the locomotives of the D and RGW. What are you doing here?"

"They're God's children, regardless," Hiram said. That was true, but then he felt compelled to tell a little additional truth. "Also, the Kimballs are Mormon."

Michael shook his head. "They're not just Mormon, they're *really* Mormon."

Sergeant Shanks raised his eyebrows. "What, you mean like, really righteous?"

Michael shook his head. "They're from one of the old families. I bet you wouldn't know the name Heber Kimball, but you've heard of Brigham Young."

"My schooling was limited, but I ain't *completely* ignorant."

"Heber Kimball was his best buddy," Michael said. "And Ammon and the rest of them haven't yet fallen so far from the tree that the boys in Salt Lake have forgotten them. You know, they're part of that whole old polygamy upper-class set."

That was more truth than Hiram would have liked to share. Michael wasn't wrong, but the fact that Hiram might be down here to help the scions of an old Salt Lake clan, as much as the miners and their families, made Hiram slightly uncomfortable. "But the point is, Mary McGill didn't shoot anyone. She was trying to get the rifle away from one of the miners. When I stepped in to help, I got shot accidentally."

"You might draw a lesson from that." Sergeant Shanks stared at Hiram and sucked a tooth. "One of the Germans, wasn't it? What was he going to do, shoot little Sammy Kimball?"

Hiram sighed. "Maybe."

Sergeant Shanks nodded. "I tell you what I *do* like, though. I like that you brought food for the miners, and not just for Ammon Kimball. Anyways, I ain't gonna let her out. We got her held on disturbing the peace, and regardless of what happens with the shooting, she's been stirring up the miners, so it's a fair charge."

"Stirring up the miners, heavens to Betsy!" Michael feigned shock. "What did she ask for, decent wages? No more seven-year-old kids sorting coal from rocks with their bare hands?"

Hiram frowned at Michael. The boy was going to get them both into trouble one day.

Michael ignored his signal.

Sergeant Shanks laughed. "Yeah, well, the state legislature don't share your views. Throw in vagrancy, she might be looking at a few months in Sugar House. But I expect it'd be alright if you wanted to talk to her a bit."

"Can Michael stay here with you?" Hiram asked.

Michael went to protest. Hiram put up a hand.

Shanks laughed some more. "Sure, I like your mouthy boy. I was a mouthy young man, myself."

"Our Father, who art in heaven, hallowed be thy name; thy kingdom come; thy will be done on earth as it is in heaven." Mary McGill clutched the first bead of her rosary between her thumb and the knuckle of her forefinger.

The cell was a standalone cage of iron strips, each strip an inch and a half wide and painted white. The strips ran horizontally and vertically, with three-inch gaps between them. A ferret couldn't wiggle between the strips, which were riveted together at every point where they crossed.

The cage had a ceiling of crossed strips, too, and it was bolted onto the hardwood floor. Outside the cage, the floor retained its shine and was colored the lovely red-brown of varnished hardwood. Within the cage, the floor had been scuffed to a dead gray trough, barely wide enough to hold two flat iron bunks, riveted to the side of the cage, one above the other, and a simple toilet in the corner.

Mary thanked God she was the only prisoner in her cell.

One other such cage sat beside hers, its bunks holding two drunk men, snoring soundly. The room had no windows and was lit by a series of electric bulbs hanging from the ceiling. The whole place smelled of bleach.

"...and lead us not into temptation, but deliver us from evil. Amen." She moved to the first of three beads, relaxing into the rosary, and concentrating on her desire that God free her from her bonds. She said three Hail Marys, then the Glory Be, and then recited the first Glorious Mystery from memory.

She heard the scraping sound of the door to the room being unbarred. She put her rosary away in a pocket, and then the man in overalls came in, the one who had got shot at the mine. Hiram. He was alone.

She stood. "I didn't mean to shoot you."

He walked to her cage. He was more handsome than she had noticed earlier, though he held himself tentatively, like a man who expected to be rejected. He took off his hat and smoothed down the few hairs clinging to his scalp. "I know. I told them that, and they don't seem to care."

She started to touch her face, then pulled her hand away and lifted her chin. "I'm with the union. The United Mine Workers. It comes with the territory."

"You seem very...ladylike...for a union organizer."

"You would prefer a hairy goon named Moe?"

He laughed a little. Just the right amount to show her he'd rather smile than frown. "I didn't say I'd *prefer* one, but that's more like what I'd *expect*. Are you not worried about, I don't know, getting beat up? Shot at?"

"My father likely wasn't thinking about my chances of being shot when he insisted on my ladylike clothing and bearing. I think he was more concerned about doing right by the wishes of my mother, God rest her soul. But then, he was a drunk, so maybe he wasn't thinking anything at all."

"I'm sorry," the man said. "I lost my mother when I was young, myself. My full name's Hiram Woolley."

"Mary McGill. Or perhaps my father thought a good ladylike posture and dress would compensate for the disfigurement I bear in my physiognomy."

"Fizzy...?"

"*Face*, Mr. Woolley. I mean my birthmark."

Hiram Woolley looked at her face as if seeing it for the first time, and appeared surprised. "I hadn't really noticed."

"God bless you, Hiram Woolley, I believe you're telling the truth."

"I *try* to."

Mary McGill looked the man up and down. His denim overalls were frayed, his hands were callused, and even the skin of his forehead and cheeks had the leathery look that comes from years of working under the sun. "I expect you do, Mr. Woolley. Tell me the truth now, then—what are you doing in here?"

"It's my fault you're locked up. I came to see if I could get you out."

"As you promised. And it wasn't at all your fault. You spoke to the policemen, and they told you to mind your business."

"True."

"Then you came in *here*." Mary raised her eyebrows to Hiram in challenge.

Hiram put his hands into his pockets and shuffled his feet. "Well?" she asked.

"I wondered if there was anything else I could do to help you."

"Bony thing that I am, you'd never believe it, but I eat like a horse. Always trying to put on more flesh so I look less like a twelve-year-old boy, and it never works. I don't suppose you have a pastry hidden in those overalls."

"Actually, I have a Snickers bar." Hiram produced the candy square, wrapped in cream-colored paper that crinkled when he touched it, and handed it over.

"Perfect." Mary took the bar, a little soft from sitting in Hiram's warm coat pocket. "A candy bar named for a horse, for a girl who eats like a horse."

"Named for a horse?" Hiram looked amused. "I had no idea."

Mary suddenly realized that she was enjoying the conversation. "There is something else, yes. Police Chief Fox allowed me one phone call when he brought me in, and I called the union's lawyer. And of course, since it's nighttime in Denver, no one answered."

"Will he give you another call?"

Mary shrugged. "Maybe."

"Give me the number," Hiram said. "I'll call the lawyer first thing in the morning."

"Denver two, twelve oh seven."

He repeated the exchange and number back to her. "And the lawyer's name?"

"James Nichols. And if he doesn't believe you, tell him Gil said Five-Cent Jimmy would never let her down."

"I never knew a lawyer who only charged five cents."

"You never knew a union lawyer, then. Haircuts are even cheaper."

Hiram furrowed his brow. "What are you doing here, Mary McGill?"

Mary sighed and sat down on the edge of the lower bunk. "It's true that I came here to organize the miners. And I thought I'd be doing it in the usual ways, and asking for the usual things. God knows they could use the usual things, at the Kimball Mine and also at all the others."

"Higher wages."

Mary nodded. "A better price for the coal they dig. No interest on the advances. Better rents on the shantytowns the mine companies have them living in. But also things like more safety equipment, English lessons for the men, for safety reasons, and for the families, because it's the decent thing to do, so they have a future. Stop child labor."

Hiram frowned. "I heard the kids pick rocks out of the coal."

Mary shook her head. "That's not all they do. They lead mules and carry messages and water. A lot of the mine owners will shrug and say they don't employ the children, it's the miners themselves who bring their kids down to help. So the companies technically don't violate the law yet benefit from child labor nonetheless."

"I can see that," Hiram said. "But sometimes a family's got little choice. Kids help on farms, too."

"Your son worked?"

"I taught Michael to drive when he was twelve. I needed him to run the tractor."

"You ever see a ten-year-old boy with black lung? A young man grown old by the age of sixteen, who has to roll back and forth on the floor at the end of the day to loosen up the phlegm in his lungs so he can cough up enough coal dust and free his breathing enough to be able to sleep?"

Hiram shook his head and looked at his boots.

"So that's why it's not enough that the mines don't employ the children. We have to ban it entirely."

"So if a man brings his son to work, he goes to prison?" Hiram asked.

"If he's a coal miner, yes."

"So I expect this is an idea you have to teach to the miners."

"And I *was* teaching them. And organizing them, at the Kimball mine and elsewhere. But then the Kimball Mine closed, and things got really bad up there."

A shadow fell across Hiram's face. "Worse than at the other mines?"

"The other mines are still open. And since the Kimball men and their families live on company land and get food from the company store, they're going deeper into debt by the day."

The shadow on the farmer's face darkened. "I've seen the miners starving. One family was trying to eat a cat."

Mary was struck by the troubled compassion in Hiram's eye. "On top of everything else, Mr. Woolley, the miners are divided by language."

"They're mostly immigrants."

"And Italians work best with Italians," Mary said, "and Serbs get along with Serbs, and Chinese with Chinese. So it's always a challenge to get them to overlook the differences of language and food and dress and church and pull together, only at the Kimball it all got worse."

"They picked sides." Hiram frowned. "Ammon has the Germans. Samuel has the Greeks."

"So at the Kimball, I stopped being able to organize for wages and safety and tried to push to get the mine back open again."

Hiram had a thoughtful expression on his face. "Samuel and Ammon both seem to have plans for operating the mine."

"Only they're different plans, the two can't agree, and each man is backed by a mob."

Hiram nodded. "I'll call Five-Cent Jimmy in the morning, and if I have to send him a buffalo head by mail, I'll do that, too. What else?"

This strange, handsome farmer was offering to be some kind of deputy. "Go talk to Ammon Kimball. If he can forgive the men rent until the mine opens, or forgive debts for food, it would be a godsend. Or even if he could get food back into the company store and offer the men credit on better terms, it could be the difference between a family making it until the mine opens, and a husband riding the rails in search of work."

Hiram slipped his hat on. "I'll do my best. I probably should get on to Ammon's before it gets too late."

Chapter Ten

SPRING CANYON WAS A WALL OF DARKNESS RISING TO EITHER side of them.

But for the Double-A's headlights, the sky above might have shown them Orion or Gemini or other features of the winter night. As it was, the truck's lamps revealed only a pale sequence of abrupt and disjointed images. A startled and sleepy cow. The corner of a brick springhouse. Rail fencing surrounded by sagging winter grass. The white hindquarters of two deer, bounding away to safety. Twice, oncoming headlights skidded past, forcing Michael to the edge of the road.

Hiram was more than ready for a rest when he realized that a small constellation of lights to the right of the truck in the darkness must be coming from the windows of Gus Dollar's shop. "Pull over."

Michael did. "You want another Coke?" he asked.

"I want to talk to the owner." Gus Dollar had craft, and he might know if there were supernatural components to the troubles at the Kimball mine.

Hiram clearly couldn't take Michael with him, because that would stop him from asking the questions he wanted to ask of Gus Dollar. Michael was aware of Grandma Hettie's wisdom, but Hettie had died when Michael was just nine years old, and Hiram had been careful to hide the fact that he followed in her footsteps.

He took the revolver from the glove box and carefully rotated the barrel, taking the hammer off the empty chamber, and putting it over a live round. Then he laid the pistol on the seat between them, near Michael's hand and pointed forward.

"This revolver is loaded and ready to fire," he told Michael.

"Okay." Michael's breathing sounded shallow.

"I'm leaving it with you."

"Yeah."

"Don't be excited. Don't be nervous. Nothing's going to happen."

"I get it, Pap. You're worried because of the fighting we saw today, and because you got shot, so you're leaving the gun with me. While you go in and, I don't know, talk with this shopkeeper some more. Because, clearly, the guy who sells Coca-Cola is secretly running everything and has all the answers."

Hiram ignored the barb. "Don't shoot unless you have to, but if you think you have to, don't hesitate. I'd rather have you dressed up for a jury than dressed up by a mortician. Keep the car running. I'll approach in the headlights, so I'm clearly visible. I won't be long."

He walked up to the deep porch in the bright yellow glow of the truck's lamps, then stepped up to the well-worn planks and examined the door and the front windows. He saw no posted hours, no sign saying either OPEN or CLOSED.

He saw again the strange curls of lead in the front windows, black in the light of a dimmed kerosene lantern sitting on Gus Dollar's countertop. What did they mean?

Hiram knocked, setting off a furor of barking within. Through the window he saw the two Rottweilers, bounding over each other to get at the door and sink their teeth into him.

Hiram waited for Gus.

The shopkeeper arrived. "Go on, shoo!" He chased the dogs into a back room, and then he let Hiram in. The dried mint and other herbs gave the room a pleasant odor, as did the sweet pine burning in a squat stove on the side.

"Evening," Hiram said.

"I like that," Gus said, a twinkle of a laugh in his voice. "You don't want to commit to the quality of the hour."

Hiram was caught on his back heel. "What?"

"Is it a good evening? Is it a bad evening? You don't want to say, so you just tell me it's evening." Gus shut the door. "Which I had already noticed."

"I'm sorry," Hiram said. "I was raised in a home where... you didn't talk about some things. I learned to listen more than I talked, in most conversations."

"Ah, yes." Gus laid an index finger alongside his nose and winked as he walked behind the counter. "I understand."

"Not just that." Hiram felt a sudden urge to explain. He felt safe here, talking with this fellow practitioner of the old arts. Gus knew the world in the same way Hiram knew it. "My father was a polygamist. Still is, I suppose, if he's alive."

"You don't know?"

Hiram fidgeted. "He left us. When I was very young."

"Ah," Gus said. "Now I understand everything."

"What do you mean?"

"You." Gus shrugged. "You were abandoned when you were very young, so now you work hard to prevent other people from being abandoned."

"No." Hiram shook his head. "I'm just trying to do what's right."

"Hmm," Gus said. "But you are, what, forty years old?"

"Forty-four." Hiram crossed the store to stand in front of Gus at his counter.

"So the practices that were mandatory when you were a child became the oddities that were winked at when you were a young man and then the crimes that are now prosecuted, when you are grown. The world you were born into has disappeared."

Hiram nodded. "How long have you lived in Utah? You sound like you know it well."

"I was in the state as a younger man," Gus said. "And then in Colorado for many years. So as a boy you had to keep the secret of your father's other wives, as well as your... lore. Were they nice to you, these other wives?"

"I never met them." Hiram's eyes stung. From the kerosene smoke? "I only learned they existed late, and I never knew their names."

Gus frowned. "Did you have brothers and sisters, at least? By the same mother, I mean?"

Hiram shook his head. How had the conversation gone in this direction?

"I see. Your mother was the disfavored wife. You were kept in a corner. Perhaps hidden from the others. You were abandoned more than once, my friend. But have you met your half-siblings as a grown man? They must be easy to find, no? All with the same name. What was it, Woolley?"

"My father stopped coming around while I was still young. Later, I learned he had moved to Mexico. The other families went with him."

"To avoid prosecution. Ah, your mother truly *was* disfavored. I am so sorry to hear of your suffering, my friend."

Hiram plucked his bandana out of the back pocket of his overalls to blow his nose. He bit his tongue and managed not to tell Gus Dollar the rest of the story: after his father had moved to Mexico, his mother had spent weeks weeping, and then months staring out the front window at the road up to Salt Lake City; then his mother had disappeared, and Grandma Hettie had told him she had died, without ever identifying a cause of death, and leaving Hiram with the unsettled impression all his life that his mother's end had been dark and maybe shameful.

"Every person suffers tragedy." Hiram cleared his throat. "I guess what matters is what you do in response to it."

"And in response to your tragedy, you became a kind of knight-errant, riding around the deserts of Utah helping the poor. And a *braucher*, we Germans would say, or you English would call it a 'cunning man.'" Gus smiled warmly. "You are not a man of this century, Hiram Woolley."

"I don't know," Hiram said. "I *do* like my truck."

"So you learned to keep secrets," Gus said. "And since we know each other's great secrets now, you thought you could share something else with me. Or ask a question, perhaps."

"I only got here this morning," Hiram said. "But I'm beginning to suspect something... occult behind the closing of the Kimball Mine. Something caused the Kimball brothers to shout at each other over the heritage of their father."

"Heirs who squabble are more common than heirs who don't." Gus shrugged.

"But these men... each was convinced that the other was lying. But they weren't."

"You have a charm?" Gus's eyes gleamed.

"I carry a stone. And Samuel Kimball seemed certain that Ammon had access to some shared piece of knowledge, and Ammon denied it. Some person they both had talked with, I think. And whatever it was, it was too sensitive for either of them to speak about it clearly. Something of their father's, or something about him."

"The stone you carry... it's a peep-stone?"

Hiram shook his head. "It's a bloodstone. A heliotropius."

Gus added a smile to the gleam in his eye. "It's a shame you don't have a peep-stone. Maybe a seer stone would give you the knowledge you seek." He furrowed his brow. "Maybe the brothers saw their father in a séance?"

Hiram shrugged, feeling tired and baffled. "That might be. Some of the men think the mine is haunted. Is it possible it's haunted by Teancum Kimball, and both his sons have seen the shade? Or it might be something more like a... document they both have access to?"

"Or you are misreading what passed between the brothers."

"Or I'm misreading it." Hiram nodded. "So this is why I've come to you. If there is something occult being done at Kimball, you might be in the best position to know it. What have you seen, Gus? What might there be between these men?"

Gus shook his head. "I'm afraid I have no idea."

"Do you know why the mine is closed?"

Gus took a deep breath. "I know enough about mining to know what sorts of things miners and their wives would like to buy, and I know *that* mostly because they ask me. I think the Kimballs have run out of money, and so they can't stock their store. It is unfortunate for them, the miners, their hungry families. I hear some have taken to banditry. All because the two brothers can't agree on where to dig."

Hiram thought about Naaman Rettig, and the offer he was being sent to make to Ammon Kimball. Might the railroad tycoon have used some means to create dissension between Ammon and Samuel? He was ambitious and driven and he wanted the land, but Hiram couldn't imagine how the railroad man could be fueling strife between the siblings. And beyond that, he didn't want them in conflict; he wanted them in agreement, and accepting his offer. Also, he hadn't seemed the type to use a hex.

Perhaps Hiram had misread *him*.

Hiram spoke in a low voice. "Maybe it would solve their problems if someone bought them out?"

"Well, you know," Gus said. "If someone bought your farm from you, you wouldn't have to worry about farming anymore."

"But that doesn't mean I'd be interested in selling," Hiram concluded. "Of course, someone else buying the mine and investing more cash in it might mean work for the miners. So that might be a solution for the workers, even if the owners didn't like it."

"Are you thinking of getting out of farming, and digging for coal instead?" Gus smiled like an imp. "I don't think it's an easier business."

Hiram shrugged. "Just thinking. I only brought enough food for the miners for a couple of days. That mine has to start up again."

What if the railroad man *was* some kind of witch? Or one of the Kimballs was? If magic was afoot, it would serve Hiram well to prepare additional defenses. Stepping to the window, he reached up and took the bunch of bay in his hand.

"I wish I could help," Gus said with a sigh. "But I don't know what's causing all the trouble at the mine."

A dull pain throbbed in Hiram's thigh and he sucked in a sudden breath.

No, not *in* his thigh. *Against* his thigh. In his pocket.

The heliotropius.

"Is something wrong, my friend?" Gus Dollar asked.

The bloodstone pulsed again.

Gus Dollar was lying to him.

The green stone was an imprecise tool. It did nothing if a person was being merely evasive. It also wouldn't tell Hiram what truth Gus was concealing, but it warned Hiram of deception.

"I hurt my back up at the Kimball Mine this morning." Hiram grunted, bringing the cluster of bay leaves to the counter. "I don't suppose you have anything I could take for it?"

"You don't mean a charm?" Gus smiled, but now the smile felt like a threat.

Hiram smiled back, and as his gaze swept the inside of the shop, he noticed things he had missed before. Lamens—metal sheets inscribed with arcane symbols—standing in discreet corners, a heavy Bible resting on a butter churn behind the door, pierced stones on leather thongs hanging as if by accident from larger appliances, the corners of a sheet of paper protruding from underneath the book of accounts, paper that looked virgin, and therefore might bear a written spell.

And in the windows, the queer twists of lead. They moved

in and out of Hiram's vision as he looked at them, disappearing and reappearing again.

Gus Dollar wasn't merely a *braucher*. There was a good chance he was a witch.

"I can do that myself, of course," Hiram said. "Maybe aspirin?"

Gus produced two yellow tins of Norwich Aspirin tablets, 5 grains each. "It says take one or two," the shopkeeper said, "but for a serious pain, I'd take as many as four, and at that rate, a tin will only last you a day."

Hiram took the tablets without setting down the bay leaves. "And the herbs."

"You're going to cook?" Gus asked.

Hiram smiled as blandly as he dared. He must bluff, and bluffing was not his strong suit. "They're a good counter magic," he said. "In case I'm right about the Kimballs."

"Of course." Gus looked at the purchases. "Make it an even dollar," he said. "A dollar for Gus Dollar at Dollar's." He laughed.

Hiram laughed too, then paid, then did his best to exit without stumbling. He stepped carefully into the beams of the headlights and approached the Double-A as evenly as possible.

When he had slid into the cab and was sitting beside Michael, he took a deep breath.

"You okay, Pap?" Michael asked.

"Yes. Drive around that corner, please."

Michael drove and Hiram looked back, until the lights of Dollar's were obscured by a wall of rock and the turn of the canyon. "Okay, wait here."

"If you're heading back to burgle the shop," Michael said, "I could go for another dope."

Hiram left the aspirin and sneaked down the cold, empty road, back to Dollar's. He crept around the darkest side, where no light shone from the windows, looking for the spot where the shingled roof came closest to the ground.

It was the porch. At the far end of the wide porch from the shop's door, Hiram carefully stepped onto the planks. Earlier, the dogs hadn't barked until he had knocked, and he counted on them to have the same response now. Taking one of the rocking chairs and moving slowly to avoid creaks, he crept to the edge of the porch and set the rocking chair on the ground.

Standing on the chair's seat, he was able to reach up and

touch the fringe of the roof's shingles. With his clasp knife, he cut away half of a shingle and tucked it into his coat pocket. The shingle was wooden; so much the better.

Then he replaced the rocking chair and crept back around the shop the other way. Only when he reached the truck did he realize that his heart rate was elevated, and his chest felt squeezed tightly, as if he were in the grip of a gigantic fist.

"It's me," he murmured as he approached Michael's window. "Wait just a minute while I climb into the bed of the truck."

Hiram carefully stowed the shingle in the bottom of his special toolbox, safely securing it all again before climbing down.

"Okay, Pap," Michael said when Hiram finally stood beside the cab. "I won't shoot you. But what were you doing back there, really?"

"I forgot something." Hiram hated the lie. "You wanted Coke, didn't you? I guess drank yours." Hunger pangs twisted in his gut. He had been fasting a full day, and was ravenous. He tried not to think of the Snickers bar he'd given Mary McGill.

"Pap," Michael said, "I have a confession."

Hiram imagined the worst. "Are you alright?"

"I already drank both our Cokes. You can't leave me sitting alone in this truck with Cokes, and expect to find them when you come back."

Hiram would have laughed, if he hadn't been so shaken by his encounter with Gus Dollar. "Did you keep the bottles, by any chance?"

"Both bottles, yes I did."

"Good. Hang on to them." Hiram slipped into the passenger seat. "Let's get up to the Kimball house."

He took a deep breath as Michael put the truck into gear. Gus Dollar was a liar, and Gus Dollar had bested Hiram already twice, luring him into Gus's store and then making him bare his soul. He'd defeated Hiram's bloodstone, to boot. Only by sheer chance had Hiram put his hand on the bay leaves and learned of the deception.

Who was Gus, and what was he up to?

And what did he have to do with the closure of the Kimball Mine?

Hiram was so deep in thought, he almost didn't notice that Michael took the hill in second gear.

Chapter Eleven

THEY SAT PARKED BY THE SIDE OF THE ROAD FOR TWENTY MINUTES while Hiram worked.

He poured all the aspirin tablets into one of the Norwich tins. In the other, he mixed the tincture with his fingers, standing beside the truck. On the farm, he would have used a mortar and pestle, but he didn't carry those in his toolbox. A flashlight, balanced on the hood of the Double-A, let him gauge the consistency. Stars twinkled overhead, but no moon.

Hiram tried not to think about the cold.

Michael, wrapped up in his coat, sat in the bed of the truck strumming his Sears, Roebuck. For being the five-dollar model, the guitar didn't sound half bad. Hiram didn't know the song, but the lyric sounded risqué: *Let me be your salty dog, or I won't be your man at all*. Hiram realized he was shaking his head, and forced himself to laugh instead. He couldn't yell at the kid for not playing "My Darling Clementine" or "The Handcart Song." And Michael's love for music had given Hiram the space to prepare the cure for Ammon's boils.

If he could cure the man's boils, that might help soften his heart.

Hiram set the shovel in the bed of the truck and placed the Central Milling flour sack next to it. The company had started making their flour sacks with patterns, so women could sew dresses from the packaging. This one had golden peonies on a blue field, but no one would be making anything out of this particular flour sack, on account of the bloodstains.

"You ready?" Hiram asked.

"I guess," Michael said. "But Pap, you giving me the gun, that was serious. How much more trouble is there going to be?"

Hiram shrugged. It was bad business: railroad men, union organizers, desperate miners, starving children, and a family torn to pieces. Throw in a powerful witch who might be causing trouble, and it just kept getting worse. Had Teancum Kimball really run off with his child bride, or was he dead? If he was, did he sleep peacefully or was he out and about causing mischief from beyond the grave?

Michael burst into laughter. "And that, ladies and gentleman, is my dear, old dad. I ask a question and he ponders it for five minutes."

"We have to be careful is all," Hiram said. "This might all be over tonight. Ammon might take Rettig's offer. Or he might agree to extend credit, go easier on the men. Either way, we can go home to the farm. I expect you're anxious to get back on the tractor."

"Yay, beet farm. Two yays for the tractor." Michael wrapped his guitar up in a wool blanket and cinched it tight with ropes tied into iron rings. "Three yays, you mixing up patent medicine with your bare fingers in an aspirin tin. You know, they can send you to jail for impersonating a doctor."

"Glad to hear you like the tractor." Hiram slid into the passenger seat as Michael got behind the wheel. "I picked it out special. And I'm surprised to hear you so down on patent medicine. What do you think Coca-Cola *is*, anyway?"

"Ambrosia, sweet nectar, drunk by the gods." Michael switched on the lights. The faint orange glow showed them the white line of the road but little else. The dark claws of trees groped toward them. Boulders piled up to squelch the light, and beyond the rocks, less distinct shapes scurried about.

Hunger gnawed at Hiram's belly. Usually, he'd be asleep by this hour on a fasting day, and he wouldn't notice the pangs.

Michael didn't take the turn left into the mining camp, but kept going and took the right, up the driveway to the red house on the hill. It was a stygian corner of the valley; the cliffs were solid midnight. No stars above; just unforgiving darkness.

A greasy yellow glow came the windows of a single back room.

Michael pulled up to the front door. "Should I give him a bit of the horn, Pap?"

"Just stay in the car," Hiram said. "I'll knock."

Michael cut the engine. "Will do. I get it. The last thing in the world you want is me shooting my mouth off with Ammon Kimball."

"The thought had occurred to me." Should he warn Michael to tone down his sarcasm? He'd never been that kind of father, but maybe he was failing Michael by being too lax.

"Okay, then, Pap. I'm right here, if you need me. I'm your muscle."

Hiram pushed open the door and winced at the cold. "Good. I'm getting too old to be the muscle. Keep the lights on."

He put the aspirin tin and Rettig's manila envelope into a coat pocket. He grabbed the blood-stained flour sack and the shovel from the back of the Double-A. The dark night and the blinding effect of the headlights would hide the shovel and sack from Michael.

Hiram approached the house. No garden, no trees, no brush to entangle him. The chill perfume of the desert night came to him, sage, the rocks sleeping, a slight moisture; maybe a bit of snow would fall.

He set the shovel and the sack next to the door, and then turned to look across the canyon at the camp. Firelight twinkled across the canvas of the tents and lights glowed in the tar-paper homes. The camp was a small city, nearly as big as Helper. The barking of dogs, the mournful scrape of a violin, and a medley of human voices drifted to Hiram's ear.

Kimball must have three hundred men desperate for work, sitting idle. And at least as many women and children.

Two days of food. If that. The Greek girl, Callista, had probably already speared the cat, and if not, the creature's doom was coming. How would a cat stew taste?

Hiram went to the door and knocked, loudly.

Ammon Kimball ripped open the door. He wore sturdy work pants and a white shirt. Deep frown lines cut down from his nose and red boils spangled his throat and neck—they had been covered by plasters earlier, but now they lay bare, all swollen and shining and a few oozing pus. Ammon's breath came in snorts with a slight wheeze at the end.

"Who are you? What do you want?"

A rough kerosene lantern dangled from his left hand. His right hand gripped something out of sight in the shadow. A shotgun? A steel bar?

Hiram took off his hat and smoothed his wisps of hair. "I'm Hiram Woolley, a farmer out of Lehi. I brought groceries to the men today, before the trouble."

"What's a Lehi man doing up here?" Ammon's eyes narrowed and shifted from side to side.

"John Wells asked me to come," Hiram said. "I don't know if you know the name, but he's in Salt Lake. Your father had friends in the leadership who remember him fondly, I guess."

Ammon's head trembled slightly, and he didn't say a word.

"But I came up here tonight to see *you*." Hiram reached into his pocket and brought out the aspirin tin. "I heard you suffer from boils. That's a terrible plague, and I have a remedy here, something my grandma taught me. And I'd like to talk to you, Mr. Kimball, about . . . about the current situation."

"A farmer? What then, beets?" Ammon laughed. "A beet farmer shows up on my doorstep to try and talk some sense into me. And to cure my boils. Well, don't that just beat all?"

Hiram nodded. "It's peculiar. But then, I come from peculiar people."

"Come in, then." Ammon stepped back.

Hiram put the aspirin tin back in his pocket. Beside the door stood a single-shot shotgun, break-action. The house smelled of sweat, unwashed laundry, and pine wood smoke.

The sitting room was full of handmade wooden furniture: rough-hewn chairs without cushions, a long low table with uneven legs, and a couch of bare wood. A grand hutch of finer workmanship, heavy with dust, towered against the far wall. Glass doors displayed some silver and some china, but none of the finery looked recently used. A few portraits were framed on the wall, people in grainy photographs. His eyes came to rest on an old man with a beard and deep-set, piercing eyes, glaring at him from a daguerreotype. It had to be Teancum Kimball, crouched next to the entrance of the mine, angry at something. Above the fireplace hung a painting, gray in shadow.

Ammon moved to the fireplace and stooped to throw in a few sticks of split pine. The wood was dry enough to catch promptly and a fire cackled into life. The new yellow light gave Hiram a better look at the painting. It depicted a canyon, bristling with cliffs and crags, and it was done in pastel pinks, oranges, and off-white colors. On one bit of cliff were some pictographs, the markings of ancient Indians found on cliffs in southern and eastern Utah. These were black in the painting; in real life, all the pictographs Hiram had seen were white.

"Is this a real place?" Hiram asked.

"Yeah. Apostate Canyon. It's just over the ridge. You can walk it from camp, or mule it. There's a bad road that takes you there in an automobile, but you have to keep on going around the mountain and it's pretty rough. That's where my corn-for-brains brother has been camping, when he's not whipping up the Greeks into a frenzy." Ammon gazed up at the painting. "When I think maybe I shouldn't be so stubborn, I look up at that picture and I remember my brother is a smoke-addled fool. What kind of man paints a cliff wall pink, when it's really orange?"

Hiram stepped closer to the fireplace and then he saw it: a rock lying on the mantel. It was a plain stone, about the size of a baby's shoe, brown with a line of white down the middle. Firelight gleamed off the mineral—quartz?—making it prettier than it would be in daylight.

It was a pretty rock, but an ordinary one such as you might find in a streambed, while hiking. What was it doing in a place of honor, on the mantel?

Could this be a peep-stone? Hiram had never seen one, though Grandma Hettie had spoken of them often. Gus Dollar had asked whether Hiram had a peep-stone, and now that question seemed suspicious.

Something about the rock unsettled Hiram. The painting, now that he stood closer, also felt wrong. The lines of the cliff edges at the top were...distorted and strange. They seemed familiar.

One of the black dots of the pictographs moved.

Hiram's mouth went dry. Another of the signs moved and then another. They crawled across the painting, little black dots. Flies were on the painting. One took off in a long buzzing saunter across the sitting room, followed by another, and then a third. The flies were big, lazy, black things, a quarter inch long, big as small bees. They buzzed away from the painting and then settled back among the pictographs.

Hiram's hand drifted to his chi-rho amulet. The ringing started in his ears. He didn't smell anything yet, but it was coming, that sweet, spicy odor.

"Mr. Woolley? You okay?"

He turned. The weak light coalesced on Ammon's boils. The yellow pus glowed and the circles around the wounds darkened from red to black.

"Yeah." Hiram took in a deep breath to steady himself and focused on the other man's eyes. The ringing diminished. "I'm fine. It's been a long day, and I'm not as young as I used to be." He didn't mention his hunger; Matthew six said it wasn't a real fast if you told people you were fasting. The Lord Divine only rewarded *secret* fasting with grants of his power. "I'll take beet farming over mining. Fresher air."

Ammon nodded. "Goddamn mine. You spend a dollar to make a dime. Sorry, I shouldn't curse. I don't want you to think..."

"I'm not as sensitive as all that." Hiram had the offer to pass on, but he had also made a promise to Mary McGill. "Mr. Kimball, the men are desperate. I only brought enough food for a couple days, and the railroad won't bring in any more. After that, I'm not sure what will happen. There's only so many deer in these hills for the men to shoot. The miners are looking for a break, maybe you could extend some store credit to them, or maybe you could forgive them rent until your trouble with Samuel is over?"

"There's no food in the store because I can't buy any more food." Ammon frowned. "You think I *want* people to starve? You think I *want* my family business to fail?"

"I only wonder...is there something you could do?"

Ammon's mouth dove into a frown and his brown eyes ignited in a livid rage. "Look around, Woolley! I ain't living in style, I ain't got a wife, and I ain't got no family. All I got is a mine I'm trying to run as best I can. You want to help? Get that idiot Samuel to stand down!"

"Samuel wants to dig a new shaft." Maybe Hiram could help Ammon resolve his feelings toward his brother. Or maybe, if Ammon got worked up enough at the thought of Samuel's meddling, he'd be more receptive to an offer that got him out of the situation entirely. "Could he be right?"

A fly lit off the painting and floated through the room with a loud buzzing thrum.

Where were these flies coming from?

The skin on the back of Hiram's neck prickled.

"He thinks we should sink another shaft down valley," Ammon grumbled. "He don't understand the cost, not a bit. Also, he's taking a shot in the dark and might miss the coal entirely." Ammon fingered a boil on his neck. "We just need to follow the eastern seam, there's still coal there, and a lot of it. The Germans get it, and Sorenson does too, but Samuel and the Greeks are bent on this new hole. Damn, and then there's Eliza."

Hiram nodded. The two flies left the painting, swirled around the brown rock on the mantle, before buzzing off.

"What does Eliza want?" Hiram asked.

"Well, I would imagine you'll get around to asking her. And you'll talk to Samuel, and God bless you, Mr. Woolley if you can break up the log jam and get the Greeks to give in. And if you can't do it, I'll have to wait until they've eaten all the deer in the county and are hungry enough to give up. So no, no more food in the store, no more credit, and no breaks on the rent." Ammon coughed out a brusque laugh.

"The hauntings your brother talks about," Hiram said slowly. "Might they be connected to your father's death?"

"Hauntings." Ammon snorted. "Bullshit."

"Yeah," Hiram said. "Most likely. I'll go and talk with your brother and your sister, and see what they say. But I have one other piece of business." He took the envelope out of his pocket, feeling his heart beat a little faster. "I can't promise you'll like what's in this envelope."

Ammon stretched out a callused palm. "Every day a new bird shits in my hand. Why should today be any different?"

Hiram held the letter. "You know Naaman Rettig, with the D and RGW?"

Ammon snorted, turned away, and took a big log from the fire in one hand. He bashed the coals off a half-burned log, cracking the wood repeatedly against the stone of the fireplace. He then flung the log into the fireplace; it slammed against the wall at the back before falling onto the embers. "And does the D and RGW pay for your work, Mr. Woolley?"

Hiram sighed. "No. But Rettig asked me to bring you his offer. I was coming up the canyon anyway." He hesitated. "Would it matter to you how much money the railroad offered?"

"No!" Ammon grabbed his lantern and stomped from the room.

There wasn't any more to be said; Hiram might as well leave. He'd failed to convince Ammon to cut his miners a break, and the mere mention of the railroad had sent Ammon into a frenzy.

He *had* learned where to find Samuel, camped out in Apostate Canyon.

With Ammon gone, Hiram couldn't resist approaching the mantel. The plain brown stone rested in shadow between two candlesticks, devoid of candles, and a music box. A blurry picture of a woman holding a baby sat in an ornate picture frame. Family knick-knacks, things of sentimental value.

Why the stone?

Unconsciously, Hiram reached between the Zippo and the clasp knife to grip his heliotropius.

That stone on the mantel must also have properties.

Ammon called to him as he reappeared in the doorway. "Mr. Woolley. You tell Naaman Rettig I'd rather dynamite every shaft of my mine than let him have it."

"I doubt he'll be surprised." Hiram moved to the front door.

"Ain't you forgetting something?" Ammon asked.

"Ah, the remedy." Hiram reached into his pocket and tossed Ammon the tin. "Put a little on each boil."

Ammon cracked open the tin and sniffed. "Rosemary and what else?"

"Rosemary, some Vaseline, a little bit of this and that." Rosemary, like bay and peppermint, warded off hostile magic. Hiram had included it in his compound to cover the possibility that Ammon's boils were caused by witchcraft.

"Why's it red?"

"This and that was red." Hiram turned the knob to let himself out.

"Why didn't you give me the letter?" Ammon asked.

Hiram turned. "You're not going to sell. Why waste time opening the envelope?"

"You're going to show the letter to my brother." Ammon's glare was dull and brutish.

"I expect he won't sign. Might not even look at it, either. Similar reasons. But then I'll have kept my promise."

Ammon stood in the doorway, not moving. His eyes went to the painting on the mantel. Or was he looking at the stone?

"Look, Mr. Woolley, if you can talk some sense into my brother, I'd appreciate it. Or even my sister. If even two of us could agree, we might be able to get the mine working again. And once we get some cash flowing in, I'll be fair with the men who stayed. I'll pay back wages, as much as I'm able. But you can't get blood from a turnip. You get me?"

"I do," Hiram said. "Good evening, Mr. Kimball." He closed the door behind him and picked up the shovel. He took it and the bloodstained flour sack into the night.

Chapter Twelve

HIRAM CREPT TO THE FAR SIDE OF THE KIMBALL HOUSE, AVOIDING the windows of the sitting room where Ammon Kimball's lantern and low fire burned.

He grimaced at the chill air on his skin. He should have brought gloves.

Hiram put the spade into the loose sandy soil, too dry to be hardened by frost. After two minutes of vigorous work, he achieved the required depth: twelve inches. He knew the measurements, from the tips of his middle finger to mid-forearm. You couldn't carry a yardstick around with you on the farm, and it was often necessary to measure off a foot. From the flour sack, he pulled the head of a rattlesnake.

He'd killed the snake months earlier, when he'd come across it on the farm. Usually, rattlers stayed higher up in the mountains; Lehi was too marshy for their taste, but this one had gotten lost and was lurking in the weeds behind Hiram's porch. As long as you knew where it was, a rattlesnake wasn't much danger to humans, but it posed a threat to his dogs, and might harm livestock, so Hiram had duly fetched a shovel from the barn and hacked off the snake's head.

Then he had scooped the snake's head into this flour sack with the shovel, not using his hands because a severed snake's head could still bite. He'd thrown the sack into the icebox, and squeezed all the blood he could from the snake's body into a little glass medicine bottle. Before starting for Helper, he'd put both the blood and the head into his toolbox.

Snakes were useful for injuries and illness. A snake regrew its skin, it was a natural healer.

That was why the tincture was red; he'd mixed snake's blood into it. The next step, the one he was undertaking now, was key. He had to bury the snake's head near the person who was suffering from boils. As the snake's head rotted, the boils would disappear.

The serpent's flesh was still a little firm from being chilled; Hiram wanted it to thaw and then rot, quickly. Fortunately, he had a Bible verse for that. He knelt to push snake's head into the sandy soil—and his fingers struck something hard.

To be certain he wasn't placing the snake's head near something that would prevent it from decaying, he brushed aside the sand. He fished his Zippo out of his pocket and flicked it on.

And saw the grin of a human skull.

Hiram took a deep breath. The skull was fleshless, which likely meant it had been there a long time. It wasn't big, so probably not a man's. He didn't think it was Teancum's.

Nor was this a bad omen. Like attracted like, that was one of the basic hidden laws of the universe that Grandma Hettie had taught him; it was one of the great secrets a person with the right knowledge could use to get things done. So when Hiram walked out into the garden with a rattlesnake skull in his hand, intent on burying it, the skull already buried in the garden had naturally and invisibly drawn him to it.

He shut his lighter and took several more deep breaths, smelling the Zippo's lighter fluid. The skull wouldn't impede his healing charm. He lay the snake's head atop the human skull, covered both again with loose soil, and then squatted. He touched the ground and whispered a verse from Job, chapter nineteen: "And though worms destroy this body, yet in my flesh shall I see God." In Sunday School, that verse was about the resurrection of the flesh. In the field, it was about rot and decay.

He said it three times. Then he stood, feeling fatigue and hunger dragging at the long muscles of his body. If Ammon were healed, maybe he'd be in a more tractable mood. Could Gus Dollar be the cause of the boils? For a witch, boils might be a simple curse.

Hiram made his way back to Michael in the truck. He tied

the shovel into its place and wadded the flour sack into a ball in his pocket.

"Did he sign the offer?" Michael asked as they drove back down to the main road.

"No. Take a right and we'll bed down farther up the canyon." He didn't want to camp too close to either the mine or Gus Dollar's store.

"No hotel room?" Michael objected. "What about my delicate constitution?"

Hiram grunted.

About a mile farther up, the canyon opened and the road split. To the left wound a road that looked as if it would climb over the hill to the far side of the ridge from where the Kimball Mine lay. It most likely led to Apostate Canyon. What would lie on the right hand, then? More mines? Former ranch lands?

"Go left," Hiram said.

A quarter mile farther up, they stopped at a place where the road crossed a broad patch of flat ground. Hiram found a good spot about fifty feet from the track, beside a dry creek. A stretch of sand beneath a leafless cottonwood was ideal for the tent they'd set up. There was no flowing water, but they had several gallons on the back of the truck; it was freezing, but they had the camp stove and piles of wool blankets.

They pulled on warm hats, scarves, and leather gloves, their fingers warmed by rabbit's fur. With their coats on and moving about, the cold wasn't too bad. They moved in frozen white clouds of their own breath.

They pulled their camping gear from the back of the truck, lit a kerosene lamp, and cut long branches off the cottonwood. They used the tree branches to form a frame for their tarpaulin and Hiram lugged over the hobo stove, a portable hunk of iron. A fire might warm them for a bit, but once the iron heated up, the hobo stove would do a much better job. Hiram had several big lumps of coal that would burn through the night. They would have to keep rolling over, with one side of their bodies always heating up and the other always going cold, but it would be tolerable sleeping.

While Hiram started the fire in the stove under their shelter, Michael undid his bedroll, then sat on his bedding with his Sears, Roebuck.

He started plucking, and yodeling in a low voice. The salty dog was gone, but now Michael was singing some sort of blues drone, promising to be some woman's monkey. Hiram shook his head.

He put twigs and dry grass inside the stove as tinder, then lit it with his Zippo. He'd put it to the side of the shelter so it would vent up and out and not fill their little space with smoke.

Once the stove was started, Hiram threw the balled-up flour sack into the flames.

Michael continued to yodel, playing another blues song.

Hiram let out a sigh. "That's enough, son."

"Not a fan of Jimmie Rodgers?" Michael asked.

"I have no idea who that is. Let's just get some rest."

Michael didn't put his guitar away. "How about this one, Pap?" He then strummed a strong series of chords, which meant nothing to Hiram, until Michael began to sing: "The spirit of God like a fire is burning…"

Hiram had grown up singing that hymn, with his mother and Grandma Hettie, and on rare occasions his father. It was an early Mormon hymn, by W.W. Phelps, written for the dedication of the Kirtland Temple in 1836. Hiram loved Phelps's hymns, and often sang them to himself while working.

Michael had noticed.

Hiram sang along now in a quiet voice, quiet, because Michael sang so much better. But for the second verse, he had to raise his voice because Michael failed on the words. They sang the third verse, finishing on a pair of lines that made Hiram's hair stand on end.

> *That we through our faith may begin to inherit*
> *The visions and blessings and glories of God.*

Michael ended in a flourish of extra-loud chords.

"Now that's a good old song," Hiram said.

"True." Michael nodded. "But you know, Pap, someday these new songs are going to be good old songs. And I'm sure a hundred years from now, some old-timer will be complaining about whatever new music there is about, and he'll say that the only good music is the old music. Like Jimmie Rodgers, for example."

"Undoubtedly," Hiram agreed. "But I don't think W.W. Phelps ever begged to be anybody's salty dog."

"So you're still a believer?" Michael asked. "Even after all the trouble we've seen here, the fighting, the greed, the insanity of the Kimballs, fighting each other over a mine that should be open, you still believe there's a God in heaven with our best interests at heart?"

Hiram stuck a hunk of cottonwood, its bark peeling away in dry strips, into the stove. The fine tendrils caught. "You think because we don't have everything we want in this life that God can't exist?"

Michael shook his head. "That's too easy. If I say yes to that, you'll point out that *you* don't let *me* have everything I want in life, so does that mean that Hiram Woolley doesn't exist? But I'm not just talking about natural disasters, I'm talking about general wickedness. Greed and theft and murder."

"So because there's evil in the hearts of men, we shouldn't believe?" Hiram asked.

"I guess I think that means that God isn't doing His job very well," Michael said. "If you gave me ultimate power, I'd make sure every kid got a meal. And I don't mean cat meat. And when people did rotten things to each other, I'd step in and straighten them out. I wouldn't let things lie until some final judgment."

Hiram nodded slowly. "If you went and intervened any time somebody did something wicked—which happens all day, every day—there would be no room for faith. If God wants us to develop our capacity to act in a world of uncertainty, He has to stay mostly out of sight."

"Faith, huh? So the whole point of life is to learn to do what you're told, even when no one can give you a good reason for it??"

"Doing what's right is reason enough," Hiram wished he could be arguing theology with a ham sandwich in his belly.

"And how do you know what's right?" Michael pressed. "Isn't it because someone tells you?"

"You might have a point," Hiram said. "Maybe God isn't good at His job. That doesn't mean He doesn't exist. Maybe He's busy doing other things, and so He leaves the work to us. That way we can develop not only our faith, but also our love for other human beings."

Michael jumped on that. "So what good is a God that doesn't do a perfect job? Isn't that the point of God? To be perfect? And if he's all-powerful, why can't he just *make* me love other people?"

Hiram felt that his mind was clear and his reasons sound. He also saw that Michael had far more energy than he did, and very strong feelings.

"If I answer this, can I go to sleep?" Hiram asked.

"I've been practicing a jazz tune about whoopie that I wanted to shock you with. But maybe if you answer my question, I won't scandalize you tonight."

Hiram stoked up the fire before he slid in a shoe-sized hunk of coal. Adult-shoe-sized, rather than baby-shoe-sized, like the stone on Ammon's mantel. What kind of stone would Ammon Kimball put on display? Not some lucky rock. Something with historical significance? Something that was passed down in the family? A stone the possession of which was evidence of status, or power, or blessing.

Had Teancum Kimball possessed a peep-stone?

"You know that bucket we had, the one with the crack in it?" Hiram asked.

Michael didn't quite guffaw, but he got close. "Sure, the bucket with the crack in it."

"Did that bucket work?" Hiram asked.

"Yeah, but it dripped, so you couldn't keep it full, and it'd get you wet if you weren't careful." Michael gave Hiram a quizzical look. "So the bucket wasn't perfect."

"No. And neither is the world. Neither are we. And maybe, somehow, neither is God. At least, the way we experience God isn't perfect. There's static on the radio, traffic on the road, unexpected bad weather, but it somehow works. Makes a mess, sure, but I didn't say God was clean. That's what some folks think. But in an imperfect world, God has to deal with both imperfect possibilities and imperfect people. Coal is dirty, but it burns long and hot, and on a night like this, I don't want to wake up with a dead fire. Imperfect choices, dirty possibilities, buckets with cracks."

"Huh." Michael didn't sound thoroughly convinced.

"Genesis says that God planted the garden in Eden, and Jeremiah says He was a potter. Do you know what gardeners and potters have in common? Dirty hands. Earth is dirt, Adam was dirt, you and I are dirt, and God is down here working among us."

"With a crack in His bucket."

Hiram nodded. "God is as dirty as we are, and most of the time, that's okay."

Whether he was satisfied or not—and probably he wasn't—Michael fell silent. Hiram stretched out on his bedroll, laid his head on a gunny sack stuffed full of his extra clothing, heaped blankets over himself, and tried to sleep.

The sand under the tarpaulin was soft, and it was easy to get comfortable. Hiram let sleep take him. His dreams never came into focus, but the bright pinks and yellows gave him the idea he was dreaming of Samuel Kimball's painting of Apostate Canyon. The lines kept blurring out of focus, and when he got close to it, the whole thing erupted into a swarm of flies.

A noise woke him.

He thought it was a howl. He lay next to the stove, which was glowing red hot. His chest was warm and sweating, his back ice.

He lay on the ground, listening to Michael's breath, coming in regular intervals. He was sleeping, but Hiram was wide awake. What had awoken him?

Coyotes probably. If they yipped and yowled once, they'd do it again. He sat.

Crack!

Michael snapped awake. "What the hell was that, Pap?"

Hiram kicked off his blankets. He didn't go for the lantern, and he wasn't about to throw a stick of wood in the stove. Either action would only make him more visible.

He groped for the flashlight in the sand, and couldn't find it.

"Who's there?" he called.

No answer.

Hiram stood now and stepped toward the Double-A, eyes straining to pierce the darkness.

He heard footsteps, and a sound that might be laughter. A high-pitched giggle.

"Jesus Christ, Pap." Michael sprang to his side. "It sounds like it might be people out there."

Hiram didn't comment on his son's profanity. The noises could be made by innocent hunters, or bandits, or animals. Could there be ghosts in the darkness outside his camp?

"Hello out there!" he called.

There was no answer. Innocent people would answer. His chiroh amulet lay cool on his chest. Was it a tad more cold than usual? He reached into the gunny sack, under his extra clothes he used for a pillow, and came out with his revolver.

He heard laughter again, high-pitched, a cackle, from something that might or might not be human.

Hiram felt a shiver trace cold fingers down his spine. "Let's get to the truck." The Double-A was about twenty feet away, sitting in the weeds, with the main road another thirty feet off.

Across the dry creek the land sloped upward into pines and rocks. Could whoever was laughing be on the other side?

But then he heard the crash of branches down the creek. With no visible moon, and only a few stars peeping here and there, the sky was pitch black. The glow of the stove didn't do much, except show their position.

Hiram smelled something out of place, a vaguely fruity smell. That cackle again, staccato, high, and then crashing into a giggle. An image of a dead girl, leering with black teeth, filled his vision. In one hand, the dead child held an equally dead cat by the tail. The other gripped a cottonwood stick spear. That was Callista, with a maniacal gleam in her eye. Was it his imagination? A hallucination?

"I'm armed!" Hiram yelled.

Silence.

"We'll get in the truck and drive away," Hiram whispered to Michael. "No sense risking trouble."

Then his ears started to ring. Ringing, and buzzing, and Hiram had the sensation that flies were crawling on the skin of his arms.

And then the smell of garlic.

He heard the sound of running footsteps. "Into the truck, now!" he barked.

As they both scrambled to get into the Double-A, the smell of garlic thickened in Hiram's nostrils. He sucked in air desperately, trying not to plunge into darkness.

In the camp they had just vacated, the hobo stove crashed to the ground, spilling coals onto the dirt. In the bloody light, Hiram saw two man-shaped shadows, coming at him from the creek bed.

"Drive," Hiram muttered.

"Pap! You okay?" Michael wasn't starting the truck. Why wasn't he starting the truck?

Hiram couldn't answer, the sickly-sweet stench overwhelming him. Mustard. He smelled mustard in the garlic.

He found himself pressed against the dashboard, not sure how he got there. Then he couldn't see, couldn't hear, he could only smell and then could do nothing but slide forward into darkness.

The dead girl's giggles followed him downward.

Chapter Thirteen

MICHAEL'S HANDS SHOOK SO MUCH, DRIVING INTO HELPER, THAT Hiram nearly took the wheel.

Given that he'd just had a fainting spell, he held back. Instead, he rested a hand on Michael's shoulder and whispered words of encouragement. "You're alright, Michael. It's okay to feel nerves after something like that, son."

Michael said nothing in return and kept his eyes fixed on the road ahead.

Hiram didn't have a charm for calming nerves as such, but he knew a passage from Isaiah forty-three, and he repeated it several times. He whispered it under his breath, probably inaudible to Michael over the growl of the Double-A, but for Michael to hear the words wasn't the point.

"When thou passest through the waters, I will be with thee; and through the rivers, they shall not overflow thee: when thou walkest through the fire, thou shalt not be burned; neither shall the flame kindle upon thee."

The scents that had overwhelmed him earlier had faded, leaving behind a bitter stink. If he thought about it, he could just find in that odor a faint olfactory halo reminiscent of picnic mustard, as if someone had broken a bottle of French's in the cab of the Double-A, and it had only imperfectly been washed out.

He realized he had dreamed. Clutching the Saturn ring, he searched his mind and found the images again. He'd raced down a desert road, calling out Michael's name in vain, as he had before. He'd also dreamed of a pit. There was no exit from the hole in the ground, and a deep voice calling a question to him over and over again.

But Hiram couldn't remember what the question was. Perhaps that was just his own fear tricking him.

"I left the stove," Michael said. "And I found the flashlight in my coat pocket."

Hiram nodded.

He took a deep breath and recited the Isaiah verse again as Michael turned onto Helper's Main Street, and the washboard rattle of the dirt road was replaced with the smooth hum of rubber on asphalt.

"Do you think we can find a boardinghouse here that *isn't* a bordello?" he said.

"I'm pretty sure we can't." Michael's face cracked into a shaky grin. "We may just have to gird up our loins and face the spiritual danger."

"'Gird up our loins' doesn't sound very good in that context."

"'Gird up our loins' doesn't sound good in any context, Pap."

"That one." Hiram pointed at a signboard that read *Boarders Welcome, Long and Short Term*. It hung on the front of a building that might otherwise have been a large brick house.

"Excellent," Michael said. "The most boring-looking front on Main Street. We shall be spiritually safe there."

"I'd settle for physically safe." Hiram shook his head.

Had someone tried to attack him and Michael in their camp? Or merely frighten them?

Who would have done such a thing? Naaman Rettig? But Hiram had been on his errand. Ammon? But he had just given the man a healing balm, and Ammon had shown him no hostility.

Gus Dollar?

And if Gus, then what was the nature of the persons...or creatures...that had invaded their camp that night?

A second sign on the boarding house said *Bufords*. Pale light shone through the first-floor windows, and when Hiram and Michael slunk into the parlor, a long hallway extended back in front of them. To the right was a door with a little sign tacked to the panels: *Mr. and Mrs. Buford. Proprietors.*

Hiram hated to do it this late, but he rapped on the door. It took several knocks, but eventually the presumptive Mrs. Buford, a substantial woman in a sleeping cap and a nightgown under a thick robe, cracked the door open and gave him a glare that could have lit coal. Through her open doorway, he saw a phone on the wall in the entryway into the Bufords' room.

Michael raised an uncertain hand. "Good evening, Mrs. Buford. Sorry to wake you."

She grunted but agreed to rent to them as long as they paid for three nights, up front.

At Hiram's request, the room was on the second floor, the street-facing side of Buford's Boarding House. When Hiram pulled back the heavy crimson curtain, he could see the Double-A, parked diagonally at the curb between a Dodge Model KC and a bright yellow convertible roadster with white sidewalls. The room had a single bed, large enough for both of them, and a porcelain wash basin on a table beneath a tall mirror. A second mirror hung on the door. There was a slat-backed wooden chair, painted black. The water closet was at the end of the hall.

Michael hung his coat on a peg on the wall. From his pockets, he removed the revolver and the extra loader.

He showed both items to Hiram, and Hiram nodded. "Good thinking."

Michael set the revolver and the full moon both on the table. Hiram sat in the chair and closed his eyes, trying not to notice the fading stench of mustard.

Michael might be right. Maybe he should get a second gun.

"We could go home in the morning," he offered.

Michael unlaced his Redwings and set them by the door. His socks were filthy, black above the ankle with the coal dust of Kimball and red below the ankle with the native soil of Carbon County.

"We came here to deliver groceries to the Kimball Mine," Hiram said. "We could get a good night's sleep and just drive back to Lehi in the morning."

"Could we?" Michael stood in front of the wall mirror. He poured water from a jug into the basin and washed his hands and face.

Michael wasn't an especially fastidious young man. What was he really washing off his hands?

What had happened while Hiram had been unconscious? He

was afraid to ask, but he had to. "While I was having my fit," he said slowly. "Did you...shoot anyone?"

"You mean *kill*, right, Pap?" In another tone of voice, it would have been one of Michael's witty barbs. Spoken as it was, flat and with a knife-like edge, the words hurt Hiram.

"Killing a man is a hard thing," Hiram said. "Wounding a man is also very hard. If you did either tonight, you did it because you had to, and you should feel nothing but gratitude that you and I are both alive."

Michael was quiet for a moment. "I shot at them. I don't know whether I hit them or not."

Hiram nodded. "Many men who came home from the Great War could say exactly the same words. Not knowing whether you actually hit the other fellow is sometimes the best source of comfort."

"I'm fine, Pap." Michael's voice relaxed slightly. "I don't need to go home."

"I could tell Bishop Wells with a clean conscience that I've done was I was asked to do."

"What's that phrase you like so much?" Michael patted his hands dry on a towel and sat on the bed. "The one where I tease you it's about burning up ants?"

"Magnifying your calling," Hiram said.

Michael nodded. "That's the one. Remind me what it means."

"It means...not just doing the minimum. It means if your responsibility is small, you can still do it well. It means carrying out the spirit of your task to accomplish great things, and not just' complying with the letter of an assignment."

"Right. So tell me again that we can drive home in the morning."

Hiram's lungs felt squeezed and breathless. "I worry about your safety."

"I know you do, Pap. You worry about *my* safety, and not your own. And you also worry about the safety of all the Kimball miners, don't you? And the safety of their families? And probably even the safety of the Kimball brothers, even though they don't give a damn about you. And whether that Greek woman and all her kids are going to eat tomorrow."

Hiram thought again of Medea and Basil, their daughter Callista, and their other children. He had injured Basil—in self-defense, but Hiram felt responsible, nonetheless. What kind of man would he be if he just abandoned them?

Michael cracked a wicked grin and looked sidelong at Hiram. "Oh, and for sure you care about the union lady."

"Mary, or Gil, I guess."

"That's the one."

"I could drive you home in the morning and come back," Hiram suggested.

"That would take you all day," Michael said. "In that time, there could be another shooting up at the mine, Gil might get attacked in prison, all kinds of bad things could happen."

Hiram hung his head, burying his face in his palms, elbows planted on his knees.

"Besides," Michael added, "you'd be preventing me from magnifying *my* calling."

"You don't have a calling. You won't even step inside a church."

"I'm your driver," Michael said. "You'd probably have another fainting spell and crash the car on the drive back here, anyway. Hell, Pap, it would be downright irresponsible of me to let you try."

"You could say *heck*, you know. Other boys say *heck*."

"No, they don't."

"Two spells in twenty-four hours would be unusual." In fact, Hiram had felt on the brink of having a spell much more frequently than usual, since coming to Helper and Spring Canyon. Was that from strain? Sleeplessness? Some malign influence?

Michael just sat on the bed, looking calmly at Hiram.

"Well," Hiram continued. "What shall we do, then?"

"Get the union lady out of jail," Michael told him. "Get the mine open. Not get killed by bandits."

Also, not get trapped by another one of Gus Dollar's enchantments, whatever the storekeeper was up to. But Hiram just nodded.

Michael yawned. "I think, though, that sleep is probably the first thing on the to-do list."

"Agreed. You hit the sack, I'll go bring in the toolbox."

"Right." Michael yawned again and lay down, flat on his back. "I've heard many times that Helper's ladies of the evening are notorious for stealing shovels and water cans."

"Before today, you'd never heard of Helper's ladies of the evening."

"True. Utah is much more interesting than I ever imagined."

And just like that, Michael was snoring.

Hiram shifted Michael just enough to get the blanket over his son, then turned off the electric light. He took the revolver with him, tucking it into the bib pocket of his overalls, and headed down to the street.

Hiram took the long steel tool chest from the back of the Double-A and carried it in both hands up to the hotel room. Once Hiram had locked the door, he lifted the top tray—with its hammer and pliers and screwdrivers and other assorted hardware—out of the chest and set it aside.

Beneath lay the chest's true, important contents. Three worn leather notebooks. A dog's tongue. Several lamens. Small sheets of virgin paper. Stones taken from the Jordan River near his farm that had natural holes in them, holes bored by the river itself, rather than by the hand of man. Two forked rods cut from the stand of witch hazel that Hiram carefully tended at the end of his farmhouse porch, and other paraphernalia.

Tools to accomplish ends, tools in their essence only very slightly different from the hammer.

Still, others would have said they were *magical*.

He looked up to make certain Michael was still sleeping.

He selected one of the lamens, an Oremus lamen, made of flattened bronze, six inches wide and eight inches long. A lamen was a written enchantment, and could be made on paper (especially virgin paper, paper of the best quality that had never been used before, and even better would be virgin parchment) or stitched into a quilt, but Hiram had a few made of metal, because he wanted them to be rugged and portable.

There was such an inscribed metal plate inside the door of the Double-A, on the driver's side. Hiram had spent an entire day figuring out how to crack that door open and fix the lamen into place, before he had let Michael drive. He'd sent Michael off on an errand first, walking to the telegraph office in town to send a message to the beet processing plant in Payson and then wait for answer. That had given Hiram the time he'd needed. The lamen in the car provided protection.

The lamen he drew from the chest now was identical to the one in the car. Hiram didn't know Latin or Hebrew, but during the Great War, he'd been briefly in London. There he'd found a copy of a volume of which Grandma Hettie had spoken highly,

Reginald Scot's *The Discoverie of Witchcraft*. The old Elizabethan squire's book, to Hiram's surprise, was a screed that railed against even the possibility of magic. In attempting to expose magic to the ridicule he said it deserved, Scot recorded dozens of charms, making the *Discoverie* an excellent resource, and the closest thing to a real book of magic Hiram had ever seen complete.

It was almost as if Scot had himself been a cunning man, attempting to pass down his magical lore in disguise.

Hiram had copied it out by hand into two leather journals he'd bought on Charing Cross Road, including all the Latin. Mostly, he ignored the Latin and Hebrew and used Scot's English charms, but he had made these two identical lamens. They read, letters and crosses carefully pressed into the bronze:

> *Fons* † *alpha & omega* † *figa* † *figalis* † *Sabbaoth* †
> *Emanuel* † *Adonai* † *o* † *Neray* † *Elay* † *Ihe* † *Rentone*
> † *Neger* † *Sahe* † *Pangeton* † *Commen* † *a* † *g* † *l*
> † *a* † *Mattheus* † *Marcus* † *Lucas* † *Johannes* †††
> *titulus triumphalis* † *Jesus Naserenus Rex Judeorum*
> † *ecce dominice crucis signum* † *fugite partes adverse,*
> *vicit leo de tribu Jude, radix, David, aleluijah, Kyrie*
> *eleeson, Christe eleeson, pater noster, ave Marie, &*
> *ne nos, & veniat super nos salutare tuum: Oremus.*

According to Scot, Joseph of Arimathea had found these words engraved on Christ's side by the finger of God Himself, and anyone protected by the words would fear no evil death, or any danger at all.

Hiram tied a leather thong through a hole punched into one end of the Oremus lamen, and he slipped the thin plate beneath the mirror hanging from the door. A close observer might see the top of the thong and investigate, but the lamen was hidden from casual view.

He wished he had one to hang in the window, too, but he didn't have enough time to take apart the door of the Double-A. And Michael had taken his boots off.

Hiram removed the chi-rho talisman from around his neck and hung it in the window.

The last word of the Scot lamen, *Oremus*, meant "let us pray." The lamen required a prayer to activate it, so on the floor of the hotel room, the only illumination coming in through the window from the marquee of the movie theater next door, Hiram Woolley knelt and prayed. He prayed for Michael's safety and the peace of Michael's soul.

While he was at it, he prayed, stomach growling, to end his fast.

Then he shut the curtain.

Thinking of Reginald Scot reminded Hiram that Scot had a charm for rest. Standing, he spoke it over Michael's sleeping form. "In the name of the Father, up and down, the Son and the Spirit upon your crown, the cross of Christ upon your breast, sweetest lady send you rest."

Michael's body sank deeper into the depths of the hotel mattress and his breathing became slow and regular.

Hiram looked at the bed and briefly considered going to sleep himself. His bones felt like lead, and he knew that if he could get even three or four hours of sleep, he'd feel much refreshed.

But he didn't lie down. Working with his own written enchantments had made him think of Gus Dollar's store. Specifically, he thought of the curious glyphs built into the store windows. He knew that for each planet, there was a written glyph that worked like a secret name; his Saturn ring was engraved with the sign of Saturn, for instance, in addition to bearing a signet he'd had made by a jeweler in Salt Lake City. Hiram knew the signs of the planets.

He also knew that angels and devils were said to have similar signs, and he didn't know those. But if the images in Gus's windows drew and focused the power of an angel...or worse, a demon of some kind...that might explain how Gus had so handily overcome Hiram's ordinary defensive charms, both to draw Hiram into the shop and also to loosen his tongue about his past and his secrets.

He had to find out more about the signs in those windows. And out here in Helper, with no library anywhere nearby, the only likely source of knowledge was the store itself.

Hiram removed his Harvesters. Like Michael's, his socks were stained by alternating layers of red and black dust. He set his boots together beside Michael's, and then took his son's footwear. From the toolbox, he took a triangular bit of leather and placed it in inside the right boot. He then put both of Michael's boots on.

Michael's feet were bigger than Hiram's. The boots were a loose fit, but Hiram could walk.

Almost as an afterthought, Hiram opened the third leather notebook, which was his dream dictionary. It wasn't really a dictionary, in that it had been written by Hiram himself, and wasn't in alphabetical order, but it collected what he knew about the symbols that could occur in his dreams. He looked up images that had dogged his recent dreams:

> FLIES—*you have many enemies.*
> VOICE, UNSEEN—*denotes you will be deluded by*
> *feigned pretenders.*
> PIT—*you face sudden surprise or danger.*
> RUNNING—*if you dream you run swiftly, you will*
> *receive a letter.*

Did it add up an interpretation of his dreams, of driving and looking for Michael, of a voice in a pit? Not that he could puzzle out. He sighed and put the dream dictionary away in the toolbox.

Hiram put the gun and the loader into the tool chest and took the chest with him. He locked Michael into the warded hotel room and headed for the Double-A.

Chapter Fourteen

ALL THE WAY UP SPRING CANYON, HIRAM CHANTED A CHARM against the falling sickness, an old name for epilepsy. Epilepsy was close enough to what ailed him. "I conjure me by the sun and the moon, and by the gospel of this day delivered to Rupert, Giles, Cornelius, and John, that I rise and fall no more."

He had no idea who Rupert, Giles, and Cornelius might be, but this was the charm Grandma Hettie had taught him. He gripped the wheel of the Double-A until his knuckles turned white and said the words over and over again.

No strange smells troubled him, and he reached Dollar's.

His stomach growled audibly the entire time.

What was it he had smelled when the camp had been attacked? The garlic and mustard smells of his fainting spell had taken him eventually, but first there had been something else, a sweeter smell that reminded him of Christmas.

He stopped the car when he was still around the bend and prepared himself. He stuffed his pockets with bay leaves. He put the revolver into the bib pocket of his overalls. He tucked the leather notebooks containing his transcription of Reginald Scot into the deep pockets of his wool coat. He took a disk of wax the size of a silver dollar, imprinted with a large cross and rimmed by a ring of flowers, and held it in his hand to avoid spoiling the impressions in the wax. He made sure he had the flashlight in one pocket and his clasp knife in another, along with his Zippo and his bloodstone.

He took the bolt-cutters.

Should he make a witch bottle, or burn the shingle he'd taken? He didn't think the time had come yet for either countercharm, so he placed the two empty Coke bottles into the lower compartment of his tool chest alongside the bit of Gus Dollar's shingle, and then shut the chest into the cab of the Double-A.

He walked quietly toward Gus Dollar's shop.

The lights were out. Gus was asleep, likely. To be sure, Hiram stood on the path at the edge of the porch and recited again the charm for rest he had used on Michael. He visualized Gus, he visualized the tow-headed children, he visualized unseen and unnamed other members of the household, and he repeated it three times.

He didn't worry about the Rottweilers.

He took time to consider what he was doing. He was about to commit a burglary. He was doing it, though, because he believed Gus knew something about the closing of the mine. The bloodstone had told him as much. And since Gus had denied that knowledge, and also hexed Hiram twice, then Gus was a man of ill will.

Peace on earth to men of good will, had been the angels' song, the way Grandma Hettie had taught it to Hiram.

Also, Gus might have a connection with whoever had attacked his camp earlier that night.

"If I am sinning against an innocent man," he prayed softly, "then stop me, Lord Divine, and keep him from harm. Amen."

On the porch, he knelt and held the wax disk up to the door. On the other side, he heard the padding feet of the dogs. He spoke his charm: "I open this door in thy name that I am forced to break, in the name of the Father, and of the Son, and of the Holy Ghost, amen." Then he blew three times across the disk and into the lock.

He stood, putting the wax back into a coat pocket. When he tried the doorknob, it turned.

So Gus Dollar was not an innocent man.

Within stood the two Rottweilers. Their jaws worked vigorously, mouths opening and closing, but no sound came out. The triangular bit of leather in Hiram's shoe was the tongue of a dog, with no special words written on it and no prayer spoken; it was old and true lore that in the presence of a dried dog's tongue, a dog could not bark.

The warm air rushing from inside the store was welcome, especially as it carried with it hints of the tins of sugar and cinnamon that Gus had sitting his shelves. The sudden stab of hunger in Hiram's belly nearly knocked him down.

He knelt again and reached out to pet the animals. Puzzled, surprised, and maybe frightened, the dogs retreated, disappearing into the back end of the shop.

Hiram stood still for a minute, until his eyes adjusted and he could make out the general outline of things in the shop: the counter, the tools, the mannequins, the washing machine.

Now for the key action, the thing Hiram most needed to do in order to stay undetected. If his guess was correct that the signs in the windows were angelic or demonic, and made Gus's magic more powerful than Hiram's, then Hiram had to destroy those signs before they undid his charms.

He cautiously moved a three-stepped stool beneath the windows and then climbed it.

For good measure, standing in Gus Dollar's window, Hiram took the peppermint leaves and stuffed them all into a pocket. Then he pushed the nose of the bolt cutters as snugly against the windowpane as he dared. Too hard, and he'd shatter the window, and he doubted the rest charm would keep Gus Dollar sleeping through a noise like *that*. Not firmly enough, and he'd have no effect.

He pressed as much as he dared, working the bolt cutter blades around the lead where it protruded most on this side of the glass and then snipped it. With a satisfying *chunk* sound, the bolt cutters bit through the soft metal.

Examining the bolt cutters' result, though, Hiram found that the sign was not completely interrupted. He applied his clasp knife to the task, gouging out additional gray twists of lead until the blade poked entirely through the window, and Hiram felt a cold squirt of air through the hole.

There. That sigil was now damaged, and its operation should be interrupted.

He moved the stool and did the same thing with the second window.

Were there other signs? Hiram checked the other windows and didn't see any. If there were painted signs, say, on the floorboard or on a wall, Hiram couldn't see them in the darkness, and of course if there were signs embedded within the walls or the door, as Hiram had done, placing the lamen of protection within the Double-A, Hiram had no way to know. But in any case, he must have interrupted *some* of Gus's power.

But what he had come here for was knowledge of what the signs meant. He studied the sigils carefully with his eye, trying to memorize the irregular curves, the curl at the one end and the arrow at the other, the way the sign seemed to creep out larger than its actual dimensions to dominate the space around it.

To be certain, he tore a scrap from the corner of an old page in Gus's account book, and with the pencil lying beside the book on the countertop, he drew the sign.

He took the nickel from Gus's revenue charm, tucking it into his own pocket. The poppet stared accusingly at him, its empty eye sockets seeming to follow him from side to side. Hiram resisted the temptation to smash the poppet flat with his fist. For good measure, he also took the Bible off Gus's butter churn and hid it on a shelf behind stacks of Henry Ford reprints of McGuffey's Readers.

Finding and fixing these little faults might keep Gus distracted.

Hiram really wanted to eat something, a cookie or a Snickers bar. He didn't. He couldn't. To steal Gus's food would be simple burglary, and a sin. Hiram's charms wouldn't work for a mere thief.

He crept from room to room, searching.

He found the dogs, lying on their bellies in a pantry in front of a wall of dried beans, tinned tomatoes, and salt crackers. They had their paws over their faces, and didn't look up as Hiram stepped past them.

He checked the windows of other rooms, but didn't see the strange glyph repeated there.

The downstairs was all store and storage, so Hiram tip-toed up to the second floor.

Around a central landing area huddled five rooms. Their doors were open, so Hiram peeped one at a time into each room. He spotted Gus, sleeping alone. There were also a couple, and a woman alone, and two rooms full of little children.

But in his squinting into the upstairs bedrooms, Hiram saw no signs of any books. No ceremonial swords or staffs, no visible lamens.

If Gus was a witch, were all his accoutrements in the store? If so, Hiram's mission was doomed to disappointment. He had learned all he was going to learn, and the curious signs in the windows would remain mysteries.

He should ask Mahonri Young. He could call from the boarding house's telephone in the morning. He could describe his sketches of the signs to Mahonri, who would be disappointed that Hiram was once again asking him questions concerning the occult, but would help, anyway.

But no, if Gus was indeed drawing arcane symbols, then he had a dictionary somewhere, a symbols list. The signs of the planets and celestial and infernal beings were simply too complex to know by heart, unless you worked with them constantly. Gus must have at least a card, a sign list. Hiram could read that, or he could take it.

He considered the layout of the building: had he missed a secret room somewhere? To the best of his spatial estimation, all the room was accounted for.

But Gus's shop stood on high ground, far above the creek. There could be a basement.

Hiram descended again to the ground floor and retraced his steps. Here, too, he could find no space not accounted for. He looked inside the washing machine, and behind the goods on the shelves in the shop and in the storerooms, and found nothing.

Standing in the pantry beside the two Rottweilers, who still pressed themselves flat against the hardwood floor, he wondered what he could have missed. Could Gus have an office in a separate building elsewhere? But there wasn't so much as a springhouse in sight, and if you were going to keep valuable ritual gear, you would store it on your person or close to you, so you could watch it.

Could a list be taped inside one of the McGuffey Readers? Hiram didn't think Gus would risk the chance that a customer might find it. Maybe in the safe deposit box of a bank? Helper had a bank. Maybe Hiram could investigate in town in the morning.

Hiram could go out to the Double-A and get one of his forked hazel rods. Did he have time to peel it, carve it, and sanctify it as a Mosaical Rod, and then still have time to use it?

Hiram sighed. He didn't.

Perhaps he'd have to come back again and search the property the following evening. Tired as he was, and having driven the truck up alone in the dark, and standing as he was in another man's house in the middle of the night, the thought was daunting.

Then he noticed the dogs.

They lay flat. Not cringing as if in fear, and not just silent, but pressed flat to the floor.

That didn't seem like the effect of his charm.

Crouching, he grabbed one dog and dragged it aside. The dog wiggled from his grasp and immediately rushed back to lie in the same space—but not before Hiram saw the outline of a trapdoor where it had been lying.

Hiram considered his options. He had to get the dogs out of the way and keep them out of the way, and they were big enough that he could only carry one at a time. And the rooms on the ground floor had no doors to shut them in with.

He could take them upstairs and shut them into bedrooms. But that might wake the people who slept in those rooms.

Hiram picked up one of the Rottweilers. It struggled, but it didn't bite him, so he carried it to the front door of the shop and pushed it outside, shutting the door behind it. Could he do it again, and put the second dog outside without letting the first one back in? It wasn't likely. The dogs were drawn to the trapdoor.

Crossing the shop, he had a better idea.

Picking up the second Rottweiler, he carried it into the shop. There he lowered it into the drum of the washing machine and closed the lid.

Thank goodness for the dog's tongue in his boot. It kept the Rottweilers from complaining.

Hiram looked outside: pale gray light suggested dawn was approaching. Given the month, it was likely that the only reason the family was still sleeping was Hiram's charm, and that couldn't last much longer.

He opened the trapdoor and shone his flashlight down. Iron rungs descended a shaft made of red stones, mortared thickly together.

There was no more time for consideration; he sat on the lip of the tunnel and then lowered himself in. Once he was fully inside, he shut the trapdoor overhead.

A whisper of air rustling up inside the leg of his overalls gave him a moment's pause; there must be a connection below to the outside. He forced himself on, and when he reached the bottom of the shaft, he shone the light around.

He was in a square-cornered basement, all of mortared local stone. In one corner, the stones had cracked apart wide enough that a man could crawl through into darkness, and that was the source of the cold breeze. A long table filled the center of the room. Here were all the things Hiram expected to see in the house of a prosperous worker in the ancient lore: tablets and paper for creating amulets, a sword, candles and matches, wax seals, stones of various colors and sizes, and alchemical flasks and tubing about which Hiram knew nothing. Resting on wooden blocks, there was a book in the process of being assembled; virgin paper, carefully cut, was bound between two metal lamens. Hiram examined the metal plates. The first was made from a yellow metal, brass or bronze, and bore sacred names and astral grids. That struck Hiram as a lamen for binding or protection. It was not lore he'd mastered, but Grandma Hettie had known such arts.

The other plate bore a series of images that Hiram thought were astrological in nature. Curiously, the plate was made of lead, which suggested that, like Hiram's ring, it was Saturnine: that might connect it with dreams, melancholy, and insight, but it might also indicate that it was destructive in intent. The lamen bore two short lines; one was in Latin, but the other was in English: *Shout, for the Lord hath given you the city.*

He knew the words. Where did they come from?

Hiram had never seen such a book, but he'd heard about them from Grandma Hettie, and he'd read of them: Gus Dollar was preparing a Book of the Spirits. The thought of Gus summoning and binding creatures beyond Hiram's craft made Hiram's blood run cold.

Ordinarily, a Book of the Spirits was used to summon and contain a spirit, and the two binding lamens that made up the covers would trap it. But this one was different. The brass or bronze lamen was likely a binding charm, but the bottom lead cover? That seemed to have been crafted to destroy something. But what?

A city? Which city had the Lord given?

Jericho. Jericho, whose walls had tumbled down when Joshua's men had shouted.

Hiram shook his head, not entirely sure what he held in his hands.

While the Book of the Spirits was still half done, there were also completed books.

He couldn't let himself be distracted. Nor could he carry away all the volumes. And, dog's tongue charm notwithstanding, might the beast in the washing machine whine loud enough to wake its master? Sweating despite the cold, Hiram grabbed the books and flipped through them. He wasn't looking for text, but for diagrams, and not just any diagrams. He ignored astrological charts, and number charts, and esoteric alphabets, and had gone through three books and was into a fourth when he finally found what he'd been seeking: the glyph that appeared in lead in the shop's windows, one of a long series of similar diagrams, each surrounded by several long paragraphs of text in tiny gothic letters.

The words were in German.

Hiram stifled a curse.

Above him, he heard footsteps. He tucked the book, which was a small volume, into his coat pocket, and stood at the bottom of the shaft to listen.

"Boys!" he heard Gus Dollar call. "Boys?"

Hiram reached into his bib pocket and pulled out the Colt. If he had to, he could shoot Gus. Gus was no innocent man, no mere shopkeeper. Gus dealt with demons and strange craft, and he was a threat to Hiram, Hiram's son, and all people everywhere.

But killing a man was a hard, hard thing to do, and a harder burden to bear, afterward. Even when the man was a witch.

Hiram eyed the crack at the corner of the room. There was a breeze, so, somehow, that gap in the wall led to the surface.

Crossing to the split, he passed the Book of the Spirits again. He couldn't leave it with Gus. He didn't want to take it, either.

And he had already left plenty of evidence that someone had been here. He tore both lamens out of the book and inserted them into the inside pocket of his coat. With his Zippo, Hiram set fire to the virgin paper. It was a desperate move. It would certainly be noticed, and it might even risk burning the shop down. Gus was awake, dealing with his dogs, so he would notice the fire. That would prevent any loss of innocent life; the old German would have counter magic against fire.

The orange flames cast only very little light ahead of Hiram as he crawled into the crack, but his flashlight let him see his path. To his relief, in a few short feet, it opened onto a passage tall enough for him to crouch in, and he waddled forward at a reasonable pace.

Small objects struck him in the face. Insects? Flying insects, beneath the ground, in February? He swatted one against his own forehead, and when he examined it in the light he found it to be a fly as large as his pinky nail.

Fear and nausea fought for control of Hiram's stomach, and nausea won. As he finished vomiting into the side of the passageway, he heard screaming behind him.

Gus had opened the trapdoor and seen the fire.

Hiram raced ahead. In another few paces, he found himself at a fork. One passage dropped steeply to his left, and the flies seemed to swarm thickly there, boiling out of the depths of the earth. The stink of rot came with them. To his right, the passage rose; Hiram felt the breeze again, and was that daylight?

He scrambled on, and when he could see the light of morning for certain, he switched off the flashlight. The passage opened in an oval-shaped egress bounded by stone, turned to face parallel to the canyon and hidden from the view of travelers by a large stone slab.

As Hiram stepped through exit, sudden pain wracked his entire body. He felt as if he had been cast into a fire, and he fell, tumbling down the scree at the base of the canyon wall.

Vision swimming, he held onto consciousness by a thread. Gus knew he had been there. Gus could be coming after him. Hiram lurched to his feet and raced across the canyon, keeping junipers between himself and Dollar's as much as possible. When he rounded the bend and found the Double-A waiting where he had left it, he heaved a sigh of relief.

Hiram started the truck and his incantation against the falling sickness at the same time, and drove as fast as he dared back toward Helper. He had reached Michael's alluvial fan and was dropping down toward the river when he realized that he smelled burnt herbs. Reaching into his pockets to examine the bay leaves and also the peppermint, he found it all dried and brittle, shriveled up, and scorched black at the edges, as if it had been thrown into a fire.

Chapter Fifteen

THE SUN SHONE DOWN ON HELPER BY THE TIME HIRAM REACHED
Main Street. He didn't want Michael seeing him, and he was too
anxious to wait any longer, so he pulled over in front of a restaurant that was clearly closed, its curb empty. There he cracked
open Gus Dollar's book.

If he'd hoped that during his drive down Spring Canyon, the
text would be miraculously transmuted from German to English,
he was disappointed.

Of course, there were plenty of Germans up at the Kimball
Mine, and one of them might help Hiram read the book. Or for
that matter, there were Germans at other camps, in Spring Canyon or in the other canyons around Helper. There were probably
German-speakers living down in Helper, running a restaurant or
working in the department store.

Only Hiram had no desire for Carbon County's German com-
munity to be talking about that strange traveler, the demonolo-
gist Hiram Woolley. If word got back to Bishop Smith . . . Hiram
preferred not to think about the consequences.

He found the sigil in question quickly and double-checked
that he had the right one by comparing it with his own sketch.
Hiram had learned a smattering of phrases as a Doughboy, and
he looked for them now. He found *isst*—wasn't that *is?* But then
here was *ist*—were they two spelling for the same word? He looked
for *gut*, and *schlecht*, and *kann*, and *muss*, and found none of

them. He gave up, but in searching for words he knew, he found two words, appearing several times each all in capital letters on the page with the glyph in question, and, as far as he could tell from a quick page-flipping, appearing nowhere else in the book.

MAHOUN.

SAMAEL.

Hiram didn't know the lore of demons. You didn't have to know such lore to cast devils out; you needed it if you wanted to summon and command them, and Hiram emphatically did *not* want a demonic ally. That made you a witch or a sorcerer.

Still, he thought he knew the name *Samael*. Samael was a demon, a fallen angel. He didn't remember whether he'd read the name alongside such names as Semyaz and Azrael in the apocryphal books like 1 Enoch, or if perhaps Grandma Hettie had told him the name in one of her rocking-chair sermons, but he was confident he knew the name.

Curious that *Samael* and *Samuel* were so similar. Coincidence?

Mahoun, though . . . nothing.

The sigil was the sign of a demon, Samael, with Mahoun maybe being another name for him. Or could they be names for two different demons? Why would Gus Dollar want such a sign? To summon the being? To channel its power? To command it?

Some combination of all of those?

A drunk staggered into the side of the Double-A, startling Hiram out of his train of thought. The sun's height in the sky told him that more time had passed than he'd planned.

The Denver lawyer might be available.

He reparked the truck in front of the Buford's Boarding House and went inside. It was morning and the smell of bacon frying and coffee dripping filled the place. To ward off the worst of his hunger pains, he grabbed a handful of mints from a crystal dish in the front hall and choked them down, almost without chewing. They were sweet, they pushed back against his hunger, and the mints had the added benefit of sweetening his stale breath.

He knocked on the Bufords' door.

Again, the woman answered and this time wore a turban. Slippers fuzzed her feet. "You again. Out late. Up early."

He winced shook his head. "I'm so sorry, ma'am. Could I possibly use your phone?"

"That'll be a nickel."

Hiram produced the coin. She let him inside the entryway where the phone was connected to the wall and snatched the coin out of his hand. "Make it quick. And keep the door open. If you come any farther into my room, my husband will give you the what-for." She retreated.

He unhooked the receiver and placed it to his ear. He spoke into the transmitter attached to the ringer box, tripping over his own tongue with the sudden flood of saliva stimulated by the mints and the smell of the bacon. When the operator asked for the exchange and number, Hiram gave her the number for B Y High.

A secretary answered, which was unsurprising, since the one telephone in the building was in the central office, but she quickly brought Hiram's friend to the phone.

"Mahonri Young."

"Mahonri, it's Hiram." Hiram hesitated. "I have a . . . a strange question."

He listened to Mahonri's deep breath and exhalation.

"What kind of strange?" Mahonri asked.

"Well, I'm not in jail, if that's what you're worried about."

The joke brought a laugh from Mahonri, and then a touch of relaxation to his voice. "Okay, Hiram. Fair enough. What do you want to know?"

"I'm looking for any information you can give me on two names. They might be old angel names, I think."

"Angels?" Mahonri pressed.

"Or something like that."

Mahonri hesitated. "I don't expect I should hope you need this information to teach Sunday School."

"I don't want to tell you why I want the information," Hiram said. "And you don't really want to know."

"I don't want to know," Mahonri agreed. "But I do want to know that you and Michael are safe."

"We're safe," Hiram said, probably too quickly. "Except I'm not so sure I'm safe from Michael. He's as aggressive and sarcastic as ever, and no closer to finding faith. And now he's taken to cussing."

"Maybe he'll find God through cussing," Mahonri said. "He wouldn't be the first, and I believe that's the *traditional* route for Catholics. What are the names?"

Hiram gave him the names *Mahoun* and *Samael*, spelling them both out. He then told Mahonri that the easiest way to contact him back was to send a telegram to Buford's Boarding House.

"I'll get back to you," Mahonri said, and hung up.

Hiram contacted the operator again.

"Denver two, twelve oh seven," he said when the operator came on the line, and then he waited.

"I heard that!" Mrs. Buford called from the other room. "Another five cents, Mr. Woolley, if not ten!"

Hiram called back, "Yes, ma'am."

A few seconds later, a woman's voice came on the line. "Law office of James Nichols, esquire."

"I need to speak to James Nichols."

"Is it about an existing matter?"

Existing matter? "I'm not a client."

"If you could just give me a few details as what the nature of the matter is, I'll know how to direct your call."

Hiram felt that privacy was being invaded, his or maybe Mary McGill's. "Please direct the call to James Nichols."

"Please tell me the nature of the matter, sir." The woman's voice had become frosty.

The nature of the matter? What *was* the nature of the matter? Hiram was exhausted. A mine was closed, two brothers were fighting over which direction to take the mine, and stirring up ethnic tensions in the process. A union organizer was being held for a bogus crime, a pride-ridden railroad magnate wanted to use Hiram as his messenger boy, and a beloved shopkeeper appeared to be summoning or planning on summoning demons, for a purpose Hiram couldn't imagine.

What *was* the nature of the matter?

"Sir?" the woman's voice shook him back to the present.

Hiram cleared his throat. "I need to talk to Five-Cent Jimmy. It isn't for me, it's for Mary McGill. And Gil said Five-Cent Jimmy would never let her down."

"I see," the woman said. "You should have said that in the first place."

"I was trying," Hiram offered weakly, but the *click* on the other end of the line told him he'd already been transferred.

"Jimmy," came a man's voice.

"Gil told me that Five-Cent—"

"Yeah, I heard that. What's happened to Gil?"

Hiram told the story as he understood it.

"Sorry, did you say that she's being held by the city police? City of Helper, Utah?"

"Yes."

"And was she arrested in the city? Of Helper, Utah? Jeebus, what kind of name is that?"

"It comes from the railroad locomotives," Hiram said.

"What?"

"No," Hiram said. "She was arrested in one of the mining camps. They're outside the city."

"Okay," the union lawyer said. "So this is a pretty basic jurisdiction problem. Cops behaving badly, think they can get away with it because they're in a small town. They won't know what hit 'em."

"That sounds good," Hiram said.

"Tell Gil to sit tight, I'll be there late tonight with the writ. First thing tomorrow, she'll be out, I guarantee it. And if they move her before that, give me a call again, will you?"

Hiram nodded, and then realized that Five-Cent Jimmy wouldn't hear the nod. "I will."

Jimmy hung up.

Mrs. Buford marched up with bacon grease flecks dotting the front of her robe. "That was two phone calls."

Hiram dug into his pocket, and produced a second coin for Mrs. Buford. He left her room and the woman slammed the door. When her turned to climb the hotel stairs, he was facing Michael.

Who was in his dirty socks.

Hiram froze. The book full of demons' signs and names felt very heavy in his coat pocket, as did the two metal lamens he'd taken from Gus's basement workroom.

"I'm disappointed," his son said.

"What do you mean?"

"When I discovered you'd accidentally walked off wearing my boots, I hoped you had at least gone to get pastries or something. You can understand my disappointment at learning that all you're doing is making a telephone call."

"Mary McGill's attorney," Hiram said. Had Michael heard his conversation with Mahonri, too?

"Yeah, I heard the whole thing. The door was open. You

know, many men get awkward when talking to a girl. Leave it to you to get all mumble-mouthed when talking to a girl's *lawyer*."

"I was telling you yesterday, I'm not a ladies' man."

"On the other hand," Michael said, "*for once*, you can't ask if I'm wearing my boots. Because *you're* wearing them."

"Sorry." Hiram retreated to a couch in the parlor, relieved that Michael hadn't mentioned Mahonri, Mahoun, or Samael. He sat and began unlacing the Harvesters.

"You have to remember that my feet are bigger than yours. That means that I *can't* wear *your* shoes."

Hiram stood and handed Michael his boots. "Now I can tell you to put your boots on. There are people I want to see in town. Eliza Kimball, for one."

"After we get some pastries?" Michael took a seat and put on the boots. The moment the right boot was laced up, Hiram felt easier.

"Pastries would be good," Hiram said. "Bacon would be better." He turned to the exit.

"Pap," Michael said.

"Yes?"

"*Your* boots are still up in the room."

Hiram grinned, blushing. Good, he'd retrieve his boots as well as the Oremus lamen he'd hid behind the mirror in their room. He wanted all the protection he could get.

Chapter Sixteen

AFTER BREAKFAST, HIRAM AND MICHAEL KNOCKED ON ELIZA Kimball's door in the Hotel Utah.

She opened it and stared. Hiram, caught off guard by the long, withering look, could only stand and endure it. Eliza had intense brown eyes sunk deep into a face that was smooth and youthful, other than faint crow's feet and a maze of wrinkles around her small mouth. She once might have had Ammon's coal-black hair, but now it was flecked with gray, tied back in a bun. Her dress and her small hat were both black.

Hiram had known actual nuns in France, but, on the score of severity, Eliza Kimball outnunned them all.

"So you're the Mormons who've been causing trouble."

Michael let out a noisy breath. "One Mormon, and one believer in science. Raised by Mormons, though."

Eliza stood unmoving in the open doorway. "I saw you two at the mine, and I confess that I was curious. Now that I've had a better look...good day."

Hiram found his mind blank.

"We have a letter you should see, Mrs. Kimball," Michael said.

God bless Michael.

"*Miss* Kimball." The woman corrected like a nun, too. She shifted her stare to Michael. "You're a bold young man, telling me what I *ought* to do. I can't have two men in my room alone. My standing in this part of the world is already so very uncertain."

127

"We could talk in the lobby," Michael suggested. "But I'm not sure you would want anyone listening in on our conversation, seeing as it involves financial matters."

Eliza tried to smile, but her mouth got stuck halfway. "Calling my bluff."

She stepped aside and waved them in.

"Thank you, Miss Kimball," Hiram said.

The sheets on the bed were tucked in tight and the bedspread arranged perfectly. The room had just enough space for the desk and a wash basin squeezed against one wall. The wallpaper matched the lobby's, gold swirls on brown. Standing against one wall was a large rectangular object wrapped in brown paper.

Like maybe a framed painting.

The place had a vaguely feminine odor, rose water perhaps, but mostly it smelled of the central heater's dust.

"You can sit on the bed," Eliza said to Michael. "And your father can take the chair."

"I'd feel better standing." Hiram removed his hat and ran his fingers across his scalp. "In the presence of a lady."

"I'd feel better if you did what I told you."

Hiram sat. He ached all over.

Michael sat, and Eliza closed the door.

"The letter," Eliza reminded them.

Hiram blushed, then gave it to her.

"Letter opener. There's one on the desk." Hiram swiveled and presented her the brass blade. She flicked open the envelope, saw the letter's heading, and threw it back at Hiram. The envelope struck his chest and fell to the floor.

"Tell Naaman Rettig the answer is no, from me, from my brothers, and from my deceased father. And even if my father's shade were in the D and RGW's pocket, we would not agree to throw our land to those vultures." She brandished the letter opener with white knuckles.

Hiram bent to pick up the envelope.

"You didn't even read it," Michael said. "What if Rettig offered you a million dollars?"

Eliza pointed the letter opener at him. "My father made that very mistake, choosing money over happiness. The mine, always the mine. Do you know what we did before he decided to sell his soul for coal?"

"Ranching," Hiram muttered.

Eliza snorted.

"You know, there are still cattle up in that canyon today," Michael said.

Eliza glared at Hiram like a hawk at a rabbit. "My earliest memories are of feeding chickens and milking goats with my mother, and riding horses into town, when Helper was nothing but a post office and a general store. Now the place reeks of debauchery, and the cliff above cringes."

"That's not a cringe." Michael smiled. "It's a bit of Cretaceous sandstone leftover from an eroding edge of the Wasatch Plateau."

Eliza's piercing gaze flashed with anger. "Young man, you need to learn your place."

Michael's smile turned wicked. "Would that place be on the reservation?"

Eliza hissed. "You should show your elders more respect."

"Please forgive us our rough manners." Hiram stepped in. "We're just farmers, and a little uncivilized in our ways. Miss Kimball, the men at the mine need work. I make it, what, three hundred men? Maybe as many as a thousand people? The mine has to be reopened. Surely, you can see—"

Eliza cut him off. "See what? See that the mine has caused my family nothing but trouble? It broke up our family, killed Samuel's mother, and drove everyone away. The unrest of 1903 ruined my father's soul. He had been a gentle person who loved feeding horses from his hand, and he became a tyrant who would hold a man's children over his head to deny him three cents a ton. And as much as a struggle as it is to discipline the children of Connecticut, they never force each other into starvation."

"Why return?" Hiram asked. "To rebuild the family ranch?"

"To set things right." Eliza stood tall above them, her spine straight as a flagpole. "To give my brothers a third option. Samuel wants to dig a new shaft because he's scared of bogeymen, and Ammon is maniacal that the east seam will be the richest yet."

"*You* want cows," Michael offered.

Eliza nodded. "And peace."

"I'm not sure Samuel's wrong about the bogeymen," Hiram murmured. He instantly regretted it.

"You can't be serious," Michael said. "Either of you."

Hiram winced.

He found himself fingering his Saturn ring and looking at the wrapped rectangle. It must be a painting. He remembered the pinks and oranges of Samuel's desert landscape hanging over Ammon's mantel, the same images that had returned to Hiram in dream.

"*I* am serious," Eliza said. "And you and your father have nothing to say about any of this. Your part in this is not clear at all."

"We came to bring the miners food," Hiram said. "Only a couple of days' worth, it turns out."

"I heard that." Eliza's dark eyes glittered. "And yet now you seem to be a pawn of the railroad."

"The beets we brought won't do a thing if we don't address the real issue," Michael said.

"And ham," Hiram murmured. "And beans and flour."

"We have to get the mine back open," Michael continued. "You might need a dozen hands to ranch, but there are hundreds of men in the camp who need work. To eat."

"That is none of my concern." Eliza lightly stuck the point of the letter opener into her palm.

Hiram cleared his throat. "Is that one of Samuel's paintings?"

"It is."

Hiram couldn't stomach the cruelty of her gaze, and he let his eyes drop. "Can I see it?"

"Art aficionado?"

Hiram shrugged.

"What's your name, child?" she asked Michael.

"Michael. But I'm seventeen years old, so if I can't call you 'Mrs.' I think you can't call me 'child.'"

Eliza nodded. "That's fair."

"And my father is Hiram. He's single. And good with farm animals."

Hiram choked.

"Michael, will you help me with the painting?" the woman asked.

Michael stood and held the frame upright. Eliza sliced open the top and peeled away the paper to reveal a painting that was dementedly framed. Warped wood painted the color of rust met at irregular angles to form a rectangle that was approximate at best, and spangled with black feathers. The nails themselves were corroded and bent, and a line of staples ran up along one side of the frame like a suture, holding nothing together.

Eliza stood to the side and gestured at the painting. "My brother is obsessed with Apostate Canyon, and the rocks and caves there. He's working as a WPA artist, now, because of his obvious talent."

It was a companion piece to the painting in the Kimball parlor, with the same array of colors. The shape of the cliffs portrayed in pink and orange bothered Hiram, causing something beneath the surface of his mind to itch.

This painting too had pictographs on the canyon walls, but there were no flies. Hiram saw figures of men, surrounded by beasts with antlers. But they didn't look quite right.

Some of the antlered beasts had only two legs.

A chill trickled down his back and the hairs on his arms stood up. Maybe Samuel had harried them in their camp. His madness could be the result of some dark league, some magic that had shattered his mind. But why would he bother Hiram? Were Samuel and Samael in league? Was it stupid to find a connection in the similarity of those names?

And then Hiram recognized the lines of the ridge. He pulled the hand-copied sign of Mahoun or Samael from his pocket and held it up in front of the painting. He compared the rough sketch to the line of the cliff in the painting...

They matched perfectly.

"Are you an artist, Mr. Woolley? Or a critic? Have you been rendered dumb by my brother's gift?"

"I visited Ammon in the red house," Hiram said. "There's a painting like this above the mantel. Your brother paints good, I'll give him that."

"Paints *well*," Eliza corrected, just as Hiram was realizing his mistake.

"Come on, Pap," Michael put in. "You have to get your grammar right. We're in the presence of higher education here."

Eliza scorched him with her eyes. "If you speak well, young man, society might overlook the color of your skin."

Hiram winced.

Michael chuckled slowly, a sound like the purr of a mountain lion. "I'm sure that if I spoke with your impeccable style, the bigots of the Earth would overlook my melanin."

"Melanin?" Eliza frowned.

Michael jerked two thumbs at his own chest. "Melanin! This boy reads *Popular Science.* Yes, prejudice would be a thing of the past if only we recipients of ethnic disdain would make use of our adverbs more correctly. Or is that correcter? Correctlier?"

Eliza, stared for several seconds, her mouth open. Then she cleared her throat and let the painting relax against the wall. "Our business is at an end. You will return to Rettig and let him know our ranch is not for sale. And I'll wish you both a good day."

Hiram and Michael stood. Eliza stepped into the corner, giving them an exit.

Michael nodded. "We don't work for Rettig, Miss Kimball. All we really want is to get the mine back open. Thank you." He left the room.

Hiram hesitated in the doorway. "Miss Kimball, I apologize. Sometimes his passion exceeds his self-restraint. I've tried to . . . give him guidance."

"You should try harder," Eliza said coldly.

"I will." Hiram swallowed. "But I was wondering about a stone on the mantel in your family home. A plain brown stone with a line of quartz through the middle. Not very pretty, but it was right there, in the parlor, as if it was important. What can you tell me about that?"

"A stone?" Eliza's voice was cool.

"Yes, ma'am, a stone. Maybe it was your father's, or maybe it's Ammon's, but I thought it was striking that such a plain rock should sit in such a place of honor."

Hiram felt keen discomfort, locking eyes with the woman.

Eliza blinked first. And nodded. "Samuel talked about a stone. Father mailed it to him, apparently just before he disappeared. Maybe it was something Father found in the mine, a memento for his son. How *that* stone would come to be on Ammon's mantel, I can't imagine. As far as I know, in any case, it's just a rock."

"So your Father mailed it to him? And Samuel came back because of it?" Hiram asked.

"Samuel came back to paint the West, paid by the WPA. Someday art collectors around the world will be glad President Roosevelt gave artists the work."

Teancum Kimball had mailed his son Samuel a stone and then disappeared. Samuel had then returned to his family home.

But then, how did the stone wind up on Ammon's mantel and not with Samuel out in the desert? Might this have something to do with the argument the two brothers had had at the mine opening? Maybe the stone had come with a letter, and the letter contained the information about the mine that Samuel was so confident that Ammon also knew?

Or... the stone was a peep-stone, a seer stone, and Samuel had had visions in it, and he believed Ammon had had the same visions. Had he given Ammon the stone?

Hiram would have to go to Apostate Canyon to ask Samuel directly.

"Thank you for your time." Hiram put his hat back on and left.

Michael was waiting for him at the end of the hall.

Hiram sighed. "Could you be a little less..."

"Caustic? Sarcastic? Opinionated? Clever? No, wait...brilliant?"

Hiram frowned.

"Probably not," Michael said. "Did you and Eliza Kimball have a moment? Is she going to be my new mother?"

Hiram guffawed, slapped his son on the back, and headed for the truck. "Come on, son, let's go to jail."

"Ah, the union lady." Michael followed Hiram down the hotel's stairs. "Is *she* my new mother?"

"I don't think you should expect to have any new mothers," Hiram told him. "But it's my fault she's in jail, and I'll do whatever I can to get her out."

"Like call her lawyer," Michael said.

"Yes."

Or employ more unusual means.

Chapter Seventeen

THE DOUBLE-A'S ENGINE REFUSED TO TURN OVER. WHEN HIRAM pressed the starter, it made no sound at all. He checked the key and the spark and tried again. Both he and Michael tried the crank with the throttle half-down and the ignition started. They inserted the metal arm into the socket in the front and spun the arm up, but the engine stayed dead.

"The good news," Michael said, "is that you just want to go to the jail next, and that's about two hundred yards down the street."

"Helper's a small town." Hiram made a face. "But if the truck won't start now, it probably won't start in an hour, either."

"Well, you've tried all the tricks you know."

"But I haven't tried all the tricks that the guy at Conoco knows."

A long whistle from a train shrieked and the city seemed to shake from the cry. Hiram took a deep breath; the train sound was *not* the whistle he had heard in the canyon. Hiram turned to lope down the street and Michael quickly caught up.

The man working at the Conoco had long arms, greasy hands, and a cheerful smile. A shock of red-orange hair peeked out from under his forest-green cap. Hiram checked the name embroidered on his shirt.

"Good morning, Bert. My Ford Double-A won't start. I'm thinking it's the spark plug, because I don't get any noise at all

135

when I hit the starter. It's parked in front of the Hotel Utah. Can you walk up and take a look at it, or do we need to get it towed here?"

The mechanic looked up from the engine of the car he was working on. "I'll get to it in about half an hour. You can just leave the keys right there on the table."

Mary McGill woke to the sound of the door opening.

The drunks in the adjacent cell had been let out as they had sobered up, each receiving a lecture about the importance of savings and sobriety, and maybe it would be a good idea to let their wives control the spending. She had been dozing and dreaming of receiving just such a lecture herself when the door groaned open, and she sat up.

Police Chief Asael Fox entered first, swaggering across the room on his bowed legs. Behind him came the tall farmer, Hiram Woolley. Fox walked right to Mary's cage and grabbed it. "This gent here says he's got a message from your lawyer."

Mary stood. "I'm glad you've let him in."

"He also admits he ain't a lawyer himself. So I think I might just sit right here and listen while the two of you talk." Fox pressed his florid face to the strips of the cage. There was something wrong with his appearance, but Mary couldn't quite figure out what.

Hiram Woolley looked flummoxed.

"That's very generous of you, Chief," Mary said.

"How do you figure it?" Fox frowned.

She realized what was strange about his appearance. Where he gripped the cage with his right hand, Mary McGill saw a thumb and, opposing it, four fingers. But where he gripped with his left, there were a thumb and *five* fingers.

Six digits on his left hand.

"When I appeal my conviction," she said, "my attorney, Mr. Nichols, will show the judges in Salt Lake City how I was denied my right to the assistance of counsel, because when he sent his agent, Mr. Woolley, the police chief insisted upon eavesdropping."

Fox stared with beady eyes. "That ain't a thing."

"Sure it is," Mary said. "It's in the sixth amendment to the U.S. Constitution." She was no lawyer and couldn't have recited all the constitution's amendments, but she knew this one. "You know, in the Bill of Rights? The first ten amendments?" Without meaning to, she held up her hands, palm out, and wiggled her ten fingers at the policeman.

Fox hissed like a snake and leaped away. He glared at her and Woolley both as if he were considering just beating them with his nightstick then and there. Hiram Woolley gazed back coolly, and the policeman backed down.

"Fine!" he called over his shoulder as he retreated. "I'll just go get myself a cup of coffee. That means you got fifteen minutes, at most!"

"Maybe you should be a lawyer," Hiram Woolley said when the policeman had shut the door.

Mary curtseyed. "When this country has the laws its people deserve, then I'll hang out a shingle and speak at the bar. Until then, I have more urgent things to do."

Hiram nodded and said nothing.

"So you spoke to Jimmy?" Mary prompted him. "As I suspected, the police chief has not let me have another phone call."

Hiram suddenly looked flustered again. "Maybe I should have written it down. Jimmy says there's a problem with . . . jurisdiction, maybe? And he's on his way with a writ right now. He says hold on, no later than tomorrow morning you'll be out. If he's driving all the way from Denver, I guess he must value you highly."

"He might be taking a train." Mary smiled. "But he didn't say hold on."

"No?"

"No, he said *sit tight*. Didn't he?"

Hiram chuckled. "He did. I guess you know Jimmy."

"This isn't my first jail, and it isn't the first time Five-Cent Jimmy has come to fish me out of hot waters. Does that shock you, Hiram?"

"No," he said.

"So I'll sit tight."

He shuffled his feet. "I'm a little worried. Jimmy told me to keep an eye on you, in case they moved you."

"Where would they move me? There are only ten buildings in this town."

"I don't know," Hiram said. "But I guess if they're willing to arrest you when they have no legal right, you being outside of town at the time, they might be willing to do other things they have no legal right to."

"I don't want to say anything that will wound your tender heart," Mary McGill said, "but it wouldn't be my first *beating*, either."

"This is going to sound odd," Hiram said, then stopped.

"Go on," Mary told him. "I just noticed that the police chief has eleven fingers. Whatever you have to say can't be odder than that."

"It might be." Hiram reached into the pockets of his coat and produced two items: a cheap copper ring and a large dried leaf.

"What is that, mint? How adorable. You've come to propose marriage, and you're offering me tea as a dowry."

Hiram Woolley blushed. For a moment, Mary wondered whether she might want to spend more time with this Utah farmer, in a more romantic environment.

"Before I go any farther," Hiram said, "promise me you won't mention these things to my son."

"Does the boy despise tea?"

"You're teasing me, but I'm serious. This is between you and me."

The flustered air had fallen away, and Hiram looked as solemn as a priest.

"I promise," Mary said.

He handed her the leaf through the cage. "You'll see writing on that sage," he told her. "Those are the names of the twelve apostles."

"Ah, which twelve?" she asked. "I spent the better part of my youth at St. Francis Xavier Academy for Females in Chicago, you see, and I know that there's more than one list."

"I prefer John, where possible, only John doesn't have a list of the twelve apostles. So I followed Matthew. Because, you know, Matthew was a tax collector, and that's kind of like being a lawyer."

Mary laughed, then caught herself. "You're serious."

"Very." Hiram nodded. "If it comes to an appearance in court, will you promise me you'll put this leaf in your shoe? Under your right heel, if possible, but in your shoe."

"You want me to wear a leaf listing the twelve apostles when I go to court."

"Under your heel. In your shoe."

"My God," Mary said. "You're a witch."

Hiram grimaced. "A witch is what you call someone who means harm. I mean you no harm, Mary McGill."

Out of shock, or tenderness for the open-faced farmer and his tough, timid ways, Mary found herself taking the leaf. "I'll wear the sage to court. And I won't mention it to the boy."

"And here's the other thing." He nodded and held up the copper ring. It had a rough inscription that read † ACHIO † NOYA †.

Smart comments flooded into Mary's mind, and she bit them all back, giving the farmer time to explain himself.

"This ring helps a person escape from prison," he said. "It will help *you*."

"Magic words?" she managed to ask without laughing.

"A special name of God that Joshua used to defeat twenty-two kings and make the sun stand still."

"I don't remember Joshua's ring from when the nuns told me the story."

"Not everything was passed down in the Bible." His gaze was so solemn and so vulnerable, she took the ring.

"How does the magic work?" she asked. "Does it turn me invisible, or help me slip through the bars?"

"I dislike the word *magic*," Hiram said. "People expect that magic means you fly, or you can catch bullets, or you throw around balls of fire. Most charms are much subtler than that."

"Okay." Mary nodded. "How does this charm work?"

"Wear the ring," he said. "You'll get out of this jail."

"I'll get out . . . because Jimmy will show up with the writ?"

"Maybe," Hiram said. "Maybe the ring will stop Jimmy from getting a flat tire, so he gets to you in time. Or maybe it will make the judge better disposed to your case. Or maybe it will make the police chief change his mind and let you go. Or maybe it will cause an earthquake, and you'll walk out of the ruins of this building."

"Like St. Peter." Mary smiled modestly. "The nuns told me that one, too."

"Will you please wear the ring?"

"I'll wear your ring, Hiram Woolley," she said. "I can see you have faith in it, and didn't Jesus say that if you had faith like a grain of mustard seed, you could move mountains?"

At the word *mustard*, a shadow flitted across Hiram's face, but then he smiled. "That's exactly right."

She put the ring on her finger. "Two charms together should do the trick, don't you think?"

Hiram nodded.

Mary smiled. "And where are you off to now, then?"

Hiram took a deep breath and blew air out through loose lips. "Now I have to go figure out what's wrong with my truck."

Hiram and Michael walked back to the car in silence.

Mary McGill's questions had Hiram thinking. Did he know a charm that would get the car started?

He knew plenty of healing charms, and healing charms were flexible. You could take a hex for warts and apply it to blisters, with a few changes. A charm that eased the pain of a broken arm could relieve the pains of childbirth, with some word substitutions.

Could he adjust one of his healing charms to heal a car?

But surely, it was a dead sparkplug, and Bert from Conoco would have it replaced by now.

Only when they reached the Double-A, they found Bert sitting behind the wheel, turning the key and pressing the starter in vain, with an expression of frustration on his face that mixed in large quantities of bafflement and was quickly mounting toward rage.

"You changed the sparkplug, I guess," Hiram said.

"This is the second plug I put into your truck, mister, and it still ain't turning over. I checked all the connections, they're good. I tried to crank her up until I nearly broke my arm. I can't figure it out."

Hiram felt a cold fist wrapped around his heart. "Let me look."

Under the hood of the Double-A, everything appeared in order. But when Hiram lay on his back in the street and scooted beneath the truck, he found what he'd been looking for: a scrap of paper, stuck to the bottom of the engine with wads of chewing gum. He pried the paper and the gum off and tucked it into his pocket as he stood.

"Alright, I'll figure this out, Bert. How much do I owe you?"

"Not a thing. I didn't get it to start."

"Can I give you fifty cents for your time?" he suggested.

"Only a fool would say no."

With Bert walking back to the Conoco with two new quarters in his pocket, Hiram climbed into the back of the truck and opened his toolbox. "Stay in the truck, will you?" he called to Michael. "I have to take care of something."

"Is that *something* finding another mechanic?" Michael climbed into the cab. "Perhaps a ... *lady* mechanic?"

"Sort of." Hiram dug into his tool chest and found the bit of wooden shingle from Gus Dollar's roof. He touched the brass plate and the lead lamen he'd taken from the old man's basement workshop, shaking his head. *The Lord hath given you the city*... what wall did Gus Dollar want to bring tumbling down? He shut the chest again and hopped down.

Then he picked a restaurant—the letter in the front window read MANDURINO's and its front door was open—and stepped inside. As he walked, he examined the paper he'd taken from the underside of the truck. It was a written *Sator Arepo* charm:

SATOR

AREPO

TENET

OPERA

ROTAS

Someone had hexed the truck. Not just anyone but, it seemed clear, *Gus Dollar* had hexed the Double-A.

He had overcome Hiram's defenses to do it. The lamen in the truck's door should have blocked the spell, or if not that, then the two chi-rho amulets he and Michael carried—one around his neck, and the other in Michael's boot.

Was Gus simply a stronger magician than Hiram?

Or had Hiram compromised his craft? Had he failed to keep a chaste and sober mind, so that his defenses failed?

Mary McGill? Did his attraction to the union organizer render him unchaste? But surely, no.

And what about Gus? He had vandalized Gus's shop, convinced he'd been justified, and then he'd stolen from the man.

Had he been wrong to do so?

Had he exposed himself and Michael to danger by wronging Gus?

And what else did the charm consist of?

He gave the hostess a friendly smile and walked back, as if headed to the restrooms. Instead, he stepped into the kitchen.

There it was, the big pizza oven, with an open mouth and with burning wood lining the inside. Hiram tore the sheet of paper right through the *Sator Arepo* grid, balled it up, and threw it into the flames. Then he tossed in Gus's shingle, too.

Burning thatch from a witch's roof was a good counter magic. Gus had no thatch, but the shingle should work.

"Thou shalt not suffer a witch to live," he murmured, and, "I am Gabriel, that stand in the presence of God." Gabriel was the archangel who had dominion over flame.

He watched a few moments to be certain that the paper and the shingle both took fire, then turned to leave.

"*Ma tu, che ci fai qui?*" a big-chested man in striped trousers and an apron yelled at him.

"Thank you." Hiram left the kitchen.

"Wow," Michael said when he reached the truck. "Again, you let me down with the food. You go into a pizzeria and don't come out with pizza. Shakespeare couldn't write a worse tragedy."

"I must disappoint you profoundly." Hiram climbed into the passenger side of the cab.

Michael shook his head. "You didn't bring the lady mechanic, either. But I know you're doing your best."

Hiram laughed. "Try starting the truck now."

Michael pumped the clutch and pressed the starter. The Double-A coughed into life.

"Let's fill up the tank and the gas can at the Conoco," Hiram suggested.

Chapter Eighteen

ON THE DRIVE UP SPRING CANYON TOWARD APOSTATE CANYON to see Samuel, Hiram debated internally. The lamen in the door of the Double-A had failed to protect them from Gus's curse.

If they got in a wreck, it would also fail to protect Michael from injury.

By the time they'd reached Dollar's, Hiram had come to a decision.

"Stop the car," he said. "Wait for me here."

"Coke?" Michael asked.

Hiram felt thirsty, too. So Gus had restored his poppet-charm and was once again besting Hiram. There was probably no way harm could come of a couple of Cokes, as long as Hiram himself chose them out of the icebox, so he didn't get doctored drinks.

"Okay," he said.

Hiram turned the knob of the front door with a heavy and conflicted heart. Making amends was the right thing to do, both because the Bible taught that he should, and because his defenses would only have power as long as he was worthy. Also, he didn't want to have Gus Dollar interfering in his activities anymore. And short of burying the hatchet with the man, he worried he'd be constantly engaged in a running battle of hexes.

And Hiram didn't *know* that Gus was working evil. He might have the German book for instruction's sake, or to satisfy his curiosity, rather than for the purpose of summoning anything.

143

Hiram couldn't let fear stop him from doing what was right.

The two Rottweilers saw Hiram, but rather than bark, they broke into a cowed whimper and slunk out of sight.

Gus Dollar stood behind the counter, frowning. "I gave your boy a free Coke."

Hiram nodded. "That was kind. And I repaid it by stealing from you. I'm sorry."

"And destroying my property."

"I'll pay the damages."

"I don't want you to pay the damages. I want you to explain yourself."

Hiram sighed. "I'm trying to get the miners back to work. And I thought... maybe... you were involved in the closing of the mine."

"And now you think it's someone else instead?"

Hiram hesitated. "I think you know something about it. Something you don't want to tell me."

"Those idiots Ammon and Samuel Kimball can't agree what to do with their mine. If they wreck it and the mine shuts permanently, you understand that I lose a third of my livelihood. Why in God's name would I do that?"

"I guess that's right," Hiram said. "But what do you know about the closing? What is it that you aren't telling me?"

Gus sighed. "The Kimball family is under a malign influence."

Hiram wrapped his hand around the egg-shaped stone in his pocket. "A witch?"

"Something older. A demon that lives beneath the earth."

Hiram thought of the crack in Gus's basement room. "And you're in league with it."

"No!" Gus's voice was firm. "No, I use my lore to protect myself against it!"

The bloodstone was inert.

"Do you know how to overcome the demon?" Hiram asked.

"I wanted to defeat it with a Book of the Spirits," Gus said. "You destroyed that."

"I'm sorry I did that." Hiram didn't offer to return the two lamens he had taken.

"I'm sorry I spooked you with my books," Gus said.

Hiram was tired, and his thoughts meandered more than he would have liked. "I also got spooked by you charming me."

"What, the customer lure? I diabolically seduced you into coming into my store, so I could give your son a free Coca-Cola?"

"That isn't all. You also got me talking, made me share a lot of private things."

Gus Dollar nodded. "I apologize. But consider it from my point of view. I am the only practicing cunning man up here in these hills. Yes, I sell Cokes and sewing needles and washing machines and canned beef, but you know what else I sell?"

"Cures," Hiram guessed. "Scryings. Love charms."

"And all the usual things. So when you showed up, and demonstrated you had some craft, I had to know more. Were you going to be a competitor? Were you going to reveal my secrets?"

"What charm did you use?" Hiram asked. "It was effective."

"And also simple." Gus held up his hand, revealing a silver ring with a sapphire.

Hiram didn't need to see the sign that must inevitably be engraved on the ring, likely on the inside of the band, or its embedded signet, perhaps cupped in Gus's palm. "Jupiter."

"Cast by myself, with a stone I selected myself from the mine, all things done during the reign of the Jovial planet. *You* wear a Saturn ring. I see the signet: a man riding a dragon, with a sword in one hand and an egg in the other. Are you a dreamer?"

"Sometimes." Hiram thought of his dreams of driving along the road, looking for Michael, and tried to dismiss them from his mind. Hadn't his dream dictionary suggested that he was supposed to receive a letter today?

"The *Picatrix* warns any man who would wear the ring of Saturn to beware eating the flesh of ducks and entering into any shadowy place."

"Duck isn't a large part of my diet." Hiram didn't want to think about shadowy places, or about the fact that he hadn't read the *Picatrix*. He knew the name, but it was an old book, such as you might find in Latin or Egyptian, and very rare. "Jupiter isn't the only influence you channel in this place."

Gus hesitated. "Yes, the seals in the windows."

"Is that the demon influencing the Kimballs? Samael? Mahoun?"

Gus nodded. "But not by my doing. I put those seals into the windows to protect myself. To protect myself and . . . maybe to channel a little power."

Hiram frowned. "That's a dangerous way to operate, Mr. Dollar."

Gus removed his glass eye and rubbed a knuckle into the empty socket. Then he sighed. "Look, this place. You're from Utah Valley, aren't you?"

"Lehi."

"Big freshwater lake there. Good fishing, there's the Provo River, all those fruit trees. It's a nice place to farm. One of the best in the state."

"I don't understand your point." Hiram put a hand into his pocket and wrapped his fingers around the heliotropius. It was cool and inert.

Gus Dollar sighed. "*This* land, on *this* side of the mountains, is different. It's dry and hot and hard. There is wealth under the rocks, but it only comes to the surface with a great sacrifice of sweat and blood. You've seen the strange stones, down by Moab?"

"The arches. Yes."

"A geologist will have a neat explanation for those arches. Ancient inland sea, wind and water erode the stone into patterns that only look strange, but are completely comprehensible when you understand their true nature. A neat explanation, but nonsense."

"I guess you favor a different view."

"Strange complex patterns that are completely comprehensible when you understand their nature?" Gus's eyes gleamed. "Of course, I do! This land was made by angels, my friend, and their signs are written upon its face."

"I've heard people call it 'God's country.'"

Gus laughed bitterly. "Wrong angels. No, there are angels here, trapped beneath the stone, but they are outcasts, rebels, sinners, angels who have become devils. *Theirs* is the strongest influence that can be channeled here in the Wastes of Dudael. Yes, I take measures to protect myself, and yes, to feed my family, to make my business prosper, to bring me the kind of affluence that lets me give your son a free Coca-Cola, I dare to channel that power as well."

Hiram thought he knew the name *Dudael*, too, but he let it lie. Was Gus insane? Likely not. Was he misled about the nature of the powers he sought to deal with? Maybe.

But the bloodstone lay still in his pocket.

"This is why you have the opening in your basement," he said.

"Power comes up through the hole. As long as my signs were

in place, the angel itself could not pass." Gus leaned forward to look Hiram in the eye. "It would be very, very bad if the angel got out."

Hiram wanted to kick himself. "I put your family at risk when I damaged your seals." No wonder his charms had stopped working.

Gus shrugged. "And yourself."

"A fallen angel," Hiram said. "You think that's what's at the root of the trouble in the Kimball family."

"Of course, it is."

Hiram shook his head. "Look, I'll be candid. I don't like what you're doing. I think it's a mistake. I think you're going to get yourself hurt really bad, and maybe some of that hurt will come down on your children and grandchildren."

"Maybe," Gus agreed. "And the hurt is more likely, if you destroy my protective wards again."

"I guess that's a fair point. But I have to ask you some questions."

"Do you wish to lay the tongue of a frog on my chest, to be certain my answers are true?"

In fact, Hiram very much liked the idea of doing just that. But he shook his head. "I've got other ways."

"Your stone."

Hiram gripped the heliotropius. "Are you causing Ammon and Samuel to fight?"

"No."

The bloodstone lay still.

"Are you trying to close down the mine?"

"No."

The stone gave Hiram no warning.

"Did you put a Sator Arepo charm on my truck, to stop it working?"

"Of course, I did. You burgled my shop. I wanted to stop you from coming back up the canyon."

True. Hiram sighed and took his hand from his pocket. "I've brought your book and I'll give it back to you."

"You mean the one you stole, of course, and not the one you burned to ash."

"I said I'd pay for the damages."

"You couldn't afford them, beet farmer. I forgive the debt."

Hiram laid Gus's German book on the counter. "I couldn't read it, anyway."

Gus nodded. "A little language skill goes a long way, in this trade. Do you know any Latin?"

"Just English," Hiram admitted.

Gus left the book on the counter, untouched. "If you're looking for a way to open the mine, have you considered divination? I assume you haven't *dreamed* an answer, or you wouldn't be accusing me."

"You mean like sieve and shears? I'd need two people to work that charm, and I don't have two people I can confide in."

"We could do it now," Gus said.

"You and I couldn't. You need two people in addition to the charm-worker, two people who have no interest in the outcome."

"You and I *alone* couldn't," Gus agreed. "But with my two grandchildren we could."

Gus was right. The two tow-headed children he'd seen running around the shop would be perfect. But he had to be careful. Could he trust Gus fully? Gus was powerful, and at the very least was willing to *channel* the energy of dark powers.

But Gus had shown good will, admitting his sabotage of the truck and his use of the fallen angel's sign, and also forgiving Hiram's destruction of his Book of the Spirits. Gus might genuinely want to assist Hiram.

And in any case, Gus's intentions were irrelevant, if he could help Hiram marshal the resources for sieve and shears.

Hiram would simply have to be certain *he* was the one doing the asking.

Hiram nodded. "I'd be grateful for your help in giving it a try."

"Children!" Gus bellowed. "Greta! Dietrich! Come help your Opa Gus for a moment!" The two children scrambled into the store like beads of water on a hot skillet, hissing and bouncing off each other. Gus leaned in Hiram's direction confidentially. "They're twins. And there is magic in twins."

Hiram nodded. Christ, some accounts said, was a twin, Thomas being his double. And James and John were known to be twins.

"Come over here, children," Gus instructed Greta and Dietrich. "Come stand on these chairs, we're going to play a funny little game. The game is to see how long you can hold a sieve without dropping it."

"Hold a sieve?" The girl picked up the circle of tin with the mesh bottom.

"That's easy!" The boy snatched the hoop from his sister.

"Hey!" the girl protested.

Gus smiled at the two. "We shall see. The great trick is that you must hold it with a pair of shears."

Gus set up the divination and Hiram considered the questions he would ask. When investigating a theft, sieve and shears was used to ask who the guilty party was. Here, the parties all seemed guilty, so he must ask a different question. What he really wanted to know, as he thought of Teancum Kimball's three children, was which one he needed to persuade.

Maybe then Gus would help him protect the mine and the Kimball family from Samael.

Gus wedged the blades of the shears around the rind of the sieve, the sieve hanging underneath the shears. "Now," he instructed the children, "when I say *begin*, you must try to hold it. But you must hold it only by pressing just your middle fingers here…and here. Understood?" The children nodded. To Hiram, Gus said, "Will you do the speaking?"

Hiram took a deep breath and knelt. "Yes."

The children put their fingers on opposite sides of the handle and pressed, holding the sieve suspended in the air. "Begin." Gus stepped back.

"By St. Peter and by St. Paul, and by the sons of Zebedee, if it's Ammon whose heart must soften all, turn about shears and let sieve fall." The line about the sons of Zebedee was improvised, and aimed at capturing the magic that is inborn in twins. It ruined the rhyme, but Hiram felt that was a good trade.

The sieve didn't budge.

"By St. Peter and by St. Paul, and by the sons of Zebedee, if it's Samuel whose heart must soften all, turn about shears and let sieve fall."

The sieve held. Greta and Dietrich smiled like cupids.

"By St. Peter and by St. Paul, and by the sons of Zebedee, if it's Eliza whose heart must soften all, turn about shears and let sieve fall."

Nothing happened. The children smiled.

Hiram looked at Gus and the German shrugged.

Hiram was at a loss. "By St. Peter and by St. Paul, and by

the sons of Zebedee, if it's all three Kimballs' hearts that must soften all, turn about shears and let sieve fall."

The sieve abruptly twisted, slipped sideways from the grip of the shears, and struck Hiram in the chest before falling to the floor. He stood.

Gus, who had been waiting and watching the shears intently, snatched them from the air before they could hit anything.

"I won," Dietrich said.

"No, I won," Greta said. "You slipped, I felt it."

"You were both very good at this game," Gus said. "So good, I believe I must award you each an animal cracker as a prize."

"I want a monkey!" Greta clapped her tiny hands together. "The monkey is cute!"

"The hippo is biggest!" Dietrich snapped his mouth open and shut in imitation of a hippo. "I want a hippo."

Gus gave his grandchildren animal crackers and Hiram stepped back, lost in thought.

All of them. *All* of the Kimballs needed to soften their hearts. With Ammon and Eliza, he'd accomplished *nothing*. Could Samuel be different? Could Samuel be the key?

"Thank you," he murmured.

"Are you and I friends again?" Gus asked.

"I don't think we're enemies," Hiram told him. "Maybe later you can help me protect the Kimballs."

Gus nodded. "Or maybe the Kimballs are safer if they move away from this place."

Feeling numb, Hiram headed for the truck.

Chapter Nineteen

MICHAEL DROVE THEM PAST THE KIMBALL MINE, AND THEN UP the winding road and the left fork. Before starting up the track that skirted the mountain to get to Apostate Canyon, they stopped at their previous campsite. The hobo stove was still there, cold and lying on its side.

Hiram and Michael loaded the stove into the bed of the Double-A and kept going. The truck bounced along the road, jostling over exposed tree roots, chugging up over shoulders of slickrock, and screaming down the other side. At one point, Hiram had to get out to soften the slope of a stone shelf by piling additional rocks to build a ramp for the truck.

For all that Hiram was sweating and his muscles beginning to ache, though, Michael grinned like a cat on the hunt.

"You can't be enjoying this, son. If we break an axle or open our oil pan, it's a long walk down."

"Ease up, Pap, this truck is indestructible and I'm the best driver there ever was."

Hiram sighed.

They finally topped the ridge. Descending into the canyon on the other side by an easier road, they saw a clearing below sharp cliffs that ran from pink to a chalky white. In the clearing lay scattered squared-off red boulders like forgotten dice from an interrupted game, and among them a camp, with firepit, tent, and even easels.

It took an hour to make the descent and by that time the sun was starting to sink behind them. The lengthening shadows brought an anxious itch between Hiram's shoulder blades. He didn't relish the idea of being out in the desert at night, exposed to another ambush.

The interview would just have to be to the point.

Hiram wanted to see Samuel's paintings, try and suss out the strange lines of the ridge, and ask Samuel about the stone on the mantel. Also, Hiram wanted to know more about Samuel's plan to drop a new shaft. Where had that come from? If Hiram was right, and the brown rock was a peep-stone, had the *stone* shown him the location for the new shaft? And why would a WPA painter care about the mine he'd run from so many years before?

He'd mention the D and RGW offer, though not until the very end.

Michael turned up and drove until he had to stop in front of two gargantuan rocks blocking the way. A narrow slit between them allowed access into the clearing beyond.

They got out of the truck; Hiram brought the revolver.

"Samuel Kimball?" Hiram hollered. "My name's Hiram Woolley. My son and I have come to talk with you."

A crow cawed in the distance. A breeze mussed a stand of pinyon pines.

"Come on." Hiram went first.

He had to turn sideways to edge his way through the crack and he had memories of the trenches, when a shell would hit close enough to collapse the wall, and you'd have to wiggle your way through the debris and the bodies.

He remembered such a collapse, when Yas Yazzie had run out of ammunition for his rifle, and had seized a dead lieutenant's Colt M1917. The six bullets in that revolver had been the difference between life and death that day, when Yas had shot the first three German soldiers over the wall and the others had turned back. He'd saved the platoon and kept the weapon, scratching his initials into it.

Of course, the Colt hadn't saved Yas in his final battle, two months later.

Hiram carried that same revolver now. He swallowed a few times, shook a drop of sweat from his nose, and finally made it to the other side.

And into a different world.

The air on this side smelled of pine, charnel house, and dust. Hiram hoped there wasn't a human corpse in the camp.

Easels stood everywhere, a couple dozen at least, some with paper flapping against their clips and others bare. One had a rotting crow strapped to it, the wings spread wide and the bird's skull showing through the rot. Another had mice nailed to the wood. Flies abounded, but not the fat flies Hiram had been seeing for the past two days.

On one canvas, Samuel had incorporated a dead cat in his painting and it dropped maggots across the drawing of the pink cliff faces. Scrawled indifferently across the canvas and the feline corpse alike was the name SAMUEL, in red paint and confused letters.

Or was that SAMAEL?

Hiram couldn't be sure.

Cow bones lay stacked in piles. A campfire smoked beneath a tripod and a boiling kettle, but Hiram smelled nothing that reminded him of food, and had no interest in seeing what might be cooking.

A neat tent, with square shoulders formed by freshly cut pine poles, stood a few paces from the cooking pit. The sun threw long shadows within and behind the canvas structure, and Hiram half expected something awful to rise out of those pockets of darkness.

He wrapped his wool coat tighter around him.

"Holy jeez, Pap. What's this guy's problem?" Michael had made it through the crack and stood next to him.

"He's an artist, son. It's why I don't want you to play the guitar too much."

"Real funny."

It was a good joke, but Hiram's stomach was twisted in knots.

"Samuel Kimball?" he called.

No answer.

"Keep your eyes peeled, son." Hiram walked up to an easel with a complete painting, but this wasn't of the landscape, though it had similar colors, pinks, creams, a little red of the sunset. Instead of a cliff face, it bore the image of a man, with a full beard and black dots for eyes. Hiram waited for a moment for those eyes to sprout wings and buzz off, then relaxed when they stayed put.

Hiram stepped closer to the painting. It reminded him of the daguerreotype he'd seen of Teancum Kimball. Below the man's forest of a beard someone had pinned a letter in rough handwriting.

> February 13, 1933.
>
> Dear Samuel,
>
> Enclosed is a stone. It's a dear thing to me and it's guided me through the more fertile parts of this wilderness. The stone assures me now that you will understand. I don't suppose you'd come home. I'm making another deal of thirty years that might change things. It might not turn out right because it's so easy to get lost down there. Either way, Ammon will need his people. God knows, few enough of us have survived.
>
> You might not love me, but we're family.
>
> Family should stick together.
>
> > Love,
> >
> > Your father.
>
> P.S. Don't talk to Eliza about this letter or the stone. She wouldn't understand.

Michael read it alongside him. "Another thirty-year deal? And where's he going to get lost...down in Helper?"

Hiram didn't say a word. His intuition was itching and if he kept quiet, that itch might turn into answers.

"The mine," Michael said. "Maybe you can get lost down there in the mine. Maybe it was a thirty-year deal about some new seam. Or he bought new equipment, modern drills or whatever. But, Pap, how can a stone guide anyone? Is this like Urim and Thummim stuff? Or the Leporello?"

What was the easy answer here, that neither opened Hiram to mockery nor led down to a conversation of Grandma Hettie's occult lore? "Yes. Like the Urim and Thummim. And you're thinking of the Liahona."

"I'm pretty sure a Leporello is something. Anyway, a guy asking for information out of a rock is obviously nuts."

Hiram shrugged, pondering the note. Another deal of thirty years? A guiding stone—well, that pretty definitively explained the rock on Ammon's mantel, at least. It *must* be a seer stone. And apparently Teancum had seen in a vision in the seer stone itself that he should send it to Samuel. Had Samuel given the stone to Ammon because of a similar vision? Was it because of visions in the peep-stone that Samuel was convinced he must sink a new shaft to save the mine, and believed that Ammon had the same knowledge? Did Samuel have reason to think that Ammon had used the same peep-stone?

And who or what was giving the Kimballs visions through their seer stone? A benign power, as Teancum Kimball seemed to have thought? Or something more wicked, something such as the fallen angel Samael?

And Michael's initial question remained. Was Teancum referring to the mine? Did he send his son the seer stone and then go down the mine, trying to make a deal but fearing he'd lose his way?

A whistle broke Hiram out of his reverie. He was far too far from the train tracks for the sound to be coming from a train. He shook his head.

Tripping down through the scree at the base of the ridge came a man with black hair and round glasses over his sunken eyes. Samuel Kimball.

Samuel was carrying an easel and a satchel hung off a shoulder. His palette was attached to the satchel by a piece of string and paint spackled his pants with every step.

He bounced into the camp and put his easel down. "You come to arrest me, sir?" His hands fluttered around his chest.

Samuel must be right around thirty. Hiram remembered someone telling him that Samuel's mother had died giving birth. Did that have something to do with Teancum's deal?

"My pap here is a farmer," Michael said. "I'm his driver. And future scientist."

"I remember you," Samuel said. "Henry Furry?"

Michael laughed, coughed, and choked.

"Hiram Woolley. Are you out here painting for the WPA?"

"I am, sir. I am." Samuel set up his easel, showing them his painting.

A shiver went through Hiram. It was a close cousin of the two he'd already seen, the same ridge, the pictographs, and the symbol that came together in the rough outline of the landscape.

Hiram pivoted where he stood, examining the ridges surrounding the camp. None of them resembled the glyph he'd copied from Gus's window at all, or Samuel's painting. To be sure, Hiram slipped the scrap of paper from his pocket and compared.

Samuel was imposing the sign in Gus's window on the landscape, over and over again in all his paintings.

Why?

The pictographs in this painting weren't of men battling beasts, but of a cyclone tossing bodies in three directions: two men and a woman, with lines for a dress. Beneath the three lay an outline that looked like the head of a snake, or a lizard.

Samuel threw out his hands. "Sir, the air is alive, can you feel it? This is Apostate Canyon, the canyon of the great rebel. I have fallen away, and yet I am reborn. You, Indian brave, can you feel it? You must. Your kind were born in the heart of the desert."

"Not *my* kind," Michael said. "I grew up in a house by the lake."

Samuel lurched forward. His glasses glowed in the light of the setting sun, and Hiram couldn't see his eyes. He'd behaved oddly before, when he'd faced off with his brother at the mine entrance, but here, in his camp, he seemed stranger still.

Samuel's fingers gripped Hiram's arm. "You know. You're a special one, I know it. And other...things...do, too. The spirits of the canyon, fallen away, to find freedom. They have a purpose for you. I have seen it!"

"In the stone?" Hiram gripped the painter's shoulder.

Samuel ignored the question. He lifted Hiram's hand and pressed his lips to it. "You've come to help me. You've come to show Brother Ammon the error of his ways. The mine is emptied out, cursed, and haunted. It is the valley of the shadow of death, and no man should tread there without fear. But I know where to find coal! The wise response to the current crisis is to dig a new shaft. I've seen what Kimball Canyon can become, what we can all become. Please, Mr. Furry, please."

Samuel seemed to be echoing what Gus had said about fallen angels, and gave the impression that he was being fed his information through the seer stone. If Gus was right and the Kimballs were under Mahoun's influence, did that mean the demon was speaking to them through the stone?

As gingerly as he could, Hiram extricated his paw from the young Kimball's grip.

Michael looked coiled, ready to spring.

"Samuel, how do you know you're right?" Hiram asked. "Is your father's stone guiding you?"

The painter stepped back and hissed. "You've heard about the haunted mine tunnels. If you've talked to Sorenson, you have. But he doesn't believe. Dimitrios, Stavros, they understand."

Another shiver slid a cold finger down Hiram's spine. "I don't have a side in this. I just want the men in the mine to make some money, get out of debt, and get their families food. Greeks and Germans and all the rest. Maybe you, Ammon, and Eliza can all sit down, and I can be there, to help you all hash things out."

Samuel reached into his pocket and got out a cigarette. In his pocket, he found a match, which he lit with the flick of his thumb. He sucked in the smoke. "Maybe you don't understand, Hiram. I thought you might. But you don't."

"You were close to your sister, weren't you?" Hiram asked.

The smell of the cigarette hit Hiram; whatever Samuel Kimball was smoking, it wasn't tobacco.

Samuel relaxed, sucking some from his cigarette. "Eliza loved my mother, begged her to escape with her, during the riots. She never had much use for me. I killed my mother."

Michael stood a few steps back, arms crossed over his chest and eyes wide.

"You didn't kill your mother, Samuel," Hiram said. "She died in childbirth. It happens a lot."

Elmina hadn't even made it *that* far.

Samuel blew out smoke. "It only had to happen to me once. My sister, half-sister really, took me in. I was grateful for it, but she was never warm to me."

"I bet if you talked to Dimitrios and the other Greeks," Hiram said slowly, "you could convince them the mine is still viable. Or at least, that you should finish mining the last of the coal in the eastern seam before dropping a new shaft. And then they could get back to work, get paid. We could bring in a priest, maybe, to put the men's minds at ease. There's a Catholic church in Helper. St. Anthony's, I think."

"You should leave, sir. The road back is rough. I've disappointed you, Mr. Furry, I feel sorry for that. I can't capitulate. Ammon will have to bend to the will of heaven. And Eliza will be irrelevant once Ammon sees the truth."

Hiram sighed, regretting that he had ever agreed to help Naaman Rettig. "The railroad has made an offer to buy the mine. You wouldn't be interested in a deal like that?"

Samuel stubbed out his cigarette and tucked it back into his pocket. "The D and RGW will never have our land. Not while a single Kimball is alive. We are sacred guardians."

Hiram glanced at the pictographs on the painting and that cyclone, killing what had to be Ammon, Samuel, and Eliza. To defend the lizard's head? *Not while a single Kimball is alive.*

Though if they all died, Naaman Rettig might get his deal.

Or would another Kimball relative appear to be guided by the stone on the mantel? Teancum had had four wives, that Hiram knew about. Apparently, many of the children had died young, while the wives themselves had fled. Could there be further living half-siblings? Or cousins?

But Hiram had a more pressing question. "Your name, Samuel. Have you ever seen it...with a different spelling?"

"Sam," Samuel said instantly. "S-A-M. Also S-A-M-M-Y. But that are kids' names, and I'm a man."

"Never S-A-M-A-E-L?"

Samuel looked at Hiram with big eyes, then started to laugh. He held his belly and kept laughing, laughed so hard he fell to the ground. And still didn't stop laughing.

Hiram left without ceremony. He and Michael returned to the truck; with Michael driving, they headed back over the ridge. The boy was quiet, and didn't seem to enjoy the tricky driving nearly as much as he had on the way in. Night fell while they were still atop the ridge; they had to slow to a crawl.

When they started down the other side of the mountain, Michael finally broke the silence. "He's crackers. Full-on Saltines, or what are those new ones you like, the ones that taste like butter?"

"Ritz."

"He's Ritz crackers. And he's convinced the Greeks that his crackers taste good. Like salty butter. And magic rocks? Please."

Hiram took a deep breath. "Maybe you're right." But what had *caused* Samuel to lose his mind? Or what was *causing* his madness now?

Rattling along the narrow crest of the ridge, the truck sputtered and died. Hiram guessed they were half a mile from their camp of the previous night.

Michael tried the starter again and the truck sat dead.

Damn Gus Dollar. While Hiram had been foolish enough to make amends, Gus had done something to the car again.

But making amends didn't make Hiram a fool. He'd gone in, as a Christian, turning the other cheek. And it was only because he was Christian that he had any power. And Gus had been forthright, hadn't he? And Samuel had seemed to corroborate Gus's words.

Hiram and Michael climbed out of the Double-A and into the cold. "Anyway," Hiram said, "I hope you've learned something about the dangers of art."

"You already told that joke, Pap. We might be sleeping in the truck tonight, you know. There's nothing but rocks around us. Besides, shouldn't you be lecturing me about the dangers of giggle-smokes?"

"No," Hiram said. "You're not that stupid." The warm car felt good against the chill.

Michael opened the hood while Hiram went for the kerosene lantern and the crank.

He had only taken two steps when he heard a high-pitched staccato laughter.

Chapter Twenty

"GET IN THE TRUCK, SON." HIRAM CREPT TO THE BACK OF THE Double-A, the revolver heavy in his hand. They'd broken down on a shelf of rock, out in the open. The moonless night sky wouldn't help, but at least it was clear.

More laughter and then a howl, but Hiram wasn't sleepy this time; he was awake and ready for them. His hand was steady and his weapon loaded.

Michael got into the truck and tried the starter again. Nothing happened.

A gunshot rang out and the whine of a ricochet rang across the top of the ridge.

More of the shrill laughter, like a cougar or a woman screaming.

Hiram wiped sweat from his brow and took deep breaths. His nose caught a strong mélange of scents drifting across the high ridge. No garlic or mustard, but there was the juniper, and the faint musk of desert animals, the oil and gasoline smell of the Double-A, and that same fruity smell he'd smelled the night before.

A Christmas sort of smell, like oranges and spice. It had the underlying alcoholic smell of a perfume or cologne, and then Hiram realized where he'd first smelled that scent.

The Greek miner, Dimitrios, had worn it.

At the mine entrance, the first time Hiram had entered Kimball.

Rettig had made a comment about knowing what went on in the camp. Was Dimitrios his spy? Or could the Greek be following Samuel's orders here?

He didn't think Rettig and Samuel could be allies—Samuel seemed too unstable to be in league with anyone.

"Get down and stay down," he whispered to Michael.

The boy obeyed. Hiram crouched behind the truck's body.

Touching his chi-rho amulet, he chanted a prayer he'd learned from Grandma Hettie. The original was in German, one of the long list of prayers she had memorized as a girl out of a book by some Pennsylvania fellow named Hohman, but Hiram knew no German, so he'd gone ahead and learned the English version.

"I conjure thee, bullet or blade, whatever is injurious or destructive to me, by every prayer of the priest, and by him who brought Jesus into the temple and said, a sword shall pierce through thine own soul, that thou suffer not me, a child of God, to suffer. Jesus. Jesus. Jesus, Lord Divine."

At each mention of the Lord's name, and again at *Lord Divine*, Hiram crossed himself. Hopefully, he'd repented sufficiently of his wrongs against Gus Dollar that the prayer would be effective.

Then he waited.

A minute later, he saw four figures coming up the rocks. In the starlight, Hiram couldn't make out their faces.

The first of the figures, a short man who seemed to be all torso, reached the hood and went around to the driver's door, on the same side where Hiram squatted.

"Hey!" Michael yelled.

The door squeaked open, and Hiram attacked. Grabbing Shorty's throat, he smashed the fellow's head into the side of the truck. He crumpled, muttering something to himself about biscuits.

The next fellow came at Hiram, and he was enormous. Something in the shape of his head was familiar; it was narrower than it should be. Hiram pistol-whipped his attacker in the face and heard bone crunch. Big Man dropped, and Hiram hoped he hadn't killed him.

Hiram had taken two down, good work, but not good enough. And where were the others?

The third attacker appeared out of nowhere, grabbing Hiram and throwing him up against the truck. He had the stink of sweat on him. He clocked Hiram, a good blow to the nose, and Hiram felt his blood gush down his lips.

And then he felt a pistol in his gut. "Gotcha, pal," Sweaty grunted.

Hiram pushed back, and Sweaty slammed him against the truck again.

Sweaty's gun made a loud *clack*. That metallic noise was the sound of the semiautomatic pistol's action jamming.

Grandma Hettie's charm had worked.

Hiram threw a knee up and caught Sweaty in his nethers. It was a cheap move, but better than blowing the man's head off. Sweaty sagged to the ground like a split flour sack.

Hiram spun and raised his revolver at the fourth man, who had to be Dimitrios. The miner stood in his cloud of cologne, hands raised. He was dressed in black and his face was darkened.

"Dimitrios Kalakis! I squeeze this trigger, and you die. Do you understand me?"

Shuffling sounds came from behind him, and Hiram couldn't afford to be ambushed. He stepped sideways, keeping the Greek covered.

Sweaty still lay on the ground, clutching himself, but Shorty was up on all fours and muttering. "Goddamn farmer saw us coming, and I said for us to wait until they camped, but the Greek, he said we should get it done..."

"Shush," Hiram said.

Dimitrios puffed out his chest. "Shoot! We Greeks, we are invincible. Do you know the story of Achilles? He was covered in fire that melted any spear that attacked him—"

"Except for his heel," Hiram said. "And a blow to his heel killed him. Only I'm thinking you may have an Achilles forehead."

Dimitrios sucked in breath and his surprisingly high-pitched voice fell silent. He'd been the one laughing.

Of the four men, Dimitrios was the only one who spoke with a foreign accent. Then it struck Hiram who the big man was. He'd been the tough working the door at Naaman Rettig's suite, the man with no neck and the sides of his head shaved.

"Mr. Kalakis," Hiram said, "does Samuel Kimball know you're working for Naaman Rettig?"

"No," the miner admitted.

Hiram kept watch out of the corner of his eye. He hoped he

hadn't killed Big Man. He hoped he wouldn't be forced to kill any of them.

"And what would your wife think about you doing this?" Hiram asked. "I'm an innocent man. My son is in the truck. He's seventeen years old, and he's scared silly because men in masks are attacking us!"

"Hey," Michael muttered.

"And for what?" Hiram continued. "So you can drive me out of town? Don't you remember that I'm the one who brought food to camp just yesterday?"

Dimitrios said nothing.

Hiram turned on the dwarf. "Does your mother know what you do for a living? Does she know you're a two-penny bravo for a railroad bandit with the ethics of a cornered rattlesnake?"

"No," Shorty said. "And that's low, talking about a guy's mom. I'm a bona-fide employee of the D and RGW."

"And yet, your mother says rosaries, praying that her son is a good man. Keep in mind, I have six shots, there are four of you. I earned medals as a marksman in the Great War, and I shot a hell of a lot of Germans on colder, darker nights than this." That was a straight run of lies on Hiram's part. "I'll kill at least two of you before you can even stand up."

Shorty and Dimitrios Kalakis both raised their hands in surrender.

Hiram prodded Shorty with the toe of his boot. "Tell me your name."

"Tyson Gibby."

"And the big fellow over there?"

"He's Frank Johnson."

"Mr. Gibby, could you check to see if Frank Johnson is still breathing?"

Gibby crept over to the big man.

"You'd better tell me your name, too," Hiram said to Sweaty.

"Lemuel Hanks," he muttered.

"Good work, Pap," Michael called from the truck.

Hiram took a deep breath. "Turn on the headlights, would you?"

Lemuel Hanks sat up. "You should've been dead. I've had that heater for ten years, never jammed on me once. You're a lucky man. And as for my wife or my mother, I don't have either, so don't try that stuff with me."

"The Lord Divine has saved you and me both from committing murder," Hiram said. "Assuming Frank lives."

The charm had worked. Hiram's repentance had been acceptable. *Blessed are ye, when men shall revile you, and persecute you*, that was one of the Beatitudes. Hiram had turned the other cheek. He had resisted unnecessary violence, he had spared the lives of his attackers.

And the Lord had given power to his charm.

But that didn't mean the truck would start now.

"He's breathing," Gibby said, "but he's out cold. Hey, Lemmy, help me drag him some. That usually wakes 'em up." Then in a lower voice, "I had an uncle who drank something awful, and he'd get so gassed he'd fall down..."

Gibby and Lemuel Hanks lugged the unconscious giant out into the glow of the Double-A's beams.

The three men stood uncertainly, looking at Hiram. Now that he had some real light, Dimitrios's single eyebrow stood out even with the black on his face.

Michael got out of the truck. "Do you believe in ghosts, Dimitrios?"

The Greek shrugged. "Maybe, I do."

"But the phantoms running the ridges up here—that's been you, all along."

Dimitrios looked down at his feet. "We frighten the people."

"Because Rettig told you to?"

Dimitrios nodded.

"But tonight you tried to attack me," Hiram said. "Rettig told you to do that, too?"

The Greek nodded again.

"What about the ghosts?" Hiram pressed the Greek. "Really, do you think the mine is haunted? The eastern seam has a ghost?"

Dimitrios opened his mouth and closed it twice before he found the words he wanted. "I have never seen a ghost, but other men swear to it. But the railroad man pays me a good pay to do what Samuel says and report to him. And since Samuel promises me Bill Sorenson's job, this is a very good work for me. Samuel says the mine is haunted, and I say, yes, sure it is. Once the railroad owns the mine, that will be better for everyone. We can all go back to work."

Hiram nodded. So Rettig had had an inside man. He tasted his own blood in his mouth, from his bashed nose. He spit.

"Dimitrios, this is what's going to happen. You're going to go back to the camp, talk with the Greeks, the Chinese, the Japanese, and whoever else you can, and tell them that there is more coal in the eastern seam, and until that coal gives out, you're going to mine it. You all need to bury your differences with Ammon and the Germans."

"They won't listen. They're scared."

"Well, you're going to try," Hiram said. "There is coal in the eastern seam, isn't there?"

Dimitrios shrugged. "I think maybe."

Hiram felt tired; he had to go down the mine. He had to confirm the presence of coal there, and he also wanted to look for evidence of Samael. If there was a fallen angel under the earth, was it even safe to open the mine again?

Which meant that he had to find out quickly.

Hiram continued. "Even if there's a whole city of coal down there, you're done, Dimitrios. You're going to take your family, and you're going to leave the camp. Do you understand me?"

The Greek nodded. "What of my debts?"

"I'll worry about that." Hiram wasn't quite sure where he'd get the money, but he wanted Dimitrios out of the picture, for his sake and for the miners'.

Frank sat up and shook his head.

Hiram felt a huge relief at the sight of Frank moving. "As for you three, you're going to go back to Rettig, and you're going to tell him I spared your life. I could have killed all of you, but I don't want trouble. Also, tell him the Kimballs won't sell. At any price. He needs to quit trying. It's your job to convince him of both."

"Why should we?" Frank asked.

"Aw, knock it off, Frankie," Gibby said. "He could shoot us now, but he hasn't."

"That all may be," Lemuel Hanks admitted sourly. "But the boss don't quit. And I don't see him quitting because I tell him to."

"We'll try, Mr. Woolley," Gibby said. "Hanks, you fool, shut your gob."

"Mr. Gibby, call your mother tomorrow and tell her you love her." Hiram shifted his gun barrel to cover Lemuel Hanks. "And you, I think you should find yourself a good woman. It'll settle you down, and if you eat right and drink less, you might not sweat so much."

Lemuel Hanks grimaced. "I'd rather die."

"Yes, but I don't want that," Hiram said. "I'm letting you go, unless you force me to do otherwise."

"I ain't forcing you," Hanks said.

Hiram pointed across the ridge. "I think that's your most direct route back to Kimball and Spring Canyon. From there, you just walk downhill."

Frank got to his feet, wobbling. Gibby and Hanks had to take an arm each to steady the big man. Together with the Greek, they took the direction Hiram indicated.

Hiram let a long breath, put his revolver back into his bib pocket, and then got out his bandana. The cold night had already congealed his blood to his lips and chin. It took some wiping, but he got most of it off.

"For the record, I wasn't scared silly. Or even scared amusing." Michael walked to stand in the glow of the headlights. Then he laughed. "You pulled the hammer back, as cool as a cucumber, and said, 'I think you may have an Achilles forehead.' And that's Henry Furry, he has ice water for blood. Damn, Pap, that was a close one."

Hiram took a deep breath.

"Don't curse, son."

Time to get the truck moving.

Hiram kicked himself for letting his guard down, and for giving Dollar back his book. The man had fooled Hiram.

Again.

But the bloodstone hadn't warned Hiram of any attempt to deceive. Either Gus Dollar's magic had been too strong for him... or Hiram had asked questions the old *braucher* could easily evade.

Had Hiram, in fact, returned Gus's book to him because Gus had hexed him?

Or was Gus wrong about his being the only magician in Spring Canyon? Had some unknown witch hexed Hiram's truck this time?

Or had Samael done it?

Hiram felt exhausted. He rubbed his eyes with his knuckles. "Okay," he said to Michael, "let me take a look."

He slapped at a fly buzzing in his ear, and missed. Flies in February. It wasn't right. He heard a distant whistle, piping on the cold wind. Hiram winced. A bad taste filled his mouth and it wasn't just blood. Things worse than men were about.

Chapter Twenty-One

HIRAM CIRCLED THE TRUCK WITH HIS FLASHLIGHT, HANDS GOING numb from the cold; he was looking for evidence of Gus Dollar's new curse.

He found it on the rear bumper, in the form of a single word, repeated three times: NEMA! NEMA! NEMA!

It was written in thick red characters. Crayon? Or lipstick? And what was *Nema?* Another demon's name?

Several flies buzzed into his face, and he waved them away.

Spitting into his bandana, he erased most of the writing in a few long strokes Then, with smaller, fastidious motions, he wiped out the last traces.

Then he stood. "Michael, I have a question that's going to sound strange."

"A strange question from my Pap! What is the world coming to?"

"You know, when you're grown, and you've figured out what you want out of this world, son...I'm going to miss your acid wit."

"Don't worry, Pap. I'll keep cracking jokes, so you don't feel deprived." Michael puffed and waved in front of his own face. "What's with these flies? They have the body of a musca domestica but are the size of a tabanus trimaculatus. Either is strange when it's this cold."

Hiram didn't get sidetracked. "While I was in the store this evening, did anyone approach the car?"

"You mean, when you forgot to get more Cokes? Yeah. I said hello, but she performed a strong Jenny Lindow impression and just ignored me. And then she picked something up off the ground and went inside."

A tall blonde woman. Dollar's daughter? While he had been talking with Hiram, Dollar had sent the woman out to put a hex on Hiram's truck. Or at least, to prepare the Double-A for Gus's hex.

Had Gus kept Hiram in the shop with the sieve and shears only to allow the curse to be placed?

"Dammit," he muttered.

"That's right, Pap. Dammit."

What was *Nema*?

Hiram brushed flies from his face. "Try the starter again."

"Nothing," Michael called back.

Hiram needed to do more. He'd already burned a shingle from Gus's roof, but he had the Coke bottles.

Hiram climbed into the back of the truck and threw open his toolbox. He had to move the brass and lead lamens, and at the sight of the lead one, he wondered again what wall Gus Dollar was trying to bring down. He snatched up a Coke bottle. He also grabbed a bundle of steel sewing needles wrapped in a swatch of cloth and a wad of modeling clay. It was only when he went to replace the upper tray in the chest and found he was unable to do it without trapping flies inside that he realized just how thick the cloud of insects was around him.

Flies. In February.

Flies, like he'd found in the tunnel below Gus Dollar's shop. Flies, like he'd encountered in Apostate Canyon.

He knew a charm against flies. It involved burying the image of a spider beneath the house you wished to protect from them, and was useless to him here. He slammed shut the tool chest and jumped to the ground, full can of gas in one hand and an empty Coke bottle in the other.

Fire was the most basic defense against evil. If he didn't know what was attacking, and didn't know who had sent it, the most useful thing he could generally do was make a fire. Fire was the lightest element, it chased away darkness, and the sun's fire nourished the earth. Fire was primitive man's oldest weapon against the wolf. In the Book of Daniel, God had saved Shadrach, Meshach, and Abednego *in* and *by* fire.

"Keep trying!" he called to Michael.

The flies were thick enough to nearly blind him now. He shoved the bottle into a pocket and lurched off the side of the road, looking for wood. He nearly impaled himself on a dry branch, and when he dragged it back onto the road, he found he had brought almost an entire juniper tree, dead and shriveled.

It would do.

Something moved out in the darkness, ahead of him and on the road. Hiram tossed the bush to the dirt in front of him and sloshed gasoline onto it.

"I am Gabriel," he muttered, "that stand in the presence of God."

He heard the crunch of footsteps, slow, heavy, and deliberate. At each step, the buzzing of the flies reached a crescendo just as the foot seemed to strike the ground. And after each crescendo, the total sound of the flies increased in volume and pitch.

Could this be Rettig's men, returning to harass Hiram again? Big Frank Johnson, making heavy footsteps?

But the footfalls were too loud. And there were the flies.

Hiram's heart raced.

He struck a spark with his Zippo—only to have the flame snuffed by a phalanx of flies, so densely-marshaled that they might have been a hand.

A second attempt met the same fate.

The steps drew nearer.

Hiram knelt, smelling the gasoline reek like an overwhelming cloud. He struck the Zippo's flint a third time—and before flies could knock it away, the juniper burst into flame.

Hiram fell back onto his shoulders. His face hurt, seared by the fire.

In the darkness and among the flies, he heard an angry shriek that resembled a train's steam-whistle more than the cry of an animal. The buzzing of the flies lessened.

"Pap! Pap, are you okay?"

"I'm okay! Keep trying!" Hiram spat flies from his mouth.

He didn't hear the engine turn over, so Hiram had no choice. He pocketed the Zippo again and removed the bottle. He made sure his back was turned to the Double-A so Michael wouldn't see what he was doing, and then he unbuttoned the fly of his overalls and carefully filled the Coke bottle with his own urine.

Grandma Hettie had explained to him the theory of the witch bottle one day when he had found a cracked glass bottle in the stone fire ring out behind the barn. The idea was that the bottle represented the bladder of the witch who was attacking a person, and the witch bottle would deliver sharp pains to the witch's bladder that would force an end to the witch's magical attack.

The flies' buzz rose in intensity, and Hiram again heard the crunching of enormous feet in the cloud. He set the Coke bottle carefully aside, grabbed the gas can, and sloshed a jet of petrol over the fire.

The *WHOOSH!* of the resulting flame felt like it might have obliterated his eyebrows, but the flies eased off. Seeing a fallen log beside the road, Hiram grabbed it and dragged it across the flaming juniper.

Then he returned to the bottle. Holding the bottle in his left hand, he bit three fingernails off his right hand and spit them into the bottle. If he were defending another person against the witch's attack, he'd use that victim's urine and nail trimmings. If he had more time, he'd add hair and other similar ingredients, but he was pressed.

He took the bundle of needles out of his pocket and dropped them into the bottle.

He thumbed in the wad of modeling clay to close up the Coke's top.

Footsteps crunched closer.

Was that the outline of a man in the cloud? Could it be Frank Johnson, after all?

But no—the silhouette suggested a man who was eight feet tall, with impossibly broad shoulders.

His hands occupied, Hiram drew on another expedient to push back the threat. "And the angel of the Lord appeared unto him in a flame of fire," he called, "out of the midst of a bush!"

The fire of Hiram's burning bush rose higher, and again he heard the whistle erupt into a terrible, injured wail that faded into a whistle.

If he wasn't killing the thing out there, he was injuring and angering it.

Could it be Samael? Mahoun? *Nema*?

Could Gus Dollar have been telling the truth? Could this be one of Lucifer's fallen angels, living out here in the Wastes of Dudael, in the hills above Helper, Utah? Had the witch summoned it and was he now controlling it?

Had Hiram himself let the thing out of its cave?

Nema, he suddenly thought. *Amen*, backward.

Nema! Nema! Nema! was amen, three times, backward.

Hiram realized what Gus's curse was, and how he could push it back.

He set the witch bottle in the fire. Activation of the witch bottle required that the urine inside be brought to a boil.

Hiram staggered off the road three times. Each time he grabbed the nearest sizeable piece of wood he could find, sloshed it in gasoline, and added it to the fire, nestling each new log as close as he could to the bottle, building up the fire there so as to be sure the liquid inside was exposed to the maximum possible heat. Each time he added wood, he shouted, "Thou shalt not suffer a witch to live!"

"Pap! Pap!" Michael was invisible to him, obscured by the flies.

"Hold on!" Hiram spat more flies out of his mouth. They were bigger than raisins and they wiggled on his tongue, causing him to gag and choke.

He emptied the gasoline on the fire, jumping back to avoid getting burned again. Then he threw the gas can into the back of the truck and lurched to the window of the cab.

"What the hell is with all these flies?" Michael asked. "And are you shouting something?"

"Shouting at flies." Hiram forced a hollow laugh. "It's like we stumbled onto a bobcat's lair, isn't it? Only it's a nest of flies. I think the fire is killing them. I'm going to get under the hood now, and I need you to keep hitting the starter until it takes."

"Got it, Pap."

Hiram lifted the hood. He couldn't see the bottle, but he trusted that it would boil any second. If he hexed Gus Dollar, that might break his curse on Hiram's truck. Now he needed the thing out in the darkness to stay away until the engine turned over.

Hiram had never had occasion to curse anyone. But he understood that one element witches used to curse their victims was the recitation of scripture, backward.

Especially the recitation of the Lord's Prayer, in Matthew, chapter six.

Hiram would counter the hex by reciting the prayer forward.

"Our Father which art in heaven, Hallowed be thy name..." The familiar words tumbled from his mouth.

The truck hadn't yet started.

Footsteps—the creature in the swarm was approaching again, and Hiram groped for any Bible verse dealing with fire. "And after the fire," he shouted, "a still small voice!"

The flames rose again, but the flies only got thicker.

He whipped through the Lord's Prayer a second time. He could hear Michael cursing inside the truck. The many hours he'd spent with Grandma Hettie, memorizing not only individual verses—what she used to sneer at as the "five-minute Sunday School technique"—but also whole chapters, and long sections of scripture, were paying off now, inside a swarm of flies and under attack by an unseen beast.

But he was drawing a blank on his efforts to think of another useful passage about fire. There were the three children, but the account said *furnace* over and over.

When would that witch bottle boil?

He heard an enormous bellow directly behind him.

If not fire, then light.

"In the beginning was the Word!" Sweat poured down his face and dripped from his body. "In him was life; and the life was the light of men."

The fire vamped again. A sheet of dead flies struck the windshield of the Double-A like limp black hailstones, bouncing off and piling up on the engine block.

He sang the Lord's Prayer again, picking up speed and pitch, without missing a syllable. "Amen!" he shouted.

The truck's engine turned over.

"Pap!" Michael shouted.

Hiram slammed shut the hood of the truck, trapping ten thousand flies inside and sending another ten thousand bouncing into the dark night.

Something grabbed him from behind. Hiram looked down and saw a hand clutching the hip of his overalls. It was gray and scabby and four times the size of a man's hand, with three fingers and a long thumb. A nail like a tent stake sprouted from the end of each digit, yellow and jagged. A smell that mixed the dry scent of dust, the cloying iron reek of blood, and the sweet, fertile stink of rotting flesh swept over Hiram from behind.

This was not Frank Johnson.

Hiram placed both Harvesters against the side of the truck and kicked, flinging himself backward. He and the thing fell together into the flies and struck the sand together, and the creature felt as if it stretched, as if Hiram had fallen back onto modeling clay, or a water balloon.

Hiram scrambled to his feet as quickly as he could, pulling the revolver from his bib pocket.

"Pap?"

A vast shape rose up from the swarm, too quickly for Hiram to see any detail, other than a face with too many mouths.

He fired the revolver at the thing. It staggered back, and he fired a second time, and then a third.

The sweet smell of crushed garlic filled his nostrils.

Oh, no. Not now.

He leaped onto the passenger-side running board of the Double-A, steadying himself with his left arm inside the vehicle.

"What the hell is that, Pap?" Michael yelled.

"Drive!" he yelled back.

The thing loomed up again in the swarm of flies and Hiram fired at it as Michael punched the Double-A into gear. The truck had a high center, which let Michael take it off the road and around the bonfire as Hiram fired twice more. The next pull of the trigger clicked the hammer down on an empty chamber.

Michael stomped on the accelerator and the truck burst out the far side of the cloud of flies, and into the cold February night.

Chapter Twenty-Two

"PAP, WHAT WAS THAT?"

"Watch the road!"

Michael jerked his eyes back around to look at the road as Hiram switched out the empty cylinder for the loaded full moon.

"You're avoiding the question! What was that thing out there? And why were you shouting Bible verses?"

Should he lie?

Should he tell Michael, his skeptical and progressive son, that he was a cunning man?

"I don't know," he said finally. "It was about the size of a bear, but I couldn't see it clearly for all those flies."

Michael cursed long and hard. Hiram didn't object.

As the Double-A rattled around the winding desert road and back down toward Spring Canyon, his hands shook beyond control. He reloaded, carefully put the revolver into the glove box, pushed his shoulders back against the truck's seat, and took deep breaths.

Turning his face out the window so Michael wouldn't hear, he chanted his charm against the falling sickness. He sucked in cold night air, and that seemed to help.

"I don't think I'm going to sleep tonight," Michael told him. "Holy shit!"

Hiram's heart was pounding, and he was grateful for an opportunity to change the subject. "Look, this cussing thing," he said. "Maybe, in this case, just say *shit*. Then you sound like a farmer."

"I sound like some other profession when I say *holy shit?*"

"That makes you sound...Italian. You know, I don't mind if you say words that are rude, but I don't want you to say words that offend God."

"Which god, Pap?"

"Come on, Michael."

"How about Ganesh, the elephant-headed Indian god?"

"Fine, also don't offend Ganesh."

Michael drove in silence for a moment. "How should I swear if I want to sound like a high-priced and extremely successful lawyer?"

"I'm pretty sure they never curse."

"Somehow, that doesn't feel right to me."

"Besides, you want to be a scientist." Hiram smiled. "Take us back up to the mining camp, please."

"I guess we'll try out the no-sleep thing for real, then."

Lawyer. Hiram could have kicked himself. Had Five-Cent Jimmy come with his writ and gotten Mary McGill out of jail? It was a long drive from Denver.

Hiram had more pressing things he needed to do at the mine. Hiram couldn't get the words of Teancum's letter out of his mind. *It might not turn out right because it's so easy to get lost down there.* Was the ghost of Teancum Kimball frightening miners, Teancum who had descended into the mine and not emerged?

Or was there, after all, no ghost, but only a demon? A demon that was now possibly on the loose because Hiram had destroyed Gus Dollar's binding charms. If the demon attacked them, it might attack others, and that would be Hiram's fault.

Hiram needed answers. He thought the mine would have them.

The lights of Kimball came into view as the Double-A rounded a bend in the canyon.

"Take us to Bill Sorenson's house," Hiram said.

"What do you think it was? That thing up there?"

Hiram didn't answer for a while, his mind scrambling after a fitting response. "It could have been a bear. Or, I suppose, a bad man, though it seemed too big for that."

Michael fell quiet.

What was the boy thinking?

Michael parked the Double-A next to the foreman's tidy home a few minutes later. Light shone inside, as it did in a few buildings elsewhere in the camp and in the big house at the north end of the canyon. "Are we staying?"

"I think so. Come inside with me."

"Are we going down the mine? You know, it's easy to get lost down there."

"*I* am," Hiram said. "You . . . you need to try to sleep."

They got out of the truck, and Hiram knocked on the foreman's door.

Bill Sorenson answered it in a sleeveless white undershirt and cotton pants, blustering before the door was fully open and shaking the rolled-up newspaper. "Is dere a problem with de mine, dat you knock on my door so late?" Then he recognized Hiram and his face softened. "Ah, you dere. Come in."

"Thank you." Hiram stepped inside. "I'm sorry to call at this hour."

"It's nothing. You know, de men are proud and dey might not want to say anything to you, but you done a real good turn here. And if deir wives knew you were in my house, well, it ain't dat dey're less proud, but dey're less stupid, and you'd get a lot of thank-you kisses."

"Aha," Michael said. "Now I see why we came back."

"I'm glad to help them," Hiram said. "And I'm hoping you'll be willing to help *me*."

"You name it," Sorenson rumbled.

"I'm hoping you'll take me down the mine tonight."

"*Ja, ja*, I can sure do dat. Don't you want to wait until morning?"

Hiram suddenly felt exhausted. He had barely slept the night before, and the effect of the last two days' physical exertion, adrenaline, and fear abruptly piled on top of him like a mountain collapsing. Also, he was starting to get hungry again. "No, I want to do it now. Though if you have a slice of cheese or a crust of bread I could eat, I'd be grateful."

"Exciting," Michael said. "Do I get to carry the gun?"

Hiram meant to ask Sorenson if Michael could stay in his house, but the Dane beat him to it. "No way, young man. Dat mine is barely safe for grown men with deir wits about dem."

"Pap," Michael objected.

"Nope, I'm de foreman here, my decision is final." Sorenson seized Michael by the wrist and slammed his rolled-up newspaper into the boy's open hand. "I'll give you dis, dough. It's enough weapon for any man."

"Great, and I can read the news." Michael unrolled the newspaper and looked at the headlines. "From 1932. The *Helper Journal*, our local informant. Hey, that guy Roosevelt won. Who knew? But what will poor Hoover do now?"

"Just keep reminding yourself," Sorenson said to Hiram. "Men with dumb kids wish dey had smart ones."

"I remind myself of that every day," Hiram said.

Mrs. Sorenson appeared in the kitchen door, wrapped in a nightgown and carrying a blanket. "The boy can relax here on the sofa, and hopefully get a little sleep. There's milk in the icebox, and I baked a pan of sweet rolls."

"Like my mudder made," the foreman said. "Only better."

"Don't let *her* hear you say that!" Mrs. Sorenson wagged a finger.

"If my sainted mudder is following me around in her afterlife, she's got much bigger concerns dan de fact dat I think she made de *second*-best smorkager since de world began."

Mrs. Sorenson kissed her husband on the cheek as he shrugged into a long coat and shoes.

"Mmm, smorkager," Michael said. "It sure *sounds* delicious."

Bill Sorenson lumbered back into the kitchen and returned shortly after with two bottles of water and three sweet rolls piled on a plate. Was the mine that deep, that they needed to carry drinking water with them? Hiram wolfed down the rolls, and then he and Sorenson exited the house, shutting the door behind them.

"Hold on just a moment." Hiram climbed into the back of the Double-A, opened his tool chest, and took out two long pieces of chalk and an unpeeled witch hazel rod.

"I'm going to do something that looks strange," he warned Sorenson. "I ask that you not mention this to Michael."

"Look," Sorenson said. "In my work, I've known men from every country under heaven, and I learned dis. Every man's got his own weird bullshit. You don't bodder me about *my* weird bullshit, I won't bodder you about *yours*. And I won't tell your son anything."

"I like your philosophy," Hiram said. "It's possible my bull is weirder than yours."

He carefully peeled all the bark off the rod with his fingers, revealing the soft white wood beneath. In an ideal world, he'd have soaked it in nightshade and dried it; in an ideal world, he'd also have something personal to Teancum Kimball to wrap around the rod.

This was not an ideal world.

He sang as he worked, and he held a prayer in his heart. Without specific words, his prayer was that he would find Teancum Kimball, or evidence that would tell him more about Teancum Kimball's fate. His song was Psalm 130, to a melody Grandma Hettie had taught him.

> Out of the depths have I cried unto thee, O Lord.
> Lord, hear my voice: let thine ears be attentive to
>   the voice of my supplications.
> If thou, Lord, shouldest mark iniquities, O Lord,
>   who shall stand?

There were other psalms that were appropriate to sing over a Mosaical Rod, but the one beginning *out of the depths* seemed appropriate in this situation. On the rod, he slowly carved three crosses, then the name TEANCUM KIMBALL, then three more crosses.

Hiram stuck the chalk into a pocket. "I'm ready."

"Dat ain't de weirdest bullshit I ever seen," Bill Sorenson said as they climbed up the slope toward the mine opening. "Not by a long shot."

Hiram didn't ask for details.

Walking up the hill, Hiram saw his own breath in a white cloud and felt the skin of his face slowly freezing. He thought he saw the shadow of a man detach itself from the mine opening, slip to one side, and disappear again into the trees. But he might have imagined it.

In a rectangular stone building just below the mine opening, they got helmets. "You ever work with a carbide lamp before?" Sorenson asked.

"Show me how."

Hiram followed Sorenson step by step through the process of lighting the brass lamps. They opened a port in the top of the lamps by swinging a little gate horizontally, and filled the lamps'

upper reservoirs with water from their bottles. Then they screwed
the lamps open through the middle, revealing lower reservoirs.
Into these chambers, they scooped dusty gray pellets like gravel,
screwing the lamps back together afterward. They pushed long
levers on the top of each lamp from OFF to ON.

"Calcium carbide," Sorenson said. "Makes a chemical reaction
with de water. You feel de lamp getting warmer already, *ja*?"

"I do," Hiram agreed. "Will the light start automatically?"

"No, de reaction just puts out a flammable gas. Now, you
cup your hand over de dish here, and hit dis little guy, just like
a cigarette lighter."

They both struck their igniters, and two fierce white flames
sprang into being.

The flames threw a long white light, but they stank infernally.

"Aren't there flammable gases down there?" Hiram nestled
his lamp into place on the front of his helmet, then put on the
helmet. He put his fedora on an empty peg.

"*Ja*, dere are. Mining ain't for chickens, son."

The Dane went to two big yellow rectangular boards nailed to
the wall. Rows of hooks covered both; one was full of brass chits
while the other was empty. Sorenson took a chit with a number
on it and moved it from the "OUT" board to the "IN" board. "If
dey wonder where I am, dey will see dis and know I'm down
below." He transferred another chit with a "V" stamped on it.
"Dat is for you, my do-gooder friend. If dere is a cave-in, dey
know to look for two bodies."

They approached the mine entrance by a trough cut straight
into the hillside, lined left and right with mortared stone that
looked just like the stone of the mine buildings. Straight up the
center of the trough ran railroad tracks. Beneath their feet and
the tracks lay a rough scree of stone and dirt, studded with many
chunks of coal. Where the hill rose steeply and the trough cut
into it, becoming an actual tunnel, a concrete lintel lay over the
opening. In large capital letters, cut an inch deep into the concrete, were the words KIMBALL MINING CO. ✶ 1891.

Down the slope from them, the long wooden tipple blocked
their view of the highway and the eastern sections of the camp.
The large building where rock was sorted out of the coal screened
out a lot of light and made the mine entrance much darker than
it would have been.

Here at the gate, the air was warmer. The dirt immediately at the opening and to either side was free of snow and the soil was relatively dry.

"Hold on one moment," Hiram said.

A correctly prepared Mosaical Rod should lead its user to find whatever it had been prepared to seek. Usually, that was water, though Hiram had heard of more than one prospector using such rods to try to find gold or silver. Hiram was looking for Teancum Kimball, either missing or dead.

But a Mosaical Rod should also answer questions, and especially questions relating to the purpose of its creation.

He gripped the rod loosely in both hands and let the pointing end rest a couple of feet above the ground. Sorenson watched, making no comment.

Hiram started with a couple of test questions. "Is my name James?"

Nothing happened.

"Is this the Latuda Mine?"

Nothing.

"Am I standing here with Vilhelm Sorenson, the foreman of the Kimball Mine?"

The pointing tip of the rod dipped sharply, pulling Hiram's hands down with it.

Sorenson raised his craggy eyebrows, visible to Hiram in a gray penumbra at the edge of his vision, but said nothing.

"Is Teancum Kimball in the Kimball Mine?"

Nothing.

Hiram felt a sharp pang of disappointment. Where had he gone wrong? Maybe the presence that haunted the mine wasn't Teancum Kimball. Maybe the old man had run off to Mexico, like Hiram's father, abandoning his family to their daily struggle.

Hiram sighed.

Bill Sorenson cleared his throat. "Can we find Teancum Kimball by going into de Kimball Mine?"

The rod dipped down.

Sorenson chuckled. "Okay, den. You heard de rod."

On the way in, they passed a tin advertising plate, rusted over its lower third, advising the miners to chew Copenhagen smokeless tobacco.

Within the mine, the air was warmer still. The tunnels were

tall at first. Sorenson pointed at the chiseled rock. "When de coal was dere, dey called it *high coal*," Sorenson said. "Dat means dat you can mine it standing up. At first, before I was here, it was all high coal, de work was easy. But you can see here, de high coal is all mined out."

Hiram swept the Mosaical Rod from side to side, careful to hold it loosely in his hands, so that if it moved, he'd feel it easily, and also so that any movement that occurred would be due to the rod, and not due to involuntary muscle contractions in Hiram's hands.

The tunnels gave opening to galleries, long rooms wide enough to hold dances in.

They passed beaten, rusty metal carts, not much larger than large wheelbarrows, standing on the railroad tracks. The mine was supported by beams climbing the walls and across the ceiling, but also by half-length railroad ties stacked in pairs in alternating orientation, creating rough wooden columns that held up the ceiling.

Sorenson slapped his hand onto one. "Dese are called cribs."

Affixed to the cribs hung brief signs in multiple languages. Many were in characters Hiram didn't know, that could be Greek or Chinese. In letters he recognized, he read one that said NON FATEVI MALE.

"Latin?" he asked. Wasn't *fata* a word that meant something like fairy? No bad fairies?

"Italian," Sorenson told him. "Dese are all safety warnings. Dey say 'be careful.'"

"None of them are in English."

Sorenson laughed. "None of my boys read English. Half of 'em don't read deir own language. Maybe you heard dis already, but dey call Helper 'de town of fifty-seven varieties.'"

"Like the beans?"

"*Ja*, like de beans. Like beans in a can, me and my men."

They walked through the galleries and passed shafts exiting left and right. Hiram continued sweeping the road as he moved. Hiram wished he'd brought a pocket watch, and thought they might have walked half a mile.

Sorenson pointed out tunnels that were only four feet tall. "Here you see where dey found de crawler coal. Same kinda coal, burns just as good, only de seam is shorter. You gotta do de work sitting on your bum, or on your knees. De work is harder, de pay ain't no better."

"You could still dig a taller tunnel."

"*Ja*, but den you do more work to get all de extra rock out. Dat's no good. But you see dat? Dis is de eastern seam, and dat's coal." He pointed at a wall of black rock. "Dat's good coal, dat can be mined, everybody knows dere's good coal down here, only de crazy Kimballs got to sort out deir heads."

Samuel Kimball had said the eastern seam was petering out? Was he simply mad? Or under the sway of Mahoun?

As he spoke, they passed an opening that was boarded over. Hiram swung the Mosaical Rod past the opening, and the rod tugged downward. He tried it again, and a third time, and each time the rod clearly signaled that he should go down that passage.

"Mr. Sorenson," he said. "Is that boarded off because it's dangerous?"

"*Ja*, sort of. It's boarded off because it ain't de mine."

"What?"

"*Ja*, in a couple of places, de Kimball mine ran into old caves. Dat ain't de mine. It's a maze down dere, you can get lost, easy, so we boarded up to keep de boys from wandering off and getting lost."

It might not turn out right because it's so easy to get lost down there.

"That's where I have to go." Hiram brushed a fat fly away from his face.

The insect lazily drifted off him and through the wooden slats. In the enclosed space, trapped under all the rock, the buzz sounded like a sawmill.

Chapter Twenty-Three

SORENSON THREW A COILED LENGTH OF ROPE OVER HIS SHOULDER, and then they ripped off two of the planks boarding up the side passage.

The walls in this new passage were rougher, with the jagged look of a chasm torn open by an earthquake fault. The planks supporting the ceiling, as well as the beams overhead and the stacks of short railroad ties, were nonexistent here.

"Something's wrong with my eyes," Hiram said.

"Tunnel vision." Sorenson laughed. "It's just because of de way de carbide lamp works. It shines most brightly in a line straight ahead of you, and your eyes focus on dat line, but dat means dey adjust to dat brightness, and everything else looks dark."

"Can I do anything about it?"

"You can avoid looking straight ahead. Den your eyes will adjust to de darkness some. Or you can just get used to turning your head to where you want to look every time."

"But never at another person's face."

"Ja, very good, you have just avoided de number one reason a man gets his lights punched out on de first day of de job. Look ahead, and down, so if you meet anudder man, your light is on his feet."

They followed the crack down. Five feet wide, seven feet tall, it was a rough passage created by the Earth itself. Sorenson lumbered ahead, slouching and half-leaping from one stone to the next. It was a steep and long descent, choked with boulders and wet with

187

seeping moisture that trickled down one wall and disappeared among the rocks at their feet. Hiram saw it all a few square feet at a time, with the entire periphery of his vision filled with darkness.

And again, a distant sound.

"If we meet another man down here, though," Hiram said, "he won't be a miner."

"Right," Sorenson agreed. "He would be an outlaw, or a lost hobo who got stupid drunk."

"You've seen outlaws?"

"Oh, sure, from time to time. De biggest was back in de early days, when old Teancum Kimball ran dis place. You know de name Butch Cassidy?"

"Butch Cassidy mined coal?"

"No, but he robbed a coal company. Pleasant Valley Coal Company, at Castle Gate. Dat's north of Helper, up in de canyon. About forty years ago, Butch robbed de payroll. Dat's why even today, every mining company in Carbon County pays its payroll on a different date every month, and dey choose de date at random. De foremen draw cards, or roll dice, or stick a pin in a calendar. It makes it harder for payroll robbers to plan."

"How do *you* pick the day?" Hiram asked.

"I got a bag of poker chips with numbers written on 'em. I pull chips out of de bag. Maybe I should switch to using de dowsing rod, eh?"

"Using a dowsing rod requires a chaste and sober mind. A prayerful heart at all times. I find it helps to fast often."

"Can you use a dowsing rod if you drink?"

"I think it *helps* not to drink."

"Okay, den I'll leave de dowsing rod to you and I'll stick to de poker chips."

At the bottom of the chasm, they entered a wide, oblong chamber. To their left, the floor gave way to a pool of water, punctuated by strawlike stalagmites reaching for the unseen sky. On the right side of the chamber, three different passages broke the cavern wall, two descending and the third boring away into darkness on the level.

"Spare de rod, spoil de child." Sorenson laughed raucously. "Come on, Woolley, pick a trail for us."

First, Hiram chalked a clear, large arrow on the cavern floor, and a second on the wall, pointing back up the way they had come, along with an estimate: *200 yds to mine.*

Then he held the Mosaical Rod and paced sideways down the chamber, facing rightward, swinging the rod back and forth to give it the chance to indicate which of the three passages would help him find Teancum Kimball.

The rod didn't indicate any one of them.

He tried it a second time, and then a third.

Nothing.

"I think you broke de rod," Sorenson said.

Hiram examined the Mosaical Rod. His carvings all seemed intact, the wood otherwise unblemished. His eyelids were heavy, fluttering perilously close to sleep as he huddled over the witch hazel.

Hiram brushed at his face. Flies? Or was he seeing things? He was sweating copiously, though the air was cool, and he was so tired that every time he shut his eyes, he was afraid he'd fall asleep standing.

"Unless, of course," Sorenson added, "de rod wants us to take a swim."

Hiram snapped back to full wakefulness. Standing, he walked in a slow half-turn on the shelf of rock—there.

A definite tug on the rod, and when he repeated the turn in reverse, the rod pulled again.

"Oh ho," Sorenson said with a chuckle. "Dis is interesting."

Hiram tilted his head down to look into the water. He felt a cool breeze on his neck, and a faint tickling sensation. In the water, small white things that might have been fish or salamanders scurried along at the edge of his view.

"Does anything … dangerous … live in these waters?"

"Not dat I know," Sorenson said. "But den, I never walked around caves like dese following a dowsing rod, so I'm learning all kinds of new stuff about de world."

Hiram took his bearings again with the rod, made another chalk mark on the stone, then stepped into the water. It was deeper than it appeared from the surface, and he sank immediately up to the middle of his thigh.

"Oh, dat's cold." Sorenson lurched into the pool beside him. "Hey, are you hearing a buzzing sound? Like bees?"

"Yes." Hiram stopped, and something like a crayfish, but totally white, crawled over his boot. "Are you armed?"

"I got a knife. In my experience, if I don't carry a gun, de boys are less likely to bring a gun to talk to me when dey're angry."

"What about for defending yourself against criminals?"

"*Ja*, well, dat's why we pick a random payday."

"I've got a revolver."

"You keep it. I'll use my knife. We'll both look really silly when we get attacked by de big white swarm of cave-bees."

Hiram pushed ahead, crossing the water. When he got closer, he saw that, where the cave wall had appeared to him to drop down into the water and end the cavern, it in fact stayed above water, and there was a two-foot tall space between the water and the ceiling, over a passage moving forward. Holding the revolver and the Mosaical Rod above the water to keep them dry, he crouched and waddled along the submerged passage.

Something slimy felt its way briefly up one leg of his overalls. Shuddering, he shook his foot and dislodged it.

He felt a tugging at his ankle. Was that a rise in the pitch of the buzzing?

But no, the tugging was only water current, and in two more steps, he had passed it, and then the ceiling rose, and in two more steps he was able to stand.

Sorenson shook himself dry like a bear with a fresh salmon in its jaws. "Give me a coal mine any day. For one thing, de mine has supports to keep up de ceiling. Here, I don't know." They both looked up, and saw that they stood inside a chimney-shaped hollow. An exit from the chimney to Hiram's right hinted at unknown further passages. "Maybe de rod will warn us of a cave-in."

Hiram laughed at the joke, but only for a moment.

"Shout," he murmured. "For the Lord hath given you the city."

"Dis ain't no city."

Hiram didn't know any charm for bringing down a wall, not the wall of a city or the wall of a cave. Such hexes existed. They were in books like Henry Cornelius Agrippa's, or the *Picatrix*. They were books Hiram had never read, and most likely never *would* read, since they were written in Latin.

But Gus Dollar read those books, and owned them. He'd created a lead lamen with quotes from Joshua on it. Was it possible Gus wanted to cause a cave-in of the mine? Yet he'd truthfully said he didn't care about the mine. Then again, these caves were below the mine.

Gus had said he was making the Book of Spirits to defeat Samael.

Climbing out of the water onto another dry shelf, Hiram found himself looking at a chunk of stone. At first, due to its blunted edges and slick appearance, he took it for a lumpy stalagmite. After a moment's observation, he realized that it couldn't be natural. For one thing, the walls here were of reddish stone, and the rock in the center was nearly white, marked by black streaks.

Also, the stone was shaped very distinctly like a lizard's head. Hiram clearly saw eyes, and the ridge of a brow; the great flat top of the stone, like the upper surface of an altar, lay behind the reptile's eyes.

As in Samuel's painting.

Only the lizard's head seemed to have three mouths.

And then Hiram realized that the streaks were stains.

"By *Gud*, de rod was right. Look dere."

In the corner of the chimney, slumped against the wall of the cavern, and beside a foot-wide horizontal crack in the stone, lay a corpse.

The body was a man's, and it was dressed in Sunday best, though wearing a mine helmet much like the one Hiram had on. Its long-bearded face was twisted in an expression of horror, which Hiram could read clearly, because although the flesh had rotted away and the eye sockets gaped wide, the body's skin and hair were intact. The skin had a bluish tint under the carbide light, but Hiram recognized the face.

"Teancum Kimball," Hiram said.

In the crook of one arm lay a collapse tangle of small bones, under a skein of desiccated skin. A lamb?

"*Ja*, I'd know dat old bugger anywhere. You want to … check his pockets or something?"

Hiram *did* want to search the body. What was he looking for? Some indication of witchcraft, maybe. Some sign of intent, a hint that it was Teancum Kimball who had ultimately caused all the trouble at the mine. Some sign it might be Teancum's shade speaking to his sons through the peep-stone, lying to Samuel, and hardening Ammon's heart. If Hiram could do something as simple as lay Teancum's body in a grave and bless it, for instance, he'd be thrilled to do it, to bring an end to all the conflict.

First, he marked the floor with chalk.

"I should have brought a blanket or a sack," Hiram said. "I don't think we can carry him out."

"If we do dat, he falls apart."

Hiram knelt. He set the revolver and the Mosaical Rod to one side. The buzzing sound was definitely louder. Gingerly, he patted down the corpse's pockets, finding keys and a billfold, which he took.

"Ffffffffff . . ."

Hiram nearly fell over, pulling away.

Had he heard the corpse speak?

"What's wrong?" Sorenson asked.

Hiram felt too silly to answer. However, if Teancum Kimball's spirit wanted to speak to him now, the easiest way to find a solution might be to listen.

Slowly, he leaned in over the corpse's open mouth. Turning his ear to the corpse meant that his tunnel vision reduced the entire cave to a single spot of bare stone wall, a few feet across. He imagined the body lurching forward to bite him, but that was ridiculous nonsense, the lurid sort of thing you would read in cheap magazines.

"Teancum," he whispered. "Talk to me."

A column of flies exploded from the corpse's mouth. It struck Hiram in the face like the kick of a mule, knocking him backward. He struck the altar under one shoulder blade and fell to the ground, reeling. Flies banged off the reflecting disk of his carbide lamp, and he smelled the bitter stink of burnt insect.

He managed not to lose his helmet.

"Jesus!" Sorenson shouted, flapping his arms to drive the flies away. The foreman staggered back to the water's edge. "Come on, Woolley, we'll do dis anudder day, bring a big basket of flypaper with us."

Lying nearly on his back, propped on his elbows, Hiram peeked into the crack. What he had taken for darkness, he now saw consisted of swarming flies. Was this the locus, the epicenter? Had he stumbled into some kind of flies' nest?

Scooting around to point his lance of light into the crack, he looked for more. Eggs? Larvae? A way through?

He saw mouths. Mouths with jagged teeth, and white slug-like larvae dripping from the mouths like slobber. Three mouths, all set in the same gray, scaly face.

Hiram threw himself backward. His helmet slipped and he grabbed it, burning his hand on the carbide lamp. He searched for the revolver and the dowsing rod, but his sight was hampered by tunnel vision. He managed to get his hand on the revolver, but felt the rod skitter away from him into the darkness.

An arm burst from the crack. It was huge and gray, and it

jostled Teancum Kimball's corpse to one side. Hiram leaped back into the water, managing to avoid the talons. His breath came in short gasps made shallow by fear and by the chill of the water.

"Dis way, Woolley! Duck!" Bill Sorenson grabbed Hiram by the shoulder and pulled him backward and down. Hiram stared at the crack, seeing the many-mouthed face once more before the dropping ceiling obscured it, and the reptile-head altar with it.

He and Sorenson dragged each other to their feet on the stone shelf on the other side, and Hiram was hyperventilating. Light speared his eyeballs, and then his vision went dark, a blackness pierced by a dull red sun that illuminated nothing.

"Woolley!" Sorenson slapped him across the cheek. "Woolley, get hold of yourself! What was dat thing?"

"I can't see!"

"Your helmet's on backward, and you looked into my lamp. Here." Sorenson adjusted Hiram's helmet, and he regained a narrow tunnel of vision, though now it was marred with bright red circles.

He whirled around to look at the submerged passage. Flies were swarming out, and the size of the swarm grew from moment to moment.

"Run now!" he panted. "Later, we talk!"

Sorenson responded by pushing Hiram ahead of him along the shelf. They followed Hiram's chalk marks. Hiram ran to the chasm, and then scrambled as quickly as he could over the boulders, slipping where they were wet and picking up a few bruises in the process. Sorenson stalked behind him.

The buzzing sound grew louder as he went.

"You're with me!" he shouted every minute or so.

"*Ja!*" Bill Sorenson shouted back.

Finally, they came to the planks barring off this chasm, and Hiram turned to run for the surface.

"Wrong way, Woolley!" Sorenson against grabbed Hiram, this time by the neck, and dragged him through the high coal tunnels, stumbling and nearly tripping over and over on the mine-cart tracks, until they burst out into the cold night air. Then he let Hiram go, and they both staggered down the stone-lined trough and out onto the hillside of Kimball Canyon.

Hiram turned and shone his carbide light into the mine opening. He saw nothing.

"What was dat?" Sorenson asked him, panting.

"Do you hear the flies?"

"No. Do you?"

"No." Hiram took deep breaths, steadying himself, trying to get control of his breathing. "I don't know what that was. I didn't get a good look." He straightened his back, raised his helmet, and ran his fingers through his hair over a scalp slick with sweat.

"Did you find what you wanted?" Sorenson asked.

Hiram considered the question. The presence of Teancum Kimball's corpse in the cave suggested that he had mailed Samuel Kimball his seer stone and then deliberately gone down into the tunnels, as his letter had seemed to indicate. He had gone dressed well, and carrying a small animal. Had he known he was going to die? Had he gone down there to face something?

The thing behind the flies?

Mahoun, Samael? The fallen angels of the Wastes of Dudael, as Gus had said? Gus claimed he wanted to defeat the demon—had Teancum done down into the caves to defeat Samael? No, he had gone down to make a thirty-year deal.

But first he'd sent the peep-stone to his son, the stone from which Teancum thought he received guidance.

Guidance from whom, or from what?

Hiram needed to take a good look into the seer stone.

"Can you check on Michael for me?" He handed his revolver to Sorenson, grip first.

Sorenson took the Colt. "Something comes for your boy, don't worry, it'll have to come through me first."

"And then just wait at your home for me to join you? I have something else I have to do, over at the Kimball house, but I'll be along shortly. And, Sorenson...Bill...if you see Ammon, don't mention me coming around. And with my son...maybe..."

"*Ja*, of course, and I won't tell your son nothing. Holy Jesus, I won't tell my wife nothing. But be careful, Hiram. Dese things that you have to do...dey frighten me." Sorenson chuckled, a bass rumble. "Hey, de mine...maybe it's haunted, after all, like Samuel says."

Hiram smiled. "How do I turn off the lamp?"

"De *on* switch," Sorenson said. "You turn it to *off*."

Hiram extinguished his carbide lamp and gave the helmet to Sorenson. He retrieved his fedora from the mine building, and he moved both their chits from the "IN" board to the "OUT" one. He then headed north across the canyon, toward the big house.

Chapter Twenty-Four

HIRAM HAD BECOME ACCUSTOMED TO THE WARMER AIR WITHIN the mine; the February night pierced his flesh and sank into his bones. His feet, damp from the water of the cave, froze immediately. He walked faster and huddled into his Army coat. Smoke from fires hung like a fog over the shanties.

He paused by the light of a window to rifle through the billfold he'd taken from Teancum Kimball's body, finding only a few ragged dollars. What kind of thirty-year deal had Teancum attempted to make with the fallen angel? And, since it was 'another' deal, did that mean he had made a previous thirty-year deal? The answers to his questions might have died two years earlier with Teancum himself.

Or had Teancum *become* the demonic fly creature?

Gus Dollar might have the answers, but Hiram couldn't test the truth of Gus's words unless he knew the right questions to ask the man.

Hiram pocketed the billfold and felt the keys he'd retrieved from Teancum's body. One should fit the lock of the Kimball house. That would save Hiram the task of working a charm at the door, and such a match would also confirm the identity of the corpse.

A man in a thick wool sweater and a hat pulled down ambled past Hiram. He wore a red bandana over his face, and Hiram recognized him from the scuffle at the mine gate. He stared intently down an alley as he walked past. Perhaps he was looking for a lost dog?

Hiram raised his hand in a silent greeting.

The masked fellow stopped and looked at Hiram.

"Evening," Hiram said. The ordinary politeness sounded strange in the wake of the evening's events.

The masked man nodded and walked on.

Hiram jogged down the hill and across the road. He approached the Kimball house past the spot where he'd buried the snake head and found the human skull.

What might the skull have to do with Teancum's planned bargain? Or had Hiram stumbled across the remains of some prospector, or a Ute hunter who had lost his way and died in this canyon, perhaps long before the house was even built?

The stone on Ammon's mantel had to be a seer stone. As a mere rock, it had no value, but a peep-stone could grant true visions which had a worth beyond price. If Teancum Kimball possessed such a stone, he might well have sent it to one of his sons as a gift, especially if he were approaching a meeting that might result in his death. Such a stone could have shown Samuel where to dig a new mineshaft, and it might even have directed Samuel to then place the stone back in his family home...perhaps with the intent that Ammon would then look into the stone.

But *whose* intent? The intent of the stone? Teancum's intent? The intent of someone who had created the stone, or a power that was connected to it?

Could the stone have guided Teancum to his death? Could the stone have told Samuel one thing, and then Ammon another, setting them at odds?

Or could the stone be giving them true visions in a difficult situation? Could the Kimballs be failing to heed the guidance of a true messenger?

Hiram shuddered. This was really not what he had expected when Bishops Smith and Wells had asked him to deliver groceries to out-of-work miners.

He sneaked around to the front of the house.

He didn't want Ammon to catch him breaking in. "In the name of the Father, up and down," he chanted, "the Son and the Spirit upon your crown, the cross of Christ upon your breast, sweetest lady send Ammon Kimball rest." He repeated the charm three times, then stepped onto the porch.

There he paused. He was an honest man. Wasn't he? And yet

here he was, breaking into someone's home for the second time in as many days. When had he become a burglar?

And breaking into Gus's home had deprived Hiram's charms of power.

Only, he had tried to speak with Ammon openly—as well as with Samuel and Eliza. And they weren't willing to budge. Could he wait until morning, and try to talk to Ammon again?

But Hiram doubted Ammon would be any easier to deal with now. He had called Samuel a thief, presumably for having their father's seer stone in his possession, even though it seemed that Teancum himself had sent Samuel the stone.

And besides, Hiram wasn't going to take anything from Ammon. He just needed to look at the stone, and confirm it for what it was. Ammon wouldn't be harmed.

Hiram chuckled, but his chuckle split into a sob.

"Lord Divine, if what I work here is sin, I beg thee to look on my heart with mercy and forgive me. But also, don't let my charms fail, and don't let me get caught. Amen."

It felt like a burglar's prayer, but at least it was honest.

He felt inclined to add, "And a special blessing on the Markopoulos family, Medea, and Callista, and help heal Basil's leg, but keep him from the temptation of banditry. Amen."

He stepped to the door and tried the key; a perfect fit.

He opened the door, the hinges whining. Closing the door produced more squeaking, and he clenched his teeth. Door shut, he waited to see if Ammon came down, forcing himself to count to a slow one hundred.

No light, no sound, no Ammon.

He probed in the darkness to see whether the single-shot break-action shotgun was by the door. It wasn't. Ammon might sleep with it under his bed. For use against burglars, presumably.

Burglars like Hiram.

But the house was quiet.

Hiram was grateful for the cloudless night, the stars, and the bare windows. He slunk across the front room to the mantel. A handful of coals glowed orange in the fireplace, but not enough to illuminate more than two feet in front of them. Hiram took off his hat.

The brown stone was only a dark shape. If it was a seer stone, Hiram might see visions. But visions sent by what power? Hiram half-hoped he was wrong, and that the stone was just a rock.

Hiram steeled himself.

He picked up the rock. It was cool to the touch. It didn't feel evil, or good, or spiritual, or powerful at all. The stone felt like a stone.

Hiram placed the stone in his hat.

He took a minute to listen again to the quiet of the house. Nothing but silence.

Hiram lowered his face into his hat.

The effect was immediate and overwhelming.

The quartz strip in the rock ignited in a blinding light that hurt to look at and he felt his body move. Vertigo seized him, as if he were flying, and a strong wind beat at his face.

A Bible passage bubbled up into his mind: chapter seventeen of Matthew, the first few verses. *And after six days Jesus taketh Peter, James, and John his brother, and bringeth them up into an high mountain apart. And was transfigured before them: and his face did shine as the sun, and his raiment was white as the light.*

Hiram knew, and felt, that he stood in front of the dying fire, faced buried in his fedora. Yet at the same time, he was standing beside himself, head up, gazing upon both his own body and the shape of a beautiful man, legs, arms, torso, head, and a face that was both indistinct and sharp. Light came from the man's body. Looking right at the figure, he couldn't make out any details. Shifting his gaze, he saw in his peripheral vision features well-proportioned and without blemish.

He and the angelic man stood atop a high mountain, clouds and light around and below them. As long as his eyes rested upon the man, Hiram could see him and the rocky landscape, but when he shifted his eyes slightly, all he saw was Ammon's furniture and shadowy walls.

Greetings, Hiram Woolley, of Lehi. I bring thee glad tidings.

Hiram's heart pounded. Something bothered him, in the back of his mind.

"Greetings, spirit. I stand ready to hear your words," he whispered.

Thy heart is troubled by the suffering of the Kimball family and their endeavors to excavate the treasures of the earth. The time of weeping will soon be over. I shall remove a keystone from the vault of the earth, and the blessings of wealth and prosperity will return to this valley.

The voice came from everywhere and nowhere.

"What is my role, messenger?"

Many are called, but few are chosen. Thy labors here are completed. I bid thee to return to thy home.

Hiram took a deep breath. Everyone wanted him to leave, including Rettig and his ruffians. At first, Rettig had seen Hiram as someone who could help him bring the Kimballs over to the railroad man's side. Word must have gotten back to Rettig that none of the Kimballs would sign, so hurting Hiram would make him just another victim and throw a scare that no one was safe in Spring Canyon. Or maybe Rettig had come to fear that Hiram would unite the Kimball family *against* the railroad man.

And of course, Michael had provoked Rettig.

Hiram saw his situation with Rettig so clearly now. Could this be a true vision of an angel? Did God want Hiram to leave?

"I can't go until I see the mine operating again," Hiram said. "The food I brought is running out." Medea Markopoulos, whose husband Hiram had run over, would starve. So would her children.

Wouldst thou argue with me? The voice in Hiram's mind rose to a thunderous roll. *Where was thou, when the morning stars sang together, and all the sons of God shouted for joy?*

The shining man was quoting scripture. That was as should be—when angels showed up, to Mary in the New Testament or to Brother Joseph in upstate New York, they quoted scripture.

And then Hiram realized what bothered him. The other piece of any true angel's introduction was *fear not*. Hiram feared, and the angel had not tried to allay his fears at all.

Was it a false spirit?

Could this, after all, be Mahoun or Samael? Could a fallen angel or a demon or a monster have pitted the Kimball brothers against each other, and was the same being now attempting to trick Hiram into leaving?

And if the spirit spoke deception, why didn't his bloodstone warn Hiram? But Gus Dollar, with his Jupiter ring and his Samael glyphs, had already proved that the bloodstone could be defeated.

"I don't mean to be difficult," Hiram said. "But I was sent to get these men fed. I brought them food, but men need to eat more than once. Tell me how I can soften the hearts of the Kimballs…Ammon, Samuel, and Eliza."

This is my work, and not thine. Go home, cunning man.

Hiram knew a way to test angels.

"Spirit," he said. "I understand. Take a grip from me in sign of our covenant." He reached out his right hand, both the physical hand in Ammon's drawing room and his spiritual hand atop the cloud-shrouded mountain.

He hoped the spirit wouldn't notice his fingers trembling.

The shining man regarded Hiram coolly.

Dost thou not fear to be struck down, as was Uzza when he dared to touch the ark of the Lord?

"What have I to fear from my Father's servants?" Sweat poured down between Hiram's shoulder blades.

So be it. The blinding white figure reached forward. Diamonds seemed to sparkle on its ethereal skin as it reached out to touch his physical body.

Hiram drew his spirit hand back. "Liar."

An angel of heaven was a creature without flesh and bone, and knew it, and would never try to shake hands with a human being. Any spirit that would attempt to touch a person bodily was a deceiving spirit—a fallen angel, a demon, or a ghost.

It was time to end the interview. Hiram tried to remove the hat from his face and couldn't. He tried to turn his feet and step down from the high mountain, and couldn't do that, either.

What is this treachery?

Hiram grunted from the exertion of will, but he couldn't move his body. He couldn't get his face out of the hat.

I will repay thy trickery with death.

Hiram felt cold fingers around his heart, and his vision began to blur. Parts of his consciousness drifted into silence, as if the memories and personality of Hiram Woolley were being wiped off of a chalkboard.

But not thy death, cunning man. I will wield thine own hand to visit horrors upon thy kin!

His own hand? Kin? What kin did he have?

He had no kin.

He was floating, a mote in a cosmic sea.

Alone.

But he wasn't alone.

Michael. The fading parts of Hiram's mind snapped back into clarity.

The demonic being was threatening Michael.

Thy son, the man-child!

The thing knew his thoughts.

"I will call upon the Lord," Hiram cried, shouting the words of the psalm at the top of his voice, "who is worthy to be praised: so shall I be saved from mine enemies!"

He couldn't take his face from the hat, but he managed to slap one clumsy hand to his chi-rho amulet.

The mountain disappeared. So did everything else, and Hiram stood in darkness, his body freezing with cold sweat. He whipped the hat away from his face, panting, and found he could see nothing. Blindly, he dug the seer stone from his fedora and managed to grope his way to the mantel again. He set the stone there awkwardly, on the lip of the wood.

Hiram gasped, shuddering to get air in and out of his lungs. He was making way too much noise for a burglar. Nausea hit him, his legs buckled, and his stomach boiled. Closing his useless eyes, he drew in deep breaths until his belly calmed down.

Finally, he opened his eyes. Tracks of light blurred his vision, and he blinked and blinked until tears stung his eyes and he could see again.

The seer stone was not divine. A malign creature gave visions through the stone. It had given Samuel false visions, and it must have given false visions to Ammon as well. The creature, fallen angel, ghost, demon, or monster, wanted the Kimballs to fight.

Hiram couldn't leave the stone in the house.

He was also loath to touch it again.

Hiram climbed unsteadily to his feet. He got out his green bandana, stained with the blood from his nose and the crayon or lipstick that had been used to write on the Double-A. That seemed fitting. He wrapped the stone up in the cloth and then pocketed it.

He left the house.

He wasn't sure whether the stone's spirit was the same entity as the fly demon, and whether either of those was Mahoun or Samael, but it seemed likely that they were all one and the same.

And the creature had threatened Michael.

He broke into a ragged run, racing across the dark valley back to Bill Sorenson's house.

Chapter Twenty-Five

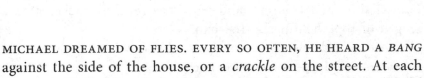

MICHAEL DREAMED OF FLIES. EVERY SO OFTEN, HE HEARD A *BANG* against the side of the house, or a *crackle* on the street. At each noise Michael started, but then nothing happened, and he'd wonder whether he'd heard anything, after all. Sleeping on the hard sofa against the wall of Sorenson's small house wasn't easy, but he tried to force himself.

The front door slamming shut finally woke him. Bill Sorenson stood alone in the door with the Colt revolver in his hand.

"Eh, you're awake. Oh *ja*, your fadder will be here soon. He's just got some udder work keeping him for a bit, at de big house. You want a beer, boy?"

"No, thanks." Michael sat up. He wasn't sure why he declined the beer. It wasn't like his pap was around to enforce the rules. It was only beer, home-brewed by Sorenson, so it probably wasn't even very strong. Or maybe that meant it would be stronger. Michael wasn't sure.

Regardless, he passed.

Within a year, he'd probably move away from the farm, and the world was full of beer. No rush.

"Water, though," he said. "Or a Coca-Cola, if you have it."

The cold night air sneaked in through the tar-paper walls of the Sorensons' house, and Michael squeezed to the end of the sofa, as close to the stove as he could get.

Why had his father given Bill Sorenson his revolver? Michael

203

knew the weapon, and if he hadn't, those initials scratched into the barrel were a dead giveaway.

Images of swarms of flies came into Michael's mind when he shut his eyes. He tried to keep his eyes open.

Behind those flies, he was pretty sure he'd seen a man. An enormous man, the size of a bear, but a man. And his father had shouted Bible verses at the man. The whole thing was odd. There had to be scientific explanation for the flies. Maybe a cow had collapsed near a hot springs and the carrion had drawn the insects. Maybe there was a thermal vent somewhere in the canyon that kept flies alive through the winter.

Sorenson brought him water in a large beer-stein, holding a second stein for himself. Michael could smell the sweet, hoppy scent of the beer. Sorenson had changed into a shapeless gray flannel shirt and trousers, and wore the revolver tucked into a length of rope holding up the pants.

Sorenson threw more coal into the stove, then sat on the other end of the sofa from Michael.

Michael drank most of his water in one long series of gulps. "Is my pap talking with Ammon Kimball, then?"

"*Ja.*" The Dane seemed deliberately nonchalant. "I guess dey had a meeting."

"In the middle of the night?"

"Haven't you noticed dat de Kimballs are crazy? Mad bastards, all of dem. I stuck with Ammon because he seemed less crazy dan Sam, but now I don't know."

"Maybe you stuck with Ammon because you could do the most good for the men that way," Michael suggested.

"No." Sorenson belched. "I don't care too much for de men. De men don't get paid, dey can just hop on de train and go find a job in Salt Lake or Denver. No, I don't give a damn about dem."

"I don't believe you," Michael said.

Sorenson shook his head. "No, it's de families I care about. It's de families dat don't eat when de man don't work, it's de families dat get left behind when a man goes to ride de rails. So if Joe's a good worker and just needs a little help, and he's got a family, *ja*, den I'm dere to help him. Every time."

"You should go into politics," Michael.

"No, politics is full of rotten bastards dat say dey want to help, but dey really just want to take all your money and you go to hell. No, I want to really help de people, and I tell you what, so does your pap."

Michael felt pride. His pap had some strange old beliefs, but he really wanted to help the poor. *The widows and the fatherless*, as Hiram Woolley himself might say.

Again, something thumped against the wall. Maybe a mule had wandered up and was butting against the house? Or kept falling and standing up again? Probably not. It wasn't a tree. No trees that close to the building. Then what was it?

The stove was heating up with the extra coal; Michael stood and walked close to the door, where he could feel a little cold air rushing in around the edges of the doorframe. Should he get his guitar from the truck? He could entertain himself, and maybe Sorenson would like to hear a little Jimmie Rodgers or Charley Patton.

Sorenson stood to get himself a second glass of beer, and Michael decided he was too tired to play.

"You have a radio, by any chance?" he asked.

Sorenson shook his head, filling the stein. "De miners' families don't have a radio, do dey? So we don't have a radio."

As he settled in to drink his second glass, Sorenson launched into a monolog. Michael could barely follow a long story about how Sorenson had been hired by Teancum because he knew how to get men to work, especially when the work was hard and the conditions dangerous. Sorenson had done it before, for the D and RGW up at a place called Soldier Summit, before he'd lost two fingers, burned off when a boiler exploded. Michael heard about Bill Sorenson's growing up on a ranch, and breaking horses, and chasing girls.

Michael longed for the mercy of flyless sleep. It didn't come.

Mrs. Sorenson appeared during the story. She pulled a kitchen chair close to the stove and sat there, working at needlepoint. She was a big woman with a wide face, though her eyes were small and merry and she moved with a lot of energy. The constant motion of her fingers and needle was a bit mesmerizing.

Fragments of his experiences over the last two days filtered in and out of Michael's consciousness. Samuel's camp had been an excursion into bizarre territory, and yet, the truck breaking down and starting again felt weirder. What exactly had his pap done that had restarted the truck? What was the thing that had attacked them? Rettig's toughs might be the least strange thing Michael had seen since coming to Helper.

But the swarm of flies? In February, with snow on the ground?

Grandma Hettie would have had an explanation for all this stuff. She had died when Michael was nine, a year before he lost his mother. If Grandma Hettie wasn't actually a witch, then she was someone who knew an awful lot about old folk magic, and seemed quite convinced that it worked. She'd tried to explain to Michael that everything had a spirit, and some spirits were ghosts and some were demons and some were angels, and that you had to watch out for the movement of the planets, and a black cat was bad luck, and that with the right stick, you could find buried treasure, if the spirits didn't take it away first.

As a small child, he'd thought she was kidding, telling him stories. But he'd realized one day when he'd twisted his ankle and the first thing that Grandma Hettie did was make the sign of the cross over it that Grandma Hettie really believed.

It was quaint and old-fashioned. Michael could imagine a day when the superstitions of the past would fade away, and scientific theory would be applied to all improve aspects of life. Tell me about a ghost? Prove it, empirically. Any axiom about god, ghost, or devil should be backed up with strong evidence or abandoned. Otherwise, it was all fairy stories, the bogeyman under the barn, and Jesus walking on water alike.

His pap might believe in silly things about God, but he genuinely wanted to do right. So Michael was proud of him, and happy to be his driver. When he went off to college, he knew he would miss their long drives, their banter, and even the good work they did together. Hiram wasn't just bellyaching about people being out of work, he was doing something to help.

Sorenson was in the middle of a story, something about a couple of Comanche stealing his horses, when he was growing up in Oklahoma after immigrating from Denmark, and how other boys made fun of his accent.

Thump.

"Do you hear that?" Michael asked.

Mrs. Sorenson's whirring fingers and the sound of the needle piercing the cloth on her lap was all they heard.

"Hear what?" Sorenson's eyes were red-rimmed and runny.

"You don't hear that?"

Sorenson shrugged and then took up where he left off, saying something about how Quanah Parker respected the courage of a man who asked for his horses back.

Michael's large drink of water had run its course through his system, and he now had a more urgent concern than likely-meaningless noises in the night. "If I have to answer the call of nature, do you have an outhouse?"

Sorenson gave him a wavering stare, opening one eye. "Call of nature? I don't understand."

"I have to...take a piss," Michael said.

The Dane chortled, his eyebrows shaking like jelly in an earthquake. "*Ja*, dat's how de miners say it! It's out back, I'll come with you."

Michael jumped to his feet. "I haven't needed help in the outhouse for years."

"I told your fadder I'd watch you." The grogginess fell away from Sorenson's face.

Michael help up a hand, backing toward the door. "You can watch, but watch from far away. Like, maybe from right here."

He slipped out the door, shutting it before Sorenson could follow him.

Outside, the wind blew strong. Passing around the house, Michael heard another *thump*. He took in a great big breath. After being inside the closed, hot room, the cold air felt good on his skin and in his lungs. The outhouse was about twenty feet away in an empty space like a lane between homes. Windows glowed with a muted light from a few of the other houses. The air was thick with the cold and the settling smoke of coal fires.

He went to the corner of the house. He heard something else now, a scratching sound followed by the thump.

Scratch. Scratch. Scratch. Thump.

What the hell? He wished he had his father's revolver.

A shiver ran up his spine and lodged in the base of his skull as an uneasy tingling feeling. He imagined Samuel, smoking marijuana and swinging a dead cat by the tail. Maybe he'd come to pin something more human to his horrid easels. Or what if Rettig's men were back?

Or what if there were really ghosts, come up from the mine?

All just stories. He'd soon see the empirical evidence. That was the only scientific thing to do.

Michael peered around the corner of the Sorenson house.

Lying on the dirt was a dog, a big, shaggy beast. It had three legs, and when it scratched itself, it fell off balance and its back foot struck the Sorenson's house. The mutt would get upright, then scratch itself until it fell over and hit the wall again.

Scratch, scratch, scratch, fall, then *thump.*

"Michael?" he heard Bill Sorenson calling from behind him.

Michael stepped forward, getting away from Sorenson. His movement surprised the animal. It leapt to its three feet and growled, showing teeth, hackles up, and tail straight back.

Michael wasn't a stranger to dogs. He crouched down and pretended to pick up a stone. He stood and cranked his arm back as if ready to throw. The dog went loping away toward the mud street in front of the house in a stutter step, two back legs working and the one front leg hopping along.

Michael dropped his arm. Just a dog.

Something struck the back of his neck; something small and moving fast, and the pain was fierce.

Michael slapped his neck, trapping something. A wasp? Buzzing filled his ears. Another sting in the palm of his hand, and more stings on the neck. He spun. Insects swarmed over him, drowning out the light, rushing down his shirt and even into his pants, biting him everywhere they found exposed skin.

He yelled and threw himself against the wall, trying to smash the swarm with his body.

"Michael?" Sorenson's voice sounded remote.

Something emerged from the shadows. For a mad moment, Michael thought it was the dog. This dark thing came forward, and he'd seen it before. It was broad-shouldered, but had the tapering waist of a man, rather than the bulk of a bear. Its skin was the color of mottled ash, and there was something wrong with its face.

Mouths. It had three mouths.

Michael backed away, but his feet got twisted under him.

He crashed forward onto his belly. The man—it had to be a man, what else could it be?—sank a knee into his back. Michael felt his hair pulled back and then his face was smashed into the ground . . . over . . . over . . . over. He was surprised he didn't hurt, just experienced a dull feeling of his head being pummeled into the dirt. The stinging hurt more, and the awful feeling of the insects inside his clothes, scuttling around on his skin to find fresh flesh to eat.

Michael vomited, then gasped in coal smoke. A tingling started in his right foot and then his whole leg seemed to be on fire. His face smashed into his own vomit. He heard a *pop* above him, saw a flash of light, maybe?

Or were those stars?

His foot hurt. It was like someone had stuck a hot coal in the heel of this boot. But he was already so dizzy, and hurt, and scared. The world went black.

Bang!

Michael woke up in surprise and in pain. Where was he?

Bang! Bang!

Gunshots. From inside the Sorenson house.

A pause. Scuffling inside the house. A final shot.

Doors of other houses flew open.

Michael staggered to his feet. He wiped the half-dried sick off his face and brushed away the dirt. His skin burned.

He went to the window. Inside, Mrs. Sorenson lay on the floor in a widening pool of blood, her needlepoint clenched in a dead fist. The left side of her head was missing. On top of her lay her husband, part of his scalp hanging off his head. Most of the scalp, however, was gone, exposing white bone, and his flannel shirt was soaked in blood.

On the floor beside them lay Pap's revolver.

Yelling, and the pounding of feet.

Michael's head throbbed.

The thing that had attacked Michael—no, the man, it had to be a man, his eyes had played tricks on him—must have killed the Sorensons. But instead, it might look like Bill Sorenson had killed his wife.

Or worse...like Hiram Woolley, whose revolver lay on the floor, had killed them both.

Or *Michael* had.

Men stomped by, not noticing Michael in the shadows. They went busting into the house, hollering. At first, the shouting was in languages Michael didn't know, but it gradually shifted into English.

"God in heaven, that's Bill Sorenson! Shot his wife! Shot himself?"

"I don't believe it. Look at the scalp. Who takes scalps?"

"That truck, it's the Mormon. And he have an Indian with him, don't he?"

"That gun, it have something on it, scratched on the barrel."

"An *H* and a *W*. Hiram Woolley. *Ja, das stimmt*, that gun is the farmer's."

"Yeah, but who is Y.Y.?"

"The other fellow must be Y.Y.! The dark guy who was with him!"

"Where is he? Where is that Indian? I bet they did it. I bet they working for Samuel and the Greeks! Make us believe it was suicide . . . but no, not Bill. Bill never!"

"Them strangers were for Ammon and you Germans!"

"No, the Indians, that Indian, they hate us white-skins. I seen the movies!"

Michael felt every slam of his heart in his aching head. He couldn't breathe.

A hand touched his shoulder and he started—but it was the Greek girl, Medea. She crouched beside him, her homemade spear in her hands. Maybe it was the way the light from the Sorensons' cast shadows across her face, but as he looked at her, Michael thought she looked like she might be his kid sister.

She jerked her head, indicating an open alley beyond the outhouse. Michael climbed to his feet and ran.

Chapter Twenty-Six

SOMETHING WAS WRONG IN THE CAMP. THERE WAS TOO MUCH noise for the middle of the night, and it seemed to be centered around the Sorensons' house. Hiram made his way cautiously through the shadows of the tarpaper shacks, cold sweat chilling his face. He sprinted up the slope and took a back way that threaded the narrow lanes between homes. He had to duck laundry lines, laundry buckets, and washboards, along with shovels, picks, axes, and other tools.

Hiram crept up through an alley on the other side of Sorenson's place. Miners had pulled their cars around to shine their lights on the big Dane's house, lighting the bare lanes on all sides. Two Ford Model Ts very nearly boxed in the Double-A. Hiram sneaked closer, staying in the darkness. He caught snatches of conversation in broken English.

Police were on their way. The Mormon's revolver. Sorenson shot his wife and then shot himself. No, that farmer shot them both. Ghosts from the mine might have driven them all crazy. Now the Dane believed, God rest his soul. No, it was the Mormon's Injun friend. Killed the Danes, took their money, and left. No sign of the Indian, but they found tracks leading away. Wasn't the Injun, it was the Mormon. You knew how they are. Probably wanted Sorenson's wife, and then shot them when they wouldn't go along.

Hiram had to rest for a minute while relief opened his lungs again. His son was alive.

He and Michael might both be in trouble with the law, and poor Bill Sorenson. Poor Eva. Bill had promised he'd protect Michael, and had died doing so. Hiram felt gratitude and sorrow, and then apprehension. Without the foreman, the strife in the camp would surely get worse.

Had one of the miners killed the Dane? Had Rettig ordered it done? Had the demon in the mine followed Sorenson home? That might make his death Hiram's fault, and Hiram found his eyes filling with silent tears.

Could Hiram show his face in Kimball, suspected by the miners, hunted by the police? And where was Michael now? Alone in the freezing wilderness and on foot, since the Double-A sat empty in front of Sorenson's house. Surely, he must be heading for Helper.

If Hiram could get to the truck and get away, he might be able to find Michael on the road. He'd have to hurry, before the police arrived—he didn't want a high-speed chase through the canyons.

The Model Ts might try to follow him.

But Hiram had learned a car-disabling charm from Gus Dollar.

The miners were clustered around the doorway, chattering breathlessly. Some of their women stood among them, arguing and waving fists, while others pulled children away from the Sorenson's house, stuffing them back into their own homes.

Hiram crept up to the back of one of the Model Ts and took a piece of chalk from his pocket. He scratched three words across the back bumper: *Nema, Nema, Nema.* Was this blasphemy? But he was only trying to escape, to rescue his son. And he didn't know the Lord's Prayer backward, so he'd say it forward and hope the Lord Divine would give life to his charm.

To his curse, that is.

Hiram whispered the prayer and then repeated the process with the second Model T.

He then drew in a deep breath. This next piece was going to be risky. *Lord Divine, help me start this truck.*

He shambled up to the Double-A, head down to hide his face, counting on the darkness to help him. Slipping into the truck with as much nonchalance as he could, he flipped up the spark, turned the key, gave the clutch a couple of pumps because of the cold night air, and hit the starter.

The truck rumbled to life.

"In the truck! The Mormon!"

Hiram slammed his foot onto the gas pedal and the Double-A shot forward. He swerved around a mustached Greek man and then took a sharp turn. He felt the truck lurch to the right and he wasn't sure his wheels were touching earth. Spinning the steering wheel, he got the vehicle onto the ground again, only to have the Double-A lurch and nearly topple over the other way.

He fought the truck into submission and he made it through the shacks and out of the camp. The Model Ts didn't follow him—his curse had worked.

His first curse.

And he'd learned it from Gus Dollar. The thought sobered Hiram.

Hiram slowed as the Ford Model Bs of the Helper police raced past him going the other way. Then he raced toward Dollar's, where he skidded onto the main Spring Canyon road. He longed to give the Double-A real gas, to keep ahead of those Model Bs with their V-8 engines, but he kept himself in check. If Hiram died in a ditch, he did Michael no good.

But it wouldn't be long before the miners told the cops that their prime suspect was on the lam and that they'd driven right past him.

He found a rough side road, little more than a dirt track, and he pulled off, going up enough distance to get out of sight. He parked the truck and crept down to the main road to wait.

All the sneaking, breaking in, and acting in a generally guileful manner didn't sit right with him. What he'd told Michael turned out to be true. It was a dirty world, and even if a man only wanted to do good, he'd likely get his hands filthy.

Soon, the Model Bs raced by again. They wanted to catch him before he reached Helper and the highway.

And if they beat him to the mouth of the canyon, they could put up a roadblock and trap him. Or could he drive out some other way? Some of these other tracks must go over the ridges and out. Samuel must have some other way in and out of Apostate Canyon—he couldn't pass his family home every time, could he?

Hiram wearily shuffled up to his truck. He hadn't really slept in two nights, and he felt fatigue now in every muscle, but especially in his eyelids.

He backed up the Double-A, did a dozen-point turn, and rolled carefully down to the road. He turned. The headlights caught the dust still swirling from the police cars.

The police might not set up a roadblock, especially if he went soon. They might chase off in the direction they imagined he'd gone. Plus, there didn't seem to be that many police in Helper. Did they really have the manpower to set up a roadblock anywhere?

Maybe they would get the Carbon County Sheriff involved.

Hiram drove slowly, searching for a sign of Michael.

A smell filled his nose, of strong garlic and sugar, sweet, spicy. His vision tunneled in, more tightly than it had in the mine. His heart thumped like a toad flopping over. "Rupert, Giles..." What was it? He couldn't remember his charm against sleeping sickness, he was just too tired.

He tried to stop the truck, get it to the side of the road, to his left, because to the right was a precipice. If he went over that, he wouldn't be walking away.

He aimed for a patch of dark green on the left side of the road. He was reasonably sure he'd pointed the truck in that direction when he lost consciousness.

Mary McGill winced when the morning sun pierced the clouds and struck a white wall of Spring Canyon, forcing the glare into her red and white Model A Ford. Her eyes stung and she blinked.

Were the tears filling her eyes the result of the light, or the events of the night before?

The evening had started out promisingly enough. Five-cent Jimmy had shown up in his best suit, wrinkled, with his gorilla arms and his necktie all out of control, just in time to drag Mary into the Helper Justice Court. To Mary's delight, Jimmy had made Police Chief Asael Fox look silly. Jimmy would fight on him on every front: acting beyond Fox's jurisdiction, censurable behavior, borderline criminal, and of course Jimmy threatened a civil lawsuit against the department if Mary wasn't released immediately and left alone.

Mary hadn't thought about the sage leaf under her heel until later, and then mostly to consider with bemusement the possibility that maybe, in some way, it *had* helped.

Jimmy left immediately—business in Salt Lake City, he'd said.

Mary had stopped to eat at the Chop Suey. A woman named

Yu Yan, whose husband worked at the Kimball mine, told her that Bill and Eva Sorenson had been murdered. The prime suspects, she had whispered, were the Mormon do-gooder and his Indian friend.

Mary had laughed that off as obvious nonsense. Still, a part of her had wanted to rush up to the mine immediately, but she had given in to her desire for a bath and a real bed.

In the morning, feeling rested, and strengthened by a bellyful of coffee and bacon, she had headed up Spring Canyon.

On the outskirts of the Kimball camp, a flash caught her eye.

Mary slammed on the brakes. Dust flooded past her. When it cleared, Mary saw thin legs sticking out from under a low Juniper a few steps from the track, and the hem of a blue dress.

Her heart hammered. She willed those legs to move, but they lay still.

Mary left her car, trying to control her breath. The images of dead children she'd seen before, suffocated in a Chicago tenement, drained bloodless in a sawmill, crushed under a fallen tree, flashed into her mind.

"Please, don't," Mary whispered. She crunched quickly across the gravel.

The child, a young woman, really, lay under the evergreen bushes. Bruises covered her arm and legs as well, but the worst were around her throat—huge, mottled, purple marks, with torn skin. Big hands had strangled her.

Flies crawled on her face.

The girl held a long, sharpened stick in her hand, like a spear.

Mary recognized her—her name was Callista, and her parents were Basil and Medea.

Mary had to tell Bill Sorenson.

No, he was dead.

She slipped into her car. She'd tell Ammon Kimball. That big red house had to have a telephone. And if not, there was Gus Dollar's store down the canyon.

But leaving the body felt like sacrilege. Mary got out, took a tarp from her trunk, and covered Callista Markopoulos's small body. The flies rose up as she whispered Hail Mary after Hail Mary.

Chapter Twenty-Seven

HIRAM WOKE UP WITH HIS FOREHEAD PRESSED INTO THE STEERING wheel of the Double-A. When he raised his face to peek above the dashboard, a bright yellow sun low on the horizon burned his eyes.

His ears buzzed, and it wasn't from flies.

He was almost certain.

He'd rammed the Double-A into a stand of junipers. Looking around, he saw now that he'd made it a hundred yards from the road.

How long had he been passed out?

He was lucky, but he didn't *feel* lucky. A fainting spell gave him no rest, so he'd missed two nights of sleep. He was afraid to stay where he was, but he was also afraid to be on the roads—there were few enough of them, it would be an easy matter to block off, say, one road up to Utah Valley and one to Price, and he'd be trapped.

Even with the small number of officers Helper had.

If he were trying to escape, he'd do it by mule.

He shook his head, trying to clear fog from his brain, and partially succeeded.

He didn't want to escape. He wanted to find Michael.

Michael was alive. He was a smart boy, and no miners would have caught him.

But the thing in the caves might have Michael. Or Gus Dollar might have taken Hiram's son, to punish Hiram for escaping

217

from his second curse stopping Hiram's truck and to continue to raise the stakes in their grindingly slow duel. Or the Helper police might have taken Michael, to warn Hiram away from interfering in their persecution of the union organizer, Mary McGill, or as a suspect in the Sorensons' death. Or Rettig or his thugs…

Hiram jerked himself awake—the sun had moved higher in the sky. He'd slept a bit, though he still felt exhausted. He willed his limbs to begin taking action.

He took his second unpeeled witch hazel rod from his tool chest; he could find Michael with it. He peeled off the rind, taking deep breaths to keep himself awake, then cut the three crosses.

And for a name? After consideration, he slowly carved MICHAEL YAZZIE WOOLLEY on the rod. Because there was room, he also carved both Michael's parents' names: YAS YAZZIE and BETTY YAZZIE. Then, after a long hesitation during which he almost nodded off, he added his own name: HIRAM WOOLLEY, and his wife's, ELMINA WOOLLEY.

He sang as he worked, the same song over and over, to a Grandma Hettie tune. Psalm 130 didn't feel quite right, or maybe Hiram didn't like using it to look for Michael because only a few short hours earlier, he had used it to go looking for Teancum Kimball, and had found the man a corpse.

He chose Psalm 67 instead, just the first two verses, and focused the prayerful desires of his heart on finding his son: "God be merciful unto us, and bless us; and cause his face to shine upon us; Selah. That thy way may be known upon earth, thy saving health among all nations."

He crawled slowly over the driver's seat of the Double-A. His hair and Michael's were very different, and no one other than the two of them had driven the truck. No, wait, there had been Bert from Conoco. Hiram closed his eyes, trying to picture the color of Bert's hair, and had to snatch himself back from the brink of sleep again.

Red hair. Bert was a carrot top.

Hiram found several long, thick, black hairs on the back of the truck's driver's seat. They had to belong to Michael. He made a very thin cut into the soft wood of the hazel rod, inserted the hairs, and then let the still-green witch hazel spring back into place to pin the hairs. For good measure, he tied them in a knot.

This would not be efficient; he couldn't operate the Mosaical

Rod while driving. He fed several test questions to the rod, getting satisfactory results, and then steeled his stomach.

"Is my son Michael alive?"

He nearly wept when the rod dipped, indicating *yes*.

It remained only to find him. Find him, and, if necessary rescue him.

He swung the rod, looking for Michael, and got a tug informing him he needed to drive farther up Spring Canyon.

He drove half a mile, hid the truck, tried again, and got the same result.

He was coming close to Gus Dollar's store. Hunkering low over the wheel—to be invisible? for cover, in case Gus shot at him?—he drove *past* the store and around the corner. When he could park the truck discreetly, he tried the rod again—and it told him to go back down the canyon.

Gus Dollar. It had to be.

Gus had his son.

He fumbled in his tool chest for his dried dog tongue and slipped it into his boot. He'd walk in the front door and didn't care if the dogs barked, but the tongue should keep them from biting him, too.

His clasp knife was a stupid weapon, but it had a locking blade, and if need be, he could cut with it.

He shook himself. No, that was a terrible idea. He'd confront Gus and demand the storekeeper release his son.

But, in the case of last resort, and truly dire need...it was strong counter magic to make a witch bleed. If he needed to overcome some last spell of Gus's, he didn't have to kill Gus, he only had to bleed him.

The clasp knife might be enough.

For good measure, he took the bronze Oremus lamen that had hung behind the mirror in their hotel room, tucking it into the inside pocket of his coat.

Mosaical Rod in hand, Hiram marched up onto Gus's porch and threw the door open.

The Rottweilers scattered.

The dowsing rod in his hand burst into flame. Dropping it to the floor of the shop, Hiram stared at the branch: the carved letters and symbols stood out briefly in blazing letters, and then they were gone as the entire hazel rod was engulfed in fire. Within seconds, the wood disappeared, leaving a trail of ash.

The floor itself remained unmarked.

Clutching his burned hand, Hiram stared into the shop. There was no sign of Gus Dollar. Behind the counter, on two high chairs, sat the twins, Greta and Dietrich. They weren't the sliding drops of mercury they'd been before. Now the pair sat still and smiled at Hiram, perfect, flawless smiles, like ten-dollar dolls from the Sears, Roebuck catalog.

Hiram's eyes shot to the lead signs of Samael, or Mahoun, in the front windows. Not only had they been restored, they had been painted over in a garish red paint. Dollar's now flaunted its wards, or association, or whatever it was, to the world.

Only it was a world no longer prepared to see the message that was being clearly published.

"Opa Gus told us you would be back," the children said together.

Hiram shook his head. He'd have sworn they'd just spoken together, mouths perfectly synchronized.

"You're the sieve and shears man," they added. They raised their hands, and their fingers glistened, as if slick with oil. Their nails and fingertips were blackened. Dipped in soot?

The hair on the back of Hiram's neck stood up. The children had been normal, happy, healthy-looking children the two times he'd seen them before. What had happened? What had Gus done? "Where's your Opa Gus?"

"Not here. No one's here but us."

Hiram could take Gus's grandchildren. That would be fair, and he could trade them to Gus to get his son back.

"Your mother?" Hiram asked.

"No one but us, sieve and shears man."

But that would be kidnapping.

But Gus had done it first. As Gus had pushed Hiram to perform counter magic by charming him first, and as Gus had forced Hiram's hand, making him commit burglary.

And something seemed wrong with these children. Maybe the old man had ensorcelled them somehow. He'd be rescuing them from Gus.

Hiram shook his head. He wasn't thinking clearly; that might be fatigue and the lingering effect of his recent spell, but it could also be Gus. Gus had influenced Hiram before, with his Jupiter ring and his other charms.

Did Gus *want* Hiram to kidnap his grandchildren?

Was Gus *trying* to get Hiram into trouble?

"Michael!" Hiram yelled. There was no answer.

He wheeled around the ground floor, crying out. "Michael!"

Silence, but for the low whimpering of dogs.

He climbed the stairs. If Gus simply shot Hiram now, he'd tell the Helper police—or the Carbon County Sheriff—that he'd interrupted a burglary in process, by a man who'd already burgled him once, and that would likely be the end of the investigation. Gus would be within his rights.

For that matter, the police might think Gus had shot the Sorensons' murderer.

"Michael! Michael?"

The second story was empty.

He turned to go downstairs and the twins stood at the top of the stairs, smiling at him.

"We told you," they said.

Hiram shivered. He wanted to lock the children in one of the upstairs rooms so they'd stop following him, but he didn't dare. Instead, he rattled downstairs as quickly as he could and entered the pantry.

The Rottweilers lay pressed to the floor on the trapdoor. Hiram grabbed each by its collar and walked back to the storeroom. The front door was open, as he'd left it, and he heaved both beasts out onto the porch, shutting the door behind them.

The twins stood watching him when he turned around.

"You shouldn't hurt the dogs," they warned him.

"The dogs are fine," he said. "Have you seen my son Michael? I'm just looking for my son."

"We haven't seen any boys here today." They continued to speak in perfect timing together. Unless Hiram was just imagining it. His head hurt. "Are you going to look in Opa Gus's secret room now?"

"What do you know about your Opa Gus's room?"

"What do *you* know about it, sieve and shears man?"

Hiram wished he'd locked them upstairs. But the Mosaical Rod had shown Michael to be here at Dollar's.

Hadn't it?

Or had Gus tricked the rod?

Or had Hiram, in his fatigue and hunger, made a mistake?

He dug into his pocket and found two quarters and a dime,

setting them on the counter. "I need ten Cokes. Will you count out ten Cokes from the ice box for me? And two Snickers bars."

They stared at him, but then turned to the red icebox in the corner and began to fetch his Cokes.

Hiram rushed to the pantry. Yanking up the trapdoor, he looked down into darkness. He pulled his flashlight from a pocket and shone it down, illuminating the ladder rungs and the stone wall of the descending shaft.

"Michael?"

Nothing. But his son could be tied up and gagged, or unconscious.

Or dead.

Or Gus Dollar could be waiting down there with a loaded shotgun.

Gritting his teeth, Hiram climbed down. Sweat trickled between his shoulder blades, and he felt a breeze blowing on the back of his neck. Fear made him drop the last few feet, landing unsteadily on his Harvesters. He whipped around, half-expecting to be blasted into oblivion.

The room was empty.

The crack in the corner of the room was gone.

Hiram's heart pounded.

He paced around the room to be sure, angry and mournful that his rod had been destroyed. He pushed at the stone in the corner where there had been a crack—under the glare of his flashlight, the wall there looked like a different color, and the mortar seemed fresh. He shone his light closer; the mortar was wet and had a reddish hue to it.

This, perversely, was reassuring. He wasn't insane, he wasn't imagining that there had once been a crack, and now it was gone.

There had been an opening, and Gus had bricked it shut.

He pounded on the stone. "Michael!"

No answer.

He went back to the ladder and looked up. The faces of the twins looked down.

Greta held an iron in her hand. In both hands, Dietrich held a heavy black skillet.

Hiram pressed his chi-rho amulet to his chest with his left hand and sprang up the ladder as quickly as he could with one hand. As he climbed, he shifted himself left and right.

The iron struck him on the left shoulder. Hiram grunted in pain, but he held tight to the rung, and pushed himself higher.

"Did that hurt, sieve and shears man?"

The pan struck him on his back. His feet lost his grip and he hung briefly over the shaft, scrabbling to get a grip. Then he dragged himself up and into the pantry.

The children stared at him with cold eyes.

Damn Gus Dollar.

The Cokes and candy bars stood on the counter. Hiram ignored them for the moment and rushed outside. He charged up to the boulders and scree behind the store, looking for the sheet of stone that screened the outside entrance into the caves that connected into Gus Dollar's workroom.

And most likely into the mine as well.

He found the stone and climbed around it, grabbing his flashlight and preparing to deal with the spell he expected to find on the cave mouth—but this opening, too, was bricked up. Bricked up, and dirt and pebbles had been piled over it to conceal it.

"Michael!" He pounded on the stone.

Nothing.

He staggered back to the store and saw a second automobile parked in front, a red and white Ford Model A. On the porch stood Mary McGill. She wore a different dress under a stylish jacket, this one a beige color accented with a maroon scarf. A brown overcoat hung from her shoulders. She stared at him with a pale face and haunted eyes.

"You don't look well, Hiram Woolley."

"Sorry to say, Miss McGill, but you don't, either."

The woman clenched her jaws and nodded. That was strange. Had she heard about Sorenson's death? Did she blame Hiram? "I bet you're thirsty."

She raised her eyebrows at him. "Pardon me?"

"You stopped here because you were starting to feel warm and thirsty, and thought you might get a drink."

"Well, I *am* thirsty. But I also came here to try to use the phone."

"I just bought ten Cokes," Hiram said. "I'll give you one."

"I'll need something far stronger than that," Mary whispered. "Someone has murdered a child up at the mine."

Chapter Twenty-Eight

HIRAM FOUGHT SORROW AND ANGER AS HE CARRIED THE TEN Cokes in an apple crate he'd taken from behind Gus's counter toward Mary's car. He'd already wolfed down the Snickers bars, which took the edge off his hunger but also made him feel nauseated. Looking over his shoulder, he saw the two tow-headed twins, staring at him from the front window of the shop. They pressed their oily, soot-marked fingers to the window and smiled dreadfully.

Bewitched by Gus?

Or by the thing in the caves? Gus was evil, but Hiram's real enemy was the fly demon, Mahoun-Samael. He'd have bet his farm that the demon was the same entity he'd seen in the peep-stone.

It was the demon that was manipulating the Kimballs.

Had it killed the Greek girl?

Fear spiked Hiram's heart. If the fly demon had killed Callista, had it found Michael as well? Had it killed his son or dragged him into the pit? He recalled his dreams...searching for Michael, the empty roads, the voice booming out of a bottomless pit.

The fear threatened to kill him. His only sanctuary was prayer. *Lord Divine, if it be thy will, bring my son to me. And please, let it be thy will. Amen.*

"Sheriff's deputies are coming up to retrieve Callista's body and ask questions." Mary opened the car door.

"Callista?" Hiram felt his heart stop.

"The murdered girl is named Callista Markopoulos. You shouldn't be anywhere around here. Word has it, you're a suspect for Sorenson's murder."

Hiram set the crate into the back seat. He looked; the twins were no longer in the store window. His stomach ached. "Do you want to ask whether I'm guilty?"

Mary laughed, and it was a bitter sound. "Hiram Woolley, I *know* you're innocent. But it sounds like you should be taking your ring back. You might just need it." She handed him the copper ring of escape.

He slipped it onto his finger; for him, it was a pinky ring.

"Let's talk in my car. It's cold out here." Mary got behind the wheel.

Hiram sat in the passenger's seat. He pulled his eyelids down with his fingertips. "I met the girl's family." He didn't mention his run-in with Basil on the road nor how the man got his leg broken.

He'd wounded Medea's husband, and now her daughter... was it Hiram's fault?

Mary sat behind the wheel. "I told Ammon Kimball," she said. "He called the police. He didn't offer to help the family, though."

"He won't." Hiram had to find Michael.

They lapsed into silence.

Finally Mary broke it. "Thank you, Mr. Woolley. Both the ring and sage leaf seemed to work. Here I am, free."

Hiram was glad for the change of subject. "Five-Cent Jimmy showed up?"

"He did," Mary replied, "and he worked his own special magic. When Jimmy tipped his hat on the way out the door, I'd swear Asael Fox wet his trousers."

"Jimmy sounds like a good friend to have." Hiram was glad Mary had escaped, but he had a hard time focusing on her freedom.

"Well," Mary said, "if you get yourself tossed into the can, be sure to wear that ring. It may summon him. And do you know who came to the hearing, bold as daylight, and sat in the back grinning?"

Hiram tried to organize his reeling thoughts. "Ammon Kimball? Gus Dollar?"

Mary McGill snorted, blowing air. "The D and RGW Director of Carbon County Operations. The railroad man, Rettig. Filthy thug didn't even try to hide his involvement."

"You think..." Hiram concentrated. "You think Fox put you in jail because Rettig told him to."

"Yes, I do. I think he's making some kind of play for the mine, and I complicated things, so he wanted me out of the way."

Hiram tried to follow the logic all the way through. "He could still buy the mine if the men working there were organized."

"Yes, but it'd be worth less, because he'd be paying the men more."

Hiram thought about the three railroad thugs and Dimitrios. Rettig wanted *him* out of the way, too. "I'm sorry."

"For what? You aren't Naaman Rettig. Oh, but I'll make that little bastard sorry, I will. Once I'm done with the mine, I'll start riding the D and RGW back and forth from Denver to Salt Lake, and I'll organize every last porter, and get them to ask for better wages, and the firing of Naaman Rettig."

Hiram managed to crack a smile. "I bet you will, too."

"And I bet you'll help Medea Markopoulos."

Hiram nodded. "I will. But I need help, myself." Hiram wanted to explain the situation calmly, but it was complicated, and suddenly he found himself babbling. "My son is missing. He was at Sorenson's house when Sorenson got killed, and I haven't been able to find him."

Mary frowned, sighed, and let her sarcasm slip. "What, you didn't try a charm?" Then she saw the expression on Hiram's face. "Ah, I'm sorry. You *did* try a charm."

"Other powers interfered," Hiram said. "I have enemies."

Mary glanced over and tried to find a smile. "I'm sorry for teasing. You must be worried sick. I want to vomit, myself. I feel so powerless. Tell me how I can help."

"A ride?"

"I'll be your chauffeur, Mr. Woolley. Let's go find your son."

Hiram's heart was heavy. "This will sound odd, but...can I bring along my tool chest?"

He hid the Double-A by driving it into a depression screened by junipers and a jagged pile of red rock. Mary followed and waited on the main road as Hiram shifted his toolbox into the trunk of her car. Moving the toolbox, he thought about the lead lamen, with its reference to Jericho. Surely, Gus intended to use it to collapse the mine.

To defeat the demon.

But that didn't mean that Gus was on Hiram's side.

Hiram hurt, the ache of sleeplessness as well as the pains he'd acquired being bruised in the cave, waylaid by bandits, and attacked with ironmongery. At Mary's suggestion, he hunkered down on the floor of the car's back seat, ready to cover himself with a ratty wool driving blanket in case they passed anyone.

A wave of fatigue washed over him so hard, he almost fell asleep immediately. "Guess I better drink a Coke. Or two."

"I thought you people weren't supposed to drink coffee and Coca-Cola," Mary said.

"Well," Hiram said, "there's more gray area than that."

He downed one bottle of cola immediately, setting the empty bottle neatly on the back seat, then held the second to nurse it.

"What's your son's name?" Mary McGill asked over the front seat, once she had started the Model A.

"Michael."

"He's the young Indian man I saw up at the mine, right?"

"Practically a man."

"What led you to adopt an Indian?"

Again, they were talking about nothing. It felt like a layer of icy normality lying over the top of a cold, wet abyss of horror. "His father and I were in the Great War. Yas was my best friend over there. He survived gas, and German bullets, and French girls, and army food. He was the toughest man I ever knew. He was a dreamer, he was very sensitive to things of the spirit. He talked about meaning and the gods and truth with an earnestness you never see, these days. And then he got killed by..."

By darkness itself, he didn't say. By fools worshipping dark old gods, trying to salvage bloody national lines and pride.

"Anyway," he continued, "his wife died in the Influenza Epidemic. It hit Indians pretty hard, I guess. But their baby son survived. It took a lot of talking to the tribal elders, but they finally let me adopt him."

"You're a good man, Hiram Woolley."

"I aim to stand before the judgment bar and say I tried, with a clean conscience. I guess I can't do much more than that."

"Where would Michael go?"

...*if he's still alive.* She didn't say them, but Hiram felt the words hanging in the air.

He considered. He'd driven up and down Spring Canyon

already. He'd tried a charm, and it seemed to have led him into a trap. Anyway, Michael hadn't been where the Mosaical Rod had indicated. Hiram doubted Michael would stick around the mine, or Kimball Canyon at all. With Sorenson dead, there were no friendly faces there. So he'd head back to town. Maybe to Buford's. The boarding house was so warm and comfortable that Hiram regretted he hadn't taken at least a little nap in that large bed.

Hiram found himself drifting to sleep, Coke notwithstanding.

"Hiram?" she tried again.

"Town, I guess," he said. "Just hopefully not one of the brothels. *Ooh-la-la*."

"Town it is."

Hiram watched the canyon walls spin slowly around the windows above him as Mary McGill turned the Model A about. He found the motion of the car hypnotic, so he grabbed another pair of Cokes.

He needed to find Michael, but there were other things he had to do, as well. If Michael wasn't dead or held prisoner by Gus Dollar—Hiram shuddered at both possibilities—then he was probably fine. He was smarter than Hiram, and he should be able to handle himself.

"Why do you think you're getting blamed for Bill Sorenson's murder?" Mary asked.

"I have a revolver. It belonged to Michael's father, Yas. Well, really, it belonged to an officer, but that fellow died and Yas used his gun to save the platoon and then everyone figured the gun should belong to Yas. He gave it to me when he died." Hiram was babbling again; he tried to focus. "Last night, I gave Sorenson my weapon so he could protect Michael with it. And then Sorenson and his wife were both murdered."

"With your gun."

"I think so. Anyway, my gun was there, and some of the miners blamed me. Or my son."

"Callista wasn't shot. She was strangled." Mary's voice became subdued. "Her body was crawling with flies."

Hiram nearly vomited.

Mary was silent—expecting a response? "I don't have any good answers."

"Things aren't going to improve at the mine," Mary said. "Dead kids have a way of making even sane people crazy."

The mine. The Kimballs. Ammon, Samuel, Eliza. If he wasn't at Buford's, might Michael have gone to Eliza? Michael knew where her hotel room was. Other than Eliza and Naaman Rettig, Michael didn't know anyone in Helper.

Eliza. The seer stone in Hiram's pocket suddenly felt heavy, and seemed to burn him through several layers of fabric. Eliza needed to be warned. She'd need to be persuaded, too, because when he told her what he knew, she would scoff.

She might not scoff at the machinations of Naaman Rettig, though.

"We need to go see Eliza Kimball," he said. "It's a long shot, but Michael might have gone to her."

"The sister. Where is she staying?"

"At the Hotel Utah. We'll want to be careful, because Naaman Rettig is staying in the same hotel."

"I know the place. It has a back stair. In a manner of speaking."

Hiram was drifting into a warm sea of mindless sleep when the car jolted to a halt, shaking him awake.

"Lie down, cover up, and hold still," Mary hissed.

He took the last sip of Coke and obeyed. He huddled under a blanket that smelled like engine oil and sweat and it cut off Hiram's air, but he lay still as a lump of coal in the back seat and waited.

A brief silence ensued.

"Hello, Miss McGill."

The voice belonged to G. Washington Dixon. Shanks.

"What's the problem, officer? I was going to drive up to mine, after hearing about the Sorensons, but then had second thoughts." Mary kept her voice even and cool.

"So you know about the murders," Shanks continued. "But we also found a girl. Not sure who done it yet, but it looks like it might be that feller who came and saw you twice in the hoosegow. Woolley."

"I don't believe that," Mary said.

"Nor do I," Shanks exhaled loudly. "Chief Fox and the railroad do, though."

The railroad? Rettig.

Mary tsked. "Surely, after getting chastised by the judge last night for exceeding his jurisdiction, Chief Fox doesn't want to go arresting anyone up Spring Canyon this morning?"

"Nope," Shanks said. "We're just helping out the Carbon County Sheriff today."

"Any other suspects?" Mary asked.

"Not one," Shanks said. "The fellow's gun is all we have, so even if he didn't do the killing, we need to talk to him. The girl...wasn't shot. I won't say more. Only that you should stay away for a bit, ma'am."

"So I should restrict my organizing activities to the other mines?"

"All these canyons are close enough, I figure you should probably stay in town for a few days. Get a hotel room, try the food at the Chop Suey. We got three movie theaters in Helper, you know, and a bowling alley."

"You're practically Coney Island. Well, as you can see, Sergeant Dixon, I'm headed down the canyon. As it happens, I have business in town, for today at least. I can't guarantee I'll stay down there. The spirit breatheth where he will, you know."

Hiram heard a metallic thumping that suggested that Shanks was pounding on the roof of the Model A. "Alright then, you drive safe."

Hiram waited until the car was in gear and traveling down the road again before he pulled the blanket away from his face and spoke. "I think you quoted John chapter three," he said.

"Ah, well, you wouldn't quite recognize the words, would you? You're stuck in your silly little King James translation, while I learned from the lovely, lilting phrases of the Douai. Deeply poetic, not afraid of the Virgin Mary like your English protestants were, and of course, rigorously checked against the Vulgate."

"I don't really know what you're talking about," Hiram admitted. "But the version I know says the wind bloweth where it listeth."

Here they were, talking about nothing again. But it felt like a breath of fresh air in the cloud of death that enveloped them.

"What's *listeth?*" she asked.

"It means *wants.* Old-fashioned. So I guess that means the same as your version. But I'm not sure about the wind and the spirit."

"Well, you know," Mary McGill said with a sigh. "Nuns."

Chapter Twenty-Nine

HIRAM KEPT LOW IN THE BACK SEAT AS THEY DROVE THROUGH town and eased down an alley toward the Price River.

His thoughts danced erratically. The demon had killed twice—three victims in total. The mine still had to be opened, but the urgency of Kimball's starving families faded by comparison with the murders. For that matter, Hiram was convinced the demon beneath the mine was the same entity as the luminous person he'd seen in the seer stone, which likely meant that the demon had been manipulating the Kimballs all along.

Rettig and his thugs complicated the situation.

Gus's presence complicated everything even more. Did he truly want to defeat Samael? But if that was *all* he wanted, why not recruit Hiram as an ally, rather than manipulate and sabotage him? And Michael seemed to have disappeared near Dollar's store.

And there remained the divination by sieve and shears, and what it had told Hiram—that he needed all three Kimballs' hearts to soften.

Mary stopped behind the Hotel Utah, pointing out a fire escape up the back. If Michael wasn't there or at Buford's, Hiram didn't know where else to turn. He had failed to find Michael, even with the Mosaical Rod, and having used up his supply of witch hazel, he couldn't try again. He could drive back to the farm and peel more branches off the bush he carefully cultivated at the end of the porch, but that would be a whole day lost.

He could turn himself in, if only to get the police's help to find his son, but Shanks had confirmed that Chief Fox was in the pocket of Naaman Rettig. He feared what the Helper City Police might do if they got their hands on either Michael or him.

Could he turn himself into the Carbon County Sheriff instead, who now seemed to be involved? But if Chief Fox was working with the sheriff, what did the sheriff think of Hiram?

He turned to Mary. "While I go visit Eliza, could you swing by Buford's Boarding House and see if Michael is there? Also, I'm expecting a telegram."

"And you think the police might be watching the boarding house for you."

"I do." He handed her the key. "It's the second floor, the room facing Main Street. Of course, they might be watching for you, too."

"Don't worry," Mary said. "If Chief Fox sees me, he'll think of Five-Cent Jimmy and run. Hopefully."

Hiram let out a shaky breath. "Let's meet back here."

Mary mock-saluted. "Sir, yes, sir. Just be careful. It would be a shame for you to end up in the Helper jail when I have only recently been released."

Hiram tried to put a brave face on his exhaustion. "Don't worry. I know the right names of the twelve apostles."

He stopped at the trunk to retrieve the wax disk from his toolbox, then jumped and pulled the swinging ladder down. He climbed up the fire escape quickly.

On the second floor, he wasn't taking any chances. He pronounced the single line of his charm, blew three times across the disk of wax into the window latch, and then raised the window.

The hotel's second-story hallway was empty. Hiram walked down to Eliza's door. Knocking before sending up from the lobby might upset her, but Hiram couldn't afford the niceties. He rapped on the door three times.

From inside he heard, "Who's there? What is this?"

He knocked again, not wanting to say his own name too loud.

He remembered his hat and removed it. He was smoothing his hair down when the door opened.

He might have caught Eliza Kimball by surprise, but she was fully dressed in her mortician's black, and her hair was pinned to her scalp.

"I'd appreciate it if you let me in," he said. "I imagine it's not strictly Emily Post, but I'm in need."

She let the door swing open and Hiram slipped inside. He turned and found Eliza staring him square in the eye, an astonished expression on her face. "And now you can explain yourself, Mr. Woolley."

Michael wasn't there.

Hiram gripped his hat in both hands. "My son is missing. Has he contacted you in any way?"

"No." Eliza shrugged. "Has he been missing long?"

Hiram shook his head. He swallowed hard, his mouth dry. "Also, ma'am, there's something else. Since I'm here, I want to talk about your family situation. About the mine. You may struggle to believe it, but there is an evil at work, here."

Her eyes iced over. "By *evil*, do you mean greed and foolishness? Because if you mean the *occult*, Mr. Woolley, the conversation ends here."

Hiram reached into his pocket and eased the seer stone out of his bandana—he preferred not to show Eliza the bloodstains—and took it out of his pocket. "You remember that I mentioned a stone, the last time I was here? This stone belonged to your father, and he mailed it to Samuel. Samuel put it back on the mantel for Ammon to use."

Her eyes dropped. "It's a simple rock. How does one *use* a rock?"

"Your father looked into it, and he saw something. Look, I know you're not a believer, but you were raised by believers. You know what this is."

The line of Eliza's jaw relented, slightly. "I know what it is."

"I think Samuel looked and saw something. Ammon too. You might be the only living member of your family who hasn't taken a turn."

"If you're suggesting I should look into that stone, stop right now." Eliza Kimball's upper lip curled into a sneer.

"I'm a believer, Miss Kimball. And I've looked into the stone, and I've seen what's in there. It isn't pretty. It appears to be an angel of light, but..."

"Stop."

Hiram took a deep breath. "Yes, ma'am. But I want you to remember the things your father believed, and the kinds of men your brothers are, and I want you to believe that your brothers are both . . . well, if you can't believe they're controlled by an inhuman evil that appears as an angel, can you believe that they're mad? Can you believe that an old family madness has taken your brothers, Eliza? Can you believe that the best thing for you right now is to help me make peace between you and your brothers?"

And soften all their hearts.

It was a long speech for Hiram, and he'd forgotten to call Eliza by her surname.

"Give me the stone."

Hiram felt a chill run up his back. "I don't want you to look."

"I'm not going to. You want my help? I'm going to help you, by throwing the stone into the river. It will end the madness."

Until someone else found the stone. "No . . ."

"That's my family's property," Eliza Kimball said curtly. "You can give it to me, or I can call the police. There's a policeman standing in the lobby, within earshot." She glared at him. "Or are you willing to overpower me and rob my family?"

Hiram felt numb. He wanted to keep the stone, because it was dangerous. He had felt the shining person reaching into his own heart, and only his chi-rho amulet had saved him. He considered jumping out the window and racing down the fire escape, but then the police would be chasing him for two reasons.

And besides, if stealing from Gus Dollar had made Hiram's charms misfire, what would stealing from Eliza Kimball do?

Perhaps, after all, the seer stone would be safest with Eliza. Her secular education and her pride might mean that the stone went straight into a shoebox and stayed there.

Or straight into the Price River.

Hiram took a deep breath and handed over the peep-stone.

"And now you may leave," Eliza said.

Mary McGill walked into the open back door of the boarding house, holding her dress up to keep it from the mud, hands trembling.

Hands trembling, and mind full of the image of two dead feet, poking out from under a juniper.

And here she was, aiding a fugitive and trying to help him find his missing son. Yet in her heart of hearts, she knew Hiram Woolley was innocent, and Mary McGill had never run from trouble.

Buford's Boarding House was warm and Mary smelled tea and toasted bread in the parlor. A policeman with big knuckles and a heavy forehead stood in the ground floor hallway, looking at Mary. After a moment, his eyes widened and he turned his head away.

She managed not to laugh.

The upstairs hallway was unoccupied. Mary let herself into Hiram's room. She moved carefully and she stayed away from the windows. The room had simple furnishings and no sign of Hiram's son.

But there were two envelopes lying on the hardwood floor, just inside the door. Curiosity about the farmer's affairs nearly got the better of Mary's manners, but she managed not to look inside the envelopes. She did see a note written in a neat penciled hand on the outside of one envelope.

> Mr. Woolley,
> A boy came twice from the Western Union with messages for you. I tipped him three cents each time. I expect to be repaid.
>
> Sincerely,
> Mrs. Buford

Mary took the envelopes, locked the door, and calmly walked out of the boarding house, nodding at the policeman on the way.

She sat in the car for fifteen minutes, watching a train slowly pull out of the station and roll up toward Price Canyon through the fogged windshield of her Model A. Two Model Ts pulled up just before the train began to move, disgorging men gray with coal dust at the residential end of Helper. Mary watched them jump onto flatcars and climb ladders to get atop boxcars, riding the rails toward Salt Lake and points west.

Miners. Fleeing Helper.

Hiram abruptly opened the car door and sat down. His face was bright red and he brought the smell of the cold river in with him.

"Michael wasn't with Eliza Kimball," he said. "Did you have any luck?"

"No sign of your son. I'm sorry. And you owe Mrs. Buford six cents." Mary handed over the envelopes.

Hiram grabbed a Coke from the back seat and drank half of it in one sustained attack. He plucked out the messages and scanned them. Mary saw the Western Union logo at the top.

Mary wanted to ask about the messages, but she kept quiet. When Hiram felt like sharing, he would. She started the car to get a little heat in and waited.

Hiram's face was gray and he sat still, staring up at the white cliff looming over Helper.

Mary fidgeted. She took a deep breath and straightened her back.

Hiram looked at her, and the bleakness of his expression caught her by surprise. "You should read this. Both of these, I suppose."

He handed her the two telegrams.

Mary read the two messages, each typed in capital letters beneath the heading of a Western Union blank. The first read:

> YOU ARE HEREBY DIRECTED TO COME HOME.
> WEVE HEARD RUMORS OF INAPPROPRIATE BEHAV-
> IOR INCLUDING WITCHCRAFT. WILL MEET YOU
> NEXT SUNDAY AT YOUR CHAPEL TO HEAR YOUR
> REPORT AND DETERMINE WHETHER DISCIPLINE
> IS NEEDED.
> I AM YOUR FRIEND
>
> JOHN

When she looked up from reading, Hiram laughed softly. "It could be worse. They don't direct me to turn myself in to the police."

"They don't know Michael's missing."

Hiram nodded. "The other one is from a librarian friend of mine."

Mary read the second:

> ACCORDING TO THE TALMUD SAMAEL IS CHIEF OF
> ALL THE SATANS. CANT FIND ANYTHING ABOUT A
> MAHOUN. MAYBE MASTER MAHAN FROM BOOK OF
> MOSES. HIRAM WHAT ARE YOU DOING. MAHONRI.

"What is a *mahonri?*" she asked.
Hiram laughed.

"That's my friend's name. Mahonri Young," he said. "He's concerned I'm mixed up in a bad business."

"And are you?"

"Yes," Hiram said. "And maybe worse than I thought. So now might be a good time for you to tell me to get out of your car, and for you to drive away."

"I can't have it on my conscience if you're arrested. Not after you helped spring me. And if I can't fix the entire world, perhaps I can help repair this little corner of it. Now, I don't remember the nuns telling me about a Book of Moses. Does Mahonri mean Exodus?"

Hiram shook his head. "No, it's one of the extra books Mormons use."

"And is Master Mahan one of the Satans in the Book of Moses?"

Hiram was slow to answer. "Master Mahan is a sort of title, I guess. It means someone who has learned to kill for gain. To convert human life into wealth."

Mary snorted. "Well, that's Ammon Kimball. And it's Naaman Rettig. A lot of people turn human life into money."

"I guess so." Hiram smiled. He shot her a glance. "So this talk of devils doesn't trouble you?"

She shrugged. "My catechism was clear, Mr. Woolley. There are evil forces in the world, and it's my duty to fight them. I must admit, I had assumed the conflict would be metaphorical."

"If only it were," he said wearily.

"What do we do now?"

"Set it right." He clenched his jaw. "All of it."

She didn't ask where they would go next. They sat.

Chief of all the Satans?

Mary laughed before she could stop herself. "Well, it seems you have trouble on every front, physical as well as spiritual. Setting it right is going to take some work, but I'm game."

"Good."

Then the man said nothing more for a long, long time.

Chapter Thirty

HIRAM SAT WITH MARY MCGILL IN HER MODEL A BESIDE THE Price River, the engine running. She must have installed a heater; Hiram felt warm air blow on him. Clouds cast shadows across the stretch of dirt behind Helper where they were parked.

"Gus Dollar. I've got to make Gus bleed," Hiram muttered.

Mary blinked. "What? That is a bit shocking. Do you mean the storekeeper?"

"Was I speaking out loud?" Hiram's own voice seemed to echo to him from far away.

"Let's pretend you didn't just say that. How many of those Cokes did you have?"

Hiram rested his face in hands. His whole body hurt. His eyes hurt. He couldn't go to sleep. "Ten, minus however many are left."

"There's *none* left. Sweet Jesus! And how many do you *usually* drink?"

Hiram shook his head, still cupped in his fingers. His hands were shaking like leaves in an August storm. "I don't drink a lot of Coke. Or coffee anymore, either. I just can't fall asleep right now. I've got to find Michael, first of all, and then the rest. The bishopric can't recall me now."

"They don't know you've read the telegram."

Hiram shifted in the passenger seat. The engine heat dried out his nose and the windows were steaming up. "But they don't

241

know. They're wrong, they've been told lies. I'm not down here working as a cunning man."

"What's a cunning man?"

"You would say a wizard, I suppose."

"You're not?"

Hiram shook his head. "I'm just . . . doing the things that I know work. And I . . . sometimes the things that work look like magic. Anyway, I'm not working. I'm serving. Religion, pure and undefiled, that's what James says. Widows and orphans, that's what I'm trying to do. Why would they object to that?"

"I don't really know your people," Mary said. "But it's my sense they don't object to the *what* so much as to the *how*."

"You mean if I just used false arrests and lies and threats and guns to solve my problems, like everybody else does, that would be acceptable?" Hiram heard the bitterness in his own voice.

"I think your Mormon bigwigs just want you to stop what you're doing here and go back. *Report*, it says."

Hiram clenched his hands into fists to stop them from shaking. "I can't, in any case. I can't leave Michael. I won't."

"You're going to get caffeine poisoning and end up with a permanent case of the jitters, if not dead of a heart attack."

"The thing under Gus's shop is behind the murders. Gus . . . is involved somehow." And, despite the fact that Gus Dollar had repeatedly bested Hiram, Hiram liked his chances with Gus better than his chances with the demon.

"Gus is the shopkeeper?" Mary asked.

"Yes."

"Who's in his basement?"

"Not who, but what. And it's not his basement, it's the . . . cave under his basement. The cave under the mine."

"The old German fellow? With the glass eye?" Skepticism tinged her voice.

Hiram remembered that eye rolling toward him across the store counter. In his mind, it seemed to be rolling toward him again now, only it was vast, a huge sphere of glass that had been cut out of the mountain without hands, and was going to crush Hiram Woolley flat.

"Yes, him. I've got to hurt him."

Mary gripped the steering wheel. After a moment, Hiram looked up and found her looking at him with a queer expression.

"Hiram...you didn't kill them, did you? The Sorensons? The girl?"

Hiram pressed his face against the cold glass of the window. "No, Mary, I...I'm exhausted. And I...I don't know what caffeine poisoning is, are you serious about that? But I don't feel good, and my son is missing. And the police want me, and I'm innocent."

"But you want to hurt an old man."

"He's not...he's not just an old man. He's a witch. And he's connected with something that's much older than he is. Something to do with the mine." A fallen angel, as Gus himself had said, living in the Wastes of Dudael? "I think he might be in league with the killer. If not, I think he'll know how to stop whatever killed Callista."

"Something much older?" she asked. "Is that the *what* in the basement?"

Hiram hesitated. "It's a demon."

"You seemed so kind when you visited me in the jail," Mary said slowly.

Hiram drooped.

Mary's voice was breathless. "Now you seem like a madman, or just a hair shy of mad."

"I don't mean I'm going to *kill* Gus," he said. "I don't want to kill him. I don't want to kill anybody. But I need to *wound* him."

"Are you hearing yourself? You *need* to wound an old man?"

"He's a witch. And he's better than me, he's been beating me at every turn." Hiram felt his eyes soften into tears, but Mary's face only looked horrified. "He lured me into his shop, and then he forced me to open up my heart to him. And then I think he tricked me into coming back, and burned my Mosaical Rod, and his grandchildren nearly killed me."

"His grandchildren. With what, guns?"

"An iron. And a skillet."

Mary frowned. "I'm on your side, Hiram, but...what kind of grandchildren are we talking about here?"

Hiram looked down at his knees.

"Jesus, Mary, and Joseph, are you telling me they're *little children*?"

"There's something wrong with them. They seemed normal before, but maybe he's bewitched them, too. I didn't hurt them, even when they tried to kill me. We can go back to the shop, you'll see them, they were healthy as can be when we left, evil, grinning little monsters."

"I'm all for battling Satan and all the demons, but I don't have a fight with Gus Dollar," Mary said. "Or his evil, grinning grandchildren. Is it possible you're so tired and so jooked up on Coca-Cola, you're actually hallucinating?"

Hiram shook his head. "Do you want the mine reopened? Do you want to stop Callista's killer? That thing has murdered three people—do you think it's finished?"

"You think Gus Dollar will help you?"

Hiram considered the question. "No," he said. "Clearly he won't. But Gus knows things he isn't telling me, and I want to know what before I have to face the thing in the pit. And I have to put an end to his hexing me before I can trust anything he says."

Mary folded her arms across her chest and took a deep breath. "Utah," she muttered. "McClatchy warned me."

"Please," Hiram said. "I don't want to kill Gus. Drawing blood from a sorcerer who is bewitching you is a strong counter magic."

"It's a recipe for chaos. If everyone thought every bit of bad luck they had was to be blamed on their ugliest neighbor, and the best way to fix it was to go break that neighbor's nose, society would fall apart in an afternoon."

"True." *That's why we need cunning men*, Hiram thought but didn't say. Cunning folk were needed so that people could resort to other kinds of defensive charms first, when there really was a witch involved.

Mary McGill shook her head. "I can't believe this tale of demons, Hiram. Your sage leaf with apostles on it—maybe that worked, and maybe it didn't. But I can't be party to you getting to the ring with an old man, not when your reason for doing so is monster under the bed."

"Under the general store." Hiram rubbed his eyes. "Will you turn me into the police, then?"

Mary seemed to consider the possibility. "No. Not yet, anyway. But this talk of monsters and madness has given me a different idea."

Hiram was almost afraid to ask. "A different idea?"

"Samuel Kimball," she said. "He's lost his mind. Might he be capable of murder in his state?"

Hiram said nothing.

"Maybe madness runs in the Kimball family," Mary said. "Maybe violence does, too."

"Teancum Kimball had a number of children die young," Hiram said slowly. Was it possible that Mary was right, and that he wasn't thinking clearly?

"I'll see how far back the *Helper Journal's* records go," she continued, "and what I can learn about the clan that may shed light on the murders. If you can calm down, I'm happy to have you come with me. Michael will probably show up on his own, and if the police find him, I'll call Jimmy Nichols."

But no, Hiram had seen the demon. He couldn't go spend time in a newspaper office, trying to find out how Teancum Kimball's children had died.

His limbs sank against the car's seat like lead bars. "I guess our paths part here. Good luck in the records."

"Whatever demons you're wrestling with, Hiram Woolley... real or metaphorical... I hope you conquer them."

"Mary..."

But she had iron in her eyes, so he stepped out of her car, removed his toolbox, and watched her drive away.

Hiram stood in the leafless trees above the river, considering his options.

What was Gus's connection with the fly demon Mahoun? He likely wanted to summon and control it, using the Book of the Spirits Hiram had destroyed. Or he already controlled it, and he wanted to channel its power to summon and control something greater. Hiram had heard tales from Grandma Hettie about witches who had begun by dominating and binding earthly and infernal spirits with the goal of summoning more celestial beings.

The stories ended badly, at least the way Grandma Hettie told them. Summoning was not the business of mortal man; devils were too dangerous and tricky to work with, and angels deserved better treatment.

And why did that Book of the Spirits include a lamen designed to bring down walls?

To stop the demon, Hiram needed to find out the truth. And that meant he needed to get information from Gus Dollar that he was certain wasn't distorted by a charm.

Time to bleed Gus.

✧　　✧　　✧

Hiram rode a stolen donkey up Spring Canyon.

He was wanted for murder, so a little borrowing of a farm animal wouldn't weigh too heavily in the scales. He picked a donkey rather than a horse for its dependable gait, and also because it reminded him of Balaam, in the Book of Numbers.

There was magic in an ass. Hiram could use any angel's warning he might get.

He borrowed the donkey and its saddle from a stable beside an adobe bungalow on the north end of Helper, underneath the stark, staring face of the white cliff. He also took a thick wool serape and a sombrero, to disguise his appearance. The sombrero went on right over his fedora.

From the same stable, he took a bullwhip.

As he crossed the river, a blast of wind scoured out of the canyon. The sky had grown cast-iron dark, and now the cutting front edge of a snowstorm rushed along the Price River and slammed into Helper. The force of the gale very nearly drove Hiram and his donkey off the railroad-tie bridge and into the waters. The serape, over his army coat, kept him comfortable, but his fingers froze in his gloves. He worked his digits to keep the blood flow going and longed for thicker socks.

Once he'd crossed the river, he cut away from the road. The wind was less once he was no longer directly before the canyon, but the snow fell thickly, obscuring the ground.

He used Spring Creek as his guide, and every bit of greenery he could as his shelter. When any cars were visible, he stuck to the trees, waiting for solitude to cross from copse to copse.

The donkey wasn't lazy, and once pointed in a direction tended to keep going in a straight line, so Hiram dozed. Fading in and out, toolbox clutched to his lap, he dreamed. In between dreams, in waking moments, he remembered his earlier dreams, of searching for Michael in vain and of a booming voice in a dark pit.

A gust of freezing wind, throwing snow, blew him awake.

He'd managed to reach Dollar's with the sun low in the sky and a storm coming on fast. Hiram checked the canyon for traffic, found none, and crossed the river. He unsaddled the donkey and picketed it to a fallen log within reach of many tufts of grass, poking up from the snow and standing up bravely to the stiff wind.

"You stay here." He stroked the beast's neck and shoulders. "I'll get you home."

He climbed up a steep bank to the edge of the road, toolbox in one hand and whip in the other. He was about to step into the tall grass on the other side, approaching the store, when he heard the tell-tale rattle of Utah's most common venomous snake. It was an irregular rasp, that started slowly, shook into full rattle, and then trailed off. The snake was barred with interlinked diamond shapes all along its body, and its head was an evil wedge-shape.

In a snowstorm in February? The snake should have been hibernating in a pit somewhere.

But if flies, why not snakes?

The rattler raised its head, twitched its tail. Hiram retreated. Circling counterclockwise to get out of that snake's territory, he walked toward the store again—and again heard a rattle.

He leaped back. Could it have been the same snake?

But no, looking left, he saw the original snake still, lying in a lazy S-shape across the snow.

Taking no shortcuts, this time he walked fifty feet to his right, and again started forward.

A rattler lunged at him from the tall grass. Only its eagerness, or its irritability, made it miss; it attacked from far enough away that Hiram saw it, and was able to shuffle aside. Darting forward, he grabbed the rattlesnake by the tail and flung it far to his right, near the base of the ridge.

Gus Dollar had surrounded his store with rattlesnakes.

Chapter Thirty-One

THE SNAKES WERE IMPOSSIBLE; THEY DEFIED NATURE'S COMMON-sense rhythms.

Gus had summoned them.

No problem. The Bible was full of charms for snakes.

Headlights flashed past Hiram, briefly throwing his shadow up against a wall of yellow rock.

He turned and saw one of the Helper Police Model Bs turning with the winding of the canyon's road. Clouds darkened the sun as it settled down behind the western ridge, but there was still enough light to make out the words HELPER CITY POLICE.

Was there enough light for the driver to have seen *him*? Police Chief Fox might or might not have jurisdiction in Spring Canyon, but he could still slow Hiram down by arresting him. Or beating him up.

The car stopped.

Hiram turned to run, and a fierce rattle reminded him that he still had a snake problem. Only he wanted to address that issue with a clear mind and heart, and not in a fear-pumped panic.

He turned and jogged the other direction, away from the store.

But had they seen him already?

He crouched behind a lone juniper tree, peering through its dark green screen.

Police Chief Asael Fox stood beside the car and scanned the canyon. Hiram's heart, already driving over the speed limit, took a ninety-degree turn and hit the brakes.

He tried to hold perfectly still.

Fox's sergeant, Shanks, was down along the bank of Spring Creek, looking at something.

The donkey. They had found the donkey.

Would Chief Fox and his sergeant now set about looking for the thief?

As if in answer to his unspoken question, Chief Fox walked in Hiram's direction.

Hiram lowered himself onto hands and knees, checked visibility, and then lowered himself again, onto his belly in the snow. Thank goodness for the serape and his gloves. His toes, though, were ice.

"The snakes," he murmured to himself. "Not toward the snakes."

If he crawled on his belly into a rattler, he'd take an immediate bite in a very painful and dangerous location.

"They shall take up serpents," he murmured, "it shall not hurt them." It was the simplest of charms for a snake. He hoped it was enough, and he repeated it several times.

He hoped the snakes were all behind him.

He dragged himself a hundred feet without to rising to check his progress or look at the policemen. Once he was curled behind two dead tree trunks leaning against a crumbling yellow rock, he levered himself up onto his feet and cast an eye in their direction.

The police chief had turned southward, paralleling Hiram's own path. Had he seen Hiram? No, he was looking at something in a tangle of gambol oak. From Hiram's position, it was clearly a faded old canvas tarpaulin, once stretched out by a traveler as a tent. To Chief Fox, it must appear to be a man in a serape.

All Fox had to do was cross Hiram's path, and the man would see his tracks in the snow.

Where was Dixon? Either in the car, or with the donkey, in either case, unseen in a twilight that grew darker by the second.

With the chief coming this direction, Hiram dared head the other way, toward Dollar's.

He started with a phrase he had memorized from Reginald Scot: "I conjure you, O serpents, in this hour, by the five holy wounds of our Lord, that you not remove out of your places, but that you stay."

The five wounds were the wounds of Christ, the manner in which the serpent had wounded the heel of the seed of Eve, bringing to its climax God's great curse on mankind. The threat Hiram was making to the snakes was their heads would be crushed, as God had warned in Genesis. He filled his heart with a prayer and focused his will on directing the snakes to remain calm.

He wished he had an amulet against snakes. He touched the chi-rho and the protective bronze Oremus lamen in his coat pocket, but their power was weaker for being broad.

Also, the old German witch had beat Hiram before.

As he neared the place where he had nearly been bitten before, in his best estimation, he tried another charm. This one came directly from the Bible, and it was the most triumphant serpent-verse he could think of: "And he laid hold on the dragon, that old serpent, which is the Devil, and Satan, and bound him a thousand years."

He shed his gloves and reached inside his shirt to touch the iron of the chi-rho talisman directly, and at the same time grasped the heliotropius with his bare fingers. He had never heard that the heliotropius had power against serpents, but it was supposed to purge poison. And if poison, why not venom? And if it would purge venom, might it also drive away creatures that bore venom?

His fingers were numb from the cold and felt like ice against his chest. Snow was beginning to pile up on the sombrero and the shoulders of the serape.

Hiram heard the rattle of a snake in the darkness, but it was slow.

He repeated the Scot incantation, and the verse from the Book of Revelation, and watched very carefully where he placed his Harvesters. He stepped forward slowly, and again . . . and again.

And there was the first snake. It sat coiled directly ahead of him, looking at him with its treacherous beads for eyes, tongue flicking slowly in and out, rattle shaking from side to side.

But the rattle's movement was slow.

". . . bound him a thousand years," Hiram said, focusing his will and his prayer on this snake in particular. It wasn't easy. His hands shook, his temples were beginning to throb—was that the cost of the intense concentration, or part of the caffeine poisoning Mary had warned him about, or from the cold?

He couldn't feel his feet.

Hiram locked eyes with the snake. If he could walk past this one, he could walk past them all.

And if this one bit him, he would turn and run, and Chief Fox would throw him in jail.

"They shall take up serpents, and it shall not hurt them. They shall pass by serpents, and not be seen."

He eased his left foot forward, placing the Redwing boot firmly on the soil beside the rattlesnake, and very definitely not on top of it.

He eased his weight forward onto his front foot.

He kept his gaze locked on the snake's eyes, weirdly visible to him in the gloom. The snake turned its head as Hiram leaned into his step, and then moved his other foot forward, shifting weight onto that boot...

And then he was past the first rattlesnake.

He took a deep breath. Dollar's was perhaps a hundred yards ahead, barely visible in the growing darkness. How many more snakes could there be in a hundred yards?

Mary McGill wanted to kick herself. Hiram Woolley wanted to assault an old man. The farmer had turned out to be...what? A wizard? A madman? A murderer?

None of those words felt right, though.

Hiram said things that sounded crazy, but he didn't seem insane. He seemed humble, and hard-working, and self-sacrificing.

And scared.

She approached the newspaper office, just off Main Street.

When she explained what she wanted, the old man standing in the door of the nondescript brick building frowned. "We don't generally open our archives to the public."

He was thin and bent as a question mark. A green eyeshade, like a bank teller's, caught light from the street, casting a green splotch on his face. It made him look like a goblin—that and his large nose and pronounced ears.

"I'm not the public." Mary smiled her most ladylike smile, trying not to wince at the knowledge that the old man was looking at her birthmark and feeling revulsion. She fought to keep her hand away from her face.

Hiram Woolley might be nuts, but he'd been a gentleman.

"You aren't Helper City government, and you aren't Carbon County. I know all *those* people. Are you someone down from Salt Lake City, then?"

There was nothing for it. "Mr. ... Bowen, did you say your name was?"

The goblin creaked his assent.

"Mr. Bowen, how do you feel about protecting the rights and improving the quality of the working man, here in Helper?"

"Ah, you're *that* kind of not-the-public. Well, you can't unionize the *Helper Journal*," Bowen said. "There aren't enough of us. Most days, it's just me."

"I mean the miners."

"Oh, yeah, well, those poor devils. Why didn't you say so? Come on in."

Ten minutes later, she was looking at a row of four filing cabinets squatting beneath a precarious stack of manila folders. Bowen was setting text at a Linotype machine in the corner, and on a card table between them stood an open bottle of whiskey and two paper cups.

"Where did all this come from?" she asked.

"Paper itself is only three years old. Most of this comes from the city's archives," Bowen said. "They were going to throw it out, and I asked if I could have it instead. I can use it for background, you see, and research, and archive photographs. In a pinch, I can fill in a few column-inches with a *Remember When?* feature. It's not official records, it's all the other stuff they had sitting around in their shelves. There's maps in there, and photos, and handbills, and paintings, and sketch books, and half a dozen journals. I was looking for a photo the other day and I found a shopping list written on the back of a receipt from Lowenstein Mercantile. There are boxes of letters and postcards and telegrams that couldn't get delivered for one reason or another, so they ended up at the city. Someday, we'll get a proper museum. God help the poor bastard who has to run it."

Mary McGill was an organizer of people, not of objects. Another person, confronted with a heterogeneous stack of materials, would have spent many hours segregating the various papers and volumes and photographs into stacks of related material, for more easy digestion.

Mary just started at the top and dove in.

She found several photographs of Naaman Rettig near the top of the pile, which made them recent. They were thought-provoking, so while Bowen was looking the other way, she pocketed them.

From handwritten journal accounts and letters dated from the nineteenth century, she got a picture of Teancum Kimball's life and dealings. Each of his three surviving children was born to a different mother. References in a picnic flyer seemed to suggest Teancum's marriages were at least partially overlapping, and that no one at the time batted an eye. For a polygamist, that seemed like a small family, and in newsletters and old announcements, she found multiple references to Kimball family stillbirths.

Teancum Kimball's children had mostly died at birth. She couldn't get to anything like a comprehensive count, digging through papers and jotting down notes in a dogeared memorabilia book, but north of twelve deaths, at least.

She found no suggestion, though, that Teancum had killed the children, or that he was insane.

Letters made it clear that, in the decades when Teancum had begun building his family and his ranch, he was loved by many, and hated by many more. He gave employment, and he acted as a local spiritual leader—Mary read more than one letter expressing some parent's gratitude for the healing of their child by Teancum Kimball, with his famous gift of the laying on of hands. She also found handwritten records of prophetic blessings Teancum pronounced on others, promising long life, wisdom, a good marriage. or success in business.

Odd. Not Mary's culture. Still not madness.

On the other hand, she found letters of complaint. Teancum had come into a valley that was already occupied by various kinds of settlers. On the basis that he was acting under the direction of Salt Lake City and its Mormon leadership, Teancum ran many of those others out of town. For immorality, or violating local custom, or criminal allegations—Teancum as local patriarch seemed consistently to end up as prosecutor and judge both, and no accused person came out vindicated. Without access to the land records, Mary couldn't see the details, but it seemed clear that Teancum at least sometimes ended up with their land, all clustered around what would eventually become his mine in Spring Canyon.

Mary generally didn't side with the landed classes in her heart, but in this case, the landed victims were prospectors, small farmers, or local businessmen. For instance, there was a Lohengrim Zoller, who had run a general store in the 1860s and 1870s, right where Teancum had eventually built his house.

And then in 1881, Lohengrim Zoller simply disappeared, and Teancum Kimball scooped up his land and added it to his holdings.

She found an old daguerreotype that seemed to show Teancum Kimball and Lohengrim Zoller together. They stood at the center of a line of women and men at a barn-raising. She knew the men were Kimball and Zoller because the surname of each person in the image was penciled in a neat script below them. Kimball had the fierce, sunken eyes of a vulture and stepped toward the photographer with one foot, as if he were about to attack. Lohengrim had hair that stood straight up, as if a micro-tornado were sucking it toward the heaven at the moment the plate was exposed, and two eyes that didn't point in the same direction.

Two eyes that didn't point in the same direction.

Mary McGill checked the date of the photo on the back. Penciled in ink that had faded to a dull tan color was the year *1881*.

She looked at the image of the two men again.

What had Hiram Woolley said about Gus Dollar having a connection with ancient things?

"No. It couldn't be."

Chapter Thirty-Two

RATTLESNAKES LAY COILED IN THE SNOW EVERY FIFTEEN FEET, all the way to the store. Hiram looked them in the eye, repeated his chants, moved slowly, and was very, very careful not to step on a snake.

They were coiled in even greater number in the flat gravel around Dollar's, and Hiram found himself trying to look two or three snakes in the eye at the same time. His legs shook and sweat poured down between his shoulder blades.

"You there!" Asael Fox called, behind him.

Hiram kept walking.

"In the poncho!"

He was only a few steps from the store. Snakes slithered back and forth atop each other underneath the porch. Snakes sat coiled on the rocking chairs, gently shaking their rattles back and forth and waiting for Hiram.

Bang!

There was no way the police were shooting at him. They didn't know for sure who he was, and even if they did, he was walking slowly up the canyon, not resisting arrest. They must be firing at the sky to get his attention.

Unless Gus had somehow bent their minds.

He turned his shoulders slowly, curious to see what the policemen were doing. The two men were running his way, jogging across the grass-speckled white field. The flurry of falling snow was thick enough that their Model B appeared only as a dim and distant glow behind a crystalline curtain.

Asael Fox was closer, but Shanks had longer legs and was catching up.

"Stop!" Hiram yelled. "Snakes! Stop!"

And then Fox shrieked and staggered backward. He screamed again, and then began firing his pistol over and over.

At the ground.

He'd been bitten. Sergeant Dixon was coming to help him, and the colored man might be the next victim, but Hiram couldn't do anything for them.

He stepped up onto the porch, conscious of the snakes tangled up with each other beneath him. A fat rattler shook its tail languidly in the space immediately in front of the door. Hiram tried to lock eyes with the creature as he slowly shrugged out of the serape. Folding the wool to double thickness and meeting the snake's gaze, he tossed the serape forward, covering the snake.

Hissing angrily, the snake uncoiled to slither out from under the blanket, but it didn't attack Hiram—it just crept a few feet to one side and coiled up again.

The lights were out in the store, but now that he was on the porch, Hiram could tell that the door was cracked slightly open. Also, he could see that a coiled rattler hung on the doorknob.

Gus Dollar was expecting him. Hiram threw aside the sombrero.

With the toe of one Harvester and the end of his toolbox, he pressed at the door, very close to the hinges. It swung inward. The snake hanging from the knob hissed but didn't so much as shake its rattle as Hiram Woolley slunk past it and into Gus Dollar's shop, mayhem on his mind.

He stopped, letting his eyes adjust the darkness. Outside, the shooting had stopped, but he was afraid to devote any more of his attention to Fox and Shanks. Crisp wind blew in through the door, throwing wet flakes in all directions.

Hiram had come to wound Gus Dollar.

He held the bullwhip coiled in his right hand. With a whip, he could strike from fifteen feet away. Also, he could cut a man's skin open with it and make him bleed, with almost no risk of accidentally severing an artery.

He didn't want to kill Gus.

"You've come thinking I will give you back your child." The

voice in the darkness was Gus's, and Hiram realized with a start that the shopkeeper was standing behind his counter.

"That's part of it," Hiram agreed.

"I pissed blood, you bastard," Gus said. "You made a witch bottle."

"You hexed my car. I had no choice." Hiram set his toolbox on the floor.

"So I did." Gus chuckled. "You know, in England they didn't burn witches. They hanged them, like they hanged other criminals. And mostly they didn't punish them for the act of magic, they executed them for the crimes they committed *using* magic. A witch would be hanged for murder or theft, not for witchcraft as such."

"Are you threatening to hang me, Gus?"

"On the contrary, I'm trying to understand your intent. Have you brought that rope to hang *me*, or merely to tie me up and force me to talk?"

"What rope?"

"I saw you in vision before you arrived, farmer. You can conceal nothing from me."

"I don't want to kill you, Gus. I *do* want my son back, among other things."

"I don't have him. But maybe there's something else that you want."

"If you don't have my son," Hiram asked, "why have you summoned a field of snakes?"

"Because I knew you were coming. And I knew you hated me. You burgled my shop. You vandalized my property. You terrified my innocent grandchildren. You are *getting in my way*, Hiram Woolley."

"If I hated you, I'd have done something to those grandkids of yours."

"No, you wouldn't have. Never." Even in the darkness, Hiram could see that Gus was shaking his head. "You're not that kind of man, Hiram. You would rather die than hurt an innocent. I admire that."

Hiram felt sick. Had his scruples doomed Michael? If he had been willing to kidnap Gus's strange grandchildren, would Michael be with him now? "You're going to tell me now that your grandchildren are there behind the counter, all hexed up again, and I shouldn't shoot because I might hit them."

"No. I sent my family away. I only...used my grandchildren in that fashion because I was desperate. I don't want them hurt, just like I don't want your son hurt. Besides..." A note crept into Gus's voice that sounded like delight. "Besides, I *know* that you don't have a gun."

"You killed Sorenson." Hiram's voice shook like his hands.

"No."

"What about Callista Markopoulos? What about Teancum Kimball two years prior?"

"No. I killed none of them. Shall we try the sieve and shears?" Gus sounded much calmer than Hiram felt. "Book and key? Clay balls? I dislike the Kimballs. They drive business away from my store. But I like the miners."

"And you hated Teancum. I don't know quite why, but it has something to do with what happened when the mine ran into the natural caves under the ridge, and they boarded the cave openings up, years ago."

"That was a long time ago, and before my time," Gus said. "I've only been here about fifteen years."

Hiram felt a pinch in his thigh.

He hadn't been thinking about his heliotropius, assuming that every word Gus Dollar said was a lie or at least misdirection, so the stone's warning twinge caught him by surprise. He'd meant to wound Gus first and then ask him questions, but the snakes had distracted him.

But the bloodstone seemed to be working.

And of all the things Gus had said, he'd lied about the caves being discovered before his time.

"Did you hate Teancum Kimball?" Hiram asked.

"No. I barely knew the man. I didn't hate him."

Another pinch.

Hiram shook his head. He was sleep-deprived, anxious, and jittery. Had he misunderstood?

"When did you first move to this area?" he asked Gus.

"Nineteen twenty."

The stone pinched Hiram a third time.

Gus's lies were clear. But that also meant that he'd been telling the truth when he'd said he hadn't killed Sorenson, the little girl, or Teancum.

"Do you know where my son is?"

"I don't. I believe he lives."

The stone didn't pinch him. Hiram asked, "Why did you build your store over the cave opening?"

"What have you got in your pocket?" Gus shot back. "Hyacinthus? Chalcedony?"

"Heliotropius."

"Ah, the rain-bringer. So your beet farm prospers, no doubt. And are you famous?"

"What's your involvement with the mine closure, Gus?"

"You never answered my question, Hiram. Are you going to hang me? This is the west, after all. It seems appropriate. The beams in my shop might not do very well, but you can find tall cottonwoods down by the creek that will serve as fine gallows."

Gus had something bulky in his hands. Was it a rifle? Hiram shifted slowly to his left, trying to get a better look. As Gus turned to follow him, more light struck Gus in the face.

His eye was missing.

Hiram shuddered. He imagined Gus hiding the glass eye under the seat of the Double-A, and then following all Hiram's movements without effort. Hiram didn't know a charm that would do that. Might Gus?

"What do you call that thing?" Hiram asked.

"The angel? Do you not have lists of angels' names to consult? Ah, perhaps not. You did, after all, steal *my* list. And apparently you couldn't read it."

"I returned it. I'm a farmer, not a magician."

"I call it *the Beast*, mostly," Gus said. "Some names are not meant to be spoken too often out loud."

"And if I spoke its name?"

"It might come. Like it came to the camp last night."

"But you're not ready, are you?" Hiram asked. "You're not in league with that thing, you're in thrall to it. And you're trying to break out. That's what the Book of the Spirits was for. You want to summon and bind it."

"I was in thrall once. I'm a stronger magician, now," Gus said. "I know two of the Beast's names, and I have the knowledge to bind it. To bury it deep under the ground."

"Mahoun," Hiram whispered. "Samael. Your Book of the Spirits was meant to crush...the Beast...underground." He thought for a moment. "So that you could take its power forever?"

A cold wind blew in through the open doorway, slamming the door against the wall. Hiram felt a fly creep across his face, a huge insect the size of a marble. He brushed it away with his left hand.

Feeling was returning to his feet.

"Don't be a fool." Gus raised his arms slightly. Hiram saw that the object the shopkeeper held was his ceremonial sword. "Find your son and leave. I don't wish to harm you, and you can do nothing to stop the Beast. You would be mere food to it. Food that it might eat very, very slowly."

"You gave it your eye," Hiram said. "That's why you have a false one. Long ago, when you first encountered it, you made a bargain with that thing and the bargain cost you an eye. What does the demon give you in return?"

Gus shrugged. "What do you bargain for? Wealth, power, the adulation of men, the satisfaction of the lusts of the flesh. But the demon only gives its blessings for thirty years."

"What did old man Teancum give it? When you were younger and first knew him? I know you knew him."

"His children."

Hiram frowned. "Ammon, Samuel, and Eliza? They live."

"The others died the day they were born. These three live on borrowed time, concessions to their mothers. The bill is due now, and the Beast is coming."

The bloodstone lay inert in Hiram's pocket, and his heart was heavy with dread.

"And my appearance worried you," Hiram said, "because you feared that I might make a bargain with the demon, and upset your plans."

Gus said nothing.

Hiram heard a car engine outside. Headlights blazed in through the shop windows, and then the car pulled to a halt. He heard the soft, scaly sound of a hundred snakes sliding out of the way and the crunching of heavy feet in snow.

"Last chance," Hiram said. "I'm not here to hang you, but I *will* hurt you. How do I stop the Beast?"

"You know enough."

Hiram shook out the whip.

Gus frowned. "That's not a rope."

Hiram whipped the shopkeeper in the face.

Gus shouted, incomprehensible words that might be German. He raised his sword defensively.

"Thou shalt not suffer a witch to live!" Hiram whipped him again, *crack*! And again. In the headlights' glow, he saw a curl of blood across Gus's forehead, and something...something else that was off about the shopkeeper's face, though Hiram couldn't quite put his finger on it.

Gus dropped the sword with a loud clatter.

"You should have left the beets and gone home, farmer!"

Gus fumbled under the counter. A gun, no doubt. Thank heaven he was having trouble putting his hands on it in the darkness.

Hiram heard steps on the porch. He grabbed his toolbox and melted back against the wall, trying to make himself invisible in the shadow of three mannequins in Sunday dresses.

The shadow that loomed through the door and across Gus was misshapen. It was tall, but also unnaturally broad in the shoulders, and its head seemed to be a giant, neckless mass. The wood of the porch bowed down and protested against the weight.

Hiram grabbed the chi-rho talisman.

Gus hissed. In his hands, he held a sawed-off, double-barreled shotgun.

"Helper City Police!" Hiram recognized the voice of Sergeant Dixon. His shadow was distorted because he held the unconscious police chief in his arms. "Put down that gun, unless you want to spend the rest of your life in prison!"

Gus eased down the weapon. Shanks hoisted Asael Fox onto the countertop. "Whisky, right now!" he shouted. "The chief here's been bit at least three times, but maybe more. I gotta find all the bites and get the poison out."

Gus grabbed a bottle and opened it. Pressed against the wall in shadow, Hiram heard the sound of cloth being torn, and then the slosh of liquor poured over snakebites and a blade to sterilize them.

He wanted to help, but he couldn't go to jail now. As Shanks bent over his chief's leg and began sucking venom out of the first of the wounds, Hiram slipped out the front door.

At the side of the police Ford, he hesitated. He couldn't do *nothing at all*. Taking the heliotropius from his pocket, he tucked it behind the cushion of the back seat. Surely, that was where Chief Fox would ride down into Helper. The stone purged poison, so it must might against snake venom, too.

Hiram trod carefully, but the snakes were gone. Maybe in biting Chief Fox, they had dissipated their force.

He found the donkey easily; it was braying from discomfort from the snow and pulling at its picket. Hiram realized that he knew a charm to cure the bite of a scorpion, a charm that involved a donkey.

He reflected briefly on the words he knew and how they would have to be adjusted. Leaning close to the ass and cupping his hand over his mouth as if sharing a secret, he whispered into its ear: "God enacted everything, and everything was good, but thou alone, snake, art accursed, thou and all thy brood." He thought of Police Chief Fox, wished recovery for the man, and crossed himself three times. *"Tzing, tzing, tzing."*

What to do now?

He would have to deal with the demon and the mine, but Hiram's first obligation was to his son. Michael was alive, at least as far as Gus knew. If Michael was alive, the boy would probably try to find his way to Helper.

Hiram climbed onto the donkey.

Chapter Thirty-Three

HIRAM CREPT INTO THE BUSHES ALONG THE RIVER BEHIND Buford's Boarding House. Underneath the bare willow branches, the air was cold and wet. The Price River was nearly invisible in the blast of snow crashing out of the canyon; twice, Hiram found rocks and crossed the icy water without getting wet.

Hiram was exhausted and now also saddle-sore. The ride down on the donkey's back had been an endless trudging into a wet, invisible curtain of snow.

The donkey had seemed considerably less bothered than Hiram, and once Hiram returned the sombrero, serape, and beast to the stable, had pushed its nose placidly into its feed trough.

Hiram had put the bullwhip, coiled up, inside his toolbox. The whip had Gus Dollar's blood on it now. Leaving that blood lying around carelessly might give some unknown third party a tool for influencing Gus, and if Hiram kept it, he thought he might find it useful.

Too tired to carry his toolbox anymore, he set it in the snow at his feet. He wasn't sure he could make his way back into the room at the boarding house. He needed to rest for a second.

The trees on the river didn't offer him any cover, but the thick bushes did, and Hiram hunkered down. He felt thwarted, baffled, and sad. He'd rarely been in more trouble in his life, and his failures troubled his heart. Evil was powerful. Had Hiram done a single thing to slow its progress here in Helper?

An unexpected voice made him jump.

"Pap!" Michael was crouched next to the thick stump of a dead cottonwood on a square of snow-covered riverbank. "I figured you'd come back to the boarding house."

Hiram stumbled through the undergrowth and squatted beside Michael. He took off his wet gloves, shoved them into a pocket, and squeezed his son's hand. "Thank God you're okay."

"Your fingers are cold, Pap."

"You should feel my toes."

"Mine, too." Michael's teeth chattered.

They needed to get somewhere warm. Hiram eyed the backs of the houses fronting on Main Street, wishing the snow wasn't blocking so much of his view. Maybe he should take Michael back to the donkey's stable. "What happened?"

Michael nodded. His face was dirty, the filth swirled into curious patterns by the flakes of falling snow. His coat and jeans were caked with mud. Thorny weeds clung to his coat, each sticker a tiny shelf catching snow now, and his hair was plastered to his skull. But Michael's eyes were bright. "I took off after Mr. Sorenson... after Mrs. Sorenson." Michael swallowed hard. "I didn't hurt them. I got knocked out by something. And there were flies."

"Was it..." Hiram thought carefully about his question. How much had Michael seen? "Was the killer a man?"

Michael hesitated. When he spoke, he sounded distant. "I'd have sworn it wasn't, last night. It seemed... like a monster, Pap. But it was dark, wasn't it? And I was tired. I'm not really sure what I saw."

Michael was talking himself out of his own eyewitness, and Hiram was inclined to let him do it. "How did you get down here?" he asked his son.

"I walked," Michael said. "It was easy. Just kept going downhill."

Hiram grunted his appreciation. "Quite a feat, still. You're a regular Flash Gordon."

"Pap, please."

"What, can't I be proud of my son?"

"Yeah, but Buck Rogers is the real thing. Flash Gordon is a total knock-off."

"Buck Rogers, then." Hiram dropped his son's hand. "Maybe it's time to go home, Buck. Admit failure and get out of town. I got a telegram from Brother Wells. Said as much."

Michael looked away into the wall of snow surrounding them and shivered. Then he looked back and met Hiram's eyes. "What's in my boot, Pap? It's what saved me from the demon, wasn't it? That was no man that killed the Sorensons."

Hiram retreated before his son's stare.

"We could get a taxi," Hiram said. "The truck is up in Spring Canyon, and I bet we could get a taxi to drop us off there." The plan might be totally insane, either for the slick state of the road or for the possibility of interception by police, but Hiram had to say something to change the subject. He also wanted to get Michael out of the storm.

"Dad," Michael said.

The word stopped Hiram cold. "Yes?"

Michael latched onto his arm. "No, Pap, we're going to talk, really talk. I spent a whole night and then a whole day sleeping in bushes or wandering through the canyons. I hid in trees, I drank snow. All that time, I thought about every weird thing that's happened over the years, and the strange things I've seen this in the last two days. I knew Hettie was a...well, she liked to say *cunning woman*. I didn't think you were...but you are, aren't you, Pap?"

Hiram felt Michael's hand like a weight on his arm. "You don't believe in magic."

Hiram turned to walk away, but Michael tightened his grip. "I know I've teased you about Grandma Hettie, but last night, when that thing grabbed me, well, that was empirical evidence of something. I don't know what. I bet you do. And I didn't use the word *magic*."

Hiram forced himself to look into his son's face. "Think about whether you really want answers to these questions. I wanted to keep you safe. I've always wanted to keep you safe and do the right thing. And I didn't want you to...I don't want you to..."

"Don't want me to *what?*" Michael's eyes, shadowed pits in the thin light drifting from Main Street, bored into Hiram.

Hiram couldn't reveal his own fears and self-doubt. His heart was in his belly, and he'd broken into a cold sweat. Michael knew.

"You don't want an old-fashioned life, son. You want to go to college and do great things, become a scientist, or a lawyer, in some city somewhere. All I have to offer is farming and old folklore."

Michael shook his head. "You're changing the subject. What don't you want me to do?"

"Leave," Hiram admitted.

Michael was silent.

"You will someday, anyway. I mean, you're old enough, and that's the way of the world. But I don't want you to run away, because you find me...ridiculous...wrong."

Michael took a deep breath. "I was nearly killed last night. The Sorensons *were* killed. The thing that killed them was big, like a bear, and it came in a swarm of insects. I believe it's the same creature that attacked you and me up on the ridge. You fought that monster by lighting a fire and shouting the Bible at it. And you got the truck started. If I'm not mistaken, you did it with a *Coke bottle*. So what killed the Sorensons? What, Pap? You know, don't you?"

Hiram's jaw trembled. "If we leave now, if we don't talk about this, we can go back to our old, normal life. If you push me, if I tell you these things, your life will never be normal again."

Michael grinned. "Normal? We were never normal. Not when Mom and Grandma were alive, and less since they passed. I've got too much melanin for the girls of Lehi and I shoot my mouth off. And you, Pap, you were born at least a century late. What a pair we make."

"Buck Rogers and...who's Buck's pal? Ming the Merciless?"

Michael coughed. "Pap, no. But maybe you can be Dr. Huer. That's kind of a match, Dr. Huer knows stuff, like you know stuff. Only you have to say *Heh!* a whole lot more."

"Heh!" Hiram would always be an outsider, with men like Smith watching his every move. Having Michael for a son didn't make him less of an outsider, because Michael, too, stood on the outside. But Michael knew his secrets—or at least, the headlines— and the world hadn't ended.

"I love you, Michael."

"I love you too, Pap. And...I respect you."

Hiram hugged his son.

He then straightened out his arms and looked into Michael's face. "The creature covered in flies is...I'm not sure. Best to think of it as a demon, maybe. But it's old and it's dangerous, and it's behind everything...the murders, the mine closures, the Kimballs' fighting. Ammon and Samuel both looked into their father's seer stone, and that demon used it to manipulate them. Hand me your boot."

Michael did. In silence.

Hiram pried the heel off with his clasp knife. He shook the secret compartment and a second chi-rho amulet fell into his palm. "That's a talisman that is good for defense against enemies. I wear one, too, around my neck. It's not perfect, but it's strong protection. Another one, or something similar, anyway, is nailed into the door of the truck. This sign is the chi-rho—its influence may be what saved you from the fly demon. And it's why I always wanted you to wear your boots."

His son's eyes widened. "Wow."

"I told you," Hiram said.

"Did you think I was in danger?"

"*Life* is danger." Hiram put the amulet back into the boot and hammered it into place by slamming the heel against an adjacent tree trunk. "At first, I figured I'd tell you about it when you were older. Then I kept putting it off, and I saw how you laughed at Grandma Hettie behind her back. Then, at some point...I figured if you didn't know about the spirit realm, you might grow up to live a normal life. Somehow, in the big city, the need for lamens and bloodstones and amulets seems less pressing."

"Lamens? Amulets?"

Hiram laughed and removed the bronze Oremus lamen from his pocket. He gave it to his son. "This is a lamen. Hold on to it. I'll explain later."

Michael pushed his fists into his eyes. "I can't believe this. Only I *can*. It's why we drive around the state when we're not planting or harvesting, isn't it? You're not just helping the poor, are you? You're also demon hunting."

"The poor need more than one kind of help," Hiram said.

The wind picked up, and the branches that were already rattling began to sound like machine-gun chatter. Both he and Michael shivered.

Michael thought in silence for a few moments. "Samuel must be behind the demon. His camp was right out of the scary part of Dante. And he was crackers. Is the shopkeeper at Dollar's the witch?"

Hiram nodded. "A powerful witch. He knows more than I do, and he has better tools. Samuel? I don't know, I think Samuel's a victim. But with everything going on, police after us, the evil of the demon, murders... I think we need to get out of town. I've been called home. It wasn't just the Sorensons. The demon murdered Callista Markopoulos."

"Callista?" Anger and sorrow flashed across Michael's face. "We can't leave, Pap. I don't care if I go to jail. And if this thing killed that girl, it could kill again."

"I will stay." Hiram knew he had to. "You should go home."

Michael touched Hiram's shoulder. "The Kimballs don't stand a chance, not without you and your magic." Michael rolled his eyes at the word. "Cripes, I can't believe I just said that."

"Maybe don't call it *magic*."

"Hexes. Charms. The occult. Lore. Wisdom. Special skills. The police are going to be useless against that thing, Pap. Unless someone calls in the Army, it's up to you."

Hiram nodded. "But you can go home."

"I'll stay." Michael's eyes blazed. "I owe it to Callista."

What had passed between the Greek girl and his son?

A car crunched through the back alley, sliding slightly in the snow. It had driven around from Main Street and now pulled to a stop not far from Hiram and Michael. It was Mary McGill's Model A, with Mary at the wheel, and no sign of anyone following her.

She stepped out stood beside her car, smoking a long cigarette, and she looked right at the river where Hiram was.

And then a second woman stepped out, from the other side of the car: Eliza Kimball. Eliza walked stiffly around the car to stand beside Mary.

"Hiram!" Mary called. "Pretty sure I saw you down here! And if there's someone in there who isn't Hiram Woolley, come out slowly, with your hands up! I have a gun."

"Just in case," Hiram told his son, "let's put our hands up." They stepped out of the bushes and into the headlights.

"Mr. Woolley!" Eliza called. "I owe you an apology, and I need your help."

Hiram lowered his hands, feeling a little foolish, but Mary smiled at him. "You don't need to apologize for anything."

"I did not behave well toward you when last we spoke," Eliza said. "Please forgive me."

"Forgiven," he said.

Neither of them mentioned the seer stone.

"I went to the big house," Eliza continued, "to speak to Ammon. I found blood and crow's feathers on the parlor carpet, and my brother gone. I fear Samuel has taken him or killed him or both!" Eliza was visibly trembling. "I don't know to whom else to turn. The men at the mine don't like me, for obvious reasons. As for the police," she gestured at Hiram, "I have been warned they are in the pocket of Mr. Rettig and the D and RGW."

"They are," Hiram said.

"Remind me to tell you something else about Naaman Rettig," Mary murmured.

Hiram felt Michael's arm around his shoulders. "Looks like we have work to do, Pap. Do we know a charm to deal with kidnapped brothers?"

Chapter Thirty-Four

SNOWFLAKES GLISTENED IN THE HEADLIGHTS OF THE MODEL A. The wind shook the trees where they stood and made it hard for Hiram to think.

"Did you find evidence that Samuel is mad?" Hiram asked Mary.

"Not in the records," she admitted. "Don't you think the kidnapping is evidence enough?"

Hiram wanted to believe that Samuel, distracted and dazed by the substances he smoked, was innocent, but he had seen the man's art...including the animal corpses. More than that, he was under the influence of the seer stone's demon. "If Samuel has taken Ammon, I believe I know where they are."

"Samuel's camp?" Eliza looked distracted, her expression torn. Shattered by fatigue and trauma, much like Hiram, no doubt.

"The mine." Hiram looked at Michael. The boy had accepted that his father was a cunning man with surprisingly good grace. Could Hiram throw him into the presence of the demon...or Gus Dollar? But was it any safer to leave him behind? The monster had come out the mine to kill. It might not be in the mine now. "Or rather, the caves below the mines. We're going to need help."

"Are you going to call out the National Guard to stop a crazy drug addict from hurting his brother?" Mary asked.

"I wish I could get the National Guard." Hiram laughed weakly. "Or even a halfway decent elders quorum. There are at least two exits out of the caves, and maybe more. I want them blocked off when I go in."

"In case Samuel gets away." Eliza smiled ruefully.

"Yes. Or Gus Dollar, if he shows up. And also, I'd rather that uninvited people not break in on us."

"Like the police." Michael grinned. Was he enjoying the idea that his father was an outlaw? Hiram resolved to look more closely at the pulp magazines that Michael was always reading. And this Buck Rogers fellow.

"Gus Dollar!" Mary didn't shout, but the sudden energy in her voice felt like shouting to Hiram. "That reminds me, I want to show you this old daguerreotype. This is why I came looking for you. I found it in the files of the *Helper Journal*. They inherited a bunch of the city's old documents, and you need to look at this one."

Hiram almost snapped at the organizer. He had no time, he was hunted, he was exhausted and cold. But he held his tongue. "Show me."

The storm had taken a break, no wind, no snow. The headlights of Mary's car lit the yellowing image Mary pulled from her purse. It was of a row of men, and one of them was clearly Teancum Kimball; he matched the old daguerreotypes in the big house, and Samuel's painting, and even the shrunken features of the corpse. Also, his sunken eyes were echoed in the features of all three children.

"Is this your father?" he asked Eliza, to be sure.

She nodded.

Another looked just like Gus Dollar. At his present age, with his straight-up hair and his not-quite-symmetrical gaze.

"Eighteen eighty-one," Mary said.

"Fifty-four years ago." Hiram frowned. "Could this be Gus's grandfather?"

"As far as I can tell on short notice," Mary told him, "there was no one named Dollar before about 1920 living in this valley. Not Gus, and not a father or an uncle or a cousin. I haven't checked the city records, though, and of course even that may or may not record the presence of any given person. I mean, if he owned *land*, he would probably show up."

Gus had given his eye to the demon. Could this possibly be Gus? If Teancum Kimball had made a thirty-year deal with the demon that ended in 1933, then Gus's deal would have had to have taken place earlier.

Something niggled at the back of Hiram's mind, and he couldn't quite figure out what it was. Something about Gus's eye.

"This is Gus Dollar," Hiram said.

Mary whistled. "But that would make him... mathematics was never my best subject... old."

"One million," Michael said. "One million years old. That makes him a dinosaur. As I suspected from the start."

Hiram's heart sank. So Gus had known Teancum, because Gus had been here in Spring Canyon, fifty-odd years ago. He'd made his deal with the demon then, and when his time was up, his place had been taken by Teancum Kimball. And now Gus was back, to master the demon once and for all.

Hiram should have killed Gus when he had the chance.

Mary took the picture back.

"The miners will help us rescue Ammon," Michael said.

Hiram wasn't sure. "What if they think I'm the murderer? Bill was good to them, he was their champion."

"You're their champion now, Pap." Michael shrugged. "Besides, you have the world's most honest face. People believe you when you tell them things. Even, let's face it, really weird things."

Mary McGill threw Hiram a surprised glance. "So... he knows now?"

Hiram nodded.

"Yeah, I know," Michael said. "Not quite sure *what* I know."

"But you *do* have a good face," Mary told Hiram.

"You could have been the world's most successful insurance salesman. Or banker." Michael grinned. "Hey, it's not too late, if this year's beets are thin."

"It's going to be a good harvest," Hiram said.

"Let's go," Michael said. "Can we take the truck?"

Eliza stood still, snowflakes piling up on her dark hair. Her brother's kidnapping had curbed her tongue.

"Sorry, Hiram, your big truck is too conspicuous," Mary said. "But four will fit in my car."

"As long as I can stop carrying this toolbox around." Hiram nodded.

"I can drive," Michael said.

"Are you assuming I can't, because I'm a woman?" Mary challenged him.

"I'm just saying I'm probably better. Not because you're a woman, but because I'm really good at driving cars."

"You know, I drove myself out here. All the way from Denver,

Colorado, and I didn't wreck my car once. Had a flat tire outside Green River. You know what I did?"

"Swooned?"

"Fixed it."

Michael nodded. "You got me."

"Ride in the back," she told him. "With your father."

"I need to grab something first." Hiram put his toolbox inside the car's trunk. He tucked the two stolen lamens—the brass plate for summoning and the lead for collapsing a wall—into his inside coat pocket.

After a moment's thought, he put the bloodstained whip into one the largest pockets, too.

Michael still had his bronze Oremus plate.

Hiram climbed into the car and huddled under the blanket. "Keep me awake," he said to Michael. "Kick me now and then or something."

But Michael didn't kick him. Hiram gripped his Saturn ring in his clasped hands and promptly fell asleep, rocked to sleep by the battling rhythms of the car's engine and the wind's blast.

Mary McGill's Model A jerked to a stop, bouncing Hiram awake. Tattered fragments of a dream escaped him—a maze of tunnels, an enthroned demon before whom Hiram had prostrated himself, and an object buried beneath the throne that Hiram would not quite see.

He needed to consult his dream dictionary.

"You should wake him up now," Hiram heard Mary say.

"I'm awake." Hiram physically pried his eyelids up with his fingertips and then pulled back the blanket. Cold night air blasted his face and neck, which helped shake him to alertness. He could only see thirty feet, for the blasting snow.

His hands shook and he felt nauseated, but if his path crossed the path of a bottle of Coke, Hiram resolved to drink it immediately.

"Pap," Michael said. "The miners are here. I . . . I think they're waiting for you."

Hiram unfolded himself out of the Model A's back seat. His joints hurt, and when his booted feet touched the frozen soil, he felt as if someone was pounding his soles with a mallet.

The miners stood under the imposing structure of the silent tipple. There was Hermann Wagner, the German leader with his blocky head, and all the Germans with him. There were the Greeks, other than Dimitrios Kalakis, lined up behind the miner who always wore a bandana on his face. There was a scattering of Chinese and Japanese and Italian miners too, and they all held weapons. They had ax handles and spades and several even held rifles, but they weren't standing against each other, and they didn't hold their weapons as if they were about to attack.

They stood as if waiting, and when Hiram gingerly climbed up the hill to meet them, a welcoming murmur rippled through the mob.

Hiram straightened his back and tried to look the men in the eye. He wished he had a stone for eloquence, or a gift for it. Instead, he just looked every man in the eye he could and spoke plainly.

"I expect some of you think I'm a killer."

"Did you murder Callista?" The voice that asked was a woman's voice, so Hiram turned, looking for Dimitrios. To his surprise, the voice came from the red-bandana man; the miner pulled the bandana down, revealing a woman's face that Hiram knew—Medea Markopoulos.

Hiram managed not to stare.

"I didn't kill her." Hiram met her gaze.

Her eyes burned with rage, but tears streamed down her cheeks.

"Did Samuel Kimball kill my daughter?" Medea asked.

"I...I don't think so." Hiram met Mary's gaze. "But I can't be completely certain."

Medea nodded.

"I didn't kill the Sorensons, either. The last I saw of Bill Sorenson was after he took me down into the mine last night."

"Ja, we know." Wagner jerked a thumb at one of his Germans. Hiram recognized the man as the foul-smelling miner who had tried to shoot Samuel Kimball. "Paul saw you."

There had been a witness? "Did you see who killed the Sorensons?"

Paul shook his head. "But I saw Sorenson take you down into the mine, and bring you back up again."

Medea sniffed and cleared her throat. "I believe Hiram Woolley."

"Ja, we do, too," Hermann Wagner added.

There followed a round of general nodding and affirmation noises. Hiram took a deep breath; a weight he hadn't realized was there had lifted from his chest.

"How did you...? Did you know I was coming?" he asked.

"I received a note from Samuel Kimball," Medea said, "telling me to guard the mine to stop you from coming in. Or rather, the note came for Dimitrios, and made its way to me."

"She's the Head Greek now," the club-footed Greek said, as if Hiram needed the explanation. "She a woman, but she smarter than us blockheads."

The Greek with the bad foot bobbed his head. "I'm Stavros."

"I received a similar message from Ammon," Hermann said. "And we got to talking. The food you brought is gone, and Herr Sorenson is dead. We are hungry and tired. Then we remembered what Mrs. McGill said, that we must work together to get the Kimball brothers to behave, and not fight each other when the Kimballs tell us to."

"The Kimballs have been..." What should Hiram tell the miners? "They haven't been themselves. I think they're going to come around, but the reason they asked you here was to stop me from trying to...fix the situation."

"Is that who's got the missing carbide lamps and helmets?" Medea asked. "Is it the Kimball brothers, down in the mine?"

"It is my brothers," Eliza said. "I'm Eliza Kimball. Let us go down into the mine, and we'll set the situation right."

"You certainly look like Teancum's girl," Stavros said.

Medea cast a narrowed gaze on Eliza.

"I need a little more help than that." Hiram sighed. "I need all the entrances watched. If anyone tries to leave—Ammon or Samuel or anyone else—I need you to hold them for me. Can you do that?"

"We will all help," Wagner said.

Medea nodded. "I'll do more than watch."

"So will I," Mary said.

"There are two more mineshafts, higher up on the hill." Hermann Wagner gestured up at the ridge above Kimball Canyon. "We can bottle those up, easy."

"What about the caves?" Paul said. "I know where there are a couple of cracks in the rock. I'm not sure, but I think they connect into the mine tunnels."

"And there's at least one near Gus Dollar's store," Hiram added. "If the shopkeeper is there, make sure he doesn't leave."

The miners floated several other locations that needed to be watched to completely bottle up the underground complex. Then they broke up into squads of four to five men each and scattered to the various openings.

Hermann stayed at the main opening, with Paul and Stavros. All three had rifles.

The German miner with a large neck goiter and a bright red waistcoat volunteered to accompany Hiram and his party. Eliza objected that the mine tunnels were narrow, and the German bellowed in response, "Den ve go in zinkle file!" He shook a pickaxe in both hands. "My name is Valter," he said to Hiram. "I apolochize for any earlier rudeness."

Medea didn't say a word, and she didn't leave Hiram's side. A blade appeared in her hands, the same sword Hiram had seen in her home. The weapon had a curving blade like a scimitar, narrow near the hilt and broader near the tip. That and her denim jeans and bandana around her neck made her look like a Janissary dressed as a cowboy.

"Why did you hide your face?" Hiram asked her. "Wouldn't Dimitrios know who you were, anyway?"

"When my Basil got injured," the woman explained, "I had to take his part. All the Greeks knew who I was, but I wore the bandana so the Germans and the others wouldn't give me trouble."

"I'm glad to have you." Hiram checked his inside coat pockets and felt the two lamens from Gus Dollar's Book of the Spirits. He had not recovered the heliotropius from the back seat of Police Chief Fox's cruiser. He handed what he hoped was a protective lamen to Mary. "Will you carry this? In a pocket, or wear it on a string?"

"From the man who wrote the apostles on a sage leaf and sprang me from jail? Yes, I will." Mary smiled, but took the lamen. She tucked it into the inside of her jacket. "It's heavy."

"It's made out of brass, I think." He didn't mention the lead plate in his own pocket, the Saturnine one with the astrological markings, the text from Joshua and the words he couldn't read. The lamen that—he thought—was designed to collapse the caves below the mine.

Hiram realized he should have stopped at the Double-A to pull his other protective lamen from the door. Too late.

Hiram took his chi-rho amulet from his neck and offered it to the Kimball sister. "Eliza, would you wear this?"

She shook her head and stepped away. Hiram felt embarrassed.

He offered the amulet to Medea and Walter both. Walter shook his head and Medea snorted, so Hiram put the talisman back on his own neck.

Turning to Eliza, he asked, "When you were a child here, did you ever learn to ignite a carbide lamp?"

"It's been a long time." Eliza's voice was dull, as if she were very tired. "Perhaps you can show me."

"One last thing," Hiram said. He quickly thumbed through the pages of his dream dictionary. There was nothing for either *king* or *throne*, but he did find one apparently relevant entry:

UNDERGROUND—*if you go underground and you are not digging, it denotes your early death.*

Chapter Thirty-Five

THE CAFFEINE HAD LEFT HIRAM'S SYSTEM. HE WASN'T SHAKING anymore, and his heartbeat was regular, and he didn't want to vomit. On the other hand, he struggled against an urge to lie down in a mine cart and fall asleep. Once the affairs of the Kimball Mine were set right, he'd sleep for a week and eat for a month.

First, he had to rescue Ammon from Samuel.

Medea and Walter had moved various chits to the "IN" board. Then they'd entered. Coming in out of the snowstorm, the mine's warmer air was a relief.

"Samuel!" Hiram called ahead of them in the darkness. With the bright carbide beams and their noisy footsteps, there was no way his party was going to surprise Samuel, in any case. "It's Hiram Woolley! Your sister's with us. Don't do anything you'll regret!"

But was there anything a drug-addled maniac like Samuel Kimball would regret?

Hiram wished he had a way to know where the demon was. He wasn't sure whether he preferred the idea that it was on the surface and therefore wouldn't attack them in the mine, or in the mine and therefore wouldn't kill innocents on the surface.

He led the way, Eliza Kimball to one side, Mary and Michael following, and the two miners bringing up the rear. He had no trouble finding the cave entrance with its removed boards, and the six of them crawled down the bottom of the boulder-choked

281

crack and onto the flat stone shelf beside the waters, following Hiram's previous chalk marks.

Mary bent over to gaze into the pool. "Ugh, it's full of little white things. Fish and insects and snakes. Why are they so white?"

"They don't need pigment," Michael said. "They've never seen the sun, not their whole lives. I read that in *Popular Science*."

Hiram looked down the three passages he hadn't stepped in before. Might they be exits? Or might Samuel have taken Ammon down one of those tunnels? But he didn't think so.

Hiram wished he had another hazel rod. "I don't think they've gone down any of those passages."

"Why not?" Medea held her sword up and to one side of her body, as if she were a warrior, entering a hostile castle. She looked competent and controlled; Walter, by contrast, nervously swung his pickaxe around with one hand as if he were strolling in the park and the pickaxe were a parasol. Hiram worried he'd hit someone.

In his other hand, at Hiram's insistence, the German carried a gas can.

"Samuel?" Hiram called, turning and facing over the water. No answer.

"Follow me." To Michael, he said: "Stay close behind me."

Then Hiram stepped into the water.

The shock of its temperature took him by surprise; he had forgotten how cold it was. At every step, the knobby texture of the walls presented a new landscape. His eyes, tightly focused by the carbide beam, interpreted those changing shadows as movement, and he continually turned his head one way and then the other, trying to find the sources of the flitting and swooping motions in his nearly-blind peripheral vision.

He wished he had his revolver.

Hiram climbed out of the pool and onto the shelf of stone with the lizard-head altar. The sound of water sluicing from his clothing and splashing all around him was loud. He wouldn't hear anyone or anything approach over that racket, he thought, but then Eliza climbed out of the water after him and was even louder.

Ammon and Samuel Kimball both sat against the wall, beside the mummified corpse of their father. The two men both stared at Hiram with expressions of horror, and then he realized that they couldn't see him, due to the power of the carbide beam.

"It's Hiram Woolley," he said.

"The witch!" Ammon gasped.

"No." Hiram sighed.

But then he realized that both men sat with their hands tied before them, and more rope knotted around their ankles. "Wait a moment." He raised a hand in warning to his friends behind him.

"So it will come to a confrontation here, will it?" A beam of light snapped on in the darkness. It shone in Hiram's face, blinding him. He held his hands up and still could see nothing but flashes of light. He knew the voice, in any case.

It belonged to Gus Dollar.

The beam came from waist height, so it was a flashlight, not a carbide lamp. It was still plenty powerful enough to blind Hiram, whose sight was already squeezed into tunnel vision by the effect of the carbide lamp on his helmet.

"It doesn't have to come to any more confrontation, Gus," Hiram said. "Let the Kimballs go. Walk away."

"You haven't come alone." Gus hissed. There was a brief silence. "You brought a warrior maiden and a jolly dwarf, I see."

"I decided I wanted reinforcements," Hiram said.

"You are a tricky old man after all," Michael added.

"I should have bound you. I would have bound you, only he stopped me."

Who was *he?* How would Gus have bound Hiram?

"What do you mean, have me arrested?" Hiram asked. "You certainly don't want a judge of the Helper Justice Court to come look at the charms and hexes in your shop and try to figure out what they mean."

Hiram shifted slightly to one side, and the beam came out of his eyes. He still couldn't see a damn, with all the blazing suns of red and green that splashed across his vision and swam in circles.

"I can see through your eyes," Gus said. "I know you think I'm pitiful, and my best weapon has been taken from me, but I've come down here to bring you to heel."

With his tunnel vision and the light in his eyes, Hiram had no idea what the others were doing. At least one of them was moving—he heard the sound of shoes scuffing on the damp stone of the shelf.

"If you can see through my eyes," Hiram quipped, "you're seeing nothing at all."

He heard squirming and whimpering noises. At first, he took them for Samuel, but then he realized it was Ammon who was wiggling and crying.

"I don't need the book," Gus said. "I've brought you here with another gift, a little tender piece of bait. You can't resist the offer of a deal, but now you've stepped inside my circle, and you are mine."

A tender piece of bait? That was the strangest imaginable way to characterize Ammon Kimball, and not much better a description of his brother Samuel.

Hiram swung his face down on a hunch, looking at the top of the lizard-head altar.

A small sphere sat there, glistening.

Flesh.

An eyeball. That was the bait.

"You're not talking to me," Hiram said out loud.

Gus Dollar hadn't been talking to Hiram at all. Who had Gus been addressing?

The skin on Hiram's neck crawled.

Was the demon present?

Gus laughed, a shrieking whoop that ended abruptly in air being sucked in through his teeth. "You're a sideshow, farmer. Your death here is incidental and irrelevant."

Hiram snapped his head back in Gus's direction. The beam of his light caught the shopkeeper in the face. Scabbed whip marks slashed down from his forehead to his chin. For an instant, Hiram felt bad for whipping the man. Then he felt revulsion. Gus retained his glass eye, but the socket which had recently housed an eyeball of flesh and vitreous liquid was now empty.

Gus had sacrificed his second eye. As bait.

The demon had to be present.

Eliza laughed, but it was a deep laugh, below baritone, below bass, a rumbling laugh like the sound of a mountain shifting from one foot to the other. A cold wind gusted from her as she laughed, and Hiram heard a buzzing of flies that rose in crescendo to a shrill whistle.

"Pap..."

Hiram grabbed in the darkness and found Michael. He dragged his son behind him, trying to put himself between the young man and either of the two dangerous figures they now confronted. Hiram grabbed the whip—it was his best weapon.

He wished he could see better.

"WHAT THEN, ZOLLER?" The voice rippling out of Eliza was titanic. Hiram turned his light to face her in time to see flies erupt from her mouth with each syllable. The skin of her face and arms bulged and rippled as she moved, as if she had too many muscles underneath. Or as if there were a swarm of flies inside her, trying to escape. "I GAVE YOU THIRTY YEARS OF PROSPERITY, AS PROMISED. WERE THEY NOT ENOUGH? WILL YOU BIND ME NOW FOR ETERNITY?"

Hiram heard muttering in Greek and German both.

In English, Mary whispered, "Holy shit."

"You allowed Teancum Kimball to run me off my land!" Gus yelled.

"YOU HAD HAD YOUR PROSPERITY AND YOUR TIME WAS UP! YOU CANNOT BIND ME!"

"I already have," Gus said. Hiram turned his light to Gus Dollar's face and saw the shopkeeper shift posture. He pulled a sword up in front of him, the ritual blade Hiram had seen earlier in the shop. "I have summoned you to this place, and now I will slay your vessel of flesh, and transfer the power of your spirit to *me*."

"FOOL." The Beast-Eliza waved an arm at Ammon and Samuel, slumped against the stone. "*I* SUMMONED *YOU*. I BROUGHT YOU ALL HERE TO FEED UPON! TEANCUM KIMBALL DELIVERED HIS OTHER SPAWN IN PERSON. I WILL TAKE THESE LAST THREE AS HIS FINAL OFFERING."

Gus's voice jumped in pitch. "I command you in the name of *Elay Adonay* to submit!"

Hiram shuddered. Invocation of any of the Divine Names was dangerous. An unworthy man who attempted it would fail, and if he was unworthy enough, might be destroyed.

Eliza laughed. She turned toward Hiram, who got a split second's view of Eliza's face. Flies swarmed her eyes, nostrils, ears, and open, leering mouth. "THANK YOU FOR DELIVERING MY STONE TO THE WOMAN."

Eliza punched Hiram. That single blow tossed him and Michael both across the chamber. He narrowly avoided the altar, with its gruesome little deposit, and fell to the stone beside Teancum Kimball.

His helmet rattled away, across the stone. He dropped the whip.

Climbing onto all fours, Hiram looked into the crook of

Teancum Kimball's arm and realized that the man wasn't carrying the skeleton of a lamb—the skeleton belonged to a very tiny human baby.

Michael yelped.

Hiram gagged, tried to vomit, and failed. Of course the Beast had found a child to kill during its rampage. It had developed a taste for it devouring Teancum Kimball's babies.

"You killed my daughter!" Medea howled.

Violence erupted into the cave, but Hiram saw it only through the crazed and shifting window afforded to him by the crossing beams of the various carbide lamps. Medea leaped forward with her scimitar swinging, and at the same time, Walter lunged and swung the pickaxe.

Eliza attacked with fists that swelled to the size of milk bottles, black masses of flies flowing like tar. Her first blow struck Walter in the face. His neck exploded, the goiter throwing a dark wave of blood across the chimney. Her second caught Medea in the stomach, and the miner dropped her blade into the water and fell to all fours.

Gus shouted in Latin, or maybe Greek.

Scrambling, Hiram found his helmet and got it back onto his head.

Eliza stepped into the water, flies bursting from the orifices of her face at the chill touch, and she towered over Medea. The miner coughed and retched into the water, helpless.

Hiram threw himself into Eliza's path. "No!"

Eliza swung a punch at him, and only a wild, last-second duck brought him beneath a blow that might easily have brained him. He fished in the water, feeling several slimy things with his fingers and the back of his hand before he found the sword's hilt.

He raised the weapon in front of him.

"You will serve me!" Gus shouted.

Hiram meant to swing the sword at Eliza, but hesitated. For all that flies now swarmed her, she had a woman's form, and not the form of an enemy.

Eliza struck him, knocking him into the water. He dropped the sword and floundered, feeling he had too many limbs until he realized he was tangled up in Walter's corpse.

Gus was still chanting.

Eliza stepped forward. She swelled to twice her normal size.

She raised enormous talons over her head for a killing blow. Was she aiming at Hiram or at Medea?

Fire sprang up behind Eliza and the Beast howled in surprise.

Gus's spell? But no, there was Michael, with the gas can. He'd lit the back of Eliza's dress on fire. The flies swarmed angrily as they escaped her body.

But as the flies exited, the sound became less and less the bellow of a wounded ogre, and more and more the shriek of a terrified woman whose body is on fire.

The flies swarmed densely, cohering into a dense, humanoid shape between Hiram and Eliza. He couldn't save her unless he moved the monster.

Standing on wobbly legs, Hiram raised his right arm to the square, elbow bent, hand up, like a carpenter's square, an ancient sign of true alignment, blessing, and oaths. And he shouted the secret name of God.

Not *Jehovah*, the silly sub-Latin English spelling of the King James Bible. Nor yet *Yahweh*, the more fashionable pronunciation that Mahonri had learned from reading those books of Biblical scholarship, and that he used when he wanted to put on intellectual airs.

Hiram used the secret pronunciation of the Tetragrammaton that Grandma Hettie had taught him. It was the only one of the Divine Names that he knew. She had whispered it to him in a closet and made him whisper it back to her until he got it right. And she had told him only to pronounce it in dire need, or else in a wind so strong it would whip the word right out of anyone's hearing, or else when passing the vital pronunciation on to an apprentice of his own.

Hiram shouted the name of God and the fallen angel Samuel, Mahoun, Master Mahan, the Beast of many names—flinched.

Five times, Grandma Hettie had told him. No demon can stand in the presence of the Tetragrammaton spoken five times with authority, by a person with a chaste and sober mind.

Was Hiram worthy? He risked failure and his own destruction.

He didn't see any other choice.

He stepped forward, keeping his right arm square, and shouted it a second time, and now the Beast darted to one side. It roared, taking shape in the cloud of flies, and tore at the sides of its head with its own talons.

Hiram wanted to keep shouting the Name, to drive the Beast out of the world for good.

But Eliza was on fire.

With the Beast to one side, he leaped forward. He tackled Teancum Kimball's only surviving daughter, pain from the fire searing his arms.

The fire splashed left and right, some of it spreading across the surface of the water and some of it still clinging to Eliza Kimball as Hiram dragged her from the pool and threw her to the stone shelf. His helmet gone again, he would have been blind but for the light of the fire, on Eliza and on the stone shelf.

He ripped his coat off and slapped it down on Eliza, patting out the flames. Remembering the lamens, he grabbed the lead one from the coat pocket. He saw the whip lying beside Eliza, and picked it up, as well.

Medea joined Hiram and together they dragged Eliza to her feet.

"Mary?" Hiram asked.

Michael pointed; the labor organizer had cut the bonds on the Kimballs' wrists and was grunting, trying to pull them to their feet. Of the six of them, she was the only one still wearing a helmet with a lamp. The beam of her lamp bounced around the cave as she moved, both giving light and baffling Hiram's vision. Shadows and flies swarmed.

The Beast lunged at Hiram, and he snapped the whip at it.

It was an awkward attack, and the Beast grabbed the bull-whip, a hand clearly visible within the swarm of flies. Then the misshapen, multimouthed face appeared, and it yanked the whip from Hiram's hand. Hiram backed away and the demon laughed.

Then it stuffed the leather into one of its open maws.

And laughed.

"Run!" Hiram yelled.

But the Beast turned around and advanced on Gus.

The shopkeeper screamed in Latin and held the ceremonial sword up in front of him, but the demon didn't slow down. Something had gone wrong with Gus's charm.

But what?

"Run!" Hiram pushed Michael into the water first, with Eliza's elbow in the boy's grip. The Kimball heiress muttered dazed gibberish. "Help her get through!"

Mary and Medea followed, each dragging one of the Kimball brothers. The men stumbled, limbs probably cramped or asleep from having been tied up.

Hiram grabbed the gas can and checked that its cap was screwed on tight. He followed last, backing along the submerged tunnel by feel and watching Gus Dollar and the Beast. He was the only witness when Gus shrieked in rage and flung his blade to the ground.

The whip, Hiram realized. The whip with Gus's blood on it. The demon had eaten Gus's blood, and Gus's hex had failed.

Exploding into a swarm of flies, the Beast fell on Gus.

Chapter Thirty-Six

BACKING THROUGH THE TUNNEL, HIRAM SLIPPED. HE PLUNGED into the icy water and lost his grip on the sword. For unreal moments he floated at the bottom of the pool, the icy tendrils creeping into his blood.

His dream dictionary had warned him of an early death.

But a beam of light from behind him crossed the stone, illuminating white creatures like scorpions and glinting off the fallen blade.

Hiram grabbed the sword, pushed himself to the surface—and smacked his head against the tunnel ceiling.

For long seconds he could see nothing, and he didn't know whether he had blinded himself with the blow to the head, or whether the last carbide light had gone out.

"Pap!" A gentler beam crossed Hiram's path.

A flashlight, held in Michael's hands. Mary, Medea, and the Kimballs huddled behind him. Medea stood in front of them with her sword in hand, rage in her eyes; the others looked terrified.

Hiram staggered onto the rocky shelf below the boulder-strewn crack leading up to the mine. Three other tunnels branched off from the chamber, and his enemy could come out of any of them. If only he could close every passageway, including the one out.

"The lead lamen," he said. "Joshua brought down the walls of Jericho. Gus came down here to fight the demon with a sword, but his original plan was to bury it under rock."

"Pap?"

"The lore is beyond me, but he was going to kill the monster and . . . absorb it. Eat its soul. It's the other lamen!" Hiram pulled the lead plate from his pocket. "Give me some light."

Michael stepped close and shone his beam on the lead plate. "Pap, you hit your head."

Hiram chuckled. "True. But I think I know what Gus was trying to do. He wanted the Beast's power, so he planned to trap its spirit in his Book of the Spirits, but destroy the body."

"And that . . . bit of plate there?"

"It's image lore." Hiram looked into his son's shadowed eyes and made a noise that was half-laugh and half-sob. "I'm sorry, I know this is all too much."

"Pap, we should run."

"We will." Hiram jabbed a finger at the writing on the plate that he couldn't read. "What does that say?"

"*In nominee patris et filii et spiritus sancti,*" Michael said. "Is that Latin?"

Mary McGill shouldered her way between them. "*In nomine,* not *in nominee.*"

"It's Latin?" Hiram said. "Nuns?"

"Nuns," Mary agreed.

"Teach us the pronunciation," Hiram said.

She said it twice, Hiram repeating it the first time, and Hiram and Michael both following along the second.

Medea stared at the passage back into the altar chamber.

Michael pulled them back on task. "Pap?"

Hiram held up the plate. "The English quote is from Joshua six, about Jericho."

"Joshua fit the battle." Michael grinned. "I can play that one on guitar."

"Shout," Hiram said, "for the Lord hath given you the city. And what shall we shout?"

"The Latin prayer," Mary said.

"And that will bring down the cave behind us, and trap the thing inside."

"It . . . will?" Michael furrowed his brow.

"It should." Willpower should not be a part of any charm. The magician didn't impose his will on the universe, the magician acted in accordance with known laws, or else the magician asked God.

In either case, faith was essential.

"It *will*," Hiram said.

"The cave *will* collapse," Michael emphasized. "It has to."

Hiram tousled his son's hair. "Back to the mine." He gestured to boulder-stuffed chasm that led upward. "As fast as you can and say the Latin words as much as you can. Shout them!"

"Anything else?" Michael asked.

"If you get to the mine, and you can find it in your heart . . . pray."

Michael hesitated, nodded, and scampered up the crack. He dragged Eliza with him. The black-clad teacher from the east was now scorched black of complexion and her hair was burnt short. The stink of fire hung about her, and she moved as if half-asleep.

"*In nomine patris*," Mary McGill said, "*et filii, et spiritus sancti.*"

"Louder," Hiram said. "Shout!"

"Mr. Woolley."

Hiram turned to find Ammon and Samuel Kimball. Both men were pale and shivering. How much had they seen? And what had their fragile minds allowed them to remember?

Samuel looked more rational than he ever had. "I'm sorry," he said simply.

"I'm sorry," Ammon echoed his brother.

"Up the rocks with Miss McGill," Hiram said. "She's going to be chanting Latin. Whatever she tells you to shout, shout it with her."

"I stay with you," Medea told Hiram, her voice flat.

The two brothers clambered up the rocks, awkwardly echoing Mary's clipped and precise Latin syllables.

A hideous roar rang out. It seemed to come from low along the icy pool, but also from two of the tunnels that opened onto the shelf. The Beast had fed, but it was coming for them.

Hiram and Medea retreated up onto the lowest of the rocks and Hiram splashed some gas down to create a thin barrier. As he lit the gas with his Zippo, he looked up and saw flies swarming from all three tunnels opening onto the shelf, and from the submerged tunnel as well. A wall of flame rose between him and the flies, but he knew it wouldn't last.

He shouted. "*In nomine patris et filii et spiritus sancti!*"

Kneeling, he wedged the lead lamen down among the boulders at the base of the crack. This was not a charm he was master of, but he thought that images written to bring down walls and cities—and mines—had to be buried inside the walls to be effective. In his dream, too, something had been buried beneath the demon king's throne.

Had he dreamed of the lamen, then?

The Beast lumbered toward Hiram, and for a moment he feared he would be flattened.

But the Beast reached the line of fire and stopped. It opened all three mouths of its eyeless face and leaned back, gaping skyward. With a sound like a horrific belch wrapped around a high-pitched whistle, three columns of flies exploded out of the Beast's maws. Hiram smelled rotten meat. As the swarms grew in size, the Beast's body dwindled, until it had disappeared entirely, and there was only the swarm.

But the swarm stayed below the flame.

Hiram raised his arm to the square and shouted the Name.

"Up!" Hiram shouted at Medea.

"Look!" She pointed below the swarm.

A pile of blood and torn flesh, and splintered bones like a demented game of pick up sticks, lay beneath the swarming flies. For a moment, Hiram wondered what it was, but then he saw the glint of a glass eye nestled in with the gore and the shattered remains.

His stomach turned. He was lucky it was empty.

"Go!" he cried.

"You go!" Medea pulled Hiram past her and sent him scampering up the rocks. He climbed breathlessly, swooning from lack of air and from effort, and had to stop to catch his balance and avoid dropping the gas can. "Lay down more fire!"

Looking down, he saw the beast re-form and lunge at Medea.

The miner was not a trained swordfighter, but the Beast had killed her daughter. She hurled herself at the Beast with such ferocity, slashing and howling, that the Beast stepped back.

Then she turned and raced toward Hiram up the chasm.

He lay down a second line of gasoline across the boulders, a little thicker than the previous one. He thought he had enough for one more wall.

The Beast bounded up on Medea's heels. She leaped from one giant stone, over the gasoline barrier, to another just as Hiram touched flame to the gas.

Whooosh! Fire leaped up, blinding Hiram.

The Beast roared but fell back.

Hiram shouted the Name at it again. It hissed and roared but didn't fall back.

"*In nomine patris et filii et spiritus sancti!*" Hiram yelled, resuming his dogged upward climb with Medea at his side. He was careful not to get his hands or feet wedged between rocks. "*In nomine patris et filii et spiritus sancti!*"

Near the top of the chasm, maybe fifty feet from the mine entrance, he saw Michael, Mary, and the others. They were shouting too, but Hiram didn't sense the slightest evidence that the cave was about to collapse.

Was Gus's hex a failure?

Had Hiram misunderstood the lamen? Was it the will of God that he fail? Was his faith too weak?

Or was he not pure enough? All charms, but especially the spells of the high court magicians, were said to depend on the magician's personal purity. A chaste and sober mind. It was one of the reasons why Hiram fasted, and tried to keep his heart free of enmity toward any.

And if he wasn't pure enough to make the lamen work, would the use of the Divine Name also fail him?

He paused his ascent and glanced up again. Medea stopped with him. Did the *others* have insufficient faith, or purity?

And specifically, they should all be as pure as possible with respect to the operation at hand. He remembered abruptly his divination by sieve and shears, with Gus Dollar and his grandchildren. Hiram had asked whose heart must change.

The answer had been: all the Kimballs.

He shouted at the Kimballs. "Ammon! Samuel! Eliza! You have to forgive each other! Forgive each other, or this won't work!"

They stared at him.

The Beast leaped over the dying flames and galloped up the chasm, its grey misshapen form shrouded in the buzz of countless flies. Hiram stopped and laid down one last line of gasoline. Twenty-five feet above, the others were yelling the Latin words, but Hiram feared the words were useless.

"You *must forgive* each other!" he shouted.

He knelt to put fire to the gasoline.

The Zippo slipped from his fingers.

Medea watched the lighter click against the stone. She cursed in Greek and leaped down the chasm to the face the Beast once more.

Hiram fumbled for the lighter. It had slipped down into a crack, and he had to stretch to get his hand down there. Something cold and dry touched his fingers and retreated, and he imagined horrible things that might eat his hand or inject him with venom.

But he grabbed the lighter.

"Medea! Come back!" He crouched again over the line of gasoline, ready to light it when the Greek woman rejoined him.

Medea struck at the Beast, and Hiram saw that she was doing no real damage. Its skin was uncut and its movements were unslowed. Then Medea turned to race up the crack, and the Beast grabbed her by the ankle.

Hiram raised his arm to the square once more and shouted the Name. Before he could shout it again, the monster swung Medea through the air, splattering her skull into fragments in a single blow against the stone wall.

Hiram felt faint. The Beast seemed to fade away into the distance and then pulse closer into his view again, and Hiram sucked in cool air, battling to stay conscious. A faint smell struck his senses, spicy and sweet.

"Pap!"

The Beast was racing toward him.

Medea had followed her daughter into death, there was nothing Hiram could do for her. But Medea's other children still lived, as did her husband, and so did Hiram's son. He lit the gasoline.

The Beast threw itself into the flames this time, but they drove it back. It wasn't the heat at work—a man could have jumped through the flames—it was the light and sacred power in the fire itself. It was the power of Gabriel.

Hiram hurled the gas can at the Beast. Flames licked around the open stubby neck of the can as it bounced off the creature's shoulder, and then Hiram shouted the Name again.

The Beast shrank and hissed, but then roared at Hiram. A column of flies shot from its open maw, slamming into the flames. Thousands of charred flies fell dead onto the stones and the fire burned on, keeping the thing trapped.

That conflagration wouldn't last much longer.

Shouldn't the Name be hurting the Beast more?

Was Hiram not worthy?

"Mary!" he shouted. "Get Michael to the surface, warn the miners! Eliza, Ammon, Samuel, I need you to stay. We can stop it."

Mary looked pale, but she nodded and they ran. Michael took the flashlight with him, leaving the flames the only light in the chasm.

Hiram scurried up to where the three Kimballs stood, trembling and staring, on a flat boulder the size of a double bed. He grabbed Eliza and shook her, shocking alertness back into her eyes.

"Eliza!" he shouted. "Samuel! Ammon! No heart is completely pure, but your hearts have been corrupted by that thing. It gave you all false visions, like it gave your father. If we are to have any chance at all, *you must forgive each other now!*"

Ammon broke first. "I'm sorry, Samuel," he said. "I'm sorry, Eliza." Then he dropped to his knees. "I didn't know the power I was serving, but in my heart, I knew I was wronging you. I forgive you, and I ask you to forgive me."

Standing above the man, Hiram noticed that he had no visible boils.

The Beast bellowed, and is if in response, Eliza threw herself on her brother's neck in an embrace. "I'm sorry I judged you! I'm sorry I gave into curiosity and looked into the stone! I'm sorry I tied you up and brought you down here! It wasn't me, but also it was! I'm sorry! I forgive you! Forgive me, Ammon!"

Samuel stood, a glazed look on his face.

Hiram could guess what might be causing the youngest Kimball's daze. "Samuel, are you on reefer right now?"

Samuel shook his head, but the motion was a shocked one. Hiram had seen it before, on the fields of France.

He took Samuel's hand and wrapped an arm around the younger man's shoulders. "Come on," he said. "I'll help you. But your sister and brother are kneeling. Let's kneel together."

Woodenly, Samuel fell to his knees. "You were never really my brother and sister," he began.

"Please, Samuel," Hiram begged. "Forgive them."

The light disappeared as the gasoline burned itself out. They were plunged into unforgiving darkness.

Hiram heard a roar and the scratching, thudding sound of the Beast resuming its climb up the crack.

"Please," he said.

"I forgive you," Samuel said. The words were simple, but they sounded sincere.

"Now one more time. Say the Latin words with me, and believe that we will be fine. *In nomine patris et filii et spiritus sancti.*"

A roar so close, the Beast might have been standing on Hiram's shoulder.

The stones beneath his feet shifted abruptly and began to give way.

Hiram took in a startled breath and heard the others do the same. "This way!" He grabbed in the darkness and found a hand—he wasn't sure whose. Placing his other hand against the wall, he groped his way up in stygian blackness. The stones beneath his feet shifted and trembled. "And keep chanting. Shout! *In nomine patris et filii et spiritus sancti!*"

Their pronunciations were no better than Hiram's, and Hiram was pretty sure that his was terrible.

"Is that a light?" Eliza asked.

It was. It was a flock of lights, rushing toward them from the mine. They ran forward to meet the lights, still chanting.

"*In nomine patris et filii et spiritus sancti!*"

The earth shook. The Beast roared. It sounded in the darkness as if it were only inches from Hiram's face.

At the boarded entrance into the mine, Hiram stopped to look. The others scrambled past him and into the arms of the miners. Behind and below the Beast, Hiram saw sudden flame and heard the deafening crack of an explosion in a confined space. Had one of the carbine lamps abandoned below ignited some subterranean gas? Or was the lead lamen simply doing its work?

A shadow lunged up to block his view of the flame, roaring and whistling.

Then the Beast's bellowing was whipped away and buried in a cacophony of crashing stone. The boards were sucked into the cave and the ground beneath Hiram's feet shook. Finally, a chunk of stone larger than the Double-A crashed into place, sealing off the natural cave.

When Hiram could see, he saw the dirty faces of the miners of the Kimball Mine. He found he was whistling, and when he recognized the tune, he laughed out loud in shock and relief.

It was "Joshua Fit the Battle."

Chapter Thirty-Seven

HIRAM EMERGED FROM THE EARTH WITH MICHAEL, MARY, AND the Kimballs, escorted by a brigade of miners.

They were met by blinding lights. The wind had stopped. Dust from the cave-in danced in shifting whorls with slow, fat snowflakes that seemed almost warm, and as Hiram stepped into the light, he heard a cheer.

The light came from headlights—three cars, at least.

A hand gripped Hiram's shoulder from behind, and Hiram heard a man's voice he didn't know. "Hiram and Michael Woolley, you're under arrest for the murders of Vilhelm and Eva Sorenson."

"Sergeant Dixon?" Hiram asked, but the voice didn't sound right.

"My name's Jefferson. Deputy Sheriff of Carbon County. I'm taking you to Price."

Hiram nodded.

"What are you talking about?" Michael snapped. "We had no reason to kill those people!"

Ammon coughed deeply, a painful sound just to hear, and spat a black wad into the snow. "It wasn't them, Deputy. The night of the murder, both Hiram and his son were at my house. I was showing them an old stone of my father's. It couldn't have been them."

"I spent all day yesterday with you." The deputy sounded irritated to the point of anger. "You couldn't mention this earlier?"

299

Tears cleared the dust and light from Hiram's eyes enough that he could see the man's face, weathered and tired. A hard-working policeman's face.

Ammon shrugged. "I was distracted. I had family business to attend to."

"Mr. Woolley is innocent." Eliza looked surprisingly dignified, with her dress scorched and burned. "As is his son."

Samuel's glasses were a sight to see, covered in dust and now collecting snow. "I also want to go on record vouching for them. You don't, don't...want to fight us on this, Deputy. We employ a lot of men in this canyon."

Samuel still sounded dazed, but he was lucid.

Mumbling a baffled apology, the deputy retreated.

Sergeant Dixon grabbed Hiram by the other shoulder. "Pretty sure you left this in my car." The policeman pressed a small object into Hiram's hand.

His bloodstone.

"Thanks," Hiram said. "How's Chief Fox?"

"Damnedest thing," Shanks said. "Got bit by a whole bunch of snakes in the middle of a February snowstorm."

"Damnedest thing," Hiram agreed.

"Best I can figure is the storm somehow knocked open a nest in the valley and woke a bunch of 'em up. I've seen enough root doctoring to guess that maybe it was that stone sitting in the back seat of the car that saved his life. Anyway, the chief ain't dead, but he's taking a nice long rest."

"Does that leave you in charge? Chief Dixon?"

"Acting Chief Dixon at most. And your gun..."

"I guess the county sheriff has it?"

"I'll get it back to you. Where did you say your farm was?"

"Lehi," Hiram said.

Hermann Wagner tottered forward, head swinging from side to side, followed by Stavros, whose foot made him lurch forward in stutter-steps. "So is the mine back open?" Wagner asked.

"It is," Ammon said. "We'll work carefully, and we'll seal up any natural caverns we encounter."

The thought made Hiram nervous, but he believed the Beast was destroyed. They'd better conduct a divination of some kind, before Ammon resumed any digging.

"We'll dig the eastern seam," Samuel said.

Eliza Kimball nodded. "We'll get started clearing out the shaft in the morning. Ammon will have to act as foreman, for now. Miss McGill, perhaps you will stay for a while?"

Mary's face was red from cold and exertion. "Me?"

"The miners might like someone to give them advice, as we get our operations started again." Ammon paused. "I think I could use a little advice, too."

"As long as you're taking advice," Eliza said, "I advise a corral of horses, a few pigs, a few cows, and of course, a chicken coop."

"As soon as we can afford them," Ammon agreed. "If nothing else, Samuel might need something to paint other than rocks."

His brother laughed.

Hiram couldn't help but smile.

Mary met Hiram's gaze. "And you, Mr. Woolley, our business isn't quite finished. If you're quite finished with the mine, I'd like a word."

Hiram blushed.

Ammon approached him and put out a hand. "Before he left, Dimitrios Kalakis said you were going to pay his debts to me. I've come to collect."

Hiram squinted at him even as he took his hand. "I believe Mary is going to argue my case. Good luck with that."

Ammon slapped him on the back and his laughter rang out across the valley.

The next morning, Hiram left Michael sleeping in their room at the Buford Boarding House. He had one little errand to run, and his son's sarcasm wouldn't help him.

Frank Johnson stood in front of the suite at the Hotel Utah with his arms crossed. Bruises clouded his face, both his eyes were bloodshot, and a narrow bandage pasted his nose into place. "Up early, Woolley?"

"Out late, Frank?" Hiram asked.

"What do you want?"

"I'd like to talk with Mr. Rettig."

Frank hesitated, but opened the door.

Sitting at his elevated desk, Rettig had his gloves on but his shirtsleeves rolled up. In front of him lay correspondence and an open book of maps. The office smelled of sweat.

Hiram stood behind one of the chairs with the legs sawed short.

"You." Rettig looked like he wanted to snarl. "Word has it that the Kimballs have become such a loving family, any chance I had of buying their mine is gone. Does that make you feel good?"

Hiram grinned. He'd slept, and he'd managed to get a few peanuts into his belly. "That makes me feel pretty good," he admitted. "You know what makes me feel even better?"

Rettig hesitated. "You'll tell me, of course."

"Buying the mine would have benefited the D and RGW, because you would have got cheap coal. You would have been the hero, so promotions and bonuses for you."

"So what?"

"So you weren't content to take that shot alone, were you?" Hiram reached into his pocket and produced just one of the photos Mary had given him the night before, when she'd asked for a word alone. The picture showed Naaman sitting at a table with several men in suits, smiling. "You had to have a second angle, another way to benefit."

"That photo proves nothing," Rettig said.

Hiram handed the photo over. "I don't aim to prove anything. What that photo shows is you meeting with the owners of the Latuda mine. I have others like it, of you at other operations."

"So what?"

"Here's what I think happened," Hiram said. "You cut yourself a side-deal, a couple of years ago, when the Kimballs were just starting to fight. You bought in to some of the coal mines yourself, personally. If you could buy the Kimballs out for the railroad, great, you're a hero at the D and RGW. But if not, the Kimball mine shuts down, and all the other mines get to raise their prices because there's not as much coal. So you get personally rich, though the D and RGW's costs go up. You'd have been cheating the railroad you work for."

Naaman Rettig scowled.

"So you'd have been happy if the Kimballs accepted your offer. But failing that, you wanted to add to the chaos and fear and stop the mine from reopening under any circumstances. It's why you sent your men around to scare people."

"Self-dealing and corporate chicanery? My men roving the countryside? You can't prove any of that," Rettig said again.

"I guess I probably could," Hiram told him. "But I don't want to. I just want you to know that I beat you. I beat your plan to buy the mine, and then I beat your plan to shut it down. You have a good morning, Mr. Rettig."

"Damn you, Hiram Woolley."

"Damn you right back."

Hiram left. On his way out, he nodded at Frank Johnson. "I'd find a different boss if I were you."

Later, after Hiram had paid his bill at Buford's, and he and Michael had eaten a pile of breakfast, they walked to the Double-A, parked beside the Price River. The smell of the water mixed with the scent of coal smoke and wood smoke from the houses and the trains.

They'd retrieved the truck the night before from where Hiram had hidden it, and it sat under a sky, dazzling blue, shining down on a snow-capped landscape. The truck wasn't alone. Other cars were there, as well as a gang of people. Mary was present, as were a few of the miners, including Hermann Wagner, Stavros, and the odoriferous Paul.

Eliza stood at the rear of the company.

"We came to say goodbye," Mary said. "And to thank you. You are something, Hiram."

He shook her hand and blushed.

Stavros limped forward. "Mr. Woolley, we don't know exactly what you did. But we thank you for it. My wife, she made a little candy for you."

"And I have some *Käsekuchen*." Hermann Wagner offered him something pie-shaped and wrapped in a gray kitchen towel.

Other miners came forward with gifts. Most gave Hiram and Michael food, but a few had brought him coins or a little folding money.

From miners who had just been unemployed, the gifts were generous.

Hiram thanked them all. Then he shook his head. "I feel bad for Walter and Medea. Without them, we wouldn't have made it out. Especially Medea. Are their families going to be taken care of?"

He thought of Callista, and her father who had taken to banditry, and now might be lame for life.

"*Ja*," Hermann said. The others bobbed their heads. "We'll take care of their families. We of the Kimball mine local will take care of our own."

Hiram said a silent prayer for the fallen, including Vilhelm and Eva Sorenson.

He gave Mary one last little smile.

She drew near and handed him the brass lamen. "You'll need this more than I will."

Hiram stuck it into his inside coat pocket. Feeling awkward, not knowing what to say, he squeezed her hand and stepped back.

Her reaction was to smile more brightly.

Eliza handed Hiram a heavy object, wrapped in paper. "I got curious, and I looked into the stone. I shouldn't have." Her face was pale and she had dark circles under her eyes. "We want you to take this and keep it safe."

Hiram took the stone. "Curiosity is natural. You didn't do anything wrong. The Beast did those things."

She smiled, for just a second, gratefully.

Hiram raised a hand. Michael said his goodbyes, and the pair drove away in the Double-A.

Hiram sat back and closed his eyes. He'd sleep, Michael would drive, and hopefully there wouldn't be much conversation.

They were going up the slope, up toward Soldier Summit, when Michael broke the quiet. "I gave Mary our address. I figure you could use a pen pal. I think you might be sweet on her. Am I wrong?"

"Not ... *wrong*," Hiram said, eyes closed. "But."

"So why didn't you kiss her?"

"It wouldn't have been appropriate."

"Nuts with what's appropriate. Come on, Pap, Mom's been dead for six years now. It might be time to find someone who's sweet on you. And you definitely were sweet on her. You squeezed her hand and everything. Wow."

"Hmm."

Michael didn't take the hint and kept talking. "Okay, so can you give me a summary of the more supernatural problems at the Kimball Mine? I can't believe I just used the word 'supernatural.'"

"I have more guesses than knowledge, son."

"Well, I have less than guesses. Share."

Hiram took a deep breath. "The Beast ... let's call it that. I hope it's been destroyed. I won't know until I make another Mosaical Rod."

"Okay."

"I guess that over sixty years ago, Gus lived here, and went by the name Lohengrim Zoller. And he met the demon under the earth—maybe he came here because of the demon, I don't know—and he struck a deal with it. For thirty years, the demon made Gus prosper. Maybe the demon also taught him magic, I don't know that, either. But when Gus's time was up, the demon made a deal with a new person."

"Teancum Kimball," Michael said.

"Teancum Kimball. And I guess that must have been right around 1903, when there were riots in the mines. So maybe the demon had something to do with the riots—it caused them, or it used them to run Gus off, or it stopped the riots when Teancum made his deal."

"Teancum gave the monster his children. All of them. And Gus gave them his eyes." Michael shuddered.

"Gus left," Hiram continued, "but he didn't stay gone. He came back around 1920, and somehow, Teancum didn't recognize him."

"I'm going to go out on a limb," Michael said. "Gus used a charm."

"Seems likely. And Gus was sensitive to the possibility that I might have a seer stone, so my guess is that the Beast gave the peep-stone to whoever made a deal with it. So Gus probably had the stone in his day, and then Teancum. And then Teancum gave it to his children."

"I want a peep-stone," Michael said. "Or at least, I want to look in one."

"Someday." Hiram considered. "My guess is, at the same time Teancum was trying and failing to talk the Beast into renewing their deal, the Beast manipulated him into sending the seer stone to his children. My guess is the Beast planned to strike a deal with Samuel or Ammon."

Michael clutched the wheel, keeping his eyes on the muddy road, blanketed with snow from the storm the night before. "So, demons, huh? How can people not know about this?"

"Many do," Hiram said.

Many others, though, were taught not to see the evidence. Or were taught to disbelieve at all costs. Or talked themselves out of belief to preserve their own worldview, or belief in their own innocence, or in the superiority of their way of life.

"Are you going to teach me the hocus-pocus?" Michael asked.

A very good question.

"Maybe if you let me be for the drive home, I might show you a thing or two. But most charms only work for a person with a chaste and sober mind. You sure you want to walk that path?"

"Chaste *and* sober? Jeez." Michael laughed.

Chapter Thirty-Eight

HIRAM HAD PUT ON HIS CHURCH CLOTHES FOR THE INTERVIEW.

It was the chapel in Lehi, early on Sunday morning before meetings started. Hiram sat on a wooden chair in a classroom, trying not to put his hand into his pocket to hold his bloodstone.

Bishops Smith and Wells sat on similar chairs facing him. The radiator hissed like a dragon, and Hiram was sweating. Outside the building, a cold snap had hit, and it wasn't going to get above freezing, but inside it was an oven.

The walls were white plaster. The only decoration they held were two framed pictures, one a painting of Jesus knocking at a garden door and the other a photograph of Heber J. Grant, the President of the Church. It shouldn't have bothered Hiram that Grant's picture was slightly larger and hung a bit higher, but it did.

The place smelled of furniture polish and prayer, and every sound started an echo that hid within it the hint of a hymn.

He had on his white shirt, which he had pressed, but which had nevertheless become very creased on the drive to the chapel. His slacks had a hole in the seam on the right leg, and his shoes, he realized, could have used more polish. At least his bolo tie was straight.

Bishop Smith sat with his fingers steepled, dressed impeccably in a brown suit and fashionably wide tie. John Wells wore a smaller tie and a waistcoat, with his jacket over the back of another chair.

"What on earth caused you to become embroiled in a murder?" Smith asked. "You were sent there simply to deliver groceries to the Kimball miners, yes?"

"Yes," Hiram said. "And I delivered them."

Both counsellors waited for more, Smith frowning, but Wells with a relaxed smile.

"Well?" Smith asked.

Hiram shrugged. "I guess I think I told you everything."

"Except why the police considered you a suspect in a murder investigation," Smith said.

"I let the man borrow my gun," Hiram said, "so it was on the scene when he died. As far as I know, that's all there is to it. I'm not a suspect anymore."

"Did they find the killer, then?"

Hiram shrugged. "You could ask the Carbon County Sheriff."

"And the witchcraft?" Smith asked.

Hiram shook his head. "I'm no witch."

Smith pursed his lips in thought.

Two weeks had passed since Hiram and Michael had driven away from Helper. Planting hadn't started yet, but Hiram was ready—the tractor was all tuned up and he'd checked his stock of fertilizer and seed.

Hiram had cut a Mosaical Rod with all the names he knew for the Beast and interrogated it about the Beast's fate. Satisfied that the being was dead, or at least would not be found again by the Kimball Corporation's miners, Hiram had telegraphed a discreet all-clear signal back to Ammon.

Ammon's response telegram had told Hiram that Dollar's was boarded up and the family gone. Where were they now? The daughter knew some craft; she'd sabotaged Hiram's truck. And the grandchildren had seemed perfectly delightful...until Gus had hexed them.

Michael had written Mary. He had better penmanship than Hiram and was far better with words; also, he had a lot to say, and Hiram didn't.

She hadn't written back.

On the other hand, Hiram *had* received a package from the Carbon County Sheriff's Department. In it was Hiram's Colt, cleaned and smelling of gun oil. Hiram was glad to get it back.

He scratched his chin, comfortable in the silence.

President Smith, though, finally cleared his throat. "The times are changing, Brother Woolley."

Hiram nodded. "Every day."

"We're getting organized. We've learned from our best stake leaders how to get storehouses together, and how to manage collective effort. Have you heard about the Welfare Program the Pioneer Stake runs? And the L.D.S. Business College has set up a Women's Sewing Center. We're going to lick this depression, and we're going to do it as a people."

"President Roosevelt would be proud," Hiram said.

Smith snorted. "We're going to do it like Henry Ford. We're building a machine, and it will take care of our people the world over. We're going to get a real organization in place. And there won't be room for men like you in it."

Hiram considered. "Farmers, you mean?"

President Smith's face turned sour. "I mean men who buck the system. Men who can't take orders. Men who so flout the public conscience that they're accused of serious crimes. Men who dowse and consult familiar spirits."

Nostrils flared, Smith stood and left.

"He's a good man," John Wells said after a brief silence.

Somewhere in the building, a choir had begun rehearsal.

"He's a good *organization* man," Hiram agreed. "He does what he's told and gets others to do the same."

"I knew a beet farmer once," Wells said. "He had a hundred sugar beets, and he had a shiny new John Deere that took care of the patch. It plowed and it planted, it weeded and it watered and it harvested, and it did very well by ninety-nine of those beets."

"Hmm."

"But there was the one beet that the combine couldn't reach," Wells continued. "And so my friend the farmer had to go out himself, to weed around that beet, water it, and keep the worms away. It look a lot of labor, but the one beet turned out just as well as the ninety-nine. Do you think my friend the farmer did right to give that beet special care?"

Hiram snorted. "I think you have no idea how to grow sugar beets."

John Wells gave a Hiram a nod. "Let Bishop Smith build his machine. It will care very well for the ninety and nine. And you and I, my friend..."

"We'll go after the one."

"We'll go after the one."

"Ammon Kimball had a seer stone. Or, really, it was Teancum's." Hiram blurted the words out. He had to say something.

John Wells nodded slowly. "A seer stone?"

Hiram nodded. "But a seer stone that was connected to... a demon."

"I suppose if I were to find such an item," Wells said slowly, "I would think it was safer in the hands of someone who believed in its power, than being given to a bureaucracy that found it to be an embarrassing piece of history, best forgotten."

That was the end of the conversation. Outside the door, Wells turned right and Hiram walked left, to where Michael waited beside the Double-A.

The next morning, Hiram rose early and cut a length of witch hazel from the bush at the end of his porch.

Michael would sleep the morning away if permitted, and on this morning, unusually, Hiram would let him do just that.

After fortifying himself with a glass of buttermilk and a couple of hardboiled eggs, Hiram opened his toolbox. From the lower compartment, he removed the peep-stone, still wrapped in paper. He didn't know whether the stone had any value other than contacting the Beast, so he preferred not to touch it.

To prepare the Mosaical Rod, he carved into it the usual crosses and the Tetragrammaton. He recited a passage from Helaman out loud as he worked: "Whoso shall hide up treasures in the earth shall find them again no more, because of the great curse of the land, save he be a righteous man and shall hide it up unto the Lord."

He pocketed his blessed knife from the tool chest as well.

Then he walked out to the south forty, the Mosaical Rod in his hand, the mud under his feet frozen in swirls. Later in the spring, once planting started, there would be hired men out and about at this hour. All Hiram saw was a lone hawk circling overhead.

He walked swinging the Mosaical Rod from side to side and waiting for it to guide him. Gradually, dipping to indicate direction, it led him to the spot.

He drew an X into the dirt with his dagger, then walked

back to the farmhouse, only to return to his X with a pile of split wood on the back of the Double-A. Above him, the Wasatch Mountains were crystalline ramparts, still white with snow over their gray rock and the dull brown of the gambol oak in their winter clothes. The snow on the peaks would stay until July, or maybe August.

Hiram got a fire going. He was grateful for the warmth himself, but also he needed to thaw out the ground before he dug. On top of that, fire was the element of intelligence, it was ruled by Gabriel, it undid enchantments, and so forth.

The fire was essential.

Hiram wasn't completely sure what spirit or angel moved the cache on his farm. Robin Goodfellow, whom Eva Sorenson had fed milk to? Grandma Hettie? A Ute medicine man who had once lived on the land? An angel who served the God of heaven?

Elmina?

Hiram's mother?

He wasn't sure who helped him, but he knew what worked. The helpful spirit, whoever or whatever it was, moved the box around, so no one could unearth it, either on purpose or by accident.

As the fire did its work, Hiram thought again of the hex he'd used to tumble down that wall in the mine. It was image magic, far beyond Hiram's lore. Hiram hadn't even been able to read the lamen without help.

Hiram's skills were woefully inadequate.

How could he possibly teach Michael?

How could he fight the demons of the land, as John Wells wanted, and keep the people safe?

Hiram took a deep breath.

He let the fire burn to coals and then waited for those coals to become ash. Sinking a shovel into the dirt beneath, he dug until he unearthed a box made of flat stones cemented together. On those stones he'd scratched every warding symbol he knew.

He should definitely learn more symbols. He should get books.

Where would he even do that?

He pulled the stone box out of the warmed, muddy ground and then knelt in front of it.

The vault's stone lid squeaked when he lifted it off. The things inside—a skull with horns, a glass bauble, a black candle, a hand of glory—were here for safekeeping. The chest kept them out of the grasp of those who might misuse them.

Which, in the case of some of the objects, was anyone who would touch them.

Hiram placed Teancum Kimball's seer stone inside and then replaced the lid. Locking it felt good. Burying it again felt even better.

Would he ever show Michael the contents of the chest? It depended on the kind of life his son wanted. Part of him hoped Hiram could pass along to his son Grandma Hettie's special skills. Yas Yazzie's ways had not been so very different, after all. Another part of Hiram wanted his son to learn the sorcery of the chemistry lab and the occult language of academic publishing.

There were other evils than demons to fight in this world.

He said another prayer to the Lord Divine. He knew that even as he finished, the guardian spirit of the stone chest was whisking it away. No one could casually stumble across the items Hiram guarded, not now, and not ever.

A voice echoed across the bare, wintery landscape. Michael stood on the porch, waving.

Hiram waved back.

He drove back to the house.

What would he say to Michael, if the boy asked why he'd been out on the back forty with a shovel?

Hiram sighed.